MW01408505

UNFOUNDED

A PRIDE & PREJUDICE VARIATION

JESSIE LEWIS

Quills & Quartos
PUBLISHING

Edited by Kristi Rawley and Julie Cooper

Cover design by James T. Egan of Bookfly Design

ISBN 978-1-956613-59-9 (ebook) and 978-1-956613-60-5 (paperback)

For anyone who ever yearned to spend a little more time with Darcy and Elizabeth.

CHAPTER ONE

CLARABELLE

Pemberley was hers. Every chamber, every passageway, every stair; each and every nook—from the attic rafters to the cellar floor—were embossed upon her mind. The house was in her blood. Indeed, there was no small quantity of her blood in the house, for one could not scrub properly without scraped knuckles to show for it, and not even the lofty rank of housekeeper had exempted Mrs Reynolds from scouring her share of grates and flagstones over the years. Her home, her livelihood, her world for the last quarter of a century—Pemberley had earned an unassailable place in her heart.

There was but one entity to which she was more devoted, and he was arriving on the morrow, bringing a large party of friends and his younger sister with him. It was vastly inconvenient, therefore, that visitors had chosen this day to apply to see the house. Rooms were aswarm with servants; labourers climbed like ants up and down ladders; deliveries of fresh produce poured into the bowels of the house by the cartful—all in preparation for the master's first return in many months. Interruptions were undesirable.

The footman who had brought her the vexatious news shifted awkwardly on his feet. "Should you prefer that I ask Mr Matthis to show them around?"

"No, there is no need for that. I shall come directly. But you had better let everybody know to stay out of the way until they are gone. And alert Mr Howes, for they will likely wish to see the gardens after the house."

With a quick nod, James left to deliver the instructions. Of course, Mr Matthis was perfectly capable of giving a tour of the house, but he considered it beneath him and preferred Mrs Reynolds to attend to all comers. It was an arrangement that suited her well. She was paid handsomely for her dedication to Pemberley, but she could never match the butler's chief qualification of being a man, nor, by the same token, ever receive equal remuneration, thus she felt no compunction in taking all visitors' tips for herself. Indeed, having no family to whom she might send funds, she had saved quite a sum by precisely those means for such a time as she was no longer able to work. A time which, of late, seemed to be accelerating towards her with disconcerting haste.

A party of three awaited her in the hall. Two were of middling years and married, if their linked arms were any indication. His brown coat, thickset stature, and sun-flushed complexion gave him all the appearance of a highly polished tea caddy. Her pale-yellow bonnet, protruding from her head like a trumpet, made her the picture of a daffodil. A younger lady accompanied them, and the eyes with which she unblinkingly surveyed her surroundings were so dark and so wide, and framed with such startlingly long lashes, as instantly put Mrs Reynolds in mind of Clarabelle the dairy cow. She curtseyed to all three and invited them to follow her into the dining-parlour.

It had long been her habit to name those who came seeking a tour of Pemberley. Such people rarely introduced themselves—something she had always considered a false conceit, since anyone whose only method of crossing the threshold of such a fine house was as a tourist could generally be but a warehouse door removed from the position of respectable upper servant themselves. Name them she must, however, for she required some method of identifying them in her letters to dear Eleanor, who never ceased to be delighted by the peculiarities of so many strangers.

"This is a fine room," Tea Caddy remarked. "Sizeable without forfeiting the acoustics. Not like the dining hall at Chatsworth that echoed every drop of a pin."

His manner pleased Mrs Reynolds. He seemed not unduly awed, only genuinely pleased. He listened with keen interest as she detailed the provenance of the vast dining table and the dinner served upon it to the king in 1764. Daffodil nodded appreciatively as she wandered the length of the room, admiring this sideboard and that ornament. Clarabelle only slightly surveyed it all before drifting to a window and staring out over the grounds. Mrs Reynolds was pleased to have a keener audience in Tea Caddy and Daffodil, else such indifference might have rankled.

From the dining-parlour, she led the party into the Venetian drawing room, a chamber always guaranteed to amaze. Though every bit as tasteful as the rest of Pemberley, it boasted the only ceiling in the house whose mouldings were gilded, and together with the vast, south-facing windows, they gave the room a lustrous, ethereal glow during the day. Daffodil exclaimed over the lightness of the space. Tea Caddy admired the elegant proportions.

Mrs Reynolds resolved not to be vexed when Clarabelle once more gave it only a cursory glance before ambling to peer outside. After all, the view was—by design—spectacular and warranted admiration. Her resolve wavered when the young lady showed the same disregard in both of the next two rooms. If all she wished to do was look at trees, Mrs Reynolds wished she had not petitioned to be shown indoors at all, for then her own activities might not have been interrupted.

There was more universal approbation of the Stag Parlour, but then, it was a difficult room of which not to approve. Its dark hues, welcoming furniture, and oversized fireplace made it a snug, intimate space that exuded cosiness and warmth.

An admiring turn came over Tea Caddy's countenance. "Now this is a room to which a gentleman could very quickly grow accustomed. I expect it is used a good deal when your master is at home—though our chambermaid seemed to think he is away at present."

Mrs Reynolds replied that he was and could not resist adding, "We expect him tomorrow, with a large party of friends." Alas—or perhaps fortunately—her allusion to the inconvenience of the trio's visit went undetected. She left Tea Caddy inspecting the tapestry above the chaise and walked to where the two ladies were looking at the miniatures that hung above the mantelpiece. As she approached, Daffodil pointed at the likeness of George Wickham and enquired of her companion how she liked it. Bristling that either woman should have singled him out over and above any of the other, finer gentlemen whose paintings were likewise displayed, Mrs Reynolds interjected.

"That is the picture of a young gentleman, the son of my late master's steward, who was brought up by him at his own expense. He is now gone into the army, but I am afraid he has turned out very wild." She pointed to the painting of Mr Darcy. "And that is my master, and very like him. It was drawn at the same time as the other. About eight years ago."

"I have heard much of your master's fine person,"

Daffodil replied. "It is a handsome face. But, Lizzy, you can tell us whether it is like or not."

"Does that young lady know Mr Darcy?" Mrs Reynolds enquired with a start.

Clarabelle admitted that she knew him a little, colouring slightly as she did—and well she might! To pry about the home of one's acquaintance while he was away was unaccountably strange. Perhaps she and the master were not on good terms, in which case, her coming was the most insolent thing in the world.

"And do not you think him a very handsome gentleman, ma'am?" Mrs Reynolds enquired. She kept her tone friendly, for she would never discredit Mr Darcy by being uncivil, but she felt a great inclination to make the young lady say something agreeable of the man into whose house she was presently intruding.

"Yes, very handsome," Clarabelle acceded, somewhat reluctantly.

"I am sure I know none so handsome. But in the gallery upstairs you will see a finer, larger picture of him than this. This room was my late master's favourite, and these miniatures are just as they used to be then. He was very fond of them. This one is Miss Darcy, drawn when she was only eight years old."

"And is Miss Darcy as handsome as her brother?" Tea Caddy enquired, coming to join them.

"Oh! Yes—the handsomest young lady that ever was seen, and so accomplished! She comes here tomorrow with him."

"Is your master much at Pemberley in the course of the year?"

"Not so much as I could wish, sir, but I daresay he may spend half his time here."

"If your master would marry, you might see more of him."

"Yes, sir, but I do not know when that will be. I do not know who is good enough for him."

"It is very much to his credit, I am sure, that you should think so," Clarabelle observed. There was a question in her expression and tone that betrayed her doubt.

"I say no more than the truth, and what everybody will say that knows him," Mrs Reynolds replied, affronted. "I have never had a cross word from him in my life, and I have known him ever since he was four years old."

"There are very few people of whom so much can be said. You are lucky in having such a master," Tea Caddy remarked.

Mrs Reynolds was aware of this and said so. "If I was to go through the world, I could not meet with a better. But I have always observed that they who are good-natured when children are good-natured when they grow up, and he was always the sweetest-tempered, most generous-hearted boy in the world."

"His father was an excellent man," Daffodil observed.

"Yes, ma'am, that he was indeed." As pointedly as she dared, Mrs Reynolds added, "And his son will be just like him—just as affable to the poor." She met Clarabelle's ill-concealed disbelief with an innocuous smile, then turned away to lead them into the next room.

She regaled the party with her usual rote of information as they traversed the music room and then the saloon. Four-and-twenty years had provided her with a wealth of knowledge about the house. There was not a painting whose artist she could not name, an artifact whose provenance was unknown to her, nor a window or fireplace whose dimensions and cost she could not recite. It was information that more commonly occasioned expressions of admiration, even awe from visitors. Clarabelle could not have shown less interest and only trailed, subdued, behind her companions. They, at least, seemed impressed.

"The family has certainly benefited from their ancestors' tastes," said Tea Caddy when they reached the principal stair hall where the Beaumont collection was hung, and exquisitely carved statuettes filled the numerous alcoves built into the stairwell.

"That they have, sir, and the present master has continued in the same vein. Nothing is brought into the house nor done to alter it that is not in the same elegant style. And the greatest of consideration is given to conserving everything that is here already. It is nothing less than such a house deserves, of course, but in my experience, there are few masters who give the same attention to these matters."

"It is clear you think very highly of him. Your commendation far exceeds any I have heard at other houses about other masters. Yours must be a rare creature indeed."

"He is the best landlord and the best master that ever lived. Not like the wild young men now-a-days, who think of nothing but themselves." Still smarting from Clarabelle's previous disdain, Mrs Reynolds cast a glance over her shoulder to see what effect this avowal had upon her, but other than listening intently, the young lady betrayed no other emotion. *Let her listen, then,* Mrs Reynolds thought, for a lady of leisure was never likely to comprehend for herself the value, nor the rarity, of a decent employer. "There is not one of his tenants or servants but what will give him a good name. Some people call him proud, but I am sure I never saw anything of it. To my fancy, it is only because he does not rattle away like other young men."

Tea Caddy made a noise of approval but was distracted when he reached the bust occupying the next alcove. It was while Mrs Reynolds answered his questions about it that she overheard a most distressing exchange between the two ladies behind her. "This fine account of him is not quite consistent with his behaviour to our poor friend," whispered the older lady to the younger, who replied that perhaps they had been deceived. "That is not very likely," was the answer. "Our authority was too good."

A lifetime in service was barely enough to keep Mrs Reynolds from releasing the indignant objection that leapt to her tongue. It was confirmed, then, that they thought ill of the master; that they had come to Pemberley, obtruded into the very heart of his family home, with naught but ill will towards him. And on whose 'authority' was this enmity founded? Recalling the manner in which the pair had cooed together over George Wickham's miniature, she was momentarily appalled, though she soon reasoned herself out of such a supposition. It was too much to imagine that they should be friends of his.

She scarcely knew what other information she reeled off as she led the party up the stairs and across the lobby into the Chesterfield room. She wished that the wretched tour be over and regretted promising to show them the gallery afterwards.

"This is another very elegant room," Daffodil remarked.

"As I said, ma'am, there is nothing done to the house that is not in the finest taste. The master was quite explicit in his instructions on how this room was to be fitted up."

"It was done recently, was it?"

"Just lately, ma'am. The master had a fancy it would give pleasure to Miss Darcy, for she took a liking to it when she was last here."

"He is certainly a good brother," Clarabelle mumbled as, yet again, she walked to the window without properly looking at anything that had been done to the chamber.

"We are all anticipating Miss Darcy's delight when she first enters the room, for she has no notion to expect the alterations the master has made. And this is always the way with him," Mrs Reynolds replied pointedly. "Whatever can give his sister any pleasure is sure to be done in a moment. There is nothing he would not do for her."

"He is better to his sister than I ever was to either of mine," Tea Caddy said with a chuckle. "I considered it my duty to plague them at every opportunity."

Mrs Reynolds gave a desultory smile and hastened the party into the picture gallery. She did not trouble herself to impart the usual intelligence about whose face was whose and left them to explore without commentary—until Clarabelle stopped in front of the master's portrait, whereupon a wave of protectiveness spurred her to give a rush of information about some of the other paintings to draw her away. It worked for but a short time; the young lady soon returned to gaze up at Mr Darcy.

"That one was taken in his father's lifetime," Mrs Reynolds told her stiffly. She received no answer and was obliged to wait uneasily until Clarabelle had looked her fill.

She limited the tour thereafter to only one of the principal bedrooms, after which she delivered the party, with as much haste as was seemly, into the waiting hands of the head gardener. Tea Caddy tipped her two shillings on his way out, and for that, she resolved to adjust the sketch of him in her next letter to Eleanor to something marginally more charitable than she had planned. Her depiction of the two ladies would not deviate from that which she had already composed in her head. It was an account she fancied would entertain her friend admirably.

CHAPTER TWO

A STATE OF DISQUIET

Mrs Reynolds did not linger to wave the visitors off and left to resume her duties before James had closed the door behind them. She had not made it across the hall before being forestalled a second time, on this occasion by Pemberley's steward.

"Mrs Reynolds, I am glad to have caught you."

"Mr Ferguson. Can I be of assistance?"

"I am looking for Mr Darcy. Is he arrived yet?"

"No, sir. He is not due until tomorrow."

"That was his original intention, madam, but—has no one informed you? He is returning today."

"Today? With the whole party? No, I assure you I was not informed. Nothing is ready!"

"No, not the whole party—just him. I managed to arrange a meeting with the architect from York at the last minute. Mr Darcy is riding ahead of the rest of the party to join us."

"I see." In a tight voice, she added, "It would have been helpful to know this yesterday. Chef has nothing planned."

Mr Ferguson gave a slight, conciliating smile. "No preparations are necessary, Mrs Reynolds. Mr Darcy has accepted an invitation to dine with Mrs Ferguson and me this evening." He glanced at his fob watch. "I am expecting Mr Jacobs in the next hour. Would you have him sent to the estate office when he arrives?"

Mrs Reynolds inclined her head, waited for him to go, then let out a heavy sigh. She supposed there were no repercussions of any great import, other than that Pemberley was not in the state of refined tranquillity it ought to be whenever the master was in residence. Nevertheless, she wished she had been given enough notice to clear the house of servants before his arrival. Indeed, she would have set off directly to see to it except, without warning, the master himself burst through the front doors.

So sudden was his appearance that Mrs Reynolds let out a cry of surprise, though Mr Darcy seemed not to notice. Indeed, he seemed not to have seen her at all, or James, whom he strode directly past before coming to an abrupt halt in the middle of the hall. There he remained, staring at the floor, his countenance a picture of confusion and his erratic breathing indicative of some vast agitation.

The possibility of his being unwell or having suffered some manner of misadventure on his journey was uppermost in Mrs Reynolds's mind. She watched him carefully as she expressed her pleasure to see him returned home safely. He only nodded absent-mindedly in her direction and glanced briefly over his shoulder at the doors before returning to frowning at the floor in front of him.

Mrs Reynolds shared a concerned look with James, then ventured, "Mr Ferguson has only this moment informed me of your early arrival, sir. I beg you would forgive the maids still being at their work in some of the rooms. They ought to be finished very soon."

"Think nothing of it," he muttered, wholly distracted. He cast another pensive look at the doors.

As discreetly as she could, Mrs Reynolds looked also, but she could see nothing out of the ordinary through the glazing, and James confirmed the absence of anything unusual with a shake of his head. A sudden apprehension beset her. "Are you expecting anybody, sir? Mr Ferguson said the rest of your party are still coming tomorrow. I trust that is correct?"

He did not answer at all this time.

"Miss Darcy?" she pressed gently. "Ought we to expect her this afternoon also?"

"Pardon? Oh—no. My sister is coming with the others tomorrow as planned."

She nodded and waited for him to say more, but he did not. Instead, he began fidgeting with his fob watch. Mrs Reynolds's alarm increased; the master was not given to inattention, and she could not recall ever seeing him fidget, even as a boy. She cleared her throat and enquired cautiously, "Was your journey eventful, Mr Darcy?"

"No. Thank you. I…" He did not finish and turned fully away from her to stare out of the front windows into the park. Mrs Reynolds wondered whether he would go back out, but though he tapped his fingers against his thigh in a restless manner, he remained where he was.

"Mr Ferguson waits upon you in the estate office, sir," Mrs Reynolds said at length.

Mr Darcy started as though he had forgotten anyone else was present. He thanked her in a voice utterly devoid of his usual sedateness and, after a quiet but observably measured exhalation, walked in that direction. So perturbed was she by his behaviour that Mrs Reynolds accompanied him—and she was no less perturbed when he did not object.

The steward came to his feet when they entered the office. "Mr Darcy. I thank you for returning early. I did not think you would wish to miss Mr Jacobs, and he is obliged to return to York tomorrow."

The master looked around the room. "Where is he?"

"I expect him within the hour. Should you like to inspect the east wall before he arrives?"

Mr Darcy looked intently at the plans laid out on the table. The moment stretched into an uncomfortable silence. Then abruptly, he said, "No. I have something I must attend to first," and left the room.

Mr Ferguson was a steady, sensible man in his late forties, who was respected by all who knew him for his mild temper and practical mind. Mrs Reynolds had rarely seen him vexed. Yet even he raised an eyebrow at this. "Do you know where he is going?"

"I do not, and if you will pardon my saying so, sir, he seemed...troubled."

"Yes, well, this problem is troubling us all, Mrs Reynolds. It requires his attention."

"I am sure he will be back before Mr Jacobs arrives. He has come this far at your summons—he is not likely to miss the meeting now."

"Let us hope not." The steward sat back down and turned his attention to his plans.

Taking it for a dismissal, Mrs Reynolds left him and set out to determine how much work had been lost to the afternoon's interruption. She could not be easy. Something was amiss with the master, and though it was not her place to pry, she prayed it was nothing serious. She did not, as she often heard it whispered amongst the other servants, regard Mr Darcy as the child she never had—she was too far removed, and he far too much the master, for such whimsical fancies. Nevertheless, she was devoted to him and did not like to see him in such a state of disquiet as he had appeared moments ago. She did not like it at all.

CHAPTER THREE

PLAGUED WITH QUESTIONS

Ferguson's dining-parlour was always dingy. More so presently with the light leaching out of the day. The gloom rendered dinner muted, colourless. It was at least cool. Blessed relief after standing about all afternoon in the August sun, staring fruitlessly at the ominous black fracture in Pemberley's wall.

"I trust your mother is keeping well," Darcy said to Mrs Ferguson.

"Remarkably well, all things considered. And Miss Darcy? I hope she is in good health."

"Excellent health, thank you."

"Did she have the opportunity to go to the seaside again this year—Ramsgate, was it?"

"No, she has been in town these past six months." He felt no alarm at the mention of his sister's summer activities. That was new. Then again, a whole year had passed, and Georgiana's brush with ruin remained a secret. From all but one. And *she* had not shunned the acquaintance in revulsion. "She may well go next summer, though. The sea air is far superior to London's," he added. Dull words, but anything sufficed that would tame the churning of his mind.

"I should like to see the sea one day," Mrs Ferguson mused. "'Tis difficult to imagine—a person must set eyes on it to comprehend, I suspect."

"It is unlikely we shall be setting eyes on the sea any day soon, my dear," her husband remarked. "Not with the work that's needed at Pemberley now."

Pemberley. Darcy shifted restlessly in his seat as Mrs Ferguson announced her leave-taking. He caught the tail end of a look between husband and wife. What it signified he knew not.

Once a servant had cleared the table and lit some candles, Ferguson poured two glasses of port and came to the point with gratifying brevity. "Were you satisfied with Mr Jacobs, sir? There are several other architects of sound reputation I could approach if you would prefer."

"No, no—he will do. You have been very thorough in checking his references. And I have heard excellent reports of him amongst my own acquaintances. Would that he had proved inept. I should much rather he was wrong."

Ferguson grimaced. "We can only hope one of his less troubling prognoses is found to be the cause. Indeed, he seemed disinclined to attribute the problem to the foundations. He remarked more than once on the area's geology making movement in the ground unlikely. To which I would add that Pemberley has stood on that spot for well over a hundred years without incident."

Darcy swirled the liquid in his glass and stared into it. One-hundred-and-forty-eight years to be precise. Six generations of Darcys. Six masters of Pemberley. And only under his superintendence were the walls crumbling. "There was an earthquake in 1795 that caused damage to buildings across the county. We thought Pemberley had escaped unscathed. I wonder now whether it did not."

"Surely, if the foundations were compromised seventeen years ago, it would have caused problems before now."

Darcy finished the last of his port and deposited the glass heavily on the table. "There is no profit in speculating. We shall have to wait and see what the investigations turn up. Have we enough labourers available for the work, or do you anticipate having to hire extra?"

"Trenches of the size Mr Jacobs was talking about will only take a few men to dig, a few more to cart away the spoil. Mr Howes ought to be able to spare enough of his gardeners. I shall have to hire a stonemason to work on revealing the lintels, though. And they will want scaffolding."

"You have informed Matthis and Mrs Reynolds that no one is to enter that part of the house?"

"I have, and alternative rooms are being readied for those guests who would have been in that wing."

Darcy nodded absently. Pemberley did not want for bedrooms, although some of the finest were in the east wing. Those which, when not in use, were kept made up to exhibit to visitors. Visitors such as those Mrs Reynolds had shown around earlier. "The embargo applies to the servants as well, not just my guests."

"Some of the footmen will need access, sir. To clear space for the workmen."

"Granted, but in general, admittance should be kept to a minimum," Darcy insisted.

"Of course. On the subject of your guests, should you prefer to postpone the work until they have left?"

His guests. Fifteen friends invited for the purpose of disguising the absence of one. One who, against every expectation and all likelihood, was not absent at all. "Let us see how disruptive it all proves once it has begun. Perhaps I shall curtail the gathering." He found himself tapping his fingertips on the table and stopped. "I ought to be going, Ferguson. The light is almost gone."

His steward graciously agreed and, after wishing Mrs Ferguson goodnight and thanking them both for dinner, Darcy left. They waved him off at the door. He walked to the end of the path and turned to touch his hat, then rounded the hedge and set off down the lane. Twenty yards along it, he stopped walking, doubled over with his hands on his knees, and expelled all the air from his lungs in one forceful breath.

Elizabeth was here!

Maintaining his composure for the interminable hours since they parted had proved taxing to the point of bewilderment. His mind had not ceased roiling, attempting over and again to dwell upon every detail of their encounter, yet he had not had a private moment to reflect on it from that instant to this. Rather, he had been obliged to pore over complex architectural drawings, listen to Mr Jacobs's catalogue of dire prognostications, and scrutinise, from every conceivable angle, the shocking fissure splintering Pemberley's stonework.

Nevertheless, it was little more than half an hour after he had seen her—half an hour of pitiful distraction and soaring hope—before Darcy understood that he still loved her. Regardless of what he had attempted to convince himself these past months, there was no refuting Elizabeth's power to render him light of heart even as he received news of a potentially catastrophic structural failure at his ancestral home.

Light as his heart was, it was nevertheless plagued with questions—and he, wild with the need for answers. Why had she come? What thought she of Pemberley? Was it too much to hope that she had forgiven him? He began walking again, his steps rapidly gaining pace as he passed the home farm and crossed the bridge.

They were on their travels, her uncle had said, visiting her aunt's friends in Lambton. Elizabeth had been emphatic in her assertions that she had been assured of his absence before agreeing to come. She need not have taken such pains to convince him of it; he had known she was not expecting to see him the instant their eyes met. Darcy huffed a small laugh of sympathy for her upon comprehending that she may not have been able to avoid the visit; her relations had likely wished it.

She had come under sufferance, then, and only after ascertaining he would not be there. This he might have taken as proof that she despised him still, except he had never seen her so abashed. Impertinent, yes; vexed, certainly—even embarrassed, but never humbled, never meek. Darcy knew from painful experience that if Elizabeth remained angry with him, she would not have struggled to meet his eye. She would have regarded him directly with the same undisguised resentment as during their last encounters in Kent.

He all but vaulted the stile before him on the path, a kernel of certainty unfurling in his mind that Elizabeth's earlier discomfiture, rather than being founded on her ill opinion of *him*, instead signified a wish that he not think ill of *her* for coming. A notion so ridiculous he almost laughed aloud. There had been no choice but for him to relinquish all hope of marrying her after his disastrous proposal, for she had spurned any possibility of an alliance. Yet the regard in which he held her had not diminished, for neither had any of her fine qualities.

In coming to Pemberley, she had given him yet more to admire, for none of her previous enmity had been in evidence that afternoon. Unlike him—and the implacable resentment to which he had so arrogantly professed at Netherfield—Elizabeth was not above clemency. How anyone could forgive the vilification of their family, situation, and worth was beyond him. Such, to his eternal shame, he had inflicted upon her. And such she had apparently forgiven, at least enough to greet him with civility, to converse without bitterness, and to consent to be introduced to his sister.

Darcy bounded up the steps to the lawn and strode towards the house, his mind leaping erratically from imagining Georgiana's delight, to calculating what time she would arrive the next day, to envisioning how the interview might go, to revelling in the possibilities such an introduction must portend. He had felt sad for so long that such unbridled anticipation was dizzying.

He wondered what Elizabeth was thinking at that moment, and whether she was as unsettled as he by their chance encounter. He hoped at the very least that she was not dismayed by it. The tentative smile she had bestowed upon him as her carriage departed gave him reason to hope not. It was unlike any she had directed at him before—sincere, with neither teasing nor challenge.

The desire to secure that cordiality, to permanently remedy her ill opinion of him—perchance to nurture a still warmer sentiment—manifested as a fire in his belly that demanded action. If he thought she would receive him, he would have turned on his heel and walked all the way to Lambton that instant. He was obliged to satisfy himself with musing how soon Georgiana might be persuaded to go there after she arrived home. And whether she might be better placed than he to extend an invitation to dinner, for he would be bitterly disappointed if Elizabeth refused as she had done his earlier offer of refreshments. There were few scenarios he had imagined more times than welcoming Elizabeth to Pemberley.

He wished the privilege of showing her the house had

been his. Interrogating the housekeeper was out of the question, but Darcy longed to know what Elizabeth had said, how she had looked, and which rooms had pleased her best as she was shown around. In the fleeting second before she noticed him on the lawn, she had been staring pensively at the building, as though attempting to make out its character. Just as she did every person she met. Darcy stopped walking and regarded it also, attempting to guess what conclusions she had drawn.

The sun had long since dipped below the horizon, and the moon was barely out. All the windows of this newly deserted part of the house were black. In the gloom, the fault that criss-crossed the wall was not visible; night had plunged the whole elevation into complete darkness. All Darcy could see was a vast black void, as though the entire east wing were missing. He shivered slightly and walked indoors to begin making plans for the morrow.

CHAPTER FOUR

MORE THAN A PASSING ACQUAINTANCE

With a firm tug, the heavy white sheet billowed into the air like a dense cloud before collapsing into a puddle at Hannah's feet. Mrs Reynolds placed a hand on the exposed mattress, pressing firmly to establish whether it was merely chilled, or the cold signified a more penetrating moisture. With a shake of her head, she wiped her hand dry on her skirt. She was not overly surprised; these rooms were seldom used, and damp was a pernicious blight. It presented a difficulty, however, for one night was not sufficient time to air a bed, even in high summer.

"We shall need the mattresses brought over from the closed bedrooms, but I'll not have any of you girls doing that. Hannah, run and see if anyone is available in the servants' hall to do it. Ask Mr Matthis if you cannot find anyone. Martha, go with her and help strip the beds before they are moved, else the sheets will all be scuffed about, and we shall have to begin again."

Both girls curtseyed and left directly.

"Edna, these fires all need lighting, post-haste. And you had best fetch some rosemary or orange peel or something to burn on them. Let us see if we can at least give the appearance of freshness. The grates will have to be done at dawn, I'm afraid, for these fires will need to be kept burning all night."

Edna set off for the stillroom with a nod. Mrs Reynolds turned to the other maids.

"Well then, girls, you know what needs doing. Mr Bingley will be in this room, and his sister in the next. Across the hall will be Lord and Lady Garroway with Miss Adams next to them in the Mahogony Bedroom. Remember, she must not have flowers in her room." With one last look around, Mrs Reynolds nodded. "I shall have the kitchen prepare you a supper for when you are finished."

Despite having been labouring since dawn, the girls set about their extra work without a murmur of complaint, though Mrs Reynolds did not doubt there would be grumbling enough behind closed doors later. It could not be helped; Mr Ferguson had given the instruction, and it was not her place to cavil.

The chef and his undercooks had returned from Astroite House on Monday, and Pemberley's kitchen was once again returned to a cacophonous hive of activity. With fifteen guests and their servants arriving with the family the next day, there was no shortage of work to be done. Supplies were strewn in every direction—still being sorted and stored according to Chef's preferences. The kitchen maids were dashing about between the great oak tables with armfuls of ingredients. Young Pip, whose job it was to turn the spit, looked fit to combust so hot did the fire blaze. It was a scene Mrs Reynolds observed with great fondness, for the kitchen was the heart of any house, and Pemberley's only beat when its master was at home.

After a quick word with Monsieur Dubois about supper for the housemaids, she took a cup of tea to drink quietly in the upper servants' hall. She discovered Mr Darcy's manservant there, eating a dinner of bread and cheese. "Mr Vaughan! Welcome back."

"Thank you." He stood, bowed formally, and sat back down, ever efficient in all things, not least conversation.

"'Tis a shame you missed dinner."

He made a movement with his mouth equivalent to a shrug. "The luggage had already been unloaded when Mr Darcy received the summons home. Took some time to sort out."

Mrs Reynolds lowered herself onto a chair. "Are you aware of the matter that required him to return early?"

"A problem with the house."

"The architect who was here this afternoon does not appear to have put anyone's mind at ease. Mr Ferguson has ordered the entire east wing closed."

Mr Vaughan frowned. "Did Mr Darcy seem concerned?"

"I must say he did. Quite out of sorts."

He gave a low grumble of unease.

Mrs Reynolds shifted her old bones about on the chair, doing nothing to make herself more comfortable. "A party of three came to the house today. One of them—a young woman—claimed an acquaintance with the master."

"Name?" Mr Vaughan enquired in a business-like tone.

"Her friends called her 'Lizzy'."

He thought about that for a moment. "There was a Miss Elizabeth in Hertfordshire—Elizabeth Bennet. Stayed at Mr Bingley's house for a few days. She was at Hunsford when we were at Rosings, too."

Mrs Reynolds bristled anew at the recollection of the young woman's coyness as she purported to know the master but a little. "What did you make of her?"

"She struck me as a pleasant girl. The colonel certainly liked her well enough, according to his man."

"She knows Colonel Fitzwilliam?"

Mr Vaughan nodded. "He was at Rosings with Mr Darcy as usual. Miss Bennet dined there with them once or twice."

And she had dined with Lady Catherine de Bourgh! "I believe she may be acquainted with George Wickham as well."

"Likely. His company was encamped near her home in Hertfordshire."

"Upon my word! Whatever can she have been about coming here in that case?" Mrs Reynolds cried, dismayed at the prospect of any friend of George Wickham's snooping about Pemberley uninvited.

"I am sure there is no cause for alarm. There are plenty of 'Lizzys' in the world. Perhaps the young lady who came today was a different acquaintance. Or a total stranger."

"He definitely knew her," said a gruff voice from the doorway. "Evening, Vaughan. Welcome home."

Mrs Reynolds jumped as Mr Howes clomped over to the table, dragged a chair noisily out from under it, and set his mug down with a loud bang. Head gardener he may be, but he had never quite learnt to leave his outdoor manners in the garden where they belonged. "What made you think Mr Darcy and the young lady were acquainted?" she asked him.

"His face when he saw her, for starters. Well, both their faces come to think of it. Never saw two people more embarrassed to bump into each other."

"*That* was what distressed him!"

"Seemed to knock him for six, to be sure. Not that he talked to her for long on that occasion."

"Was there another occasion?"

"Well, there's the other reason I know they are acquainted. Because if he did not know her, then how do you explain his coming back out around the lake to find her and her friends and take over the tour of the park from me?"

Mr Vaughan raised his eyebrows but said nothing and returned his gaze to his plate. He never partook in speculation directly relating to the master, even among the upper servants. Neither did Mrs Reynolds in the usual course of things, yet she could not allay her disquiet where this young woman was concerned. She fancied that if Mr Vaughan had witnessed Mr Darcy's distress in the moments after that first encounter, he might share her unease.

"Well, all I can say is we must be thankful she has gone and nothing worse came of it."

CHAPTER FIVE

TALKING OF POSSIBILITIES

Mrs Whitaker's parlour was reminiscent of Longbourn's with its comfortable but slightly worn chairs and bundles of sewing paraphernalia scattered about. There was a similar hubbub of lively conversation, too, as Mrs Gardiner reminisced with her old acquaintance. The scene afforded a soothing sense of familiarity that Elizabeth vastly appreciated since it was in stark contrast to the riot of confusion occupying her head.

He was not supposed to have been there! The chambermaid in Bakewell had confirmed it, his own housekeeper had confirmed it—yet Pemberley was where Mr Darcy had very much been. There, also, had *she* been, caught gazing at his house as though calculating the worth of every brick she had forfeited! She winced at the memory of it, mortification reasserting itself with the same force as it had then. How she wished they could have met under different circumstances!

"And so, Miss Bennet is your niece on your husband's side?"

"Mrs Bennet is Mr Gardiner's sister. She—both his sisters, in fact—live in Hertfordshire."

"Oh? Whereabouts? I have an uncle near Bishops Stortford."

Elizabeth refocused her gaze and discovered her aunt and Mrs Whitaker regarding her. "My godmother used to live in Bishops Stortford. My own home, Longbourn, is farther away, near Meryton."

She was relieved when this proved enough to satisfy her company. They moved on to discussing the whereabouts of various other relations, leaving Elizabeth at liberty to reflect on her previous train of thought.

Four-and-twenty hours ago, she would not have said that she wished to meet Mr Darcy at all. She had come to comprehend that he was far from unfeeling, it was true. The letter in which he explained his history with Mr Wickham and her own retrospections had taught her that. She would even admit to a good deal of regret for her conduct towards him, which had been proved petulant and vain. Nevertheless, she had not previously harboured any desire to rekindle the acquaintance. If asked, she would have said that such an encounter could only occasion pain to both parties.

That was before she heard his housekeeper's praise of him, a more generous account one would be hard pressed to invent. Before he showed such solicitous attention to her aunt and uncle, relations he had formerly derided as reprehensible connexions. Before she witnessed the startling alteration in his behaviour, his pride all gone, replaced with civility and gentleness.

"Will you dine with us tomorrow?" enquired Miss Tanner, Mrs Whitaker's spinster sister who had been sitting mutely at Elizabeth's side for the chief of the evening. "Rosemary is excessively anxious to see you."

Mrs Gardiner sat up straighter in her chair, her countenance a picture of delight. "Rosemary is in Lambton?"

"She returns tomorrow. We were none of us quite certain when you would arrive or how long you meant to stay, but she will be delighted not to have missed you."

"We mean to stay until the beginning of next week at least."

"We may be obliged to stay longer now, my dear," Mr Gardiner said. "For as well as your ever-expanding circle, we must also apparently find time to make the acquaintance of Miss Darcy."

Mrs Whitaker and her sister both exclaimed at the notion. "Miss Darcy? You jest, surely."

"No, indeed," Mrs Gardiner replied. "Mr Darcy asked Lizzy just this afternoon if he might make the introduction."

"When did you have occasion to speak to Mr Darcy? He hardly ever comes into town."

"No, we met him at Pemberley."

"You never mentioned you were Mr Darcy's guests at Pemberley!" Miss Tanner said reverently.

Mr Gardiner began to chuckle. "We were not, madam. We applied to see it just as we applied to see Blenheim and Chatsworth. We were not there by invitation—though Lizzy does boast a trifling acquaintance with its owner."

The sisters both looked to Elizabeth for confirmation.

She smiled weakly. "He stayed for a few weeks at a house near my own last autumn. I saw him at a few dances."

Mr Gardiner explained that they had encountered Mr Darcy on the lawn at Pemberley. "He did us the honour of escorting us around the lake."

"Faith!" cried Mrs Whitaker. "You must have made quite an impression at those few dances, Miss Bennet."

Elizabeth stumbled over a reply and was grateful for her aunt's determination to have her say in the conversation.

"Lizzy's cousin is also parson to Mr Darcy's aunt, Lady Catherine de Bourgh. And you saw him again while you were visiting Mr and Mrs Collins in the spring, did you not, Lizzy?"

"Yes, once or twice."

Mrs Whitaker was unconvinced. "We are cousins to Mr Darcy's own parson, but he has never walked either of us around his lake. Has he, Jenny?"

Miss Tanner shook her head. Elizabeth felt the weight of their gazes and, worse, that of her aunt, who was regarding her with new interest.

"He may simply have felt obliged to make the application for the sake of civility," Mr Gardiner opined. "He offered that I should fish in his lake whenever I desired, too, and I doubt he meant that either. Or at least, he likely forgot it as soon as we were out of sight."

Elizabeth's uncle had said something similar earlier in the day, and she had not contradicted him then. She dared not now either for fear of rousing her aunt's suspicions further, yet she felt for the second time that Mr Gardiner had quite mistaken Mr Darcy's character. The master of Pemberley might be many things, but impetuous was not one of them—an offer made by him was an offer meant.

"You think it was pride that induced him to be civil?" Mrs Whitaker enquired doubtfully. "I would have thought pride more likely to make him uncivil, and not notice you at all."

"Is that how he more commonly behaves?" asked Mrs Gardiner. "We had heard reports that he is rather above himself."

Her friend shrugged. "If he is, I daresay he has a right to be. He moves in far higher circles than we ever will and owns just about everything as far as the eye can see. But I did not mean to accuse him of being ill-mannered—quite the opposite if he singled your party out for attention as you describe." She cocked the smallest of suggestive nods at Elizabeth. "Do help yourself to more coffee if you would like some, sir."

Mr Gardiner, who had been peering forlornly between the coffee pot and his cup, thanked her. "We met a few of his servants today," he said as he poured. "They certainly had not a bad word to say about him. His housekeeper in particular seemed determined that we should think well of him. Went to great lengths to convince us of his affability to the poor. He is evidently a liberal master, and that, no doubt, disposes her to assume he will be equally generous abroad, but these great men all delight in proclaiming charity and very few follow words with deeds."

"To be fair to the lady, she is best placed to know, for it is her whom Mr Darcy tasks with distributing clothes and food amongst the poor once a quarter. It was his mother's tradition originally, but he re-established it after his father died."

"And you know, he endowed the alms-house at Kympton," Miss Tanner added to her sister's evident surprise.

"I did not know that! Though I did know he paid for the new schoolhouse in Shepsbrook."

Mrs Gardiner raised her eyebrows, which saddened Elizabeth to see. Upon leaving Pemberley yesterday, she had related to her aunt and uncle some of the particulars of Mr Darcy's dealings with Mr Wickham, explaining that the former's character was by no means so faulty as it had been considered in Hertfordshire. It shamed her to comprehend how injurious her previous censure must have been that Mrs Gardiner should still be surprised by reports of his charity.

For herself, she was disinclined to be shocked. She knew from his letter the care Mr Darcy took of his friends and relations, and from those friends and relations themselves in what esteem he was held by them. She had no reason to doubt his housekeeper's account and every reason to believe him capable of such generosity as Mrs Whitaker and Miss Tanner described. Rather than surprise, Elizabeth felt a fresh wave of shame for ever having disliked him.

"What can you tell us of his sister?" she enquired.

"She is even less well-known than her brother—hardly ever comes into Lambton. Some say she is too above herself, and that is as may be, though I expect she spends most of her time in London anyway," Mrs Whitaker answered.

"I do not blame her for that," said Miss Tanner, "for she cannot have many friends hereabouts. The nearest estate must be three or four miles away from Pemberley, she is not yet out, and I cannot imagine she would be permitted to associate with other young ladies her age in the local towns or villages. It must be a lonely existence in that huge house all cut off from the world."

Exceedingly lonely, Elizabeth privately agreed. It was unthinkably cruel that Mr Wickham, one of Miss Darcy's few childhood friends, had used her so ill as to attempt to persuade her to elope at just fifteen years old. Pity allayed some of the guilt Elizabeth felt for agreeing to be introduced to her. Miss Darcy was the young lady who had usurped her dearest sister in Mr Bingley's affections, but she hoped Jane would not object to the meeting. Her sister was too kind to blame a naïve, young girl for the carelessness and caprice of men.

That Mr Darcy wished to introduce his sister was something of a marvel. She would not have blamed him for doing everything in his power to keep them apart after her obstinate and ill-founded defence of Mr Wickham. Yet, not only was he desirous that they should meet, he also averred that so was Miss Darcy.

Such a wish could only have been born of her brother's recommendation, giving rise to a suspicion in Elizabeth's mind of Mr Darcy's attachment to her remaining so steady that all her credulity and petulance had not been enough to completely erase his good opinion. She could not but be gratified by anyone admiring her so well, though she did not think it warranted the eruption of warmth that overspread her cheeks. She looked around her company to see whether she was discovered, but nobody was paying her any attention.

"What are your plans while you are here?" Mrs Whitaker was asking.

"We thought to keep our time free to renew some old friendships," Mr Gardiner replied.

"You are very accommodating, sir. My late husband would not have been so obliging, I am sure. He always wanted to be off shooting, or drinking, or riding somewhere."

"Time spent in good company is no hardship, madam. Besides, my wife has allowed me more than my share of entertainments on this trip. And you never know, I may yet find myself fishing at Pemberley." He winked as he said this, evidently still not believing it likely.

"What about you, Miss Bennet? What do you hope to see while you are in this part of the world?"

Elizabeth was not expecting the first thought to pop into her head to be Mr Darcy. "Other than a bit of walking, I am at my aunt's disposal."

It was rapidly settled that the whole party would return to Mrs Whitaker's establishment for dinner the next day, where Mr and Mrs Heyworth and a few other of Mrs Gardiner's erstwhile neighbours would join them. After that, the evening seemed at a natural end, and Mr Gardiner excused their party.

It was a short walk to the inn where they were staying, and Mrs Gardiner was too full of rejoicing over the evening's success to allow talk of anything else. That suited Elizabeth well; she walked arm in arm with her uncle, happy not to be called upon for more than the occasional nod or smile.

Her mind was engaged wondering what Mr Darcy was thinking at that moment. Now that enough time had elapsed for the shock of seeing her to wear off, had he remembered to be angry? She was amazed he had not been angry the moment he set eyes on her; she well knew how that sentiment looked on him, yet she had seen nothing of it in his countenance earlier. On the contrary, all she had perceived in him, other than embarrassment, was what appeared to be a concerted eagerness to please.

She smiled into the night. What she truly wondered was, after everything that had transpired between them, whether it was possible that Mr Darcy still loved her—and how she would feel about it if he did.

CHAPTER SIX

A LONG-AWAITED INTRODUCTION

The first of Darcy's guests arrived as he was still eating breakfast. He did not need to look out of the window to know whose carriage he could hear rolling up the drive. He knew Miss Bingley would have obliged her brother to leave Derby unreasonably early to ensure they were here before all the others and able, therefore, to boast a greater intimacy with the family. He only hoped her desire to ingratiate herself had extended so far as to invite Georgiana to travel with her.

"Alas, no, Mr Darcy. Miss Darcy preferred to travel with Miss Ada today."

"I do not believe she will be far behind us," Bingley said, stepping around his sister and reaching to shake Darcy's hand. "Most of the party were up and about by the time Caroline and I left. Except Pettigrew and Sedrick. I should not expect them until later if I were you."

"Late night, was it?"

"I left them to it at one. And I should have gone to bed a

darned sight earlier had I known I was to be dragged from my pit at such an ungodly hour."

Miss Bingley tutted. "Somebody had to leave first, Charles, and it might as well have been us. We should have been waiting there all day if ours had not been the first carriage out of the stables."

"I ought to have made Louisa travel with you and come at a more reasonable hour in Hurst's carriage."

Darcy noticed his housekeeper hovering nearby, waiting for the Bingleys to cease squabbling, and indicated that she should come forward.

"Thank you, sir. If I might just acquaint Mr and Miss Bingley with the alteration to their usual rooms?"

An increasingly familiar sinking feeling weighed in Darcy's stomach at the reminder of the threat that now loomed over Pemberley. Bingley's eyes widened as Mrs Reynolds explained that the east wing was off limits to all guests. Miss Bingley was more concerned with how much wardrobe space she would have in her new room, and, to Darcy's relief, the housekeeper offered to take her there to inspect it.

"Upon my word, that sounds serious," Bingley said when they were gone.

"It is precautionary only. I do not yet know the cause or the extent of the problem."

"What *is* the problem?"

"A crack in the stonework."

Bingley made a face that betrayed his ignorance as to the significance of such a defect even before he breezily remarked that he was certain it would all turn out for the best.

Not for the first time, Darcy considered how uncomplicated his friend's existence must be with no greater accountability than to ensure his sisters did not outspend their inheritance before they married. "How far behind did you say you thought Georgiana might be?"

"Not more than half an hour, I should think."

It was closer to three hours, by which point Darcy was seething with impatience. In that time, he welcomed Aldridge, the Hursts, and even the Coxes, despite Cox's wife being a notoriously late riser. Templeton and his eldest sister arrived without either their younger sister, Miss Ada, or Georgiana in their carriage.

"Ada is travelling with Miss Darcy and Mrs Annesley in your carriage," Miss Templeton explained, with her brother adding, "They were fussing over clashing bonnets when we left."

Garroway came next with his wife and sister, receiving the same information from Mrs Reynolds about bedrooms that Bingley had and requiring Darcy to repeat his disagreeable account of the damage to the east wall. Even Pettigrew and his brother, Sedrick, staggered biliously over the threshold before Georgiana made an appearance.

When, finally, one of the footmen informed him that his sister had arrived and gone directly to the breakfast room, his insides jumped with anticipation so great, it was an effort to maintain his composure. He left those of his guests who had gathered in the saloon and made his way to see her. She was dining with her travelling companions, both of whom he met with forced civility, making all the requisite enquiries as to their journey and good health as he waited for them to be done.

The looks passing around the table gave him cause to suspect he was not disguising his impatience well, but it could not be helped. No sooner had Georgiana laid down her knife and fork than he begged her companions to spare her and held out his hand to pull her to her feet.

"Come with me," he whispered as he tucked her hand

into the crook of his arm and led her away from the others to somewhere they might talk privately.

"Is something the matter?" she whispered.

"Yes, you are late."

"Am I? Forgive me. Ada and I—"

Darcy waved away her apology and pulled her up the stairs, unable to keep from smiling.

"Is the problem Mr Ferguson wanted to talk to you about less serious than you thought, then?"

"It is too early to tell. What made you ask that?"

"You seem far less troubled today than when you left Derby yesterday."

His smile broadened. They reached the top of the stairs, and he nudged her into the nearest room, pulling the door closed behind them. "I have something to tell—" It was his turn to be silenced.

"Oh, Fitzwilliam! It is beautiful!"

"What is?"

"This room! Did you do this for me?"

He became aware, belatedly, that he had brought her to the Chesterfield room, which he had, indeed, had fitted up for her pleasure. He wished he had taken her somewhere else, for the further delay was excruciating. "I did, and I am pleased you like it, but—"

"Oh, I do! This wallpaper is exquisite! And these sofas—they are not the same, are they? Or are they? They look so different now the room is lighter!"

"I had them reupholstered. Georgiana, please—"

"Is this mother's writing desk?"

"Yes. Would you—"

"How well it looks in here! And this chair is the perfect match—Oh, Fitzwilliam, you do spoil me! I do not think I shall ever want to leave this room again."

"I hope you will, for I should like you to come to Lambton with me."

"Lambton? When?"

"Now."

At last, Georgiana ceased dashing about the room and looked at him. "But I have only just got home."

"I know, but there is somebody there I should like to introduce you to." He took a deep breath. "Miss Elizabeth Bennet is staying at the Plough and Horseshoe."

The room instantly lost all its appeal, and he became the sole focus of his sister's attention. "I thought you said it was unlikely that I should ever meet her."

"She is visiting the area with her relations. We happened across each other on my return yesterday."

"Then of course! I should dearly love to make her acquaintance. Only..."

"What?"

She began twisting her fingertips together as she always did when she was nervous. "Are you sure she will welcome it? I do not know the exact nature of your parting, but I hope you will pardon me for saying that it seemed rather final. I should not like to obtrude on Miss Bennet's notice if there were any chance that she would resent my doing so."

Darcy knew not whether to grimace or triumph. That his sister had guessed the acrimonious end to his relationship with Elizabeth was unfortunate, yet he savoured the thrill of being able to reply that she had already agreed to the introduction. Georgiana's sweet smile gave him even more cause to rejoice. He knew he had disappointed her when his letters from Rosings abruptly altered from promises of a dear new friend to the curtailment of any such hope.

"Then we absolutely must go," she said gently. "I confess, I am relieved. You made her sound so kind and so sensible that I feared someone at Rosings must have offended her somehow to induce such a sudden change of heart. Cousin Fitzwilliam perhaps—he can be a little careless when he is in a sportive humour—or our aunt more likely."

No. Neither of them.

Darcy absorbed the sting of her unintentional indictment in silence. It was nothing for which he had not already berated himself a thousand times, and sting it should, but Georgiana was wrong on one count. Elizabeth had not had a change of heart in Kent, sudden or otherwise. He had only mistaken—nay, neglected to even consider—what her feelings were. If she had undergone any change of heart, it was since then. For the Elizabeth he left in Kent would never have consented to this meeting.

A spike of alarm cut through his urgency. Had he mistaken her again? Had it been naught but civility that made her agree to the introduction? Evidently mortified to be caught at his house, perhaps she had felt obliged to consent and was now dreading his visit. He despised not knowing. He was used to being master of all he surveyed, the answer to every quandary if not in his grasp, then within his power to discover. Uncertainty and indecision were anathema to him. That was the problem with Elizabeth. He always felt utterly out of control around her, with no idea what she would make him feel or do or say. It terrified him, but by God he felt exhilarated by it—enlivened in a way he had never known possible until he met her.

"That was careless of me, Fitzwilliam, I apologise. I did not mean to give you any alarm. I am sure nobody insulted her."

He smiled and shook his head. "Miss Bennet is more than capable of prevailing against anyone's insults, I assure you. Now, do you wish to change first, or shall we leave directly?"

"Leave? Where are you going?"

Darcy cursed privately to see Bingley saunter into the

room. He had no wish to share this introduction with anybody, least of all the man he had gone to such lengths to separate from Elizabeth's sister. A more manifest reminder of the foundation for her antipathy he could not imagine.

"Lambton. To see Miss Bennet," Georgiana answered before he could prevent her.

Bingley's ears pricked like a bloodhound's. "Miss Bennet is in Lambton?"

"Miss *Elizabeth* Bennet, yes," Darcy said carefully. "She is travelling with her aunt and uncle. We bumped into each other yesterday and agreed that I would bring Georgiana to meet her."

Bingley's disappointment was plain to see, though, in his inimitable fashion, he soon found another way to be cheerful about it. "What a turn up! It has been far too long since I saw any of my friends from Hertfordshire, and she will have all the news we could hope for. I wish you had said sooner, Darcy, I should not have bothered changing. If you will wait for me to get my boots back on, I shall come with you."

There was nothing for it; Darcy could not refuse. So be it, but he was determined to give his sister her moment first. "You will have to make your own way there, for I mean to take Georgiana in the curricle. Miss Bennet is staying at the Plough and Horseshoe." He did not give Bingley time to object and ushered Georgiana out of the room, down the servants' stair, and out through a side door to avoid detection by anyone else who might waylay them.

CHAPTER SEVEN

INAUSPICIOUS ENCOUNTERS

Mrs Reynolds paused to catch her breath, flinching at a new and sharp pain in her side. It passed as quickly as it had come on, which was just as well, for she had not the time for infirmity this day—or any other, for that matter. With a determined puff and a firm nod, she pushed away from the dresser and continued into the servants' hall.

She was met with pandemonium, so many guests and all their people only adding to the usual bustle. Not every visitor had servants travelling with them. Some were sharing a manservant, lady's maid, or both between their party; others were borrowing from Pemberley's roll. In total there were seven extra bodies, and most of them appeared to have gathered in the servants' hall to protest or enquire about something.

"Mrs Reynolds?" called poor Hannah from the centre of the throng. She excelled as head housemaid but was not of strong character. She was visibly floundering in the face of so many demands.

"How may I help you all?" Mrs Reynolds said evenly, inserting herself into the melee.

"The bell-pull in my mistress's room is not working."

"No, nor mine."

So appealed the maids for Miss Bingley and Lady Garroway, both of whom had been moved into the scant-used chambers on the upper floor.

She might have guessed some negative would arise from the last-minute alteration—an excellent illustration of why she abhorred unpreparedness. "I shall have it seen to directly."

"Are there strawberries on tonight's menu? Miss Adams cannot so much as touch a strawberry without coming out in a rash."

"Chef is aware. And pray advise Miss Adams to avoid the kitchen gardens and conservatory."

Mr Aldridge's manservant wished to know where the luggage had been taken to, for he was one box short.

"In the porter's lodge, sir, though I believe your box is on the dresser out there in the corridor."

"Might I trouble you for some pomade? I have forgotten to pack Mr Templeton's."

Mrs Reynolds looked at the unfamiliar young man who had asked this. "You will need to speak to Mr Matthis about that, sir. I do not stock gentleman's pomade in my store cupboard." She did, as it happened, but she had no intention of handing out Pemberley's supplies to anyone so unworthy as to forget their master's own.

She espied one of the footmen striding past the doorway and called to him. "Andrew, none of the bell-pulls along the upper north corridor are working. Will you run and let Mr Matthis know."

"I'm on an errand for Mr Hurst at the moment, ma'am, but I'll see if I can find Thomas or William to do it." He made to leave, then paused to add with a grin, "Master just showed Miss Darcy the Chesterfield. Right pleased wi'it, she were. Right pleased."

He went on his way, and Mrs Reynolds returned to answering questions, a strong feeling of gratification warming her from the inside. The late Lady Anne would have been as proud as punch to see the way her son cherished the daughter she did not live long enough to love herself. He truly had grown into quite the most generous young man. And she was pleased to have advised him to choose the lighter wallpaper, for she knew it to be Miss Darcy's preferred colour.

"Ah, Mrs Reynolds," said a new voice. "I am glad I have found you. The bell-pull in Mr Bingley's new room does not appear to be working."

She looked back around to assure Mr Bingley's manservant that the matter was in hand.

"Excellent. And might I enquire what time dinner will be served today?"

"The same time as it always is, sir."

"Right-ho. I thought I had better make sure, for Mr Bingley has just gone out with Mr Darcy and his sister, and I thought there might have been a change of plan."

"Out?"

"Yes, to visit Miss Bennet in Lambton."

Mrs Reynolds prided herself on authority that verged on omniscience where the running of the household was concerned. She therefore asked no further questions and kept her expression neutral, though not without some effort, for she was sorely vexed. Enough guests had just descended on Pemberley to fill almost every bedroom that was still available for use, every one of them expecting to enjoy Mr Darcy's company—something this 'Miss Bennet' knew full well, for Mrs Reynolds explicitly told her and her friends yesterday.

She could not like that this was the moment the young woman deemed appropriate to declare herself at home to callers and lure the master away.

"Miss Bennet is in Lambton?" Miss Bingley's maid said derisively. "Well, there is a happy coincidence for the lady. The same as when she chanced to show up at Grosvenor Street when we were in town over winter as well."

"It is her sister, Miss Elizabeth, I understand," Mr Bingley's man corrected her.

Miss Bingley's maid screwed up her face. "My mistress would tell you that is even worse news."

Mrs Reynolds pressed her lips together to prevent herself from asking why, though she was vastly relieved when Lady Garroway's maid asked instead.

"Because the older sister is just your common or garden fortune hunter. But the younger one, Miss Elizabeth—she is the worst sort of impertinent country coquette. As soon quarrel with a man as flutter her eyelashes at him—preferably both at once. No manners whatsoever by all accounts."

"Not *all* accounts," said a stern voice.

Miss Bingley's maid blushed deeply as Mr Darcy's manservant entered the hall. "I am only repeating what my mistress told me, Mr Vaughan. Miss Bingley said Miss Elizabeth plagued Mr Darcy with arguments at every opportunity."

"What your mistress said to you at Netherfield is of no interest to anyone here. You are at Pemberley now, and Mr Darcy does not tolerate parlour-room tittle-tattle amongst the servants."

"Quite so. Thank you, Mr Vaughan," said Mrs Reynolds, more to save face than to express any real gratitude. It ought to have been she who quieted such talk—and would have been under any other circumstances—but on this occasion, she wished Miss Bingley's maid had not been silenced. She would hear the worst of the charges against Miss Bennet. Better the [redacted] you know, after all, and though there would be precious little she could do to prevent it if the woman chose to cut up the master's happiness, at least she could be prepared to help ease him through any difficulty from afar, as she had done for him many times before.

CHAPTER EIGHT

FORCED CONFIDENCES

Elizabeth had hoped the discomposure that beset her upon seeing Mr Darcy's curricle approaching the inn would subside once the introduction with his sister had taken place. Alas, almost half an hour later she was no less agitated than when he initially entered the room, looking disquietingly well turned out and much taller than she could ever remember him being. An innocent glance to compare his and his sister's appearance had flustered her almost beyond recovery from the outset, for her appraisal had concluded very much in the brother's favour.

His collected behaviour ought to have aided the restoration of her own, for throughout the meeting, he betrayed no awkwardness, nor any indelicate display of regard to make her uncomfortable. Regrettably, it had the opposite effect of emphasising the alteration in his character from proud and disagreeable to civil and attentive. The prospect that her reproofs should have induced such a change only heightened her bewilderment.

Miss Darcy was evidently vastly uneasy, and her discomfiture might ordinarily have moved Elizabeth to focus her energies on putting the young lady at ease. Instead, it begged the question what Mr Darcy could possibly have said about her to provoke his sister to be so embarrassed. Thus, all curiosity as to his affections was further fuelled, increasing the weight of his gaze each time it came to rest upon her.

Mr Bingley's arrival, sudden and exuberant, brought with it yet more uncertainty. His vivacious cordiality made it easy to overlook any vestige of anger she felt towards him for abandoning her sister. It also made it impossible to discern whether his interest in her family was a veiled search for news about Jane or merely good breeding.

To all of this was added the undercurrent of Mrs Gardiner's scrutiny. Though Elizabeth was sure her aunt thought herself subtle, her every exchange with Mr Darcy drew Mrs Gardiner's hawkish observation. It was enough to make even the most disinterested person nervous and was abrading what little equanimity she had remaining.

"Are you alone in travelling with your aunt and uncle? Are all your other sisters at Longbourn?" asked Mr Bingley.

Elizabeth tried her best to attend to him, but as he asked this, Mr Darcy said something to Mr Gardiner that put such a look of surprise on her uncle's face as made her desperate to know the particulars.

"I should be delighted, sir," Mr Gardiner replied. "Though I shall have to take you up on your offer of borrowing a rod and tackle."

The offer to fish at Pemberley had been repeated! Elizabeth was gratified to have been right about Mr Darcy's sincerity—if so wrong about everything else. How different he now seemed. Never had she seen him at such pains to please—and never had she thought to see that effort expended on any relation of hers!

She turned from Mr Bingley to join in the other conversation. "Aunt, will we ever drag my uncle home again, do you suppose? A spot at that beautiful lake and a fishing rod in hand, and he might very well decide to stay here forever."

Mrs Gardiner merrily concurred with the very real prospect of having to go home without her husband, then took up Mr Bingley's mention of Longbourn and began speaking to him of her children, who were staying there.

"You are kind to say the lake is beautiful, Miss Bennet," Mr Darcy said quietly while the others were talking together. "I meant to ask whether you enjoyed the park."

"I did, very much."

She would have elaborated on how well she liked the informality of the landscape but for the fear of saying anything that sounded covetous. It seemed enough to gratify Mr Darcy. He sat back in his chair with a smile that she remembered to have sometimes seen when he looked at her in Hertfordshire—a small, unassuming curl to his mouth that changed an otherwise severe expression into one of contemplative contentment. It was an understated, almost private display—particularly when juxtaposed to his friend's effusiveness—but now that she knew what to look for, she could scarcely any longer see the disapproving, superior man who had slighted her at the Meryton Assembly. He looked simply happy. Happy to be there. Happy to be with her.

Her heart gave a silly flutter, and she hastened to speak to distract herself from it. "Miss Darcy, I imagine you must enjoy Pemberley's grounds very well. I know your cousin Miss de Bourgh likes to tour the park at Rosings in a phaeton. Do you share her fondness for driving?"

"N-no. I-I never took to it well."

Mr Darcy leant forward with an encouraging smile for his sister. "Georgiana likes to draw the various views from around the park. She has produced some exceedingly fine sketches."

"Then I am not surprised at your aversion to driving around it, Miss Darcy. A moving carriage is absolutely the worse place from which to compose a sketch."

"Oh, I did not—"

"Miss Bennet is teasing."

It was gratifying that Mr Darcy understood as much, but Elizabeth was nevertheless sorry to have unsettled his sister if she was not used to sportive conversation—which she could well believe was the case. She was on the verge of apologising when Miss Darcy let out a soft laugh.

"Some of my early attempts did look as though I drew them on the move."

Elizabeth grinned. "I might take up telling people that is how all my sketches were made. It would go some way to excusing the results."

Mr Darcy announced their departure not long after this, calling on his sister to join him in expressing his wish to see their party at Pemberley before they left the country.

Miss Darcy blushed deeply and made her appeal to the floor. "Um, y-yes. We should like, very much, if you would join us. For dinner. If you please."

Miss Darcy's embarrassment was obvious, but Elizabeth was quite sure her own was greater as she considered the implications of such a request. Mr Darcy wished to prolong the acquaintance even further; he did not seem troubled by the prospect of Mr Bingley hearing more news of Jane; he wished to introduce her aunt and uncle—the very relations with whom any intercourse a few months ago would have been a disgrace—to his 'large party of friends,' all of whom she supposed hailed from the same elevated sphere as he. She could explain it by no other means than that he must still love her.

It was a conclusion by which not even the bravest person could remain unaffected, and she turned away to compose herself before she must meet anyone's eye. She did not summon the courage to look up again until the whole company had said their goodbyes. She managed only a fleeting smile and a brief curtsey before the door closed behind them, at which point, Mrs Gardiner turned directly to stare at her.

"What did you think of Mr Bingley?" Elizabeth enquired before her aunt could voice the question sitting openly on her face.

"I thought him a thoroughly pleasant fellow," her uncle replied. "Very easy manners indeed."

Mrs Gardiner agreed. "I approve of him quite as much as the next handsome, rich young man. He has shown himself to be no more careless and inconstant than the rest of them."

"You are severe upon my sex!" her husband complained.

"Probably, but of Mr Bingley I say only what is true. It was easy for him to be in love with Jane when she was there in front of him, but away from her, his head was quickly turned. It always goes off the same." She gave Elizabeth a peculiar look and added, "Usually."

It was too much; Elizabeth announced her intention to dress for dinner and hurried from the room.

Mrs Gardiner was sufficiently distracted by her friends' company throughout Mrs Whitaker's soiree that Elizabeth dared to hope all curiosity had been forgotten. Her heart sank when, after retiring for the night, her bedroom door opened, and the light of a candle emerged around it.

"May I come in?" Mrs Gardiner enquired.

With her own candle still burning, Elizabeth could hardly pretend to be asleep. She pulled her knees up to make room at the foot of the bed for her aunt, who began far more seriously than she had anticipated.

"Lizzy, is there anything amiss between you and Mr Darcy? Anything about which I ought to know?"

"No, I assure you. There is nothing for you to worry about."

"I am relieved to hear it. Still, it is evident that you are better acquainted with him than you previously let on. Just as it is evident that you esteem him."

"What makes you say that?" Elizabeth said—too quickly. It made her aunt smile pityingly.

"You did well at saying as little as possible at dinner, I grant you. But you rather gave yourself away when you spoke up to defend him—vehemently, I might add—against Mr Wickham."

"And rightly so! Mr Heyworth was implying that Mr Darcy treated Mr Wickham poorly when it was entirely the other way around."

"Yes, yes, so you informed me yesterday. But you never said whence this new intelligence originated. You certainly could not have inferred so much from that one trifling remark of Mr Darcy's housekeeper, surely?"

"No, of course not! I have it on much better authority."

"Whose authority could possibly be better than Mr Wickham's?"

"Mr Darcy's." Elizabeth clamped her mouth closed in exasperation when she saw the triumph flashing in her aunt's countenance.

"And pray, what business had Mr Darcy in telling you about Mr Wickham?"

Elizabeth had neither the courage nor the inclination to explain that Mr Darcy had divulged his history with Mr Wickham in a bid to defend his character after she hurled a litany of unfounded charges at him, accusing him of defying his father's will, and of casting off his childhood friend. She was ashamed enough already; she had no desire to witness her aunt's disappointment also. In the end, however, she was not required to confess anything. Her aunt guessed.

"It is because he did not wish you to think ill of him, is it not? Because he is in love with you. Now do not attempt to deny it—any fool could see he was overflowing with admiration this morning."

Elizabeth did as she was bid and refrained from denying it. Her heart was racing to hear it said aloud by another person.

"You do not seem pleased by it though. I got the impression today that you had come to like him more. Was I wrong?"

"No, I do not dislike him. I do not know what I feel for him, but it is not dislike. Would that I did know, for the last thing I wish to do is hurt him again."

There was a pause, then Mrs Gardiner said, cautiously, "Again?"

Elizabeth held her breath for a moment while she contemplated her options, then blew it out in surrender. With her forehead resting on her knees, as though that would shield her from judgment, she whispered, "Mr Darcy proposed to me in Kent." She looked up when she heard her aunt gasp. "I refused him. I refused him in the most hurtful, petulant way imaginable. Pray do not ask me for the particulars. It is enough to know that he and I parted on exceedingly bad terms."

Mrs Gardiner was fixed in disbelief. "Why did you not tell us? We would never have gone to Pemberley if we had known this. What must he have thought to discover us there?"

"I did not know how to tell you. Then, when everybody

we asked told us he would not be there, I thought I would not have to."

Her aunt looked supremely displeased with this answer. "That was selfish, Lizzy. Your uncle and I have worked incredibly hard to establish a good reputation for ourselves. You might have undone all that in one morning if Mr Darcy had been less forgiving."

The accusation cut all the deeper for the truth of it. Elizabeth had never once considered the consequences to her aunt and uncle of being discovered at Pemberley—only her own discomfort in going there. Then, though it was her aunt's wounded gaze that held hers, it was her own voice she could hear as she recalled viciously deriding Mr Darcy for his 'selfish disdain for the feelings of others'. And whereas he had subsequently been proved innocent of any such defect, she had betrayed an even greater want of consideration.

"You are right," she whispered. "I am sorry."

Mrs Gardiner sighed deeply, observably dispelling some of her anger. "There has been no harm done, and I do see that it has been difficult for you. Besides, it seems we have all been exceedingly fortunate, for he has obviously forgiven you."

"I know, and I could not have been more astonished to discover it. Though I know not what to make of it. I should hate to give him false hope. Until I know my own feelings, it would be cruel to encourage his affections."

"Perhaps you might be careful where you direct your high spirits until you better know your own heart, then, but he seems a sensible man. I am sure we may dine with him as friends without issue. I doubt we will even see him when we go tomorrow."

"Tomorrow?"

"We must return Miss Darcy's call, Lizzy."

Elizabeth found she was not averse to such a visit.

Despite her shyness, Miss Darcy had seemed a most agreeable young lady—certainly as nice as any of her aunt's acquaintance on whom they would no doubt call if they did not go to Pemberley. It would be as pleasant a way to pass the morning as any. And her aunt might be wrong; they might see Mr Darcy while they were there.

The prospect did not displease her, and she gave her agreement to the scheme.

"Aunt, I beg you would not tell anyone about this. The situation is delicate enough, without raising anyone's expectations."

Mrs Gardiner assured Elizabeth of her secrecy and departed, leaving her niece even wider awake than she had been before she came in. Having prided herself all her life for being an excellent studier of character, retrospect had shown Elizabeth she was far from a good judge—woefully unqualified to yield the power, which her fancy told her she still possessed, of bringing on the renewal of Mr Darcy's addresses.

CHAPTER NINE

A SPHERE LESS CONCEITED

Darcy privately conceded the competition when Hurst pulled his fourth carp out of the river before an hour had passed. His heart was not in it anyway. From this spot on the bank, he had a clear view of Pemberley's easternmost wall, where an ever-shifting lattice of cracks seemed to dance over the stones beneath the passing clouds. The actual fissure was not visible from this distance, though it might have been better if it were, for his imagination was playing merry hell with his eyes.

He had met before breakfast with Ferguson, who had informed him that neither of the stonemasons who customarily served the estate were available to take on the necessary work. Rather than wait, Darcy had instructed his steward to set about finding another, but these things took time, and the delay was troubling at best. He was attempting not to brood upon the worst.

"Is that another, sir?" called Pettigrew as Mr Gardiner hefted his net aloft to proudly reveal his squirming catch.

"Watch out, Hurst, you'll lose if you are not careful. Mr Gardiner here is proving to be a dab hand!"

Darcy tipped his hat at Mr Gardiner in compliment but allowed the others to carry on the conversation with him. Having Elizabeth's uncle among the party was perhaps the chief reason he could not concentrate on fishing. The man had shown himself to be intelligent, amiable, worldly, and sporting—everything, in fact, Darcy had dismissed him for not being, and he felt the full weight of Elizabeth's reproofs for the injustice. Therein lay the problem: Mr Gardiner presented a constant reminder of his niece, and that made everything else that might have occupied Darcy's thoughts ten times less urgent and a hundred times less interesting.

"Bingley tells me you live in the city, Mr Gardiner," said Cox, who had long ago abandoned his rod in favour of wandering up and down the bank, smoking cheroots. "Not much fishing to be had thereabouts—not for anything still alive, anyway. Where did you learn to hook 'em like that?"

"The river Stort," Mr Gardiner answered. "I hail from Hertfordshire originally."

"What brings you to Derbyshire?"

"Happenstance. My wife and I had planned a tour of the lakes this summer, but my work kept me in town a fortnight longer than planned, so we have been forced to curtail our travels."

Darcy tensed. Though a hard lesson indeed, he had come to be deeply ashamed of the self-consequence that once induced him to scorn Elizabeth's relations for their condition in life. Nevertheless, he knew not how his friends would receive the intelligence that Mr Gardiner lived by trade. He watched quietly, ready to interject should it seem as though any censure might be forthcoming.

Cox, like Bingley, had the markings of trade heavily imprinted upon his own fortune and was the least likely to object—and indeed, he raised nary an eyebrow. Pettigrew, egged on by Hurst, was far too interested in his sport to spare a thought for how any fisherman as competent as Mr Gardiner made his money. Pettigrew's younger brother picked up on the mention and glanced Darcy's way in askance, though a dark glare was enough to banish his interest. Sedrick was here only at his older brother's request and had too little consequence and much more sense than to question the master of Pemberley about anything.

The remaining three were of most interest to Darcy. Aldridge, whose family was almost as old as his own, looked surprised, though not wholly displeased. He, above all Darcy's acquaintance, valued excellent understanding, and he seemed satisfied with the lively debate already compassed with Mr Gardiner about the standard of editorship at the *Times*. Templeton also looked taken aback, though it became clear when he quietly remarked, "Mellowing in your dotage, eh?" that it was not Mr Gardiner's occupation that astonished him so much as Darcy's own tolerance of it.

Garroway's countenance gave nothing away. A baron, he was the only titled guest in attendance; and with an estate of a similar size to Pemberley, and his mother a great favourite of Lady Catherine's, he was very much of the same circle as Darcy. If any among the party were likely to share his former, conceited prepossessions, it was Garroway.

"And what is your business, Mr Gardiner?" he enquired.

To his credit, Elizabeth's uncle neither equivocated nor cowered, though he must have been aware of the derision behind the question. "I own several warehouses in the city."

"And in what way did that impinge on your travels?"

Mr Gardiner gave a grunt of dissatisfaction. "It was Castlereagh's announcement back in June that he meant to repeal the Orders in Council that did it. Everyone lost their minds and began sending cartfuls of wares to the docks as though all trade with the United States would instantly resume. The wharfs began clogging up, which led to a backlog of domestic traffic that delayed more than half my stock, most of which comes from the midlands." He picked up his rod and began preparing to cast again. "Of course, it was all for nothing. Now Madison has declared war, the ministry has impounded all American ships in port anyway."

"If Liverpool had repealed the Orders when Madison first requested it, there would *be* no war with America, and we might not be facing even higher excises to pay for it," Pettigrew grumbled without looking up from the spot where his line entered the water.

"That might have saved Mr Gardiner's tour of the lakes, but it is not likely to have staved off the conflict indefinitely," Darcy said grimly.

Mr Gardiner agreed, adding, "If Lord Liverpool is serious about mending relations with the Americans, he might wish to address his government's policy on impressment."

Sedrick, who had an opinion about most things, had one about this, and he came to sit next to Mr Gardiner to tell him about it.

Garroway turned to speak discreetly to Darcy. "He is an eclectic addition to the party, but not without promise. I daresay we shall survive. Where did you find him?"

"I am acquainted with his niece."

"Oh?" he replied, all intrigue, but Darcy gave him nothing more and after a brief pause, Garroway conceded. "Understood—none of my business. Have it your way. But I will say this." He tipped his chin at Mr Gardiner. "He is a distinct improvement on your other uncle, the late, prostrate Sir Lewis. He was never awake long enough to form an opinion, let alone express it."

Darcy's remorse was complete. Beyond a few raised eyebrows and some pointed questions, none of his friends—

friends whom he had been certain would ridicule and censure any suggestion of an alliance with a family of such low connexions—had any serious objection to Mr Gardiner's presence among them. He was not unaware that his own liberality had likely influenced theirs, or that there were those in society who would be less forbearing. Still, it shamed him deeply to see that the pride he once thought under good regulation was not typical of the sphere he grew up in but rather a product of his own, unregulated vanity.

"How are your wife and niece passing their time this morning, Mr Gardiner?" Bingley enquired.

"They planned to return Miss Darcy's call. They are probably at the house as we speak."

Darcy spent the next few minutes staring at nothing and listening to no one until at length, the prospect of appearing ridiculous began to seem a lesser evil than forfeiting the opportunity of seeing Elizabeth, whereupon he muttered something about arranging refreshments and set out for the house at a pace.

James directed him to the saloon, where his sister had received Elizabeth and her aunt. Miss Bingley and Mrs Hurst had joined her, and though initially vexed that more of the ladies had not troubled themselves to be sociable, Darcy soon decided it would have been better if neither of them had come either. Mrs Hurst added nothing to the conversation, and Miss Bingley's only notable contribution was a snide remark about Wickham's company having left Hertfordshire.

It served her less well than he was sure she hoped it would. Elizabeth answered calmly and collectedly that the militia's departure had caused neither her family nor the neighbourhood in general any distress beyond a scarcity of gentlemen with whom to dance at the next assembly. She looked at him as she said it, and her small, earnest smile turned Darcy's insides over. She believed him, then. His account of Wickham's true character, so indignantly, so angrily dashed off in a letter in the hours after her rejection all that bitterness she had overlooked and chosen to take him at his word. The gratitude, the sheer relief this stirred in him eclipsed Miss Bingley's paltry meanness and put a cheerful spring in his step as he escorted Elizabeth and Mrs Gardiner to their carriage.

"It was very good of you to return my sister's call, Miss Bennet. She will be delighted to have received a visit."

"As were we by hers, and so soon after her own arrival."

"She was eager to call. She has long been desirous of making your acquaintance." He was not discouraged when Elizabeth looked away, for she had not turned her head so far that he could not see the little lift at the corner of her mouth. "Have you any plans for the rest of the day, Mrs Gardiner?"

"My husband intends to take us to see the Roman lead mine at Lower Kympton this afternoon."

"If he ever decides he has caught enough of your fish," Elizabeth interjected.

Mrs Gardiner laughed awkwardly and glanced expressively at her niece as though to admonish her for such forwardness. "And tomorrow morning, we thought we might walk along the river to Dedman Gorge. I would see whether it is as beautiful as I recall."

"Be sure to cross to the west bank before you leave Lambton. You can no longer access the gorge from the other." Darcy could also have told them where the otter holts were usually to be seen and the best resting places were to be found, but since he was already forming an idea to accompany them on their walk, he kept the information in reserve and only wished them a pleasant excursion. "I look forward to seeing you all at dinner tomorrow," he said as he handed both ladies into the open carriage.

"Yes," was all the reply Elizabeth gave as she took her seat and fixed him with a curious look. He withstood her attention with thundering heart, more than happy to be the object of her scrutiny.

The carriage lurched into motion, and for the second time in as many days, Darcy was overcome with a bewildering array of emotions as he watched Elizabeth depart. Yet of one thing, he was absolutely certain: he still wanted, with a passion that was almost alarming in its intensity, to make her his wife.

CHAPTER TEN

OVERHEARINGS MORE TO THE PURPOSE

"I think Miss Bennet might be more than the master's friend, Edna."

"What makes you say that?"

"'Cause he defended her when Miss Bingley tried to do her down. Said she were the handsomest woman of his acquaintance and then stormed out of the room, all in a lather."

"I never heard of Mr Darcy storming anywh—"

"I've got to go!" William interrupted, and go he did.

Mrs Reynolds stood away from the door, straightened her skirts, plucked a jar from the shelf—any jar, for it served no purpose other than to give her the appearance of having been otherwise occupied—and left the storeroom. She did not reprimand Edna for gossiping, for which the obviously startled maid looked deeply relieved. She only returned to her sitting room in furious silence.

This was the second conversation she had overheard in the last hour that was not meant for her ears. The revelation that the master held Miss Bennet in high esteem would not have been welcome news even before that morning, for the young woman scarcely inspired admiration. With a reputation for being a quarrelsome coquette, she had come uninvited to the house, scorned every commendation given about the master, and made no secret of her acquaintance with the despicable George Wickham. She was not worthy of Mr Darcy's notice, let alone his affections; that she had managed to engage his heart was cause for the greatest concern.

This news, however, was rendered infinitely more alarming by the previous snippet Mrs Reynolds had chanced to overhear. About half an hour earlier, as she made her way discreetly through the house along the unseen service corridors that framed her world, she witnessed James answer the front door to two ladies. Miss Bennet and her companion, Daffodil, had called on Miss Darcy, and while the footman went to inform that young lady of their arrival, a damning discussion had passed between the pair.

"I should not have come—this is cruel," the younger had whispered to the older. "What if he thinks I am trying to throw myself in his path?"

"'Tis a little late to be worrying about that," had been Daffodil's response. "Your intrigues have landed you front and centre of his notice." She had taken a good look around before adding, "But you will receive no more censure from me. There are very few people with integrity enough to turn their noses up at all this."

James had returned at that moment to escort them to the morning room, but Mrs Reynolds had heard enough. Miss Bennet had revealed her design to captivate Mr Darcy, just as her sister had reportedly attempted to do to Mr Bingley. And the master, it seemed, had thrown all his usual discernment to the wind and allowed himself to be drawn in. It made Mrs Reynolds sick to her stomach to see so excellent a man fall prey to such duplicity. No doubt this woman saw Mr Darcy's wealth and assumed his life was one of ease and indulgence —ripe for the picking.

She knew better. She had seen first-hand the effect of death after death upon the family. In particular, she had watched the young master's travails after his father's sudden demise and witnessed with her own eyes his unstinting efforts to learn what he must to do for his tenants in a time of unprecedented national unrest. She had observed his devotion to his young, orphaned sister—and the devastation wrought upon him by what Mrs Reynolds suspected was her near ruin at the hands of his once treasured childhood friend.

Though she knew no details of what passed at Ramsgate the previous summer, she had surmised enough to know it was dire. She had brought to bear every ounce of her not inconsiderable influence to suppress all mention of it in the Darcy households. She regretted that her influence did not extend to allaying the profound sadness Wickham's betrayal had provoked in the master. That Miss Bennet thought to use him so ill again was the cruellest thing in the world, and Mrs Reynolds railed that her station in life made her utterly powerless to intervene.

As if intending to exasperate herself as much as possible against the young woman, Mrs Reynolds chose for her employment the examination of all her most recent letters from Eleanor, in every one of which her friend made some mention of her goddaughter. Dorothy—or Dot, as Eleanor called her—was the young lady responsible for Mrs Reynolds's long-held opinion that, unless another woman existed who possessed the same inimitable virtues, then there could be no one else who was good enough for Mr Darcy. For years, she had read Eleanor's proud reports of Dorothy's accomplishments and triumphs, and she had long wished to see the master settled with a woman half so deserving. Instead, this young upstart had insinuated herself into his affairs, and Mrs Reynolds could do nothing but watch in dismay as the dear man fell further and further under her spell.

The next morning did not so much dawn as emerge reluctantly from the long, uncomfortable night. Aches and pains kept Mrs Reynolds tossing and turning in her bed through all the hours of darkness, giving her far too much time to worry. There was, as always, plenty about which to fret. The bell-pull in Miss Bingley's room still stubbornly refused to work, two casks of redcurrant wine had spoiled, and there was mildew in one of the linen cupboards. Mr Hurst was up to his old tricks, attempting to bribe the footmen to steal liquor for him, and she had a strong suspicion that one of her maids was secretly stepping out with the new groom. Problems such as these, more irksome than truly distressing, nevertheless loomed large at three o'clock in the morning. Of late, however, more pressing anxieties had begun to obtrude.

She was not well. It was not something she could any longer deny. She knew what ailed her: the same thing as had taken her mother and both aunts. An unnamed, insidious end that she supposed she must be grateful had, in her case, waited until the advent of her seventh decade to show its hand. She was familiar with the course it would take, and she was resigned to it.

She was less able to reconcile herself to the peril overshadowing her beloved Pemberley. Two days ago, the problem with the house had been an inconvenience: extra work for already busy hands. But Mr Ferguson's uncharacteristically dour humour and Mr Vaughan's more than common guardedness concerning Mr Darcy had alerted her to there being a more serious problem afoot. She rarely walked around the eastern end of the house, for the servants' quarters were in the opposing wing. Thus, the previous evening, she had stolen a few minutes to view it for herself.

It was a startling sight; a deep wound in the fabric of the building that she felt as keenly as the ominous pangs afflicting her vitals. It imprinted all her dreams that night with tentacular crevasses until she gave up on sleep entirely and removed to her desk, where she set out all her qualms in a letter to her friend.

Revered though any housekeeper worth her salt must be, she was denied the luxury of friendship within the household over which she ruled. Such relationships eroded one's authority. Eleanor, an intimate companion since childhood, was the only person in whom Mrs Reynolds could safely confide, and so she had done in the early hours of that morning.

Her dismay at the deterioration of the house had been set down in but two lines, for what was there to say but that she hoped it could be repaired? Of her own health, she had written nothing. On the present danger to the master's happiness, she had dwelt with warmth for several pages. Eleanor liked to joke that she knew Mr Darcy better than his own mother ever had, so much had been revealed to her by this method over the years. While Mrs Reynolds had never divulged anything that might injure the master, she had written more often than she liked of his loneliness and melancholy. He was the best of men, but the happiness he deserved cruelly eluded him at every turn.

Never had he seemed sadder than these months since his sister's misadventure in Ramsgate. Whatever had passed in those few, significant days, whatever that scoundrel Wickham had done, had taken a terrible toll. When Mrs Reynolds received word that he was to bring a large party back to Pemberley with him this month, she had hoped it was with the intention of finally choosing a bride. A faithful companion, who would fill his empty house with children on whom he could dote as he had done his young sister, would be just the antidote to his solitude.

Alas, when she received the list of names, it appeared as though he had gone out of his way to invite as many married couples and male acquaintances as he was able. The only single women of marriageable age in the party were Miss Bingley and Miss Templeton. The first, despite the lady's most tenacious efforts, had failed to endear herself to him in all the years of their acquaintance. The second might have been considered a contender, had not James witnessed her embracing Mr Pettigrew enthusiastically in a dimly lit anteroom the previous evening. The dearth of eligible women had given rise to vexatious ramifications and her complaints to Eleanor on the subject had been lengthy and bitter.

Instead of either of these desirable ladies, it is Clarabelle who has insinuated herself into his attentions, exploiting his loneliness to extract an invitation to dinner. Thus, rather than the pleasure of overseeing a grand feast for the future mistress of Pemberley, I am reduced to appeasing Mr Matthis's disgruntlement at being required to serve a tradesman and his family at table.

CHAPTER ELEVEN

ARTS & ALLUREMENTS

Once the breakfast service was finished, Mrs Reynolds set out for Lambton with several bills to settle, a jar of Pemberley honey for the goldsmith who had promised to mend a link on her chatelaine gratis, and a handful of other correspondence from the house, saving whichever of the footmen was on post duty that day from making the trip. She delivered the chatelaine and honey first, then presented herself at the post office with her letters.

The postmaster was hunched over a letter, eyepiece in hand, squinting at the address. He looked up in surprise when she wished him good day. "Mrs Reynolds! Come in, come in. Perhaps you can be of assistance to us. None of us can make out the address on this letter beyond that it says Lambton—and even that is in some doubt, for it has already been mis-sent once."

Mrs Reynolds took the letter he held out to her and examined it. She sucked in her breath upon recognising the addressee and thrust it back at him as though it had burnt her. "This is for Miss Elizabeth Bennet. She is staying in town, though I am afraid I do not know where, precisely."

"Well, that is a good deal more information than we had before. Madam, you are a godsend."

She hoped all talk of Miss Bennet was done, but at that moment, the young lady herself walked past the window with her relations at her side, and Mrs Reynolds felt obliged to point them out to Mr Biggleswade.

He exclaimed at the good fortune and turned to one of his assistants. "Arthur, run it out to her quickly, before you lose sight of her." He shoved the letter at the boy, the boy grabbed for it, and the missive crumpled between their colliding hands, the wax seal snapping in half with an audible pop.

Mr Biggleswade growled with displeasure. "Never mind. Get on and catch up with her!"

Arthur ran from the shop and out of sight after the departing trio. The postmaster sighed wearily and apologised to Mrs Reynolds, who assured him there was no need and passed him her own letters to be stamped.

"There's another addressed to Miss Bennet here," announced another assistant, plucking a letter from the pile he was sorting and holding it aloft.

"Any more legible than the first?" Mr Biggleswade enquired, but before the boy could answer, Arthur burst back into the office, red-faced and out of breath.

"I can't give it to 'er now, Mr Biggleswade. Mr Darcy has just ridden into town and stopped to talk to 'er. I daren't interrupt. I'd be horsewhipped!"

"Then get out there and wait until they have finished talking! You have broken the seal on that letter now, boy. I'll not have open correspondence lying around my post office for any Tom, Dick, or Harry to nose at."

"But they're walking away! You can't mean for me to follow them through t' town?"

"If that is what it takes to get the letter delivered, then that is what you'll do! And take this one with you, while you're at it. 'Tis for her as well." He snatched the second letter from one boy and waved it angrily at the other.

Arthur took it, but when he made no move to leave, Mrs Reynolds took pity on him and held out her hand. "Give them to me, young man. I shall deliver them to Miss Bennet. How much is the postage?"

Both letters were pre-paid, it transpired, which information, along with the postboy's repeated and breathless thanks, almost made the dubious privilege of becoming Miss Bennet's personal Letter Carrier bearable.

"They went along Mill Lane, towards the bridge," Arthur told her as he pressed the letters into her hand.

Mrs Reynolds nodded, and with the postmaster's additional professions of gratitude, returned outside and set out in the direction of the river. The open letter felt even more as though it were burning her now—a searing hot temptation that only pride gave her the strength to resist. No matter that Miss Bennet was a woman of inferior birth with a flagrant dislike for the master and a reputation as an unprincipled self-seeker, Mrs Reynolds was not the sort of woman who read other people's correspondence.

At least, she had never been before, but human curiosity is a force to be reckoned with, and what began as a cursory glance of the ill-written address progressed, quite without volition, to a quick glimpse of the seal. She did not recognise it, but by then, her eye had gone to the inside lip of the folded paper, for it was unusually tight with words, written right up to the edge in an untidy hand as though added as an afterthought. It was there that her gaze struck upon a word that crowded her mind with alarm: Wickham.

She clapped the letter closed between her palms. Somebody bumped into her and shuffled off, grumbling at her for having stopped in his path. She looked up to call an apology to him, but the words died on her lips when she espied the scene before her. At the end of the road were Miss Bennet's relations, standing on the bank of the river, talking to another couple Mrs Reynolds did not recognise. Mr Darcy and Miss Bennet were on the bridge. She was looking at the river, pointing at something downstream. He was looking at her, and in a way that made it very clear it was too late to prevent him falling completely into her trap.

With slow deliberation, Mrs Reynolds turned in the direction of the haberdashery to settle the first of her bills. Miss Bennet's letters she slipped into her pocket. Curiosity had quite deserted her, leaving only profound sadness in its wake. Since she first met him when he was a sweet, unflappable little four-year-old, Mrs Reynolds had been endeared to the master. That he had grown to become a venerated and liberal landlord, that by his generous superintendence her own life had been given purpose and security, only increased her devotion. For four-and-twenty years, she had done everything in her limited power to care for him from afar. In the scheme of things that was little enough, but whatever she could do, from helping his mother hire the best nursemaids to burying ruinous gossip, she had done it.

It had all been for nothing; he would be made miserable after all. She walked away as though her bonnet were made of lead—her head bowed, her shoulders slumped, and her eyes filled with tears. Whatever arts Miss Bennet had condescended to employ to captivate a man she did not even like, they had worked, and it was too cunning, too despicable a thing to watch.

CHAPTER TWELVE

UNINHIBITED LIVELINESS

Darcy wished he knew what Elizabeth thought of his obtrusion onto her outing. The Gardiners seemed pleased with his company, but he had no faith whatsoever in his ability to discern Elizabeth's feelings correctly. It was regrettable that his offer to act as their guide had been all but impossible to decline. Two of Mrs Gardiner's acquaintance had happened by just as he suggested it, and it was they who expressed astonishment and delight at the honour of his condescension, the Gardiners only accepting thereafter.

It was precisely the opposite of what he intended. He had meant to demonstrate the sincerity of his regard to Elizabeth and show humility to her relations, not to flaunt his rank by rendering the townsfolk awestruck.

"Well, my dear, is it as pretty as you recall?" Mr Gardiner enquired as they descended into the narrow valley.

"It is deeper than I remember," his wife answered. "I did not think the sides were so steep or so high as this."

"It is usually the other way around for childhood memories," Elizabeth remarked. "Things you revisit as an adult tend to look smaller than you remember them, not bigger."

"Your aunt is uncommonly short though, Lizzy. You must make allowances," Mr Gardiner quipped.

Darcy smiled, beginning to enjoy the Gardiners' sportive way of talking to each other and comprehending that it was likely from them Elizabeth learnt her talent of teasing without any meanness at all.

"Very droll," Mrs Gardiner replied. "But, as your uncle knows perfectly well, I was not a child when I lived in Lambton, Lizzy. I came here when I was eighteen, after my mother died, and my father sent me to live with my aunt and uncle. I remember your father coming into my uncle's workshop one day, Mr Darcy. His fob watch—his grandfather's—had come loose as he rode through the town, and it was caked in mud, and the glass cracked. He was so pleased my uncle managed to salvage the workings that he sent all his watches and clocks there afterwards."

"Your uncle was Mr Henrick?" Darcy asked. When Mrs Gardiner confirmed it, he turned around, lifting his fob watch on its ribbon, and holding it in his palm for her to see. "The very watch he mended. He is no longer in Lambton, though."

"He and my aunt moved to Anglesey some years later, and I was sent to live with another uncle in Bishops Stortford. That is where Mr Gardiner and I met."

"Fortunately for me, my wife has a surfeit of uncles," Mr Gardiner observed.

"That I do," she agreed. "My father was one of seven boys."

Elizabeth had grown exceedingly quiet, and a quick glance revealed her head to be bowed, the rim of her bonnet not wholly concealing her blush. Darcy did not wonder that she was uncomfortable; she was no doubt anticipating that he would despise Mrs Gardiner yet more for her family's condition in life.

"It must be pleasant to have a large family," he said. "My father was an only child, so I have no aunts or uncles on his side. My mother was one of three, though she occasionally expressed envy at my father's want of brothers and sisters. But Miss Bennet has met my aunt, so she will comprehend that sentiment well enough."

Elizabeth's incredulous amusement banished any regret he ought to have felt for such a coarse and disloyal remark.

"I *have* met Lady Catherine," she agreed. "I have also met Colonel Fitzwilliam. So, tell me, which of them is your uncle most like—his son or his sister?"

"Neither really. Lord Matlock is very quiet, very self-possessed."

"More like his nephew, then."

Her comment drew his gaze to hers. He dared not presume she meant to compliment him, but neither did he think she meant to censure him. "Yes, I suppose so."

"Everyone tells me I am like my aunt Wallis, which is silly, because she is not a real aunt, but I suppose we are similar in temperament."

"Then I am sure I would like her very well."

Elizabeth grinned, although it looked as though she was trying not to. "I am not sure she would approve of you."

Mr Gardiner cleared his throat. "Lizzy's aunt Wallis does not like anyone, Mr Darcy. You must not take it personally."

Elizabeth's secret grin broadened into a full smile, and she leant sideways to whisper conspiratorially, "She has a very low opinion of my mother." She straightened, but after a second or two, added, "On second thoughts, maybe you *would* get on."

Thoroughly ashamed by his previous censure of all Elizabeth's relations, Darcy opened his mouth to deliver a sincere and long overdue apology. He stopped when she looked at him, and he saw the mirth on full and glorious display in her expression. She was extraordinary—truly unlike anyone he had ever known. He could think of no one else with compassion enough to forgive the vilification of their own mother, grace enough to admit the truth of it, and humour enough to laugh about it.

"I say, are these Lilies of the Sea?" Mr Gardiner enquired. Darcy and Elizabeth both turned back to find him peering at an outcropping of rock that obtruded onto the path.

"Undoubtedly—they are ubiquitous in these hills." Darcy stepped aside to allow Elizabeth to see.

"Lilies of the Sea?" she asked.

"They are known colloquially as Derbyshire Screws, for their shape, though I know them as Astroites, which they are called for their star shape in cross section. You are familiar with them, Mr Gardiner?"

"I have never seen one in situ before, but a handful of specimens have passed through my hands over the years. They are gaining popularity as curiosities. People have begun to question their mineral properties. I believe there was some chap in the seventeenth century who thought they might be petrified plants."

"Martin Lister," Darcy confirmed, yet again humbled by Gardiner's knowledge of the world.

"I have never seen anything like them," Elizabeth remarked.

"My house in town is built from Derbyshire limestone and named for them—Astroite House. You can see them dotted about the walls."

"How extraordinary! I should like to see that."

Darcy doubted Elizabeth meant it, but that did not prevent his insides jumping with anticipation of taking her there to show her.

"Look, there!" Mrs Gardiner exclaimed. "Was that an otter? In the ferns, by the water." She, her husband, and her niece all peered hopefully at the riverbank.

Darcy watched Elizabeth. He did not even pretend not to and did not care who caught him doing it. He watched her, watching the riverbank, and marvelled at her total want of affectation. Unlike most women of his acquaintance, she did not position herself to better show off her figure or feign interest—or disinterest—in things to make herself more fascinating. She went through the world artlessly, vivaciously, and wholly unaware of her own allure.

He had never wanted a woman in the same way—body and mind. It was like an obsession. His thoughts were full of her, all the time, but he wanted her approbation as much as he wanted her touch. He wanted her company as much as he wanted her kisses—and he wanted those more than any gentleman would admit. When she craned her neck to peer over the water's edge, his gaze trailed along the line of her jaw, the rest of him aching to trace her other curves—until she leant too far, and alarm pierced the haze of his desire. He instinctively reached towards her, then someone shouted, and Mrs Gardiner tripped into his arms.

For a few, confusing seconds, Darcy had no idea what was happening. He righted Mrs Gardiner and was almost knocked over himself by her husband, who was leaping about from one foot to the other, shouting inarticulately and flapping his hat at his feet. Darcy turned in panic to locate Elizabeth—and there she was, unharmed, unafraid, and laughing unrestrainedly at their expense. She noticed him looking and made a vague attempt to school her hilarity, but it lasted only until her uncle cried, "Not an otter, Mrs Gardiner! Not an otter!" whereupon her laughter redoubled.

"Please forgive me, Mr Darcy," Mrs Gardiner said, red-faced. "It ran directly towards me."

"What did?"

"A rat," Mr Gardiner answered. "A very large rat. I am glad you find it so amusing, Lizzy!"

"I am sorry," she replied, with negligible contrition. "It was just so funny when you screamed like that."

"So would you have if it had been your leg for which it was aiming!" he replied, though his grumbling was good-natured. "You must excuse us, Mr Darcy. We are not usually so uncivilised."

Darcy dismissed his apology with a shake of his head and was earnest in thinking none was necessary. He might have disliked such an exhibition under other circumstances, but there was something about Elizabeth that reduced all such qualms to moonshine. Who could care a whit for propriety when she flouted it so exquisitely?

He never laughed as she was laughing now; he never cast aside restraint or allowed himself to take pleasure in the ridiculous. Her uninhibited liveliness was beautiful and invigorating to behold. Indeed, he did not think he had ever felt as happy as simply watching her laugh. All he could think was how dearly he loved her, and he dared not say anything else for the certainty it would be those words that spilled out before any others. He merely offered her his arm and exulted privately when she took it without hesitation and resumed their walk, silent but smiling unmistakably for him.

CHAPTER THIRTEEN

NATIVE SURROUNDINGS

Fully anticipating that Mr Darcy's friends would match Miss Bingley in their contempt for her society, Elizabeth was delighted to discover at dinner that they were perfectly agreeable, some exceedingly so. If they disliked the disparity in rank, none of them betrayed it, and Elizabeth did not think they could all be such good actors. Her aunt and uncle appeared to be faring well, as pleased with the company as the company was accepting of them. Dinner itself was not entirely without ceremony; precedence was rigorously observed, and she was sure there were more servants than guests in the dining-parlour. Nevertheless, the general mood was one of relaxed harmony.

None seemed so at ease as Mr Darcy himself. Elizabeth had been astonished and astonished again at his demeanour thus far, for never had she seen him so animated. It had not previously been unusual, particularly in Kent, for him to go ten or twenty minutes complete without opening his lips. Of course, she had come to understand it was his feelings for her that kept him quiet then, but that made her gladder than ever for the chance to see him in his element.

Though too stately to be a contender for liveliest of the party, she yet found him the most engaging. He was interested in what everyone had to say, conversant on every subject, and by far the most frequently deferred to by all his friends. Indeed, with such a constant stream of applications for his opinion, his knowledge, and his approbation, it was easy to see how he had come to value his own judgment so highly—and harder to blame him for it.

Even so, Elizabeth perceived none of that old conceit in him this evening—only gentleness and good humour. Miss Bingley had once said to Jane, no doubt to demonstrate her familiarity with him, that Mr Darcy never spoke much unless among his intimate acquaintance. It provoked a strong sensation of warmth in Elizabeth's breast to consider that, by implication, she might now think of herself as among Mr Darcy's intimate acquaintance.

That feeling of warmth flared hotter each time their eyes met, and that was just about every time she looked at him; it seemed as though his gaze never left hers. She was almost relieved when it came time for the ladies to withdraw after dinner, for she was certain the suspicions of the whole party were awakened against them. Most of Mr Darcy's friends had spent the evening looking as though they were attempting not to notice his preoccupation. Some had done a poorer job of disguising their interest, and a few had been overtly amused.

Elizabeth was not afraid for herself beyond a little discomfort, but for Mr Darcy she was exceedingly anxious. It was too soon to know whether the burgeoning esteem she felt for him would advance into affection, but she did feel a real concern for his welfare and abhorred the thought of exposing him to ridicule amongst his friends. It made her guarded in her responses to the other ladies, whose probing remarks were less than subtle, and was possibly what provoked Miss Bingley's simmering jealousy into an outright attack.

"What a delightful evening we are having," said Lady Garroway, a young lady of about Elizabeth's own age. "I must say, when I met Mr Darcy in London earlier this year, he did not seem quite so amiable. I *had* worried he did not like me."

Elizabeth could not help but laugh at that. "I comprehend your sentiment. Mr Darcy has a satirical eye."

Miss Templeton gave Elizabeth a shrewd look. "I suppose that could be said of him, though it does not appear that much is displeasing him this evening."

"He seems in an uncommonly good humour," agreed Mrs Cox. She was a slightly older, slightly quieter member of the party, though no less friendly for it.

"I noticed no great difference in him," Miss Bingley said tightly. "He is always excellent company."

"Nobody is suggesting otherwise, dear. Do not be prickly. We are only saying that he seems more than usually complacent." Miss Templeton patted her friend on the arm consolingly as she said this, though she continued looking pointedly at Elizabeth.

"He does," agreed Mrs Cox. "However should we account for it?"

Their rather graceless insinuation was disarmed by their good-natured smiles, and Elizabeth replied in the same spirit. "I expect it is his being here. We are all more comfortable in our own homes, are we not?"

"I should certainly be comfortable if my home were as delightful as Pemberley," Lady Garroway remarked.

"Oh yes! I forgot that your ladyship has not been before," Mrs Cox replied.

To Elizabeth and Mrs Gardiner, Lady Garroway explained,

"Lord Garroway and I only married in the spring. He has known Mr Darcy for years, but this is my first visit to Pemberley. I thought his lordship's house was impressive, but it is nothing to this. It is quite the grandest place I have ever stayed."

Conscious of saying anything that might appear grasping, Elizabeth agreed that Pemberley was very handsome but did not elaborate. Her answer was evidently too ungenerous to satisfy Miss Bingley.

"It is Miss Bennet's first visit, also. Pemberley is a good deal larger than Longbourn, is it not?"

"It is a good deal larger than most houses, Miss Bingley."

"Is it true there are secret passages?" Lady Garroway enquired. "I heard there were."

Miss Bingley gave a small, reluctant shrug, as though unhappy not to be an authority on the matter. "You would have to ask Mr Darcy. Or his sister."

"What a shame Miss Darcy is not still here. She might have even shown us."

Elizabeth, too, regretted that Miss Darcy had retired, but all three of the young ladies who were not yet out had been shepherded upstairs by Mrs Annesley after dinner. She had remarked to her aunt that she thought it an unnecessary formality, and they had both agreed on the violence of Lydia and Kitty's protestations were they to be similarly banished.

"Has your ladyship looked into the family chapel yet?" Mrs Cox enquired. "It is definitely worth seeing."

"I have not yet, but I must while I am here. His lordship raves about Pemberley's stained glass."

"I can show you *that* if you like," Miss Bingley offered.

"Oh do, Caroline," said Mrs Hurst, giving her sister an encouraging nudge with her elbow.

"Would you?" Lady Garroway implored. "I should dearly like to see it. Would not you, Miss Bennet?"

Elizabeth would much rather see it with Mr Darcy. "Would it not be better to view the stained glass in the daylight?"

"Oh yes, I suppose it would."

Miss Bingley stood up. "Do not be dissuaded, madam. I know the house intimately, and there are plenty of other things I can show you."

"As long as it is not the secret passages," Miss Templeton said with a snort. It was an obvious tease, but one Miss Bingley just as obviously disliked. "Will you join us, Miss Bennet, Mrs Gardiner?"

Elizabeth sent her aunt a beseeching look, which Mrs Gardiner acknowledged with the slightest of nods.

"Thank you, but we have seen a lot of the house already," she said to Miss Templeton. "We were shown quite a few of the rooms by the housekeeper on Tuesday."

Miss Bingley's mouth curled into a satisfied smile. "Even more reason for you to come, then, for you will only have seen what is shown to visiting tradespeople."

There was an awkward pause, during which Elizabeth fought to keep her countenance, then Lady Garroway came to her feet. "Come, Miss Bennet. Let us explore together."

"I shall stay here and keep Mrs Gardiner and Mrs Hurst company," Mrs Cox added, settling the matter beyond refusal. "Off you go and see the house."

Elizabeth followed in unhappy silence. She could not but think that Mr Darcy would disapprove—not only of Miss Bingley's presumption, but of the missed opportunity to show off his own house. A man as proud as he must surely take satisfaction in exhibiting such a heritage and so much good taste. She felt like an intruder, sneaking about darkened rooms, having every priceless vase pointed out to her as though she were preparing to plunder the place.

They passed outside the dining-parlour, where the

gentlemen were enjoying themselves with audibly less restraint than had been on display while the ladies were present. Elizabeth could not hear Mr Darcy, but she had not expected that she would. His voice was deep and resonant, but he never raised it or laughed coarsely as some of his friends were presently doing. He was too dignified.

She smiled to catch herself thinking of him in such terms and deliberately turned her attention to her surroundings as Miss Bingley led the party onwards. They passed through some rooms she had already seen, and some she had not, some lit and some not, until at length they reached the chapel.

"Oh."

Elizabeth pressed her lips together to avoid laughing at Lady Garroway's disappointment. How splendid the windows might be was impossible to tell, for the space was cavernously dark, and the effect of the few candles they had brought with them was only to make everything around them blacker still. Miss Bingley was not to be put off. She sallied forth and wafted her candle overhead, where it did indeed reflect a glimmer of green light off a window.

Elizabeth perched on the arm of a pew. It truly was a magnificent house, elegant with no useless finery, a comfortable home despite its vast size. It astonished her more every day that Mr Darcy had wished it to be *her* home. Of all the women he must know—all the heiresses, accomplished ladies, pretty sisters of lifelong friends, and single cousins of excellent fortune—he had chosen her to share this with him. Even with most of the house obscured by shadows, the compliment—and yes, she would admit, the honour—felt immense.

"This way."

Elizabeth jumped and hastened to go with Miss Bingley out of the chapel and through another darkened room.

When no one followed, she enquired after the other two ladies.

"They have gone back to the drawing room," Miss Bingley replied irritably.

"Should we not return as well?"

They went through a door; the light changed, and Miss Bingley came to a halt. "We could, but I thought you might like to see this."

Elizabeth glanced at her surroundings, her heart sinking as she realised Miss Bingley had brought her to the library. "Thank you, but I really would have preferred Mr Darcy to show me this."

Miss Bingley sighed sharply, and it sounded awfully like she had stamped a foot, too. "I have gone out of my way to show everyone the best rooms in the house, and nobody has betrayed the least gratitude. I should have thought *you* would at least appreciate this room, being such a *great reader*."

Elizabeth let out a long, quiet breath and inclined her head in capitulation. She would never like the woman, but she felt some sympathy for Miss Bingley's failed attempt at playing the part of Pemberley's mistress. She duly walked farther into the library, looking properly this time. Away from Miss Bingley and the light of her candle, the room revealed more of itself, and the moonlight, which shone through the windows on this side of the house as it had not done in the chapel, lent everything it touched an ethereal glow.

"Impressive is it not?"

Elizabeth nodded. She was not, in fact, a great reader, at least no more prolific than the next person, but even the most ardent hater of literature could not be unmoved by the sight of so many books in one place. She trailed her fingers over the spines as she walked the length of the room. It was a vast space, and beautiful—though beautiful in a masculine way. A strong, dark, inscrutable landscape that promised secrets and knowledge of the world. So much like its owner that she was utterly entranced. Looking at it felt as intimately familiar as looking at Mr Darcy's portrait in the picture gallery.

Someone—a man—cleared his throat. Elizabeth turned around, half hoping it was Mr Darcy himself, but only the butler was there. Miss Bingley was not.

"I must ask you to leave this room at once, madam. This part of the house is not open to you."

If Elizabeth had thought herself mortified the first time she was caught snooping, uninvited, around his house, she could scarcely bring herself to contemplate what Mr Darcy would think to discover she had been doing it a second time. "I beg your pardon. I was taking a turn with the other ladies and lost my bearings. I shall return to the drawing room this instant."

"Allow me to escort you."

She gave a tight smile and followed him, silently, back to the drawing room.

"There you are!" Miss Bingley exclaimed when she returned a few minutes afterwards. "I looked for you everywhere. Where did you go?" She was not wholly successful in concealing her glee.

Elizabeth gave the same excuse she had given the butler and turned away. Her earlier sympathy had soured into hard pity, for Miss Bingley must truly be desperate to go to such lengths to discredit her in Mr Darcy's eyes.

She had not as much time as she would have liked to recover from the misadventure before the gentlemen appeared, several of them exclaiming over the merriment of the evening. She was pleased to see her uncle still smiling—a good indication that the other men's forbearance had not diminished along with their sobriety. Mr Bingley seemed in particularly high spirits as he seated himself in the chair next to Miss Templeton and signalled for more wine.

Mr Darcy came directly to sit next to Elizabeth. "Have you ladies kept yourselves well entertained?"

"We have certainly not been dull, sir," she replied sardonically.

He frowned, but any more discussion of the matter was prevented when Miss Templeton, with a rebellious smirk, said, "Do not be glum, Mr Darcy! We were only just now discussing your uncommonly good humour this evening."

"That will be because he bested every one of us at the shoot today," grumbled Mr Hurst.

"Aye, although I do not know how, for he only joined the party halfway through the afternoon," Mr Pettigrew remarked. "Where were you, Darcy, sleeping?"

Elizabeth assumed he would prevaricate and was amazed —and not a little gratified—when he answered without a shred of embarrassment that he had been with her and the Gardiners. "We walked downriver to Dedman Gorge."

"Upon my word, you do find yourself in some interesting places, do you not, Miss Bennet?" Miss Bingley said. She dipped her head to pick at some imperceptible fleck on her skirt and added, just loudly enough for Elizabeth to hear, "And all of them so far removed from your native surroundings."

"It certainly was interesting," Mr Gardiner agreed, and proceeded to detail his discovery of Sea Lilies in the limestone.

Not wishing to acknowledge Miss Bingley's pettiness, Elizabeth fixed her gaze on her uncle and pretended to listen to his tale. Mr Darcy had never explained his true purpose in coming to Lambton, and she had not been brave enough to ask, but she suspected it was simply to see her. Knowing he had guests expecting his company made the several hours he had spent with her still more valuable. They had not been at liberty to discuss anything meaningful in her aunt and uncle's presence, but that they had talked with ease, that they had made each other laugh and smile, seemed of far greater importance.

Since he was sitting close to her uncle, Elizabeth could not help but notice that Mr Bingley was not even pretending to pay attention to the discussion of the gorge. She had spent some time watching him in Hertfordshire, attempting to determine whether he returned Jane's affections, and had been convinced, then, that he must do. It therefore struck her forcibly to see him with the same expression of attentiveness, the same eager smile as he had shown her sister, only this time directed at Miss Templeton. It threw all her hopes for Jane into doubt.

"Are you well?" Mr Darcy enquired quietly.

"Oh—yes, quite well, thank you," she stumbled, startled out of her reflections.

He turned his gaze to where she had been looking, but if he guessed where her thoughts had tended, he showed no concern over it, asking instead, "Were you studying more characters?"

"The practice would not do me any harm, would it? I have been exposed as having rather lamentable discernment."

"You have indeed," Miss Bingley interjected, tittering loudly, and drawing the attention of the whole room to their private exchange. "Your attempts to make out everybody's character in Hertfordshire were especially unsound. You accused poor Charles of being capricious!"

Having only recently been deliberating on that gentleman's whimsical civilities, it was on the tip of Elizabeth's tongue to reply that he *was*, but Mr Darcy intervened, saving her from the necessity of giving any response.

"*I* said that Miss Bingley, not Miss Bennet."

"That's right, Darcy, you did!" Mr Bingley added with mock affront. "You were quite undeserving of Caroline's defence of you—you are far from perfect if you ask me."

"Charles!" his sister cried, her cheeks colouring. "I said no such thing. I merely said Mr Darcy had no defects at which Miss Bennet might laugh."

Mr Templeton surprised everybody by snorting wine out of his nose. He sat up straighter, dabbing at his face with his cuff and shaking his head. "You have revealed yourself there, Miss Bingley. What is it they say—love is blind?"

The lady's countenance went from pink to puce in an instant.

Miss Templeton raised an eyebrow. "Of what would you accuse Mr Darcy that Caroline was too polite to mention?"

"Oh no! If I begin pointing out Darcy's faults, he will start on mine, and then I shall be done for. Miss Bennet will hate me forever." He winked at Elizabeth in a way that made her feel like another of his sisters, and she liked him very well for it.

"You are right to be cautious," she told him. "There are very few people capable of graciously accepting reproof. It is remarkably humbling when you meet one." She looked deliberately at Mr Darcy. His face moved very little but for a subtle smile, identical to the one in his portrait, every bit as enigmatic as the moonlight in the library.

"If we are forbidden from making sport of each other, might we at least have some music to pass the time?" cried Lord Garroway. "Darcy, you do not mind if my wife plays, do you?"

Neither Mr Darcy nor Lady Garroway had any objection, and the instrument was opened. In twisting away from her to better observe the performance, Mr Darcy's shoulder came to rest, just barely, against Elizabeth's own. She could easily have broken off the contact—reached for her cup, leant to talk to her aunt, yawned, anything! She chose to remain still, never in her life so aware of another person's proximity. It made her hot; it made her silent; it made her utterly inattentive to the music. She wondered whether Mr Darcy were even aware they were touching, for he had made no attempt to distance himself. Indeed, he had not moved at all. He was so still, in fact, that she would almost say he must be holding his breath.

It was as though a spell had broken when Lady Garroway came to the end of her aria. Mr Darcy sat forward, applauding along with everyone else. In a daze, Elizabeth watched his back as he stood up and called for a footman to bring the harp forward for Mrs Cox to play.

She felt a fool for having imagined he would be similarly affected—until he turned around and pierced her with a look of such fierce yearning, she could almost feel it. His handsomeness, always present but never before at the forefront of her consciousness, asserted itself in her mind with new and startling significance. It made her wish to reach out and touch him again, and *that* was so disconcerting a thought that she looked away in confusion.

She knew not where he got it, but in the next moment, Mr Darcy was pressing a glass of wine into her hand and sitting back into his own seat. Mrs Cox began to play soon after, and by the time she finished her performance, Elizabeth had composed herself tolerably well. Her heart was less obedient and felt as though it would never stop racing again. Not while she took her turn at the pianoforte, not while she bid everyone goodnight, certainly not while Mr Darcy handed her into her carriage. Not even as she climbed into bed in the early hours of the next morning and drifted into dreams filled with feelings that were entirely new to her, and not entirely unwelcome.

CHAPTER FOURTEEN

MORE THAN STONES & MORTAR

Darcy paced the hall, stopping at every pass of the doors to check for the return of his carriage. He generally had more presence of mind, but that was precisely what Elizabeth had robbed him of almost from the first moment of their acquaintance. It was one of the reasons his feelings for her had alarmed him so at first, for never, before he met her, had he felt paralysed with despair or drunk with desire, nor any of the other emotions she mercilessly wrung from him. Pacing was a meagre frailty in comparison to some of the others to which she had driven him.

At last, he heard horses' hooves and the rattle of traces and made his way outside, heart racing absurdly in anticipation. It seemed to take an inordinately long time for the carriage to come to a halt, the door to be opened, and the steps folded down. All the while, he could see Elizabeth's anxious glances.

"Good morning," he said, handing her down. "You are looking for my sister, I think?"

"Yes. She sent me a note—and a carriage!—inviting me to drink tea with her."

"And pray be assured, she is greatly anticipating your call. I had only to mention the idea and she wrote the invitation directly."

She started. "*You* sent the carriage?"

"I did. And I beg you would allow me to steal a moment of your time before I take you to Georgiana, for there is something important I would say to you first."

He regretted phrasing it thus when Elizabeth's eyes widened in alarm. It was a sobering sight. Despite having forgiven enough of his past offences to resume the acquaintance, despite the electrifying moment that passed between them after last night's dinner, Elizabeth was clearly not ready to receive a renewal of his addresses. He felt a stab of disappointment, though no surprise. The impression of him that he carelessly allowed her to form in Hertfordshire would have been difficult enough to undo; it was inevitable that it would take longer to atone for the insults, personal and unfeeling, that he thoughtlessly directed at her in Kent.

And now he must correct another slight, layered atop all the others last night through no fault of his own for once. With a gesture, he asked her to walk with him and led her away from the front door and onto the path that ran parallel to the front of the house towards the east wing.

"It has come to my attention that you were spoken to somewhat brusquely last night by my butler." Relief and confusion warred with each other on Elizabeth's countenance, giving her a charming appearance of innocence. "In the library."

Embarrassment instantly eclipsed all her other sentiments. "I beg you would forgive me, sir. Some of the other ladies wished to explore the house, and—"

"There is absolutely nothing for you to apologise for," he

interrupted. "I know what happened. Bingley overheard his sisters discussing the matter after you left. It seems Miss Bingley… took steps not to be discovered."

Elizabeth rolled her eyes. "I suspected as much, though I could not conceive of a reason why she should."

"Because she knew neither of you were supposed to be in there. Which brings me to the reason I wished to speak to you." They had turned the corner of the building, and he directed her off the path and out onto the lawn. Partly to avoid the gaggle of labourers standing with a glum-faced Ferguson beneath a library window. Partly because the stark black scar in the wall could be better seen from farther away. He knew the moment Elizabeth saw it, for she let out a soft gasp.

"That crack appeared last month," he explained. "It is what brought me home early. My steward and I met with an architect on Monday to discuss it."

"Can it be repaired?"

"It is too early to tell. Work is due to begin on Monday to try and determine the cause. For now, I have ordered this entire wing of the house closed off."

Comprehension dawned on Elizabeth's face, vindicating Darcy's decision to bring her here, for she evidently *had* been distressed by her unceremonious eviction.

"I wished for you to see for yourself, so you would understand the urgency with which Matthis ejected you from the library. It is not safe—or rather, it is potentially unsafe. But I would have you know, you *must* know, you are welcome in every part of Pemberley. Especially the library."

"Thank you," she said after a long pause. He knew not whether it was embarrassment or some other emotion over which she stumbled; it was gone before he could place it. "I did not see much of it in the dark," she said more brightly, "but what I could make out was very impressive indeed. You told me once it was the work of generations, but I still had not imagined anything quite so extraordinary."

"I hope to show you in daylight as soon as the site is secured. Though I have no idea when that will be." Quite a while if Ferguson's present fretting was any indication.

"What will the work involve?"

"Inside, they must assess the state of all the roof and floor timbers and remove some of the plaster from the walls to establish the integrity of the window lintels. Out here, trenches will be dug to expose the foundations and establish whether they are compromised. I beg your pardon, Miss Bennet, would you excuse me for just a moment. I must have a quick word with my steward."

He hated to abandon her, but Ferguson had progressed from shaking his head to glancing his way every few seconds with an expression that made it clear he wished to interrupt. Elizabeth assured him she did not mind, and Darcy strode to the foot of the wall. "What is it?"

"Another crack, sir," Ferguson replied without preamble, and set off immediately towards the rear of the house.

Darcy followed, not a little alarmed that a second fault should have appeared so far from the first. He was obliged to peer closely to see what was causing Ferguson such consternation, but when his eyes found it, his stomach sank. Unlike the first crack, which had arced up the wall with such devastating force that a dozen or more of the heavy stone blocks of which Pemberley was built had been cleaved in two, this one zig-zagged more innocuously between the stones. There were places where mortar was crumbling out of the wall, however, preventing anyone from mistaking it for superficial.

"It might not be new. It could very well have been here for as long as the other one," Ferguson went on. "'Tis difficult to see, what with ashlar mortar joints being so thin."

That did not account for all the head shaking. "But?"

"The other crack will have begun in the same way. I shall write to Jacobs for his opinion, but I should think it will need shoring."

Darcy nodded sombrely and hoped he did not look as bilious as he felt. He left Ferguson to make the necessary arrangements and returned to Elizabeth. "My apologies for the interruption. Allow me to take you to my sister."

Elizabeth did not begin walking. "Did your steward have bad news?"

He grimaced slightly, wishing that Ferguson would bring him any news that was *not* bad. "He has discovered another crack. Not as serious as the one you can see but every flaw increases the possibility of collapse before it can be repaired."

She looked unexpectedly troubled by the news. When she whispered, "Your beautiful home!" it was so soft, Darcy could believe she had not meant to say it aloud, and her use of the word 'home' twisted the ever-present knot in his gut uncomfortably tight.

"The damage appears to be limited to this section of the house, at least. It is built on an E-shaped footprint, and this wing is effectively the bottom arm of that E and is the only part showing deterioration. Which is fortunate in one regard, but it is adding considerably to the mystery of it."

"I hope you find the cause—and a solution."

"As do I. A lot of people depend on my doing so."

She fixed him with one of her searching looks. "I confess, I never truly comprehended what a burden being master of all this must be."

"It was not my intention to sound self-pitying."

"I did not take it so. There *are* a lot of people depending on you—your housekeeper made that very clear when she spoke to us on Monday."

Darcy knew not whether he was more indignant or

disconcerted to hear that Mrs Reynolds told anyone *anything* about him. "And pray, what else does my housekeeper say of me to visitors?"

"You need not look so horrified—she was very complimentary about you," Elizabeth said with a grin. "My comment about burdens relates to something she said about your tenants and servants. It made me consider how many people's happiness must be in your guardianship. And here," she gestured towards the house, "is proof of how far that guardianship extends beyond people. It is a vast responsibility."

"It is not an unwelcome one. Indeed, it is more privilege than burden."

"Pemberley is fortunate to have such a conscientious master. Not all landlords are so dedicated. My father has certainly not taken the same care with Longbourn. I do not presume to compare the two houses, but even in relative terms, Longbourn has not flourished under my father's superintendence as Pemberley is clearly doing under yours. Perhaps because it is entailed…" She shook her head. "I do not know, but yours is a very fine legacy."

Darcy did not answer. He ought to be delighted she should think so, but it was as though, with the sentiment, Elizabeth had torn the rug from beneath his feet. He had been concerned by the appearance of the crack, of course—deeply so—but his primary object had been policy: hazards and consequences, materials and labour, timings and costs. Elizabeth had articulated precisely that which had been sitting at the pit of his stomach, gnawing at his equanimity, the thing he had been stoically ignoring for days: his family seat was crumbling, and he was unutterably sad about it.

"I am sorry if I have said something to pain you. The last thing I would wish is to add to your distress."

Elizabeth was regarding him anxiously, one hand

hovering halfway between them as though she had reached to comfort him and thought better of it. He resisted the urge to take her hand in his own, though he longed to feel the consolation of her touch.

"If there is any burden upon my shoulders, it presses more heavily from the past than all present concerns. Pemberley is, as you say, the work of generations. The prospect that it might fall under my curation is difficult to bear."

"It is not as though you have gambled away your fortune or wilfully allowed the house to fall into disrepair. This is entirely out of your control."

"That makes it worse. If I had done something, it could be more easily *un*done. As it is, I know not what the solution ought to be, if I can afford it, or if it can even be done. I find myself faced with the real possibility that this could be the beginning of Pemberley's downfall."

"Oh, but I quite disagree!" she replied fervently, almost crossly. "Pemberley is manifestly more than stones and mortar. Nobody could think otherwise who has seen all this —" She made a sweeping gesture with her arm that took in the grounds as well as the house. "Or heard your friends and family and servants speak of it, or witnessed the pride you take in it, and the care you take *of* it. If the whole house were to fall down, you would still be the master of something of real importance to a great many people, both past and present, and I daresay future. And walls, you know, can be rebuilt as easily as they can be knocked down."

Darcy savoured the familiar upwelling of admiration he had used to feel whenever she locked horns with him in the early days of their acquaintance. She had done it again: induced him to say, to feel more than he intended, but by God he could get used to having such a fierce advocate! Fierce, and devastatingly alluring with it. He considered her handsome at all times, but in high emotion—be it obstinacy, anger, or, as now, defiance—Elizabeth's beauty was captivating, her complexion radiant and her dark eyes flashing fire.

"You have a most effective way of making a person see the truth before their eyes," he admitted. Such she had done when she accused him of selfishness, conceit, and ungentlemanly behaviour—all demonstrably true, all in dire need of correction. "Pemberley is far more than the sum of its parts. I welcome your assurances. Indeed, I am persuaded that I ought to take steps to preserve some of those parts and have this wing emptied." He gave her a small, wry smile and made yet another confession. "I have been putting it off."

"Until your guests left?"

"That is the reason I avowed to myself, but in truth, it felt too much like an admission that there was any real danger."

Elizabeth gave him an encouraging nod and set off back towards the front of the house. "It is always better to take charge than sit about, waiting for Fate to play its hand. And that must be especially true for those with a strong inclination to have things their own way."

It could have chafed but, said as it was with a playful, sideways glance, the tease gratified Darcy no end. "Purpose is always preferable to irresolution."

"Oh, absolutely. If only buildings were as complying as people, you could simply *tell* the wall not to fall down. Have you tried? If you gave it one of your very severe stares, it might work."

To distract himself from imagining what it would be like to spin her around and kiss her until she begged him to marry her, Darcy asked whether her plans were yet determined for the rest of their travels.

"My uncle had decided we would leave on Tuesday, but my aunt has been invited to a recital that afternoon, so I think he may be persuaded to stay until Wednesday."

"In that case, might I impose on you all to join us on Monday? With the work beginning here, I thought it would be prudent to take my guests away from the house. We are to have a picnic at a spot on the far side of the estate. You would like it, I think. It has a charming view over the Derwent valley."

Darcy was anticipating a repeat of Elizabeth's embarrassment from three days ago, when Georgiana invited her to dine with them, or her quiet reticence on their walk to the gorge. Instead, she answered directly that she would very much like to attend, only becoming embarrassed upon belatedly recalling that she would need to confirm with her aunt. She promised to send a note, and he delivered her to Georgiana, who had this time been joined by several of the other ladies, he was pleased to see. Then he went in search of Mrs Reynolds, principally to give the instruction to begin emptying the east wing, though the thought crossed his mind to triple her salary for whatever it was she said that worked such a change on Elizabeth's opinion of him.

CHAPTER FIFTEEN

RESOLVED TO ACT

Mrs Reynolds had not intended to read Miss Bennet's letters. It had been her design to hand them to her when she and her party arrived at Pemberley for dinner. Yet one, then another interruption occurred, and it was not until she undressed for bed at the end of the long night that a faint rustling recalled her to the charges in her pocket. The solution was simple; she would take the letters with her when she returned to Lambton the next day to collect her chatelaine from the goldsmith.

That endeavour turned out to be unnecessary. Miss Darcy informed her after breakfast that Miss Bennet would be coming to Pemberley again that day for tea. Mrs Reynolds's revised plan to return the letters at that point was also waylaid, for the young woman's arrival coincided with the delivery of a much-anticipated reply from Eleanor, which distracted the housekeeper from all else.

Dearest Agnes,

Your letter, as always, gave me a good laugh. 'Daffodil' is one of your best names yet, though I think my favourite is still 'Bagpipe' for the man with two walking canes and a tartan waistcoat.

Clarabelle sounds utterly delightful. What a charming mix of guile and impudence for a young lady to possess! I pity you, having to suffer so many of these petty-minded women of 'Quality'. I blame idleness; too little industry has turned their minds to rot. Her connexion to George Wickham is something of which to be wary, to be sure. I have not forgot your philippic for that other friend of his, Mrs Younge, nor your regret for not detecting her treachery in time to obviate it. I hope, for all your sakes, you see no more of this latest parvenue.

There were a further two pages of other news, but Mrs Reynolds could not concentrate on any of it, not with the comparison of Miss Bennet and Mrs Younge reverberating in her head.

The latter had presided over Miss Darcy's establishment in Ramsgate the previous summer, and her abrupt dismissal was proof enough for Mrs Reynolds of her involvement in whatever evil Wickham had perpetrated there. Before that, necessity had required the two women, both in charge of Darcy households, to be in regular communication, but Mrs Reynolds had never liked her. She was surly, evasive, and dismissive of authority. An endless stream of trifling concerns, raised by everyone from Miss Darcy's lady's maid to her pianoforte master, had somehow always been explained away, always in some way mitigated, preventing Mrs Reynolds from reporting her misgivings. How she had regretted her inaction when Miss Darcy returned to Pemberley brow-beaten and contrite, and the master had plunged into a steadily worsening state of despondency.

Her self-reproach was interrupted by a sharp rap at the door. Something in her side spasmed painfully when she hauled herself to standing, but she could not remain seated, not when Mr Darcy himself entered her sitting room. He seldom came into this part of the house, but her surprise was summarily answered: he had come to her to save time, for his instructions were urgent.

She was to oversee the emptying of the entire east wing, beginning at once. Not a stick of furniture was to be left behind. The contents were to be moved to other, vacant parts of the house where possible, or sent to Astroite House if necessary. He did, as was his way, acknowledge the onus of such an endeavour but assured her she had his full confidence and that she would receive whatever assistance she required. Then he left, in a significantly more buoyant mood than the situation warranted.

Mrs Reynolds's discomfort did not abate as she made her way, stiffly, towards the servants' hall. The entire east wing! It would have been a vast undertaking under any circumstances, for that part of the house encompassed the library, the master's study, the picture gallery, numerous guest apartments, and a labyrinth of attic rooms. At present, however, with so many guests in residence, such a quantity of dinners, shooting parties, and picnics to arrange, and a pernicious fatigue dogging her every move, Mrs Reynolds suffered an unprecedented moment of doubt in her ability to see the business done.

"Are you well, Mrs Reynolds?" asked Mr Ferguson, coming towards her from around the corner at the end of the passageway.

She ignored his question. "I was on my way to find you. Pray, has the situation with the house worsened?"

His heavy eyebrows drew closer together. "No. Has this to do with emptying the rooms? Mr Darcy has sanctioned the hiring of as many extra hands as you need."

"Thank you, sir, although we would not need any extra hands if we were not so busy with the house party. If the danger has not increased, can it not wait until his guests have gone?"

Temperate as ever, the steward betrayed no displeasure in either his tone or his expression, though the reproach in his few words was unmistakable. "The master wishes it done now, Mrs Reynolds."

He continued on his way, and she sagged against the wall, one hand pressed to her side and her face flaming. Mr Ferguson was a fine steward, but there were times she despised his authority, which was conferred upon him by dint of his sex alone, for he could claim very little knowledge of Pemberley beyond her own. Only a man would be comfortable making a woman more than twenty years his senior and with experience at least equal to his own feel like a naughty schoolgirl. She pulled herself upright when Hannah poked her head out of the women's workroom.

"Did I hear correctly? The *whole* east wing?"

Mrs Reynolds nodded. "And I should like to know why the sudden urgency."

Edna's round face appeared next to Hannah's. "Perhaps that Miss Bennet said something about it when they were out there just now. She's supposed to have come to see Miss Darcy, but William says she went with the master to look at the outside of the library first. Bet she put the idea in his head."

"Do not conjecture, Edna," Hannah scolded her. "The master does not require his sister's callers to tell him about his own house."

Edna shrugged. "She was in there last night, too. Mayhap she saw something then."

Mrs Reynolds could feel her displeasure rising like gorge in her gullet. "Please explain what you mean, Edna."

"William said Mr Matthis had to kick her out of the library last night. Seems she went nosing 'round the house after dinner while the men was all drinking. Miss Bingley had to warn Mr Matthis, 'cause she saw her heading in there all on her own."

Mrs Reynolds maintained a blank expression and ordered both girls back to work. There was no way of knowing why Miss Bennet had ventured, unaccompanied and in secret, into the closed wing. But Mrs Reynolds knew better than anyone that it was a room never shown to strangers who applied for a tour of the house. Being presently off limits, it would have remained unchartered even to an invited guest. Miss Bennet's only opportunity to evaluate its treasures was a clandestine visit. That she had followed her exploration, less than four-and-twenty hours later, with a suggestion to relocate the contents in case of disaster, savoured so highly of fortune-hunting, Mrs Reynolds felt faint.

So it was that she found herself back in her sitting room, tearing open the letters she had meant to return, decorum entirely subsumed by the dread that something terrible was being plotted against the master.

Eleanor was right; Miss Bennet's connexion to George Wickham was a cause of the deepest concern. He was a reprobate of the worst sort. Mrs Younge was not the first person he had embroiled in a scheme to injure the master, and Mrs Reynolds would be in no way surprised to discover that he was making another attempt, with another conspirator. The presence of his name in one of Miss Bennet's letters, coupled with her unashamedly rapacious behaviour, was more than enough justification for alarm.

What the letters revealed was an even uglier connexion than Mrs Reynolds had suspected. Ugly enough that she could no longer sit back and obediently observe her station in life while misfortune and misery careened headlong towards the master. Reminded by Eleanor's words just how profoundly she regretted not acting to protect Mr or Miss

Darcy from Wickham before, Mrs Reynolds resolved not to fail them again.

Instead of returning the letters to Miss Bennet, therefore, she instead returned them to her pocket and set out to visit somebody she had not seen for an exceedingly long time and would have preferred never to set eyes upon again.

CHAPTER SIXTEEN

ONE GOOD DEED

She let herself in to the little cottage when her knock was answered with a thin, reedy voice, telling her the door was open. It was dark inside, and her old eyes did not immediately adjust to the gloom.

The occupant was at no such disadvantage. "Look at what the wind blew in."

Mrs Reynolds peered into the corner of the room to where a vague form filled a chair, though swathed in enough shawls and blankets as to better resemble a pile of laundry than a person.

"How long has it been?" came the same, quivering voice. "Four years? Five? You look much older."

"You look the same as always."

"What do you want, Agnes?"

Mrs Reynolds chafed that she should presume to still use her name, but she let it pass. That was not the battle she had come to fight. "I need to find George."

There was a pause, followed by a wheezy cough. "Now why on earth would you want to do that?"

Mrs Reynolds did not answer.

"You cannot expect me to help you without knowing why."

"It matters not why."

"You may think not, but I cannot agree. I am sure I can think of no good reason why you should wish to renew the acquaintance of a person you make no secret of despising."

"Why are you protecting him? For heaven's sake, he tells people you are dead."

"You've not changed a bit, have you?" came the sullen response from the mountain of blankets. "Does it give you pleasure, lording it about the place, belittling the likes of me for what we've lost? Well, it gives me none, so take your Pemberley airs and leave me alone."

Mrs Reynolds bit back several rejoinders, not least that Mrs Wickham had lost very little that she and her son had not themselves squandered. Instead, she pulled a chair out from the table beneath the window and sat down defiantly. "Believe me when I say that I take no pleasure in this errand whatsoever, but it must be done. Your son has persuaded a young girl of but fifteen years to leave all her friends and run away with him. You and I both know she will no longer be intact, yet he is refusing to marry her."

"Can't say as I blame him. She sounds wanton."

"Then they ought to be well suited," Mrs Reynolds retorted without thinking. Then, hastily, she added, "Lucy, please. Her whole family is in disgrace. Can you not see, George must be made to marry her."

"What is this girl to you that you care so much?"

"My interest in the matter is irrelevant. A young girl's life is about to be ruined, and you have the opportunity to do something good for a change and save her."

Mrs Wickham made a clicking noise with her tongue and leant forward in her chair. "Agnes Reynolds, I don't care how important you think you are, but there is plenty you do not know, and you have seriously miscalculated here. It makes no difference that George has forged his own path away from me, nor that he is imperfect. He is still my son. You could not possibly comprehend a mother's love, being childless yourself, but I'll not give my boy up to goodness-knows-what-fate just because you've waltzed in here and demanded it without explanation or inducement. Either you tell me why it matters to you that he marries this girl, or my lips will remain shut."

The childless slur never failed to wound; Mrs Reynolds sat quietly until the sting faded. At length, and with waning energy, she said, "I have reason to believe the girl's sister is close to securing an offer of marriage from Mr Darcy."

"Oh? And since when did Pemberley's exalted housekeeper involve herself with the family's private business?"

Mrs Reynolds baulked. Mrs Wickham was right; it was not her place. Never in all her years serving them had she presumed to interfere in the Darcys' private affairs. But it was simply unthinkable that Miss Elizabeth Bennet should be mistress of Pemberley! Over her dead body would she allow the master to ruin himself over such a woman, from such a family! Regrettably, that did not leave her much time to act. "She does not love him. She has drawn him in with her arts and allurements. I would ensure he is not ill-used."

Mrs Wickham crowed disdainfully. "Now it becomes clear! You believe that if George marries the one sister, your lord and master will have nothing to do with the other, and by that means, he will be kept safe from her money-grabbing schemes."

Mrs Reynolds made no attempt to deny it.

Mrs Wickham sucked in her breath between what few teeth remained in her gums. "Very sly. Very unlike you."

"Perhaps, but unlike *you*, I happen to think Mr Darcy is

worth protecting. I ought not to be surprised that you do not. You never cared a whit about him. No matter that he was the best friend George ever had. No matter that he took beatings for your son's wickedness. No matter that it drove a wedge between him and his father that they never overcame. All this you and your sorry husband knew, and yet you said nothing because it profited you to stay quiet."

"Bah! Mr High-and-Mighty ought not hold grudges over childhood squabbles."

Mrs Reynolds slapped the table angrily. "They were not children last summer! But I suppose you know nothing about what happened then, what with George never speaking to you. Your precious boy is *still* scheming to ruin Mr Darcy's happiness, so now you tell me who is bitter?"

She took a deep breath and fought for a measure of composure. In a calmer voice, she asked, "How can you not care, Lucy? Sitting here in your comfortable cottage with your widow's pension, all courtesy of his good will." She pointed to an upholstered chair with a scene of Pemberley embroidered upon it. "You have even furnished your house at his expense." Indeed, the more Mrs Reynolds looked around, the more items she saw that seemed familiar. A pair of ornate candlesticks that had once adorned the sideboard in the breakfast room; a framed architectural drawing that had used to hang in the late Mr Darcy's study; a fire screen whose twin stood in the Lady Anne room. "None of this is yours!"

Mrs Wickham's shawls moved in a way that suggested she had shrugged. "'Tis only what he owed us."

"He owed you nothing, then or now! But you and your son owe him everything. I am not asking much. George chose to run away with the girl—I only wish to make sure he sees it through."

At last, there appeared a trace of hesitation in the wall of obstinacy before her.

"I cannot make him marry if he opposes it," Mrs Wickham said grudgingly.

"I can well believe it. You could never make him do anything."

"I do not see how you think you will manage any better."

"At least I will have tried. But I need you to tell me where I can find him."

"Are you going to hurt him?"

"Do not be ridiculous. I am a sixty-year-old woman."

"Are you going to have someone else hurt him?"

"Of course not! I only want to make sure he does the right thing. The girl is a gentleman's daughter. He will have a far better outcome than he deserves, I assure you." She shuffled forward in her seat and poured all her fears for the master into her plea. "Do this, Lucy, I beg you. Do this to atone for all the times you stood by and did nothing. After all the misery your family have given him, will you not help me save Mr Darcy from yet more?"

Against her expectations, Mrs Reynolds left the cottage with a list of all George Wickham's most recent addresses in her possession. They were not many, and the latest was over a twelvemonth old, but it was a start. Her parting words to her erstwhile friend were not warm, but since she was not wholly without gratitude that Mrs Wickham had, at the last, conceded to do this one good turn, she had not demanded that the embroidered chair be returned.

She hobbled slowly into town, weary in both body and mind, and after a bit of a struggle, pushed open the heavy door of the goldsmith's.

Mr Lynton looked up from his work, over the top of the magnifying spectacles that made him look forty years older than the strapping young man that he was. "You have excellent timing, Mrs Reynolds. I finished your chatelaine not half an hour ago."

"You are very good, sir." Mrs Reynolds reached into her reticule and withdrew her purse.

"Now, now," he objected. "I told you—the honey was payment enough."

She smiled and did not attempt to prevent her fatigue from showing in it. "Yes, but I have another favour to ask of you, and this problem requires a good deal more than a trifling repair. Honey will not suffice."

"I am intrigued. But I am thoroughly in your debt, for goodness knows you pass enough work my way from Pemberley. If I can help, I shall, most willingly."

"It gives me great comfort to hear you say so. I wonder, sir, when your work will next take you to London?"

CHAPTER SEVENTEEN

LEAD BALLOONS

"Here, look—Bingley, if you stand on this corner, and Aldridge puts his foot there, then I move Ada's chair—" Miss Ada let out a squawk when her brother hefted her chair, with her in it, two feet to the right. "There we are! That ought to do it."

Mr Templeton's purpose was to pin down one of several blankets, all of which had been flapping about wildly in the wind, knocking over drinks and spilling the contents of plates since they arrived. The day had dawned overcast and a little chilly, but the arrival of several cartloads of workmen at Pemberley had been encouragement enough for Mr Darcy's guests to persevere with their planned excursion.

Elizabeth had learnt much of her own feelings by the magnitude of her relief upon receiving Miss Darcy's note to that effect. She was further thankful to discover that the silvered skies had in no way diminished the view, either. Mr Darcy had been correct when he conjectured that she would like this spot. She was quite enraptured.

"Am I to remain here for the rest of the afternoon, do you

think, Miss Ada?" Mr Bingley enquired, standing gamely to attention, and winking at the young lady.

"You are if I am," Mr Aldridge replied from the opposing corner of the blanket.

"I think you might serve the function of paperweight just as well sitting down, Bingley," Mr Darcy suggested with mild amusement.

"Better, I daresay," added Mr Hurst. "For your foot is not nearly as large a weight as your—" His sentence ended with a soft 'oof' as his wife elbowed him in the ribs.

To Elizabeth's right, Mr Gardiner gave a single, high-pitched bark of amusement. She smiled with him, though her thoughts were chiefly of Jane. She found it hard to suppose what her sister would make of such a scene. The camaraderie and good will would, undoubtedly, appeal to her, for Jane was never happier than when all those around her were content as well. Elizabeth was less certain what her eldest sister would think about Mr Bingley's behaviour.

Though never as rigidly self-possessed as Mr Darcy, Mr Bingley had still never conducted himself with so little formality as he was presently displaying. In Hertfordshire, his attention had been so firmly fixed on Jane, it had been difficult for him to appear interested in anyone else. Here in Derbyshire, he was markedly more liberal with his attentions—particularly towards the ladies.

It was, perhaps, a natural consequence of a sociable disposition amongst familiar company, and Elizabeth attempted not to conflate it with the cessation of his enquiries about Longbourn. There were only so many questions one could ask of a static situation, after all, and as no letters had come from home since her arrival in Lambton, she had no new intelligence to impart. She could not blame her family, for she had hardly been diligent with her own correspondence, but she wished she had something more to offer Mr Bingley than repeated assurances of Jane's well-being.

A hue and cry went up when another gust of wind threatened to lift Lady Garroway's skirts, and Lord Garroway, in his gallant leap to help preserve her dignity, overturned several full glasses and an empty chair. Mr and Mrs Cox both managed to roll out of the path of destruction, leaving Mr Connelly—an addition to the party, and apparently one of Mr Darcy's nearest landowning neighbours—to soak up the brunt of the spilt wine.

"Gads, sorry about that, Connelly," his lordship said, laughing in a thoroughly uncontrite fashion. "I do hope your breeches are not ruined."

"Better my breeches than your wife's honour," Mr Connelly replied amiably. "Rum idea to have a picnic in a gale anyway. What were you thinking, Darcy?"

Mr Darcy flicked his gaze to Mr Connelly and smiled very slightly. "That it would have been much less like a picnic indoors."

It was a simple exchange from which both gentlemen swiftly moved on, yet Elizabeth felt a small thrill to observe it, for she was coming to greatly enjoy Mr Darcy's understated humour.

"I understand you and Mr Darcy met in Hertfordshire last year?" This was from Miss Reid who had seated herself on the blanket having dismissed the notion of sitting in a chair at a picnic as being 'like going to a ball and refusing to dance'. Elizabeth had taken an instant liking to her.

"Yes, at our local assembly."

"An assembly?"

"You are surprised?"

"I have never heard of Mr Darcy attending a public ball. We have enough trouble trying to persuade him to come to our private ones."

"I do not think he would have attended this one if his friends had not insisted." Elizabeth indicated the Bingleys with a glance. "He was certainly not inclined to dance with anyone outside of his own party."

"Oh yes, poor Miss Bingley. Her brother is excessively fond of dancing, and she is forever being called upon to save his less-eager friends when they are unable to escape the obligation of a set."

Elizabeth suppressed a smile, though not without some effort. "I did not get the impression she objected in this instance."

Miss Reid looked fleetingly surprised before giving in to a smile. "No, you are probably right." Lowering her voice, she added, "It is, after all, as close as she is ever likely to get."

Miss Templeton abruptly detached herself from her own conversation, twisted around, and inserted herself into theirs with an equally low voice. "Leave Caroline alone, Fenella. There are few of us who have not set our caps at Mr Darcy at some point or other. Indeed, I am surprised you never have."

Their familiarity evidently allowed for this level of rebuke, for Elizabeth could perceive neither vexation in her tone nor affront on Miss Reid's face.

"Me?" the latter replied, clearly amused. "What a waste of my time it would be to pine after a man who would never have me."

"I do not see why he would not. You have fifteen thousand pounds and *that* face."

"But I am not clever. Not clever enough, anyway. Although, cleverer than your friend Miss Bingley, for she has not been so easily put off."

"Oh, do stop," Miss Templeton replied, though she smirked all the same. To Elizabeth, she said, "Caroline is not that bad you know. She can be a little spiky, but she is perfectly amiable once she decides she likes you."

"I shall have to take your word for that."

Miss Templeton and Miss Reid both delighted in this but quieted when their mirth drew curious looks from the other picnickers, the lady in question included.

More quietly, and with a knowing smile that removed any concern for it being meanly meant, Miss Templeton said, "Well, we all know why she does not like *you*, Miss Bennet."

Elizabeth felt herself blush and tried, somewhat inelegantly, to change the subject. "It sounds as though you know the Darcys well, Miss Reid. You must visit Delamont Hall often."

"Oh, I live there. Hamish's—that is, Mr Connelly's—mother and mine are sisters and were both widowed in the same year. We have all lived together at Delamont since. So yes, I have known the family for some time now. Mr Darcy was such a good friend to Hamish when my uncle died—his death was unexpected, and my cousin was woefully unprepared. Mr Darcy spent hours and hours showing him what to do with the estate. Hamish thinks the world of him. We both do."

This was a report Elizabeth received with great satisfaction, and for more reasons than hearing yet another fine account of Mr Darcy's character. That was, perhaps, the thing that surprised her the least, not because the testimony of a friend was not valuable, but because she was coming to expect that people who knew him would speak well of him. There was also some amusement to be had in seeing one of those acquaintances whose sensibilities Mr Darcy had been so averse to injuring by marrying her, now commending *him* to *her*, for all the world as though to promote the match.

Most significantly, however, Elizabeth was delighted with Miss Reid herself. She was young, good-natured, and seemed as sensible as she was lively. Just the sort of person Elizabeth imagined would make a charming neighbour, should she one day find herself living in the vicinity—

She caught herself and felt her cheeks reddening again. It still felt outrageously presumptuous to think it, even privately. When Miss Darcy suggested that they all walk to the ridge to take in the view, Elizabeth was the first to leap to her feet to escape her embarrassment.

"Who fancies a game of Lead Balloons?" Mr Connelly said when they reached the vantage point.

"Oh, I have not played that since I was a girl!" cried Mrs Gardiner. To her husband and niece, she explained that the objective was for everyone to find the lightest object they could, and all drop them over the ridge at the same time, with one person stood on the ledge below to judge which landed last and declare the owner of it the winner. "The first item to land is the Lead Balloon, naturally."

"Naturally," Mr Gardiner echoed, smiling indulgently.

The whole party spent several minutes searching the hillside for suitable projectiles. A few lucky ones found feathers, others picked leaves, grass, and flowers; two ladies chose to sacrifice lace handkerchiefs, and Mr Pettigrew produced a piece of paper from somewhere on his person. Elizabeth took off her bonnet and began to unthread a ribbon from the trim, turning as she did to see what Mr Darcy would use. He was speaking to a footman who, as he listened to his master, broke into a broad grin, bobbed his head several times in apparent thanks, and took off down the escarpment. Mr Darcy then walked directly to a gorse bush tucked away in the nook of the rocky outcropping, from which he unsnagged a wad of sheep's wool.

"You did not search very hard for that, sir," Elizabeth called to him. "One might be forgiven for thinking you prepared for this game in advance."

He looked up, and for a moment said nothing—only

stared at her with an intensity that stilled her hands, stilled everything. Then he moved up the slope towards her, and the wind resumed; hastening clouds on their way and tousling her hair once more.

"I knew there would be wool somewhere," he admitted. "One of my tenant farmers brings his sheep up here to graze."

Elizabeth freed her ribbon and replaced her bonnet, asking as she retied the bow, "Might I enquire, if it is not too impertinent, what you said to your footman just now that made him so happy?"

It was evident the question took Mr Darcy aback, but he answered without objection. "I promised to double whatever the other gentlemen tipped him at the end of the day if he went down to the lower path to judge our game."

"That was generous."

"Adjudicating parlour games, albeit outdoor ones, does not fall within the usual remit of his duties. Besides, I am in an exceptionally good humour."

It showed, Elizabeth thought approvingly.

They were called to attention, along with everyone else, by Mr Connelly, who seemed to have assumed the role of umpire. With several warnings to take care, for it was ten or twelve feet to the next ledge down, he bade them all line up along the ridge of the bluff with their arms outstretched and their objects at the ready. On three, they all let go, and within seconds, Miss Adams's parasol—thrown by her brother—had been declared the first lead balloon. Lord Garroway was duly disqualified from the game. The other items were retrieved and re-thrown again and again; the competitors whittled down one at a time.

Elizabeth played along, hoping the chaos of her thoughts was not apparent. She kept thinking of Mr Darcy's letter, in which he had laid out all his dealings with Mr Wickham and motivations for separating Jane and Mr Bingley. It had overturned her conviction that he lacked compassion and forced her to acknowledge his good intentions. Even so, it had not much improved her understanding of the man behind the words or induced any great desire to know him better. Its effect had rather been to shine a light on her own character, exposing all her own defects.

It was only now, as more and more facets of him were revealed to her, that the caricature of polite society into which she had turned Mr Darcy was falling away to reveal a man of exceptional depth. He had faults, yes—but he had that in common with the rest of the world. He also had friends, family, responsibilities, pleasures, and problems, just as every other person did. Indeed, his problems seemed greater than many people's. The look on his face as he told her about Pemberley's uncertain future had made Elizabeth's heart heavy for him. The desire to comfort him in that moment had been overwhelming. To be the woman to whom Mr Darcy turned for comfort in every moment of need was a privilege Elizabeth suddenly wanted very, very much.

She could feel the pulse at the base of her throat and knew her heart was racing, but as for the other sensation, fluttering at the top of her stomach beneath her ribs, prickling at the edges of her mind—*that* she could not name. Though she could guess.

Her hand shook slightly as she held out her ribbon for the next round. When it was pronounced to be the next lead balloon, Mr Darcy asked if she would like to return to the picnic area for a drink. He watched her as they walked, obviously concerned, and Elizabeth was sorry her distraction had banished his earlier complacency, for it had looked well on him. That thought only rattled her more, however, and feeling as though she would burst if she did not speak, she stopped walking and blurted the first words that came to mind.

"I am sorry."

"What for?"

"For what I said to you in Kent. For what I said *about* you in Hertfordshire. For the way I misjudged you. All of it. Everything."

He said nothing, seemingly fixed in astonishment. Several others overtook them on the path in a dash. They called something as they passed, but Elizabeth did not hear what. Neither did Mr Darcy, judging by the intensity with which he continued to regard her. It endeared her to him further still and persuaded her not to wait for him to reply.

"I am heartily ashamed of what I said, and what I thought. I would have you know, I do not think it anymore."

At last, he opened his mouth to reply but was distracted by one or two drops of water landing on his face. They both looked up, just as the heavens opened and let forth a deluge of rain; huge, fat drops that seemed wetter than water ought to be and filled the air with the smell and deafening patter of a summer squall. Elizabeth tucked her shoulders inwards as though they might fit under the rim of her bonnet. A cataclysmic roll of thunder made her shriek and drop her ribbon, then laugh as she bent to retrieve it. She quieted as something came to rest around her shoulders. When she straightened to her full height, Mr Darcy pulled the lapels of his coat closed under her chin.

She held her breath. His was such a presence!—his clenched hands resting, gentle but hot, on her collarbone, his beautiful face inches from hers, rain dripping from the curls plastered to his forehead, and his eyes as stormy as the sky. The air between them shifted, and for the space of one, shocking heartbeat, Elizabeth thought he would kiss her. Then his hand was at her back, and they were running together towards the carriages, joining in with everyone else as they tussled and harried each other out of the downpour.

The rain on the roof of the carriage was too loud for conversation on the way back to Lambton. Mrs Gardiner dozed lightly; Mr Gardiner squinted through the gloom at his book. Elizabeth watched the storm-capped hills roll past the window, feeling it was an unjustly dreary end to a momentous afternoon. Indeed, were it not for the fact that she was still wearing Mr Darcy's coat, she might have thought she had imagined the most exhilarating few minutes of her life.

Quarter of an hour after arriving back at the inn, she would have done anything to return to dreariness. Instead, shock and dismay were her new attendants, along with something much more visceral that ached tangibly in her breast.

A letter had arrived for her uncle while they were out. It signalled an end to all their engagements in Derbyshire, an end to their holiday, and an end to many more things besides.

My brother Gardiner,

I hope you are sitting down. Your children are all fine—be not alarmed on that score. I regret that your nieces are not all so easily accounted for. My youngest has lost what little reason she had remaining to her and eloped with one of Colonel Forster's officers—Lieutenant Wickham. You met him at Christmas, I believe, and liked him as well as we did. Alas, we have been unhappily deceived in his character.

The pair left Brighton last Saturday and were traced as far as Clapham but no farther. They have certainly not gone to Scotland. I came to town on Monday and have been searching for them since, to no avail.

Jane has, I understand, written to Lizzy more than once, appealing for your swift return. I suspect, from the want of any reply, that her requests were too subtly made. Mine will not be. I implore you to come home. I need your knowledge of London; Jane needs Lizzy's help at Longbourn; your sister needs a degree of patience that I suspect only your dear wife can provide; Lydia needs all our prayers. I fear she is lost, Brother. I am sick with guilt. I hope to see you in London very soon.

Yours &tc.,
T Bennet

CHAPTER EIGHTEEN

OFFICIOUS INTERFERENCE

"Sugar?" Mrs Reynolds enquired. Mr Ferguson did not often take it with his tea, but he looked singularly fatigued that evening, and cold and wet to boot. He nodded, and she added two lumps. "Should you like something to eat?"

"I thank you no. Mrs Ferguson is expecting me for dinner. I shall get off as soon as the rain eases."

"I take it the rain put paid to any significant progress on the dig," said Mr Matthis.

Mr Ferguson nodded glumly. "An inauspicious first day."

"Bit of rain would not usually see my lads falter," Mr Howes grumbled. "But digging in this sort of weather is no fun for anyone."

This many of the upper servants rarely gathered together. They were typically too busy, and their work hours and places too disparate for it. The rain had interfered with everyone's plans; all outdoor work had been brought to an early, sodden halt, and dinner had been delayed until the guests recuperated from their drenching at the picnic.

Unusually, therefore, Pemberley's steward, butler, housekeeper, chef, head gardener, and the master's manservant were all crowded into the upper servants' hall at once. It felt smaller as a consequence, and Mr Ferguson and Mr Howes's waterlogged clothes had added a vaporous, dank air to the space.

The dampness only worsened when the head gamekeeper entered, dripping wet and wringing his cap onto the flags.

Mr Ferguson greeted him with a nod. "Is there a problem?"

"We have caught ourselves a poacher. Well, more found than caught, I suppose, for he was injured and in no fit state to make a run for it."

"Injured? Not in a trap, I hope."

"No. Slipped and turned his ankle. I am not surprised, either, for there is a torrent coming down over the rocks on the north slope."

Mr Howes frowned. "There is no watercourse on the north slope."

"There is today. And now I've a soggy, lame scoundrel in my cabin, and I should like very much to know what to do with him."

"Have you informed Mr Darcy?" the steward enquired.

"Mr Darcy was not in a humour to listen."

Mrs Reynolds frowned. "Perhaps he was busy, Mr Sheldon. He has only just returned from a day out, and he has a large number of guests to attend to."

"Then perhaps he ought to send them home, for this is not a good time to be distracted," Mr Ferguson snapped, to everyone's astonishment, for he rarely showed his temper. "Pray excuse me. Only he was in no humour to hear my report earlier, either, and I am used to him being more attentive to estate matters."

"Mr Vaughan, is the master ill?" Chef enquired.

Mr Darcy's manservant shook his head. "No, Monsieur, he is in perfect health."

"Then what can be the matter with him?" he replied, directing the question to the whole room.

Mrs Reynolds said nothing. She would not have dignified such an enquiry with an answer in any case, but as it was, her lips were pressed firmly together in displeasure. She had a strong suspicion what was consuming the master's attention. What a good thing the *distraction* would soon be gone.

"Come now, Mr Vaughan," Chef coaxed. "It is just us. None of the young girls or boys are here to listen to what we say. You can tell us what has got into Mr Darcy, *non? Est-ce cette jeune femme?*"

Mr Vaughan replied in French, and whatever he said did not please Chef, who returned to his kitchen with a snarl and a spattering of other foreign phrases muttered under his breath.

Mr Ferguson stood and retrieved his coat—still sodden—from the chair in front of the fire. "We had better summon the magistrate. Howes, will you join us?"

The head gardener agreed that he would, and the three men trudged unhappily from the room to return to the rain.

"You had better make amends with Chef before you go back upstairs, Mr Vaughan," Mr Matthis said mildly. "You know how he likes to sulk."

"The man is an incorrigible gossip."

"I shall not argue. Mr Darcy ought to be allowed the odd bit of flirtation without being accused of neglect, even if he is hopelessly preoccupied. But pray, for the sake of all our appetites, make amends with Monsieur Dubois."

The door abruptly burst open, and Hannah leant around it, her manner urgent. "Beg your pardon, Mrs Reynolds. Sarah has knocked over the scuttle trying to light the candles in the Stag Parlour. There is coal dust everywhere."

The housekeeper was plagued by none of her usual aches and pains as she strode through the house. Indignation fuelled her steps and oiled her stiff joints; it stole her patience as she directed the maids in their work and put a sting in her voice as she reprimanded Sarah for carelessness.

Never, in all her years working for him, had Mr Darcy prioritised something or someone before Pemberley. Never had she heard his perennially loyal servants complain about him. It was all, *all* Miss Bennet's doing. Every moment of doubt she had suffered these past two days since visiting Mrs Wickham was banished—she was more certain than ever that she had taken the necessary, the only possible, action.

"I think there is someone at the front door," Hannah said hesitantly.

Mrs Reynolds did not think it likely, for it was long past the hour for calls and still pouring down outside. "James will answer it, if there is."

"James was in the kitchen just now, having a glass of milk."

Mrs Reynolds sighed sharply. "Keep on with what you are doing, girls. I'll not be long." She heard the banging herself as she exited the parlour and almost decided against answering it, thinking it might be better to fetch James or Mr Matthis if there were an angry mob to be repelled. But then she reached the hall and saw, through the glazing of the front door, that it was no violent stranger, no wild beast outside. A threat to Pemberley, certainly, but not one she was unable to deal with herself. She swept across the hall, incensed by the sheer audacity of the woman, and opened the door by no more than an inch.

"The family are not presently receiving guests, madam. I am afraid you have had a wasted trip."

She faltered as soon as the words were said, her heart pounding and her doubt swimming nearer to the surface once more. For all her anger, it felt entirely wrong to meddle so brazenly in the master's concerns. She ignored the sensation; little point baulking at turning away callers after the lengths to which she had already gone to banish Miss Bennet from his life forever. With Mr Lynton in London on an errand to see the marriage between George Wickham and Lydia Bennet done whatever the cost, all connexion between Mr Darcy and the rain-soaked and windswept woman presently banging at his door would soon be dissolved.

Miss Bennet looked thoroughly deflated to be refused entry. She was clutching something to her chest, and she fumbled with it awkwardly as she began to speak. "I would never presume, under any other circumstances, only something has...There is a...I find I must return home immediately. I would take my leave of the family before I go if I may."

It was too much to hope this had anything to do with Mr Lynton's assignment—it was too soon—but she was leaving, and all doubts aside, that could be nothing but a source of relief.

"As I said," Mrs Reynolds repeated firmly, "the family are busy at present."

"Is there no way you could let Mr Darcy know I am here?"

Mrs Reynolds did not need to feign her shock; such shameless impropriety would scandalise the most liberal of minds. "This is most irregular. Perhaps if you waited until a more sociable hour and called on *Miss* Darcy?"

Miss Bennet flushed scarlet. "Or Miss Darcy—I meant that. Both of them—either of them. Forgive me, I am...This is...Please, if you would just let one of them know I am here."

"Tomorrow would be more acceptable."

"It cannot wait until tomorrow. We are leaving now."

"Perhaps you could write to Miss Darcy when you reach home, then. *If* the young lady has agreed to a correspondence, of course."

Miss Bennet shook her head slightly, her countenance twisted with what looked like genuine pain. But then, she had put so much work into her scheme; it must be unbearable to give it up at this stage. Mrs Reynolds held firm.

"Lizzy? We must go now."

The housekeeper started at the deep voice and peered out into the driving rain. She had not noticed the carriage at the foot of the steps, nor Miss Bennet's uncle, leaning out of it, gesturing for his niece to make haste. She had not come alone, then, and her call was not quite as scandalous as it had first seemed. Doubt immediately crowded back into Mrs Reynolds's mind—but no! The woman was all but in league with George Wickham! She forced herself to give a thin, unpleasant smile. "It seems you must go."

Miss Bennet's shoulders slumped in defeat. "I do have a note for Miss Darcy. I was hoping for the chance to explain… Never mind. Would you be kind enough to give it to her? And pray, tell her how very sorry we all are that we must leave without a proper goodbye."

Mrs Reynolds accepted the note but made no promises.

"And this belongs to Mr Darcy." She held out the bundle of cloth in her arms, which turned out to be one of the master's finely tailored coats, scrunched into a soggy ball.

Mrs Reynolds shook it out disdainfully and made a point of draping it carefully over her arm. "I shall see that he gets it."

Miss Bennet did not move, which might have worked, for Mrs Reynolds had neither the strength nor the gall to physically evict her. But then she attempted, surreptitiously, to crane her neck and peer into the house for a glimpse of her quarry, and Mrs Reynolds made up her mind. Though it opposed every ounce of her training and every principle of her position, she shut the front door in Miss Bennet's face. The young woman's eyes widened in disbelief, then she shook, as though she were sobbing, and turned and ran to her uncle's carriage.

Mrs Reynolds clutched her shaking hands together. There was no way of dressing up what she had just done as acceptable. The business with the younger Miss Bennet was one thing—that merely required George to finish what he had already begun. This was different. This was deliberate and officious interference in the master's private affairs—and in direct opposition to what she knew would have been his wishes.

The weight of self-reproach reminded all her limbs of that fatigue which resentment had earlier made them forget. Feeling every one of her sixty years, she crossed the hall, expecting with every step that Mr Matthis would appear and demand an explanation. No one came. Neither the butler, nor the footman, nor any of the girls cleaning up the spilt coal dust. The steward was off, dealing with the poacher. Most of the guests were in the saloon on the other side of the house. If any had seen the carriage from their bedrooms, she would discover it soon enough, but for now, it seemed there had been no witnesses to her aberration. And Miss Bennet was gone.

She checked on progress in the Stag Parlour, assured the maids there was not a murderer hammering at the door, then retreated unsteadily to her sitting room. Her hands still shook as she unfolded the note for Miss Darcy. She made no attempt to excuse it to herself—it was a despicable invasion of privacy. Yet having come this far in her endeavours to evade all cunning, she had no intention of overlooking any more.

The note appeared entirely innocuous—merely a repetition of Miss Bennet's apologies for her precipitate departure and a hope that they would see each other again. Mrs Reynolds threw it on the fire. After several deep breaths to allay a wave of nausea, she pulled the master's coat onto her lap and checked its pockets for hidden communications. There were none, which surprised her again. Queasiness and misgivings bubbled back up to haunt her.

It would not do. She must not allow the ugliness of the last few minutes to cloud her purpose. She opened the drawer of her writing desk and pulled out Eleanor's most recent letter.

I have not forgot your philippic for that other friend of his, Mrs Younge, nor your regret for not detecting her treachery in time to obviate it.

As always, Eleanor's words steadied her. *This* was why she had acted. Yes, it sat badly with her; yes, she felt sullied by the underhandedness of it, but when her time came, sooner rather than later, she would die knowing the master would not be ill-used.

"A servant just brought this over from Lambton," she said as she handed Mr Darcy's coat to Mr Vaughan. Then she returned to her duties and hoped nobody would notice her still-shaking hands.

CHAPTER NINETEEN

GONE

The months following Elizabeth's rejection had been some of the most wretched of Darcy's life. He had wasted many months prior to that moment, tormenting himself with all the reasons he ought not to marry her. In the end, when his feelings had grown too strong to master, he had allowed himself to imagine what it would be like were Elizabeth his wife.

Desire had already left its mark on his nocturnal dreams, but his waking imagination centred on their happiness in marriage, teasing him with the hope of replacing solitude with solicitude. It was not something he had known he wanted until he met Elizabeth. He had not comprehended how desperately he needed it until she denied it to him.

Exacerbating that most painful of forfeitures had been the coinciding bereavement for the man he once believed himself to be. That he might have won her affections had he troubled himself to be more modest, more forbearing, more considerate—more *gentlemanlike*—was a regret that tortured him still. He could not, he would not, repeat his mistakes.

The ground was a quagmire after yesterday's storm, forcing him to ride slowly. A good thing, for it gave him time to consider what he would say—and a very bad thing for the same reason. He could not conceive of a worse method of declaring himself than his previous attempt, and that had been the product of altogether too much deliberation. But he would try and find the right words, for speak to her he must. He was uncertain of his reception—what man who had already been rejected once would not be? Yet by the end of the previous day, he had committed to his purpose.

Elizabeth had driven him almost to distraction at the picnic, scarcely taking her eyes off him the entire day. More than once he had convinced himself he could feel the heat of her gaze and chided himself for such foolishness, only to turn around and find himself looking directly into her eyes. It had stirred his blood more each time, and he longed to know what she had been thinking, though he could not believe she observed him with disapprobation. He had seen what displeasure looked like on her, and this was as far from it as was possible.

By the time she came to be standing toe-to-toe with him, soaking wet, wrapped in his coat, and staring up at him with naked admiration, he had been ablaze with desire. Never had he wished to kiss anyone as much as he wanted to kiss her in that moment. He had not allowed his thoughts to go further; nevertheless, it had still been necessary for him to retreat into privacy to regain his equanimity when he returned to Pemberley, proving what he already knew—that if he never succeeded in winning Elizabeth's hand, he would be utterly useless to the rest of the world.

As he had climbed into his bed that night, desire had been replaced with a different but equally intense longing. He had missed dinner, making do with a light supper in his room, for his evening had not gone at all to plan. The first part of it was passed in the gamekeeper's cold, damp cabin, along with his steward and an exceedingly disgruntled magistrate, deciding what was to be done with a poacher Sheldon had apprehended. After that came Ferguson's grim report of the fiasco at the dig, a brewing disagreement with the stone mason over rates, and the difficulty of finding suitably secure storage for the contents of the library.

Such was ever the way. There were always problems to solve, always decisions to be made. He no longer wanted to make them alone. He wanted Elizabeth there to reassure him with kind words or to comfort him with her touch. He wanted, instead of climbing into an empty bed after a difficult night such as that, to climb into her arms. He had resolved, before he closed his eyes, that he would not allow her to leave Derbyshire without knowing his affections and wishes were unchanged. As he turned his horse onto Lambton's main thoroughfare that morning, he hoped to God it would be enough.

"What do you mean *gone*?"

"They left yesterday, early evening."

"Are they coming back?"

"They did not say so. Mr Gardiner settled his account in full."

It required every ounce of Darcy's self-control to keep his voice steady. "I understood they were not planning to leave until tomorrow. Was there some emergency?"

"None they deigned to tell me about, sir."

"Did they seem distressed?"

"They were keen to be gone, but nothing out of the ordinary."

"It was pouring down with rain—they must have had good reason to travel in such bad weather."

The innkeeper reddened. "Begging your pardon, Mr Darcy, but this is an inn. People come and go all the time."

Darcy felt his dismay begin to spiral towards panic and forced himself to ask collectedly, "Do you know where they were headed?"

"I do not, sir. Shall I ask the chambermaid?"

Darcy gave a curt nod and waited, fist clenched rigidly around his riding crop, while the innkeeper left to make his enquiries. A dream-like quality overtook proceedings; everything moved too slowly, nothing quite made sense, and disaster seemed to be waiting, eager, in the shadows.

The innkeeper returned. "Nell says she heard them talk about going to either Chesterfield or Sheffield after they left Lambton."

North? "Not Hertfordshire?"

"Not by the sounds of it."

"They left no forwarding address? No messages for anyone?"

"None that I know of."

Did the man pay attention to nothing that went on in his own establishment? Darcy wanted to shake him until he remembered something, *anything* of use! The innkeeper backed away slightly as though he, too, thought a rattling might be imminent, and Darcy knew he must leave.

He mounted his horse, a thousand misgivings flooding his head as he turned homewards. He hoped there had not been some problem that necessitated their immediate departure. It dismayed him to think of Elizabeth in distress—and that she had felt either unable or unwilling to come to him. Yet he could not imagine, even if their situation were dire, that none of the party would have left word.

A prickle of apprehension cut through him. People who did not take their leave generally did not intend to maintain the acquaintance. Was not that why neither he nor Miss Bingley called at Longbourn before they followed Bingley to London last autumn? *Damn!* Had he misunderstood again? Was it merely a rapprochement Elizabeth had sought, and instead, he almost kissed her? No wonder she ran away!

He did not want to believe it. It was too appalling to allow that he could have been so egregiously mistaken a second time—but what, then? Had Elizabeth told him they were leaving yesterday, and it slipped his mind? In which case, was that meagre goodbye at the picnic, shouted through the carriage door as her uncle pulled her out of the rain, the best for which he could hope? Was that why she had stared at him all day—had she been waiting for him to declare himself before she left?

Damn, damn, damn!

She had apologised! Dear God! As though she were in *any* way to blame—and he had said nothing. *Nothing!* A gentleman would have dismissed her apology as unnecessary, told her how profoundly he regretted every reprehensible thing he had ever said to her, explained that he was attending to her reproofs. A sensible man would have told her he still loved her. He had only shoved her into a carriage and sent her on her way without so much as a promise to call the next day. Why *would* she leave word for such a man?

Darcy pulled his horse up and closed his eyes, his breathing laboured and a palpable hollowness in his chest. Elizabeth was gone, and there was no way of knowing why and no easy way of finding out. Even if it were sensible to follow her and ask what went wrong, he would have to wait until he could be sure she was returned to Longbourn, for he had no idea where she was at present. Whether that *was* sensible, he was in no state to judge. If she had left to get away from him, he ought to let her go with dignity on both sides, but every fibre of his being revolted against giving her up. He knew only one thing: he could not leave matters as they were. He would go mad. Indeed, he felt as though he were most of the way there already.

CHAPTER TWENTY

JUST AS WELL

By mutual agreement, card tables were set up in the saloon that afternoon. Darcy played and lost, and played and lost again, and played and received a ribbing for his bad form, and played some more, and maybe won, or maybe lost this time; he was not paying attention. He excused himself from the next round and went to look out of the window. The sky was cerulean blue with not a cloud in sight, as though nothing worse could be happening in the world than Mrs Hurst losing a fish in a card game.

He adjusted his gaze to the reflection in the window. All his guests were present, and it was a large party, but they might as well all go home. There were not enough people in the world to disguise the chasm left by Elizabeth's absence.

"You are very quiet, Mr Darcy," Miss Bingley called—very loudly. "I hope whatever it was that required you to miss dinner is not troubling you still."

"It is not, but thank you, madam."

"I am pleased to hear it." She paused. "Though, we were

all rather wondering what was so urgent that it could not wait."

Darcy did not answer. *Let her wonder.* Too late, he caught the glint of cunning in her countenance.

"Will our friends from Lambton be gracing us with their company today? Perhaps, if your urgent business took you to see them last night, you would know better than the rest of us what their plans are."

Darcy glanced around the tables and observed more than one fixed expression as his friends all awaited his answer. Well, that was no more than he deserved, was it? One did not lavish such attentions on a woman without raising expectations. What was it of which Elizabeth had once accused him? Exposing Jane Bennet to the derision of the world for her disappointed hopes. Was this his comeuppance? It was exceedingly effective, if so.

A new possibility occurred to him: that Elizabeth had left because, regardless of her own sentiments, she could not forgive him for separating her sister from Bingley. He almost bared his teeth in anger at all the consequences of his own ill-considered interference.

"I was with my steward and Lord Felixstowe last night, Miss Bingley. But Miss Bennet and the Gardiners will not be joining us. They have departed on the next stage of their travels."

Bingley looked up sharply. "I should have sent my regards to her sisters at Longbourn if I had known that was the last we were to see of them."

"The whole party were delightful company," said Mrs Cox. "I hope we shall see them at Pemberley again."

Darcy did not answer. Next to Mrs Cox, Georgiana sat quietly, regarding him with an obvious question in her countenance. He gave the slightest shake of his head; she gave the merest nod of hers and returned to her cards. They would discuss it later, though heaven only knew what he was to say to her. He returned to looking out of the window.

After what seemed like an interminably long time, the low murmur of conversation returned to the room. If it was more subdued than before, there was nothing he could do about it. There was precious little he could do about any of his present troubles. He had never felt so powerless.

He saw in the window that Bingley was approaching and steeled himself for an uncomfortable exchange. He knew his friend had noticed his partiality for Elizabeth—had caught him frowning at it more than once. A lesser man would have demanded to know why a connexion with the Bennets should be no obstacle to the master of Pemberley when it had been presented as such an evil to himself. But Bingley was not one for recriminations. He would never presume to interfere in Darcy's affairs as Darcy had done in his.

"Did you know yesterday that the Gardiners were leaving today?" Bingley enquired quietly.

"No."

"I thought not. 'Tis a shame. I should have liked to ask—" He exhaled noisily. "Miss Elizabeth did not say anything to you this week, did she? About her sister?"

Darcy stared hard at a tree in the middle distance and kept his countenance blank. Several times over the last week, he had considered confessing his misapprehension of Jane Bennet's regard. The only thing that prevented him was Elizabeth's silence on the matter. Surely, if her sister were still enamoured of Bingley, she would have found a way to let it be known? Yet she had not mentioned it, thus neither had he, for fear of it no longer being true.

He shook his head. It was not, strictly speaking, a lie—Elizabeth had spoken to him about Jane in April. Still, he disliked the disguise.

"Probably just as well."

Darcy refrained from looking at Bingley in surprise. *Just as well?* Was that apropos of his own warning against the Bennets, or had Bingley's regard begun to wane?

"I had wondered whether *you* might be—" Bingley began.

In the periphery of his vision, Darcy could see he was peering at him expectantly. His gut clenched, dislodging the cloud of numbness that had crept over him since that morning, threatening to expose the turmoil lurking beneath.

"You are right," he interrupted. "It is probably just as well. Excuse me." He did not take his leave of the rest of the room and did not care what anyone made of it. He yanked the door open and swung it closed behind him, obviously startling his footman, then made his way with purpose towards the stairs.

"Wait!"

He halted, mouthed an oath, then turned reluctantly to face his sister.

She hastened to him, all tender concern—the worst sort. "What happened?"

"She left."

"She did not tell you she was going?"

He shook his head.

"Something must have happened. Nothing else would induce her to slight us, to slight *you* in such a way. It is obvious she admires you."

Darcy's heart leapt into this throat, only for reason to swat it back down again. His sister was scarcely an impartial observer—hers was not a sound assessment. "Her unannounced departure rather discredits that theory." Her face fell, and Darcy abruptly reached the limit of what he could withstand. "Return to the card tables, Georgiana. Your friends will be missing you."

She nodded sadly, but to his consternation, before she

left, placed a hand on his arm and squeezed. "Do not give up hope."

A weight fell inside him as though he had swallowed a stone. He gave her a desultory smile and escaped up the stairs to his dressing room. Vaughan was there already, laying out his clothes for dinner.

"My coat and boots if you would, Vaughan. I am going for a walk."

"Of course, sir." He glided silently around the room, removing Darcy's discarded house shoes from sight and setting his boots on the floor beside him in one fluid movement.

Darcy watched him work and refused to allow any other thoughts into his head. Questions were too many, and answers entirely lacking. Vaughan helped him into his boots, gestured for him to turn around, then did the same with his coat. Darcy waved off his attempt to fasten it for him, too impatient to be gone to wait for the bother of button hooks. Yet, as he strode to the door, he caught a glimpse of himself in the mirror and froze on the spot.

"What is this?"

"Your green coat, sir. The black had mud on it after your ride this morning. It is not yet dry."

"I can see it is my green coat. I mean, where did you get it?" The last time Darcy had seen it, it had been wrapped around Elizabeth as her carriage drove away. He met his man's eyes in the mirror and understood immediately that Vaughan knew the cause of his distress. It was in his voice, too, when he answered.

"A servant brought it to the house last night, sir. From Lambton."

"With a message?"

Vaughan's face said it all. There was no need for him to reply, "No, sir."

That was it, then. Elizabeth had returned his coat with neither thanks nor farewell, but her message was loud and clear, nevertheless. She wanted nothing more to do with him. He knew not how or why, but he had lost her all over again. Feeling alarmingly close to high emotion, he opened his mouth to dismiss Vaughan, but his man had already gone. Darcy was utterly alone. Again.

CHAPTER TWENTY-ONE

NOTHING TO BE DONE

Longbourn was strangely muted, given the extraordinary circumstances. Mr Bennet remained in London, and thither, too, had gone Mr Gardiner. Mrs Bennet kept to her chambers. Without her favourite sister to conspire with, Kitty made a good deal less noise than she was generally wont to do. Elizabeth, Jane, and Mary, all conscious of the implications for them of a sister's fall from grace, were vastly subdued. The whole family was avoiding social engagements, and by such means, all difficult questions.

The only liveliness in the house came from the Gardiner children, and their mother spent most of her time attempting to dampen that, for fear of upsetting the rest of the household.

"Shall we take them out to play in the garden?" Elizabeth suggested, seeing the littlest of her cousins begin to work himself up to tears upon being hushed for the fourth or fifth time. Mrs Gardiner readily agreed, and between them, they bundled all four children, several toys, and a blanket outside.

The three eldest children dispersed across the lawn, whilst little Matthew began lining up his toy soldiers on the hills and valleys of the blanket-landscape.

It was a mild day, not cold but not sunny either, and the stiff breeze picking at the corners of the blanket reminded Elizabeth of the picnic at Pemberley. That had been less than a week ago, yet it felt a lifetime removed. Separating that moment from the present were three miserable days of rain-plagued travel, followed by two even longer days spent absorbing all the distressing details of Lydia's elopement. Elizabeth would not have been surprised had she woken that morning to discover her entire stay in Derbyshire had been a dream.

She wished she had kept Darcy's coat. It had smelled wonderful. She would have taken solace in wrapping it around herself, perchance to pretend she was in his arms as she had come so close to being.

"I hate to see you so downcast, Lizzy," Mrs Gardiner said gently. "I am more used to you finding the humour in things."

"I do not know that things have ever seemed less humorous."

"These are not ideal circumstances by any stretch of the imagination. But I am sure your father and uncle will find Lydia."

"Then you are more confident than I am." Elizabeth righted several of her cousin's soldiers that had fallen over. They all toppled over again directly, for she was too angry to place them with any care. "Stupid, stupid girl! To go, and go willingly, into such a situation—and with such a man! What possessed her?"

"Youth. Fancy. Inclination. Do not fool yourself into believing that passion is the sole province of men. Women are just as susceptible."

Elizabeth did not need to be persuaded of that. When Darcy had pulled her towards him in his coat and looked at her as though she were a siren from whose song he was struggling to break free, her body had responded compellingly. Sensations she had never felt before but were instinctively understood left her flushed, light-headed, and unsatisfied. She had wanted him to kiss her with a fervency that startled her still, so yes, she knew very well what it was to be carried away by passion. She knew it so well, had dwelt on it so long, in fact, that she had begun to doubt her understanding of everything else.

She fretted that she, like Lydia, had allowed her fancy to overtake reason—allowed herself to see admiration where, in truth, there was only civility. For she knew now that Darcy could be so very attentive, so very gentle, so very generous. It was perfectly possible that he had not wanted to kiss her at all; that he had meant only to shield her from the rain; that, not wishing to appear resentful, he had merely been tolerating her company all along.

"Perhaps he is relieved I am gone. He certainly will be when he finds out what has happened."

"Who?"

"Mr Darcy."

"Oh. We are talking about him now, are we?" Mrs Gardiner had taken over straightening the fallen soldiers, passing every other one to her son for him to position. It nevertheless seemed that her small smile was not for him. "If you are lucky, he will not find out."

"Lucky?" Elizabeth said with a bitter laugh. "I suppose it would prevent him discovering yet another reason to object to my family, but it would not explain to him why I left, just when—" She bit off her words and exhaled in exasperation. There had been no question of explaining the matter in her note to his sister—the risk to Lydia's reputation hardly as great a consideration as the pain to Miss Darcy that any mention of Mr Wickham's name must give. It had never been her intention to leave without any explanation at all, though. Not when she and Darcy had seemed so close to an understanding. She could not bear to think what his feelings towards her must presently be. "Would that I could have talked to him."

"I know you wanted to, and that your uncle and I agreed to it, but in retrospect, I am not sure it is a bad thing that you did not get the chance. What would you have said?"

"That I—That Lydia—Oh! I do not know!"

"Exactly. It is better this way. Let us find your sister and bring her home first. Then, once everything has settled down, your uncle can write to Mr Darcy and invite him to dinner when he is next in London, and the acquaintance can be renewed that way."

"Only if Lydia is not married to Mr Wickham. If she is, it is all lost." It was not to be supposed that Darcy would have anything to do with her if she were connected so closely to the man he so justly scorned.

"If she is *not* married to Mr Wickham, it may still all be lost."

Her aunt's sombre tone was humbling.

"Forgive me, I do not mean to be selfish. You must know I am concerned about what will happen to Lydia. But I cannot pretend it does not pain me that Mr Darcy does not know why I left. He will think I do not care."

"Oh, Lizzy. We could all see that you cared. If he could not, then he must be blind."

Elizabeth shook her head emphatically. "He assumed I admired him the first time he proposed, and I spurned him. He is not likely to risk making the same mistake again. He cannot have lost that much of his pride."

"But did you not say in your note to Miss Darcy that you hoped to see him again?"

"I did, but what good will that do? He will not seek me out while there is any doubt as to my feelings, and my uncle will not write to him while there is any doubt as to Lydia's virtue. My only hope is that Lydia can be found unruined and unmarried. And soon." Or that, by some miracle, the message she *had* sent to Darcy would be sufficient to convey her feelings. The strength of those feelings was somewhat alarming, considering their newness, but she did not question them. She had never missed anybody so much that it physically hurt, not even Jane. That was not something she could disregard.

Her aunt squeezed her hand gently. "Your uncle can write even if they are married if that is what you wish."

Elizabeth took a deep breath, and another. At least that way, she supposed, Darcy would know she had not abandoned him willingly. "I should like that. Thank you."

"Look what I found in the parlour, Matthew."

Elizabeth looked up in surprise as Jane folded herself elegantly onto the blanket and handed Matthew a toy soldier.

"How is your mother?" Mrs Gardiner enquired of her.

"Much the same. Hill has given her some tonic to help her sleep. Who is my uncle writing to?"

Mrs Gardiner glanced at Elizabeth in question.

"Mr Darcy," she admitted.

"Mr Darcy?" Jane exclaimed. "Why?"

"To explain our sudden departure."

Confusion clouded Jane's countenance, but Thomas, Mrs Gardiner's other son, chose that moment to run across the blanket, knocking soldiers in every direction and drawing a shrill scream from his brother. Mrs Gardiner announced that she would return both boys to the house and after a sympathetic glance at Elizabeth, took them both by the hand and led them away.

"Lizzy, I have been very remiss," Jane said at once. "I have not asked a single thing about your travels since you got home, but now I am anxious. What on earth happened that requires my uncle to write to Mr Darcy, of all people?"

There had scarcely been a minute these past few days when the conversation was not centred on Lydia's plight, and neither had Elizabeth been sure how much she ought to say of those people she had met in Derbyshire, for fear of giving her sister any distress. Yet the longer she was away from Darcy, the more certain she became of her heart, and she could never withhold sentiments of such moment from her dearest sister. Beginning with Mr and Mrs Gardiner's fateful decision to visit Pemberley on their way to Lambton, Elizabeth relayed the events of the last week, concentrating on her dealings with Darcy and making no mention, for now, of his friends.

Her sister could not conceal her astonishment, and by the time Elizabeth came to describe her confrontation with Pemberley's housekeeper on Monday afternoon, her hands were firmly in Jane's clasp.

"Poor, poor Lizzy. I am sure our uncle will smooth things over when he writes. And I am not as convinced as you that Mr Darcy will not come sooner than that. Not if he loves you as much as it sounds as though he does—which is only as much as you deserve."

Jane's compassion made Elizabeth suddenly tearful, and her voice wavered as she replied. "I wish I could send word myself, but I dare not write to him, and it would be unpardonably cruel to embroil Miss Darcy in anything in which Mr Wickham is involved."

"What has Aunt Gardiner advised?"

"Only what you heard—that our uncle will write to Mr Darcy once Lydia is found."

"Have you written to Mrs Wallis? She always has sound advice."

"Not yet, but I owe her a letter. I have not written to anyone since before I went away. I shall not do it today, though. My head is too jumbled. I thought a few days would clear it, but—" She sucked in a deep breath to prevent a sob. "I think I love him even more than when I was there."

Jane tilted her head and smiled kindly. "Then I pity you, Lizzy, for I know that feeling all too well."

A shard of guilt pierced Elizabeth's sadness. She adjusted her grip so that Jane was no longer holding her hands, but she Jane's, and squeezed them tightly for a moment while she gathered her courage.

"There is something else. Mr Bingley was among the friends staying with Mr Darcy." She allowed a few seconds for that news to sink in, then continued, "I do not know what I can tell you except that he is still single, and I was right about him and Miss Darcy. There is nothing between them."

Jane nodded. She had gone quite pale. "Did he ask about me?"

"Yes."

"Do you—do you think he still loves me?"

It was the question Elizabeth dreaded, but she answered as honestly as she could. "I do not know. He did not say so, but I would not expect him to tell me if he did. I looked for it, but it was impossible to tell without you there. I am sorry."

"Oh, do not be sorry for me," Jane said with a sigh. "I have had plenty of time to become accustomed to my disappointment. Yours is much fresher." She tucked Elizabeth's hair behind her ear and cupped her chin. "But I am confident you will not be unhappy for long."

Elizabeth did not feel consoled. "We shall never see either of them again if Lydia cannot be found."

"Of course she will be found! She and Wickham must make a handsome couple—*somebody* will remember seeing them."

"What if she is not with him anymore?"

"You cannot believe him so bad as to abandon her!"

"I am sorry to say it, but I do."

"Oh, Lizzy!" Jane covered her mouth with her hand. On anybody else, the gesture would have looked affected. It made her sweet, unsuspicious sister look truly horrified.

"I know," she whispered. "She is so naïve. She would not understand the danger she was in until it was too late."

"I cannot bear to think what that would do to Papa. You should have seen him when the express came. I never saw anyone so shocked."

"I cannot bear to think what it would do to any of us, Jane. There would be no gentlemen callers from Derbyshire or anywhere else. We would all be ruined. And as for our poor, reckless sister? Well, we had better pray that our uncle knows where to look for her. It is the only hope for any of us."

CHAPTER TWENTY-TWO

THE PRICE OF HAPPINESS

The library was the largest room in Pemberley, bigger even than the great hall, yet not until now had Mrs Reynolds considered it to be imposingly so. Hitherto, its walls of books, abundance of reading chairs, and two fireplaces had made the cavernous chamber welcoming, in spite of its grandeur. As its shelves were slowly emptied and its furniture removed, the space felt ever less familiar.

She patted the wall next to her and whispered. "Poor old girl. I know how you feel."

She did, too. It was another damp day, and her ailing body ached and groaned in new places and foreign ways. It no longer responded to instruction as it had used to, and she found herself, on occasion, staring up a flight of steps or at some other obstacle, wondering when her limbs had become so truculent. When she tried to walk away from the wall, her feet were disinclined to obey, and she staggered slightly.

"Mrs Reynolds, are you well?"

She glanced behind her, mortified to discover that the

master had observed her frailty. "Quite well, thank you, Mr Darcy."

He pierced her with an unnerving look. It was one he had mastered at an exceedingly young age, and which she had observed him use on countless people in her time. She could not deny its efficacy. "It was just a little turn. It will pass."

He immediately signalled for two footmen, who were marching towards the door with a wing back chair slung between them, to bring it to him instead; then he insisted that Mrs Reynolds sit in it. She did, knowing the pain in her side would ease faster that way.

Mr Darcy beckoned the nearest maid. "Hannah, fetch a glass of wine for Mrs Reynolds, please."

After a quick, concerned glance at her and a curtsey for him, Hannah hastened from the library. Mr Darcy perched on a nearby stack of crates. It looked neither dignified nor comfortable, and Mrs Reynolds suspected he did it only to make her feel less conscious about sitting down herself.

"I am terribly sorry, sir. I shall be as right as rain in a moment."

"Do not apologise. But be frank with me—is this all too much?" He gestured to the wider room.

There certainly was a good deal going on. Three of the housemaids were in here, packing books into crates. Since very few of them knew their letters, each had been paired with a clerk, hired from the village to inventory the contents of every crate. Two footmen were stacking furniture by the door ready for collection. Two more had lowered one of the library's huge chandeliers onto a wooden trolley and were detaching it from its pulleys and ropes. A man she did not know was up a temporary scaffold, hammering at the wall above one of the windows. And she had come, as she did several times a day, to ensure the smooth running of things, to check that all was well with the house. A little like visiting a dear old friend in their sickbed.

"I have never been frightened of hard work."

Mr Darcy gave her a small but sincere smile. "I am well aware. But your stumble just now—I hope you are not overfatigued?"

Mrs Reynolds hesitated. She would have to tell him at some point that he would need a new housekeeper, but not when the poor man had so much else with which to contend. "I should say I am more melancholy than fatigued. It is difficult to see Pemberley being pulled apart in this way."

His expression softened, revealing a sadness in his countenance she had not noticed before. "But of course, this has been your home for almost as long as it has been mine."

"I daresay I am as fond of it as you are, if it is not impertinent to say so."

"I should be a strange sort of employer if I considered loyalty an impertinence. Be assured, I shall do everything in my power to save the house. Though, as a wise woman once said to me, Pemberley is more than stones and mortar. It will endure, no matter what happens to these walls."

They certainly were wise words, and Mrs Reynolds took solace from them. She wished they had afforded the same comfort to the master, but he looked almost haunted by them, staring sombrely at the ground, his mind evidently off elsewhere entirely. She cleared her throat. "Did you come to the library in search of me, sir?"

"No, I came to see how the clerks were getting on. But I do need to speak to you, as it happens. Mrs Annesley wishes to expand Miss Darcy's understanding of household management. She will begin with arranging the dinners, so you will be dealing with her instead of me each morning—a much pleasanter task for you and Chef, I am sure." He gave another small smile as he said this, though it contained no real joy.

"I am sure Miss Darcy will excel at the task." She caught the barest hint of scepticism on his face, which she knew from experience she would not have seen if he had not intended her to; thus, she permitted herself to add, knowingly, "I shall make sure to acquaint her with everybody's favourite dishes, sir."

"Just do not allow her to put foie gras on the menu, I beg you. And please remind Monsieur Dubois that Miss Darcy is fluent in French, so he must watch his tongue. Ah, good, here we are."

Hannah had returned, and the master gestured for her to hand over the wine directly.

Mrs Reynolds took it, sipped it, and did indeed feel restored. "You are very kind, sir. And now I really must get on." She set her glass down and put her hands on the arms of the chair, but before she could push herself up, she found herself all but lifted to her feet by Mr Darcy's strong hands. He did it so quickly, and so discreetly, that she was standing before anyone else could see what he had done.

If she had been his mother, she would have cupped his face and told him what a dear boy he was. She was not, so she could not, but there were other means by which she could reward him. She had not previously thought it appropriate to share her memories of his family, but she would be gone soon, and then there would be no one left alive who could tell him the stories.

"Mr Darcy, would you allow me to tell you my fondest memory of this room?"

He looked surprised by the request but acceded to it, nevertheless.

"It was about half a year after I began working at Pemberley. You stole out of your nursery after the nursemaid was asleep and came in here. The alarm was raised in the morning, and of course the whole house was in uproar. It was your father who found you—curled up, asleep, in front of the atlases. He bought you a globe for your next birthday."

Mr Darcy stood motionless for a moment or two, and Mrs Reynolds could almost see him sifting this new information into place amongst his own memories. At length, he smiled, but so sadly, it hurt her to see it.

"I recall my father giving me the globe. I did not know that was why. Thank you."

She bobbed a curtsey and turned to leave, but the master forestalled her.

"You must take care, Mrs Reynolds. Let Mr Ferguson know if you need extra help. I cannot lose my housekeeper as well as everything else."

"Mr Darcy will take a tray in his room later."

"Again? Is he unwell?"

Mrs Reynolds did not like the way Mr Vaughan paused before answering "no." It allowed the doubts that now lurked permanently at the back of her mind to nudge their way forward. She had been certain Miss Bennet's departure would rid the master of his preoccupation and return him to his usual vigour and diligence. She had not foreseen that he would become steadily more inattentive, more withdrawn, more unhappy.

"He will be missed at dinner."

"No doubt." Mr Vaughan was apparently not inclined to elaborate and left.

Mrs Reynolds pursed her lips and pulled the chair next to her back under the table, wincing as the legs scraped on the flags. She straightened the tea tray in front of her, so it aligned with the grain on the table and stared at it. It was no good; her qualms could be ignored no longer, and she was unable to keep from saying to Mr Matthis, "Something must be wrong—do you not think? It is most unlike the master to be such a poor host."

The butler lowered his paper to frown at her. "It is unlike *you* to criticise him."

"I am not! But I *am* concerned for him. His guests will begin to comment if he continues to neglect them. They have not come all this way to dine alone."

"I doubt any of them came with the sole purpose of watching Mr Darcy eat, either. Besides, it is hardly singular. Mrs Hurst has eaten dinner in her room three times since she arrived, and the younger Mr Pettigrew misses breakfast every time he overindulges the night before, which is most days." In a gentler tone, he added, "I know you have a particular regard for the master, and nobody could dispute your devotion, but I think you are concerning yourself over nothing."

"Let us hope so. 'Tis bad enough that his servants have begun speaking against him. I should not like to see his own circle doing so."

Mr Matthis set his paper aside. "Which of the servants? You ought to have brought this to me sooner. I shall stamp it out directly."

"I doubt it, unless you have suddenly gained authority over Mr Darcy's steward."

"Mr Ferguson? What has he said against the master?"

"Oh come, sir, you were here when he said it. On Monday. He sat in that chair and complained that Mr Darcy was not paying attention to estate matters. He was most unhappy about it, too, for when have you ever heard Mr Ferguson raise his voice?"

Mr Matthis did not quite roll his eyes, but a dubious expression came over him. "Correct me if I am wrong, Mrs Reynolds, but attending to estate matters is what a landlord pays his *steward* to do. Still, I daresay we should make some allowance for the fact that Mr Ferguson was wet through and late for dinner with his lady wife when he made the complaint." He sipped his tea. "In any case, Mr Darcy *did* attend to the matter."

"He did?"

"Indeed. Not long after the conversation to which you refer, he came looking for Mr Ferguson, and I directed him to Mr Sheldon's cabin. And from what I hear, he did a remarkable job of placating Lord Felixstowe, who was fuming to have been called out in a storm only to be told he was not needed."

"Why was he not needed?"

Mr Matthis leant forward with an elbow on the table, his aversion to gossip always quite forgotten whenever the information pertained to matters outside of the household. "The poacher turned out to be old Peter Mason from Edgeley Farm."

"Whose son died last winter?"

"The very one. He has fallen on hard times since, only Mr Ferguson did not know it was him when he sent for the magistrate. Fortunately, Mr Darcy was able to persuade his lordship not to impose a fine. He let Mason keep the birds he caught, paid for the surgeon to splint his ankle, and sent him home with a warning that if there is a next time, he will see him imprisoned. You see? Mr Darcy is not neglecting Pemberley at all."

Mrs Reynolds took a deep breath. That sounded much more like the generous, sensible young man she knew and esteemed. When she exhaled, she let go as many of her doubts as could be persuaded to release their grip on her conscience.

The conversation buoyed her to such an extent that she agreed to give a brief tour of the house to the couple who called shortly thereafter, despite it being a Saturday, when the house was not usually open to tourists. She named them Wisp and Wasp, which she thought Eleanor would enjoy, for one was balding but for the tufts of fine hair above his ears, and the other had her waist cinched so tightly as to make it seem impossible that her torso could be attached to her legs. With so many guests in the house and the east wing closed, there were few rooms she could show them, but they tipped her extremely generously nevertheless, and she headed back towards the servants' area feeling still more sanguine.

Martha looked up from her stitches when Mrs Reynolds entered the women's workroom. "You missed Mr Lynton. He waited for as long as he could, but he had to go."

Mrs Reynolds's complacency evaporated. "Did he leave a message?"

"Yes. He said the business with which you tasked him in London has been concluded satisfactorily, but that the going price was equal to what you supposed it would be. He said he would come back next week if he did not see you in his workshop first."

"Thank you, Martha. Is everything in order here?"

All the girls nodded.

"Then I shall leave you to your work."

Mrs Reynolds clutched the coin in her hand tightly as she made her way to her sitting room. It would not do to lose the last half crown she had to her name. Her steps were light, though, and she could not keep from smiling. The master's future happiness was secure, and that assurance, she was perfectly satisfied, was priceless.

CHAPTER TWENTY-THREE

FUTILITY & INDECISION

The week following Elizabeth's unexplained disappearance hastened by in a blur. Pemberley's east wing was gradually being reduced to a shell as every treasured heirloom and prized artifact that had been proudly displayed there was boxed and carted away. Floorboards had been lifted, scaffolding erected, and intricate plasterwork hacked off walls as though it would not cost a small fortune to reinstate. Hammering and shouting echoed rudely around the empty space, and dust settled like a second skin on everything that remained.

The rest of the house was alive with the usual bustle and excitement of a country house party, only here, it was carpets that were rolled back to enable dancing, musical performances that rang through the halls, and banquets of exquisite repast that were demolished.

For a week, Darcy existed fully in both worlds. Be it up ladders on scaffold planks, shooting game in the park, peering into holes in the ground, or listening to readings of poetry in the drawing room, life swept him along on its bow wave, demanding his attention on every matter under the sun but the one he most wished to dwell upon. Ferguson wanted to erect a tent and procure an inordinate quantity of beer for the labourers. Connelly and his cousin wanted him to come to dinner and were disinclined to accept no for an answer. Another neighbour, Lord Hutchinson, wanted his vote in the upcoming by-election. Garroway's sister was indisposed, having wandered too close to a gooseberry bush or something equally inexplicable. His sister wanted a new gown.

Darcy could not refrain from thinking, each and every time some new problem arose, how much easier, pleasanter, better it would be to resolve it with Elizabeth at his side.

Not helping to allay his melancholy in any way, was his cousins' shock upon arriving at Pemberley the following Monday and being shown the progress of works. Viscount Linseagh and Colonel Fitzwilliam had come for some shooting, and either Darcy's account must have been wanting or they could not have taken seriously his report of the disruption at Pemberley, for both seemed horrified by what they saw.

"Good grief, Darcy! Your letter said a crack, not a ravine!" exclaimed Colonel Fitzwilliam as they walked towards the men at work.

Darcy shook his head ruefully. They had approached from the back of the house, where the smaller fissures were not visible at a distance. From this angle, the most shocking sight was the raked shoring, jutting out from the wall like spindly buttresses, and the sizeable channel that had been dug along the foot of the wall. He indicated for them to follow him around the corner. There, on the easternmost wall, was the original fault, still as shocking to him as the first day he laid eyes on it.

"*That* is the crack I wrote to you about."

At his side, Linseagh blew out his breath in a muted whistle. "That is a distressing sight and no mistake."

"Have they established, then, that it needs underpinning?" Fitzwilliam asked. "For it looks as though they have already begun."

"That is only to expose the foundations for the architect to assess. Though, it looks more and more likely that it is subsidence."

"On solid limestone?" Linseagh queried sceptically, echoing the doubts of everyone before him.

"Well, it is not the lintels, rafters, or joists. They have all been pulled apart for nothing."

"And the roof?" Fitzwilliam enquired.

Darcy looked at him sharply. "I sincerely hope there is nothing wrong with that."

"What is the scaffolding for, then?"

"To stop the whole lot falling down."

Fitzwilliam gave a dismayed exhalation identical to his brother's. "You ought to have been more explicit in your letter. Father would have come with us if he had known."

"It was not this bad when I wrote. Matters seem to be going downhill with alarming rapidity."

"And the architect is returning on Friday, you say?" Linseagh asked. When Darcy confirmed it, he continued, "Then we shall stay until then and hear what he has to say. I shall send word to Branxcombe for my father to co—"

"Do not trouble him," Darcy interrupted. "Jacobs knows his business, and your father is not well enough to make the journey." He did not add that he, too, knew his business. He wondered sometimes how his cousin would manage when Lord Matlock eventually succumbed to one of his many ailments. Though four years Darcy's senior, Linseagh still tended to defer to his father in most matters. His own father having been dead for above five years, Darcy had learnt to be considerably more self-sufficient. Moreover, his aged and sickly uncle was likely to be more hindrance than help, and he had no need of any more difficulties.

"Does it not present a problem having so many people in the house?" Fitzwilliam asked.

"No indeed. They are taking my mind off things," Darcy replied. His cousins did not need to know it was not the work on the house from which he needed to be distracted.

"Rather you than me. I would find so many loiterers a royal pain in the backside," Fitzwilliam persisted.

"It is easy enough to keep everyone out of this wing. Besides, Georgiana would not thank me for sending her friends away. And Bingley has not found another house to go to yet. Cox's is being renovated. Garroway's sister is confined to her bed. And Aldridge has been waiting all week for you two to arrive. And *I* certainly have nowhere else to be."

He must have allowed too much bitterness to creep into his voice at the last, for it drew a curious look from Fitzwilliam. "We had better go in and dress for dinner, or we shall be late," he said quickly and walked away before his cousin could ask him what he meant.

"What did you mean, when you said earlier that you have nowhere else to be?"

Darcy repressed a sigh. He ought to have known Fitzwilliam would not let it go. "Precisely what I said."

His cousin grunted. "Funny thing to say."

Darcy played his turn at billiards and did not answer. Only his cousins and he were present; everyone else had either gone to bed or was still playing cards in the drawing room. Linseagh was, as always, taking the game far too seriously, and proceeded to score a run of cannons and hazards while Darcy stood by and watched.

Fitzwilliam was sitting out, having lost the previous game to his brother. "I shall tell you another funny thing. Bingley told me at dinner that Miss Elizabeth Bennet was here last week," he said from his seat in the corner.

"Did he," Darcy replied flatly.

"He did. And I was wondering, as I am wont to do, for I am a philosophical sort of fellow, why you did not mention it yourself."

Linseagh struck his cue ball noisily, potting all three balls and scoring the maximum of ten points. He made a small noise of triumph before laying his cue down and turning around to lean against the table with his arms folded. "Somebody is going to have to enlighten me as to who Miss Bennet is, and what is the significance of her being at Pemberley."

The fire crackled and popped as though quieting the room for a speech. The dimness outside of the glare of oil lamps above the table made it hard to see his cousins' expressions, though Darcy could feel both sets of eyes on him. He gripped his cue tightly. There was a time when he had been unwilling to speak of his affection for Elizabeth because he was ashamed of loving her. The only shame he knew these days was for the conceit that had made him think in such preposterous terms. He cared not if the whole world knew what she meant to him now, yet that made it no easier to speak about.

Fitzwilliam began for him, his voice considerably gentler than it had been moments before. "She is a young lady Darcy met last autumn, while he was staying with Bingley in Hertfordshire. She has four sisters, no connexions of which to speak, and no money, but her father is a gentleman—he owns an estate in Hertfordshire. Her cousin is Mr Collins—Lady Catherine's parson." He hesitated between each new fact, as though waiting for an instruction to stop, but Darcy said nothing. "She was visiting Mr Collins and his wife when Darcy and I were at Rosings at Easter. We both spent quite some time with her. She is an exceedingly lovely young lady, but Darcy holds her in *particularly* high regard."

There was a longer pause, then he said abruptly, "Darcy, I am going to finish this tale if you do not say something."

"Finish it. I have no stomach to tell it myself." Darcy tossed his cue down next to Linseagh's and stalked to lean against the mantelpiece with his back to the room.

"Very well," Fitzwilliam acceded, somewhat warily. "Our cousin made Miss Bennet an offer, but it transpired she did not return his regard. In short, she said no."

"Ouch," Linseagh said quietly, neatly summing up the entire *débâcle.*

"Indeed," his brother replied. "I understand there were recriminations on both sides. In fact, they parted ways in a manner which, at the time, seemed as though it would preclude all future contact."

"Then how came she to be at Pemberley?"

More silence.

"I cannot tell this part, Darcy!" Fitzwilliam said with exasperation. "In case it escaped your notice, I only arrived today. I do not know what happened last week."

"Neither do I!" he snapped, turning around to glare at his cousin. "She was here, she was perfect, and then she was gone. Would that somebody could explain it to me, for I sure as the [redacted] do not know what went wrong."

He knew that would not satisfy them, thus he stationed himself in the nearest chair and yielded grudgingly to a stream of questions as they wheedled out of him all his dealings with Elizabeth the previous week. He disliked the discomfort of so personal a disclosure but held on to the hope that his cousins might perceive some motive or justification he had overlooked himself. Regrettably, they were both singularly unforthcoming in that regard.

"Most odd," Linseagh said.

Fitzwilliam agreed. "It is, considering that Miss Bennet is not exactly backwards in coming forwards. If something had upset her, she would have told you, I think, would she not Darcy?"

Darcy could not help but chuckle slightly at that. "Probably."

"But not to leave word—even for Georgiana? That seems unkind."

"If she was offended by something I did, I would not expect her to give greater consideration to my sister's sensibilities than her own." Except Darcy could not help but think that she would.

"And you are absolutely set on her?" Linseagh asked, immediately holding up a hand to convey his sincerity. "I ask with no ulterior meaning. Only to confirm that you do want to find out what has happened. Because you could walk away from this now without a spot on you."

"I have walked away twice already. I keep coming back to it, one way or another." He twisted impatiently in his seat. "Linseagh, *my* wishes are not in question."

"Quite right. Though I hardly know how you ought to proceed when you do not know what hers are."

Darcy closed his eyes and wished he had gone to bed when the others did.

"You could write to Mr Gardiner," Fitzwilliam suggested.

"Do not be ridiculous," Linseagh interjected. "You would have the grandson of an earl write to a tradesman, begging to know whether his niece holds a candle for him?"

Darcy could not deny the prospect was unappealing, though he might have done it anyway had he no other reservations preventing him. "Mr Gardiner has not written to me, either, which I can only presume is because he—or his niece —would prefer to drop the acquaintance."

"*Would* he write?" Linseagh queried. "He sounds clever enough. I doubt he would presume to take the liberty."

"Or, more likely, he is ignorant of his niece's interest in the matter," Fitzwilliam opined. "Could not you ask Georgiana to write to Miss Bennet?"

"That would be unfair, if it turns out Miss Bennet did leave to get away from him," Linseagh argued. "What a disappointment it would be for our poor cousin to write to a lady she thought might become her sister, only to have her olive branch spurned."

"Or for the lady who left to get away from me to be hounded by all my relations," Darcy added quietly.

"Well then," said Fitzwilliam, decisively. "You must go to Hertfordshire and speak to Miss Bennet in person."

Darcy discarded his glass on the nearest table and rubbed his face with his hands. "I cannot go to Hertfordshire. Not yet, in any case. Miss Bennet continued north when she left Lambton. I have no way of knowing when she will return to Longbourn, and with things as they are at Pemberley, I cannot spare the time to sit about in Meryton awaiting her return."

"But she cannot travel forever—and you said yourself Gardiner has warehouses that require him to be present. So, go in a few weeks."

Linseagh gave a murmur of ambivalence. "I do not know. What if Miss Bennet really does not want anything to do with him?"

"Then I ought not to mortify her by chasing after her," Darcy replied.

"Well, what do you propose to do, then?" Fitzwilliam cried.

Darcy gave a bitter bark of laughter, retrieved his glass,

drained it, and put it back down. "I have no idea, and you two have been no help whatsoever."

Jacobs arrived at the end of the week as planned and delivered the verdict that by now was a surprise to no one: Pemberley's east wing was subsiding and must be underpinned in its entirety to prevent a catastrophic collapse. Furthermore, the architect recommended that the exploratory trench be extended to determine whether whatever was causing the problem posed a threat to the rest of the building.

For Darcy, the worst thing about this news was not the cost, nor the way Fitzwilliam looked at him, as though concerned that he, too, might begin to crack under the strain of such devastating news. It was that this event, more than any other, made him feel Elizabeth's absence most keenly. He fancied he could weather any difficulty, bear any bad tidings, if she were by his side. He craved her companionship more than anyone else's he had ever met—more so after those few, sublime days when she had seemed equally pleased with his society. Being without her was unbearable. Yet he knew not how, or whether, he would ever win her back.

CHAPTER TWENTY-FOUR

FOUNDED ON MISTAKEN PREMISES

Very rarely did something happen that Mrs Reynolds had not witnessed before in some iteration or other in her sixty years. This was perhaps why, despite her dearest wish to believe she had acted in the master's best interests, her misgivings lingered. Had Mr Darcy's behaviour resembled, in any way, what it had always been before; had his conduct mirrored that of other men, even, Mrs Reynolds might have been easy. Yet his strange sort of melancholy was unfathomable to her. Her initial apprehension that he was neglecting his responsibilities had altered to a concern that he was instead applying himself with uncommon—and unnecessary—industry. Her worry that his slight disappointment was persisting overlong had been replaced by the certainty that he was profoundly unhappy.

Several days earlier the news had arrived that the cause of subsidence had been determined. The incident of Mr Mason slipping on a 'torrent' on the north slope the night he was caught poaching had prompted the groundsman to investigate the area. A hitherto unidentified natural culvert had been found—and moreover, revealed to be blocked. Nobody knew how long it had been directing rainwater down towards the house rather than away to the vale beyond, but the resulting movement in the substrate suggested it must have been many years. Nevertheless, it had been discovered and could therefore be remedied, preventing further damage to the house.

This wondrous news—received to much fanfare and celebration amongst the rest of the household—had not lifted Mr Darcy's spirits by even the slightest margin, and Mrs Reynolds was no longer able to pretend that the problems at Pemberley were the cause of his suffering.

She tried to convince herself that, regrettable though his evident heartache might be, it was preferable to the lifetime of misery to which he would have been condemned had she not intervened to prevent him being Miss Bennet's dupe. Yet her doubts had received an unlikely exponent the previous day: a letter from Eleanor, containing the most distressing news—both in its very nature and in its unnerving familiarity.

With what violent indignation do I write to you this day! It is my turn to beg of you some wise counsel, and a large measure, if you will, of that practical advice which is your particular forte. Dot, my precious, undeserving goddaughter, has been dealt the most unjust and injurious of blows. Her youngest sister has eloped! Or attempted to, at any rate. It is no surprise that she fudged the undertaking since the thoughtless, empty-headed peabrain has disappointed in every conceivable way since arriving on this Earth.

About three weeks ago, in the middle of the night, the fool girl appears to have fallen into an Ann Radcliffe novel and stolen away with the most useless man to hand at the time. She left a letter of no little triumph for her friend, openly stating her intention to travel to Scotland, which has placed the secrecy of the whole affair in the hands of a bored army wife—not ideal, I am sure you agree. The rapture with which the note was written did not outlast the second change of horses, however, for the pair made it only as far as London before apparently forgetting their purpose entirely.

In town they languished for over half a month; God knows how or where they lived, but we all know what they were doing. Their memories, it seems, were rudely jogged when they ran out of funds. Only at that juncture did it occur to the halfwits that they might be better off if they were, in fact, married—but rather than trouble themselves to complete their flight to Scotland, where the affair might have been concluded both simply and legally, they instead took it upon themselves to pull the wool over the eyes of the Lord and the law, and claim an authority they did not have—to wed in England. It is now a matter of official record that they married <u>*with*</u> *her father's permission—a fact that cannot be refuted without drawing attention to the disparity between the date of the nuptials and the date which all her friends know her to have run away.*

You are wondering, I suppose, why I am not pleased that the marriage did at least take place. I might have been, had the bottlehead thrown her lot in with a man worth having. Alas, she abandoned all her friends and family in favour of a penniless soldier. Indeed, not even a soldier, for he has resigned his commission. I cannot see that there is any point to him at all now. The daft peacock has no title, no profession, no money—and according to Dot, no scruples whatsoever. One must suppose he is pretty, else there can be no reason but lunacy for the sister to have behaved in such a way.

In my humblest opinion, they deserve each other and whatever comes their way. But Dot has more compassion than I, and she cares deeply what will happen to her sister. Her father has agreed to give what little subsistence he can, but it will not be enough to keep two such ignorami in clothes and out of trouble. A more resourceful woman would find herself work, but Peabrain scarcely has the wherewithal to fasten her own boots, so we may discount any such recourse. Dot despairs of her running a prudent household, for she has not the slightest education in housekeeping. I have not the heart to point out that, if Peacock is as cruel as all that, then Peabrain's woes will not end with an empty larder

As to the rest of the family, their respectability hangs tenuously in the balance. The disgrace of a ruined sister appears, for now, to have been averted, although their neighbours are already whispering, and they are all living on tenterhooks for not knowing whether the original elopement or the fraudulent marriage vows will be discovered. The grief of a sister abandoned by her husband seems all too likely a prospect to me. Dot writes that her father has been made ill by it all. She fears for his heart. I fear for <u>*hers*</u>*, for in her letter, in the words she used, it sounded broken. Write to me quickly, Agnes. Tell me what I can do to help her. In truth, I know there is nothing to be done, but I ask all the same, for I am powerless to do anything but grasp at straws.*

Yours Affectionately,
E. Wallis

At first, Mrs Reynolds had been too stupefied to know what to think. The similarities between Eleanor's tale and her own recent dealings were striking, yet it was impossible. Of all the people in all the world, it was inconceivable that the two sets of individuals should be the same. Nevertheless, dread had arisen in her throat as she considered what it would mean if it transpired that Eleanor's goddaughter and Miss Bennet were one and the same.

As the seconds had ticked by, and her heart slowed to a less panicky rhythm, reason had re-established itself. Eleanor's goddaughter was in the Lakes this summer—Eleanor had written of it explicitly, for she was eaten up with jealousy not to be going with her. Miss Bennet had been here, in the Peaks. One's given name was Dorothy and the other's Elizabeth. They were different people, and there was no feasible way they could be mistaken for each other. One was kind, rational, witty, and clever. The other was a cold-hearted, conniving fortune hunter, whom Eleanor herself had advised should be kept away from Mr Darcy. It could only be coincidence. Evidently there were more men like George Wickham in the world than anybody needed.

The letter had been refolded and set aside to be answered when she had more time—and time was not something she would have any more of this day. The guests were departing on the morrow, and a 'last hurrah' feast had been planned to see them off in style. She wished that, in between all the errands she must complete in preparation for it, the image of Miss Bennet, sobbing in the rain, would not keep darting into her head.

CHAPTER TWENTY-FIVE

DOROTHY

After checking the dining room fire had been correctly laid and patching up a kitchen maid with a cut hand, Mrs Reynolds set about allocating Pemberley servants to attend those guests whose own maids would be travelling ahead that evening. As she looked about for the correct face in the busy hall, it was the memory of Miss Bennet's visage that accosted her, yet again, and she could not help but reflect on how unexpectedly genuine the young woman's distress had seemed that day in the rain.

"Miss Cotton, will you have time to see to the two Miss Templetons as well as Miss Darcy tonight and tomorrow morning?"

Miss Darcy's lady's maid assured her the extra work would present no problem, then returned to talking to the footmen sat either side of her. "The young miss is ever so sad to see everyone go—and not just for her own sake. She is worried there will be no one but her left to keep her brother's spirits up. It is a shame the colonel cannot stay on."

William, without looking up from his polishing, shook

his head. "I do not see why the master should need his spirits lifting. Not now the house is saved."

"It is not saved yet," Mrs Reynolds said. "It still needs work, and that will be costly and disruptive."

"Yes, but even so—you'd think he'd be happy."

"I do not think that is what is making him *un*happy," Miss Cotton said.

"What is then?" James wished to know, but Mr Darcy's manservant cleared his throat and looked pointedly at Miss Cotton until she closed her mouth and turned her attention to her needlework.

The uncertainty in Mrs Reynolds's breast was not so easily silenced, and before she knew she was going to say it, she blurted, "Please do not tell me it is the departure of that awful young woman!"

"Miss Bingley?" asked Miss Cotton.

"No! Miss Bennet."

Miss Cotton's amused smile vanished instantly. "Miss Bennet? But she was lovely. And Mr Dar—"

Mr Vaughan abruptly stood up. "Miss Cotton, we had better leave now if we are to be ready for the master and his sister."

Mrs Reynolds watched them go. There were times she envied Mr Vaughan's access to the master. It was far easier to look after someone when you were privy to all their secrets. She had done the best she could by Mr Darcy, but it was difficult, acting blindly. She could only pray that she had not erred in her methods.

"Miss Bennet seemed like a most agreeable young lady to me," said Mr Matthis.

Mrs Reynolds looked at him in consternation. "Was it not you who complained of having to serve her at dinner?"

"I disliked that we were entertaining a tradesman at the same table as a baron, but Mr Gardiner conducted himself perfectly well in the end. He was certainly no bad reflection on his niece, who was very popular with the master's other guests."

"Have you forgotten that it was one of those very guests who was obliged to warn you of Miss Bennet's snooping about in the library later that evening?"

He raised an eyebrow. "Who told you that?"

"Edna. And she heard it directly from William."

The butler glanced darkly at William, who shrank slightly in his chair. "I only said what I saw, Mr Matthis."

Mrs Reynolds was dismayed. When had she begun to pay heed to idle reports?

Mr Matthis was evidently just as displeased, for his lips were pursed and his colour heightened. "Miss Bingley took Miss Bennet into the library quite deliberately. She did not see me, for I was in the north stairwell, but I saw them go past and heard Miss Bennet say she thought it a poor idea. I was on an errand for Lord Garroway, but once I had seen to that, I went back to ask the ladies to leave—but Miss Bingley found me first. What William witnessed was her feigning alarm that Miss Bennet had wandered into the library unaccompanied."

He paused and regarded her as though attempting to determine whether he was yet believed. "I do not know where she then went, but she only returned to the drawing room after I had escorted Miss Bennet back there, whereupon she claimed to have been looking all the while for her lost companion."

"I see." Mrs Reynolds felt her cheeks flaming.

Maintaining a severe expression, Mr Matthis stood and left, calling for James and William to go with him. William dawdled behind to say guiltily, "I am sorry, Mrs Reynolds. I hope I've not caused you any bother."

"It is my own fault for listening to gossip."

"I weren't gossiping. I wouldn't have the nerve to make up a story as unlikely as the truth, anyhow. Goes to show, even rich people get jealous, and they can be just as daft as the rest of us with it."

"I sincerely doubt that Miss Bingley was motivated by jealousy. She had absolutely no reason to be envious of Miss Bennet."

"You did not see them together. Mr Darcy and Miss Bennet, I mean. Always talking and laughing with each other, they were. And you should have seen how the master defended Miss Bennet this one time, in the morning room. Miss Bingley can only dream of the master liking her that well."

Mrs Reynolds bristled. "Miss Bennet certainly did not like him so well when she first came to the house."

She clamped her mouth closed when Mr Bingley's manservant entered the hall. He walked slowly to the table and sat down, glancing between Mrs Reynolds and William in a way that made clear he was aware of his interruption. "William, is it? I think Mr Matthis is looking for you." He waited for the footman to scamper away, then turned to Mrs Reynolds and said carefully, "Mr Darcy has not always been kind to Miss Bennet, you know." He held up a hand to stay her angry retort. "Even Mr Bingley was exasperated by the way he behaved towards her in Hertfordshire."

"And pray, what way was that?" she demanded indignantly.

"He argued with her—often. Other times he would simply ignore her. He refused to dance with her the first time they met. Said openly that she was not handsome enough for him. That really did embarrass Mr Bingley. Especially as he was attempting to woo the older sister."

"Miss Bingley's maid said it was the Miss Bennets who were doing the chasing. She said they were fortune hunters."

He looked at her disbelievingly. "Yes, well, irony is as lost on Miss Bingley's maid as on the lady herself."

Mrs Reynolds felt as stupid as he must think her. It was well-known that Miss Bingley had been hankering after the master—and his house—for years. Why in heaven's name had she paid attention to the whisperings of either woman?

Mr Bingley's manservant began to unfold his newspaper. "I do not mean to speak ill of your master. I only think it unfair that Miss Bennet should be blamed when it was Mr Darcy who was the antagonist."

"Well, she seemed to have grown on him by the time they met in Kent," came a booming voice from the doorway. Sergeant Jeffers, the colonel's batman, stalked into the hall with his customary halo of pipe smoke wreathed about his head. Mrs Reynolds watched him snatch the newspaper away from Bingley's man and take it with him to sit in an opposing chair. "Shame he got to her first, because I think the colonel might have been tempted to offer for her if his cousin had not."

Offer for her! "Are you suggesting that Mr Darcy proposed to Miss Bennet in Kent?"

The sergeant affected a look of feigned innocence and did an approximation of standing to attention without rising from his chair. "I am not saying anything, Mrs Reynolds. I know how you Pemberley folk despise gossip." She must have made a face of her own because he capitulated straight away. "Very well, yes, he did."

Mrs Reynolds stared at him. "You must be mistaken, sir. I would know if Mr Darcy were engaged."

"I did not say he was engaged." He drew deeply on his pipe and smoke billowed from his mouth as he added, "Miss Bennet was not inclined to accept his offer, apparently."

"But he is the master of Pemberley!"

"That did not seem to matter to her."

Mrs Reynolds gripped the back of a chair and squeezed her eyes shut against the clamour of her doubts. 'There are very few people with integrity enough to turn their noses up at all this'—so she had overheard Mrs Gardiner say. She had taken it to be an acknowledgement of how tempting Pemberley's luxuries were, and Miss Bennet's intention to acquire them by nefarious means. Had she, instead, meant to credit her niece for refusing that temptation, for refusing the chance to be mistress of Pemberley, for want of the proper feeling for Mr Darcy? In which case Mrs Gardiner was right: people with that much integrity were uncommon indeed. She knew barely any. One of those few was Eleanor's goddaughter.

"They would have been well suited," Sergeant Jeffers said.

"Miss Bennet and Colonel Fitzwilliam?" Mr Bingley's man replied.

"No, she and Mr Darcy."

"You might be right. She seemed to have come around to him on this visit. But then, he went to extraordinary lengths to give a better account of himself this time. Morning calls, dinners, picnics—quite the gallant."

"Is that so? Ha! The colonel will like to hear that."

"Do not tell him you heard it from me."

"He will know it came from you. All the best gossip usually does. I say, are you perfectly well, Mrs Reynolds? You look as though you are going to fall over."

She did not answer. She only made a vague, dismissive gesture with her hand and left. Horrible, gnawing certainty eroded her composure further with every step. By the time she reached her sitting room and locked the door behind her, she was shaking from head to toe.

Neither she nor Eleanor had children, but they had each been blessed with a younger soul to cherish. She had Mr Darcy; her friend had her goddaughter. Through their constant correspondence over the years, they had shared all their news, hopes, and pride for both, until each was as fond of the other's charge as they were of their own. It was not unsurprising, therefore, that a tacit wish should have arisen for Dorothy and Mr Darcy to one day meet. Eleanor had often remarked that Mr Darcy would make an excellent husband for Dorothy, and little in the world would have given Mrs Reynolds more pleasure than for Mr Darcy to meet a lady with as fine a character as Dorothy's. The prospect that they had met, that they had loved each other, and that she had torn them apart, was too dreadful to contemplate.

At the back of Mrs Reynolds's cabinet were several bundles of Eleanor's letters. Not every communication warranted keeping, only the most diverting or meaningful, but there were still plenty. She took them out and began running her eye over the pages for references to Dorothy. Mentions of her abounded—as did allusions to her home, which Eleanor referred to as 'Bedlam,' and her mother, whom Eleanor had never called anything other than 'the Termagant'. For the first time in their longstanding acquaintance, Mrs Reynolds rued her friend's delight in giving everyone and everything she encountered a ridiculous name. She could find no hint, anywhere, of Dorothy's surname, nor where she lived, nor any salient information at all.

What she did uncover, was the letter Eleanor had sent in April, bemoaning the detestable man—dubbed 'Starch'—who had proposed to Dorothy in the most contemptible, hurtful manner imaginable. Mrs Reynolds recalled very clearly the reply she penned at the time, decrying the blackguard's conduct, and begging Eleanor to keep her goddaughter safe from all such heartless men. It had not been dissimilar to Eleanor's recent advice to keep Mr Darcy safe from Miss Bennet. She set all the letters aside and pulled out a fresh sheet of paper.

There were a thousand incongruities—unexplained acquaintances, mismatched locations, ambiguous remarks—but Mrs Reynolds asked just one question of her friend: Who is Dorothy? She did not explain why she wished to know. She could not bring herself to admit it, but she knew. In her heart of hearts, Mrs Reynolds knew that she had ruined, perhaps forever, that which she had devoted almost half her life to preserving: Mr Darcy's happiness. Dorothy's, too—and possibly Eleanor's. Potentially that of all Dorothy's relations as well. And Miss Darcy's. Probably even George Wickham's. She sealed the letter and shuffled painfully to put it out for posting.

The grand dinner passed in a blur. Mrs Reynolds had never felt so old or so ill, and she retreated to her bed as soon as proceedings permitted—though, not to sleep. She did not think she would ever be able to sleep at night again.

CHAPTER TWENTY-SIX

A RARE AFFECTION

"Lydia, you do not seem to understand what we are telling you. One-hundred pounds a year between two people is barely enough to get by. One or both of you will have to find work."

"I do not see why. Plenty of people live on a lot less."

"Not people who need to employ a cook because they have never learnt to make their own supper. Or people who wish to travel twenty-four miles to show off their wedding rings. Do you even know how much your fare from London cost?"

Lydia shrugged. "Two shillings?"

Mary closed her eyes and shook her head, but Elizabeth persevered. "One pound and sixteen shillings." Seeing her sister was unmoved, she pressed, "That would be doubled for a return journey. If you visited Longbourn three times a year, that would be over a tenth of your annual income spent on travel." She realised her mistake when her sister's eyes grew vacant. She changed tack. "You will not be able to afford to make long journeys."

"Then I shall make only short ones."

"And you will not have the use of a carriage whenever you want it, as you are used to."

"Then I shall ride."

"You will not have enough money to keep a horse."

"That is well by me. I do not like horses anyway. They smell."

"In which case, you will have to walk a lot more than you do now."

"What of it? *You* walk everywhere, and I do not hear you complaining about it."

Elizabeth took a deep breath, wishing profoundly that her aunt Gardiner were still at Longbourn to help make Lydia understand. "Do you know how much a new pair of walking boots costs?"

"Yes, I do! Two pounds. I saw a pair in Meryton yesterday." At the mention of shopping, her sister forgot to be defensive, and a softer look overcame her countenance. "They had little bows on the top edge, and red laces, and—"

"Two pounds would be a whole week's allowance!" Elizabeth interrupted. "Would you go without food that week to pay for them?"

Lydia flounced in her seat. "Why are you being such a bore?"

"We are trying to prepare you for what your life will be like now," Jane said, her tone softer than Elizabeth's. "You are going to have to learn to live more frugally. We only wish to make sure you understand what it takes to make ends meet."

It was a mission the three eldest Bennet sisters had taken upon themselves when it became clear that their mother would not. Mrs Bennet had spent the last two decades fervently applying herself to the task of seeing all her daughters wed and wasted not a whit of attention on what would come afterwards. Now that the deed was done—Lydia having returned home of her own volition the previous Tuesday afternoon, quite unaided by either her father or her uncle, and with her new husband in tow—the problem was more immediately before them.

As well as persuading her father against annulling the marriage for fear of the ensuing scandal, Elizabeth had also convinced him not to throw Mr and Mrs Wickham out directly, that she and her sisters might have more time to instil in Lydia some sense of parsimony, some understanding of wifely responsibilities, or at the very least, to teach her how to boil an egg before she left for her new life. Alas, Lydia wore her ignorance like a suit of armour, and not even the stoutest good sense could penetrate it.

"This cottage in which you say you will live—will you tell us about that?"

"It is in Clerkenwell—"

"An awful place."

"How would you know, Mary?" Lydia retorted. "You have never been farther than Longbourn churchyard, so you can shut your bone box."

"Lydia!" Elizabeth admonished.

When Jane gently suggested that it would be more helpful to encourage Lydia than chastise her, Mary lost all patience and quit the parlour.

"Clerkenwell is not so very bad," Lydia said with a pout. "There are clockmakers and a print shop. And you cannot even *see* the prisons from our street."

Elizabeth closed her eyes. She almost wished Lydia could remain this innocent forever, but reality would obtrude upon her notice soon enough. "Do you know when the rent is due?"

"Oh, not for two years. We have ages before we must pay that."

"Two years? Why has Mr Wickham paid for two years of rent when you did not have coin enough in your pockets to pay for the chaise from London?"

"It was stipulated in the lease agreement, Sister." They all looked up to see Wickham saunter into the parlour. "Decent lodgings are not ten a penny. When they become available, it is prudent to secure them by whatever means are necessary."

Jane assured him they understood. "Is it a comfortable cottage, then?" she asked Lydia.

"It will do. The landlady lives next door and is very friendly. She said if we ever have any difficulty, we are to ask her. Indeed, you were with her for over an hour the other day, were you not, Wickham? Something to do with the roof, was it? Or the chimney? I cannot recall. Anyway, she is exceedingly obliging. If ever I cannot find Wickham, I always know he will be next door with Mrs Younge."

Elizabeth froze. She glanced at Wickham; he was smiling, and if she had not been looking for it, she doubted she would have noticed how fixed his expression had become, or how wary his eyes. Fury, pity, nausea all pinned Elizabeth to her seat. Mrs Younge, the same woman who aided Wickham's failed attempt to seduce Miss Darcy, was now Lydia's closest neighbour and, from the sounds of it, her husband's lover. Wickham abruptly looked her way, and his slight frown made it clear he had perceived her alarm, and suddenly there was a good deal more agitation in the air.

"That is good," Jane said, oblivious to it. "It will be easier starting out if you have friends around you."

Elizabeth really thought she might be ill. "I wonder whether Mary is right, Lydia. Perhaps you ought to find more suitable lodgings."

Lydia rolled her eyes. "We have told you, we cannot. We have paid two years' rent."

"If lodgings are in such short supply, I am sure Mrs

Younge will find another tenant easily. She seems fairly undiscerning."

A glance at Wickham revealed his usual, self-satisfied smirk to have distorted into something a lot more like a snarl.

"Where should we live then, Lizzy?" Lydia enquired.

"You would do better the farther away from London you go. Perhaps the Outer Hebrides."

"There is not much work to be found there," Wickham said.

"You *do* intend to find work, then?"

He cocked his head. "Or Lydia may."

Lydia thought this a fine joke and snorted her appreciation of it. Then she stopped laughing and sprang to her feet. "Look! Pen and her mother are coming along the drive. They must have heard my news." She squealed with delight and rang the bell, declaring that they would have tea and cake to make it more of a celebration.

Elizabeth stole quietly out of the parlour. She would apologise to Jane later for abandoning her, but she could not partake in another spectacle such as those that had been occurring all week. Every day, at least one of the neighbouring families would call. Lydia would strut about, brandishing her ring and gloating of her good fortune. Her mother invariably joined in. Their visitors would nod, smile, and feign interest, all the while casting amused glances at each other and smirking behind their hands. Their whole family was the object of ridicule—an only marginally better fate than being shunned altogether from society.

She changed her shoes and exited the house via the kitchen. As she walked around the corner of the house, she saw Wickham coming towards her on the path. She turned and walked away across the lawn, but he caught up with her in two strides.

"There is little point in being vexed with me, Lizzy. We are brother and sister now, and there is nothing you can do about it. You or Mr Darcy."

She inhaled deeply, comprehending why he had sought her out. He wished to know how much danger he was in from that quarter. While it was true that Darcy neither could nor likely would wish to intervene, Wickham did not deserve the relief of having it confirmed. "Why did you marry her?" she asked. "You clearly do not love her."

"What a quaint notion, that one should marry for love."

"Do you love Mrs Younge, then?"

He laughed unpleasantly. "I have a very great affection for Mrs Younge's talents and connexions. It would not do to lose her good will."

Elizabeth fought to conceal her revulsion. She recalled with abhorrence her attempt to defend this man's character to Darcy—and at such a moment, as he laid bare his most intimate feelings. How he had found the heart to forgive her for it, she would never know.

"I have shocked you," Wickham said. "I confess, I thought you rather more practical. When I directed my attentions towards Miss King earlier this year, you declared it a wise and desirable measure for both."

"I assumed you felt *some* affection for her. I know better now. I know you felt none for Miss Darcy, either. You certainly cannot feel any for Lydia, since you have set her up next door to your mistress. And what of *her*? I have no reason to think well of Mrs Younge, but neither can I approve of your refusing to marry her whilst taking full advantage of her 'talents'. Do you feel no shame in treating people so coldly?"

"Why should I? Will Darcy feel shame for marrying a rich heiress?"

"Who says he will?" she replied, struggling to repress a surge of feeling.

"How else will he replenish the Pemberley coffers when his precious sister does, eventually, marry? You are aware, I take it, that her fortune is thirty thousand pounds? Darcy must pay that from the estate. It is a vast amount to find, but find it he must, and since he will never condescend to selling off land, you can be assured he will marry a lady whose fortune matches his sister's. You see, he is really no better than I am."

Elizabeth stopped walking and glared at him. "You have said many things with which I disagree, sir, but none that I have objected to as much as *that*."

"Oh yes, I forgot that your opinion of him had improved. I would advise you not to like him too well. You are not rich enough for him."

"I was not rich enough for *you* a few months ago, and I am no richer than Lydia, so I ask again, sir, why did you marry her?"

"Would you believe me if I said I liked her better than you?"

"Yes, quite easily, but it does not answer my question."

"I think it does."

It did not—it made no sense at all! "How will you provide for her—for your children, when they come along?"

He smirked grotesquely. "Perhaps I shall join in your mother's prayers for the rest of her daughters to marry well."

Elizabeth strove to emulate Darcy's calm demeanour, though every part of her wished to rail at her new brother. "Regrettably, your actions have made that considerably less likely."

She walked away. Her legs itched with the urge to run, and she was beyond relieved when it became clear Wickham meant to let her go. He watched her, though, and she directed her steps towards the hermitage at the other side of the garden, desperate to be out of sight before her equanimity shattered.

Darcy would not come for her now. The more she saw of Wickham's true character, the more certain she was that no sane person would voluntarily allow such a man into a sister's life, even as a brother. It was why she had refused her aunt's offer, made again the day she departed for London, for her uncle to write to him. Elizabeth could scarcely tolerate her new relationship to Wickham; the thought of what Darcy's feelings on the matter would be left her cold. She would much rather he remembered her as she was in Derbyshire.

This was not a new source of sorrow, however; Elizabeth had understood that all hope was in vain the moment Lydia stepped down from her carriage, wafting her wedding ring under their noses. But Wickham's mentions of Miss Darcy's fortune had compounded this grief with yet another cause of regret. How ignorant, how childish she had been to blame Darcy's reservations about marrying her on pride alone. He certainly had been proud, there was no denying that—but in offering for her, he had overcome far greater concerns than a trifling dislike of what society might say. He had effectively forfeited his sister's fortune.

Elizabeth had been to Pemberley; she had seen how many people relied on Darcy for their livelihoods and homes. She had discovered what the house itself meant to him, and how conscientiously he cared for it. For the first time, she properly understood the responsibility he bore to marry well, for the sake of the estate and all its hundreds of dependents. That obligation was even greater at present, for he must pay for the repairs to the house as well.

In disregarding that onerous duty, in choosing her, he must have decided that she was more important to him than any of it. Remorse wrung her heart, for nobody was fortunate enough to be loved in such a way twice in one lifetime. She would never feel such devotion again, and it was a bitter truth to swallow.

She sat alone with her regret until she could be sure the visitors would be gone, then returned to the house, only to find everything had worsened. Jane had sent for the apothecary to attend their father, whose condition had deteriorated upon reading a letter recently arrived from their cousin in Kent. Mr Collins, it seemed, had heard from his wife, who had heard from her family, that Lydia was now Mrs Wickham, and he had written with barely concealed contempt for her choice of husband and her method of ensnaring him. Elizabeth dared not suppose what Mr Collins had discovered of Lydia's 'methods', but if news of her dalliance with ruin had reached Kent, then all hope of containing it was lost.

Mr Bennet's declining health and the exhaustion of her own forbearance induced Elizabeth to press for Mr and Mrs Wickham's expeditious departure. They left Longbourn the next morning, and it felt to her that they stole all her dreams with them.

CHAPTER TWENTY-SEVEN

AN UNEXPECTED TRAITOR

With the east wing off limits for the foreseeable future, Darcy had taken over the Argyll room, at the opposite end of the house, as his permanent study. It was a poky space by Pemberley's standards, made even less welcoming by the pyramids of upended furniture and crates presently lining the walls.

For an hour, he had been picking his way through the unremitting stream of trivia and trouble that was strewn across his desk. None of it ought to have taken this long to review, yet of late, he struggled to apply himself to anything, too occupied with the effort of ignoring the hollowness eroding him from within.

He snatched up another letter. This one was from Jacobs, expressing his professional reservations that even a decade's worth of rainwater run-off could account for the severity of the damage sustained on the east wall. 'Redirect the culvert, by all means,' was his position, 'but do not rely on it resolving the underlying issue.' Would that Jacobs had applied himself as assiduously to identifying 'the underlying issue' as he had to decrying every solution Darcy's own men had thus far proposed!

He closed his eyes and sucked in a deep breath. 'Manifestly more than stones and mortar'—so Elizabeth had said, and so he kept repeating to himself. Alas, such comfort as it gave was always countered by the misery induced by all reminders of her. God knew Pemberley would be manifestly more if she were here, making it a proper home.

Someone knocked on the door, and he called an instruction for them to return later, then ran a hand over his face and forced himself to pick up Jacobs's letter to read again, for it required an answer. He had forgotten the first knock entirely by the time the second came.

"Not now!" he repeated, this time allowing his displeasure to bleed into his voice. To his consternation, the door opened anyway. He prepared to deliver an angry remonstrance but bit it back when his housekeeper edged nervously into the room. "Mrs Reynolds. I can only assume you did not hear me when I said I was not to be disturbed."

"I did hear you, sir, forgive me, but I must speak to you. About something of the utmost importance."

Darcy could not recall ever having cause to be angry with his housekeeper, and the sensation was not in the least agreeable. "Whatever your concern, Mr Ferguson is quite capable of dealing with it. There is nothing I can assist you with that he cannot."

"I am afraid that is not so," she said in a quavering tone. "This has to do with Miss Elizabeth Bennet."

"What?" The word tore from his lips before she finished speaking. He regretted his discourtesy when Mrs Reynolds appeared to shrink from him. Her shoulders folded inwards, and her countenance crumpled as though she might weep, which was most unlike her. "You had better come in," he said more collectedly.

His alarm increased when she shuffled into the room as though the weight of the world were bearing down upon her. He waited with simmering impatience for her to come to a halt in front of his desk, but once there, she did not say a word. She only fidgeted with her chatelaine and took the occasional deep, shaky breath. It was as though someone had kidnapped his assured, competent housekeeper and replaced her with an awkward, inexperienced housemaid.

"Madam?"

"I beg your pardon, sir. It is difficult to know where to begin."

"Well, I should be grateful if you would begin somewhere."

She nodded and raised her head to look him in the eye. "I have made a terrible mistake."

It took all Darcy's restraint to wait in silence for her to gather enough courage to continue.

"When Miss Bennet first came to Pemberley, several things happened that made it appear she was not a friend to you."

"And since when has it been your place to have an opinion on such matters?"

She ducked her head. "Never. I beg you would forgive my presumption, only it seemed very much as though Miss Bennet did not care for you beyond—that is, I had very serious cause to believe she was attempting to—that she would make you exceedingly unhappy. I know now that I was wrong, but I only wished to do the best by you, sir."

"What have you done?"

She visibly swallowed. "I did not pass on her message to you."

"What message?"

"That—that she was sorry to be leaving so suddenly. And that she—she hoped to see you again soon."

It was becoming increasingly difficult for Darcy to remain calm. Fury, elation, despair, disbelief—they had all been whipped up at once, and he knew not which to respond to first. "When did she give you this message?" he said when he could be sure of his own voice.

"On the afternoon of the picnic."

"And when did you have the opportunity of seeing her that afternoon?"

"She came to Pemberley, while you were with the magistrate."

He launched himself to his feet. "Miss Bennet came here, and you did not see fit to tell me?" Darcy could scarcely believe what he was hearing. Mrs Reynolds, whom he had known since he was four years old, who was gentle and kind, and who never allowed anything to go awry at Pemberley, had sabotaged everything. He all but snarled a demand for her to tell him every word that was said and grew more enraged with each revelation.

"She asked to speak to you or Miss Darcy. I-I told her the family were not receiving visitors. She asked me to give you the message I have just relayed. Then she gave me a-a note for Miss Darcy, which said the same thing."

"You *read* it?"

"I did, sir, heaven preserve me, I did. Then she—she returned your coat—"

Darcy spun away from her and gripped his jaw to prevent himself roaring at her in anger. *Elizabeth* had returned his coat! Not a servant—Elizabeth! In person, in the rain, seeking to see him before she left. And she had been sent away! "Where is the note she gave you for Miss Darcy?"

There was a pause before Mrs Reynolds eventually whispered, "I burnt it."

"Good God!" he cried, beyond caring for manners. He whirled back to face her. "Why?"

"Forgive me, sir. I thought I was protecting you."

"From what, exactly?"

"From Mr Wickham."

Darcy recoiled as though struck. "What the [redacted] has Wickham to do with this?"

"He is the reason Miss Bennet was obliged to go home. He eloped with her sister."

The room was not large enough for the surge of furious bitterness that overtook Darcy. The sound of his own, barely controlled breathing bounced back at him off the walls, and his voice, when he spoke, seemed to resound like thunder on the air, though he had not spoken any more loudly.

"Which?"

"The youngest I believe. Miss Lydia."

"When?"

"At the beginning of August. They are married now."

Darcy shook his head in disgust. "Miss Bennet revealed all this to you, and still you turned her away? You who know what sort of man Wickham is!"

"No, sir—she did not tell me any of this. She only asked that I pass on her farewell."

"How do you know of it, then?"

Her entire frame slumped, and she exhaled feebly. "I stole her correspondence."

Darcy had no capacity for shock remaining. He felt only bone-deep disillusionment as, with this ugly confession, one of the most trustworthy, respected, and enduring figures in his life revealed herself to be a total stranger.

Mrs Reynolds glanced up at him, and away again hastily, squeezing her eyes closed against whatever she had seen in his countenance. "The postmaster asked me to pass them on, but the seal on one was broken. I saw Mr Wickham's name written, and I know he has given you nothing but pain. I was anxious that if Miss Bennet was connected to him, she should be kept away from you."

Darcy's lip twitched, baring his teeth. "You have surpassed yourself in that case. She is gone. And I am struggling to comprehend why you are troubling yourself to reveal any of this to me now, given the extent of your success."

She had begun crying, he noticed. Not sobbing, but tears were spilling down her wrinkled and hollow cheeks. With his boyhood affection for her ripped away, he saw for the first time how frail she had become with age. He wished her senescence had not arrived hand in hand with treachery.

"Because they are not doing very well. Mr and Mrs Wickham have no money and no prospects, and there is unkind talk, affecting the whole family. Miss Bennet's father has been made unwell. And I thought you would want to know. Because I understand now that my fears were unfounded—that Miss Bennet is not who I thought she was. That she is important to you. I thought, perhaps, you might be able to help her. That it might not be too late for you to—"

"Get out."

"Mr Darcy, I cannot express the depth of my regret. I only wanted to protect you, to protect Pemberley—"

"Enough! You have done more damage to Pemberley by denying it Miss Bennet as its mistress than if every single wall crumbled to dust. Now *leave*!"

She did as he commanded. It was neither a hasty nor a graceful exit. She fumbled and shuffled her way to the door, by which time, Darcy's control had run out entirely. Leaving Mrs Reynolds to hobble down the passageway, he wrenched open the opposing door and stormed instead through the billiard room, drawing room, and dining room into the hall, throwing doors open before him and leaving footmen scrambling to attention in his wake. He charged up the stairs and into his bedroom, where he paced furiously back and forth, attempting to put everything he had been told in order.

He ought not to have been surprised to discover Wickham was involved—the man tainted everything in his path—but Elizabeth's *brother*? How in blazes had that come about? He wished to rail at Miss Lydia but could not without censuring his own sister for the same frailty. He knew, without a doubt, Elizabeth would think this was why he had not come—that a connexion to Wickham would extinguish his regard for her. She would think that, because she did not know that he had loved her so deeply, and for so long, that his feelings had permeated every sinew of his body, every facet of his mind, and every fibre of his soul. She had no way of knowing that a thousand ignoble relations could not injure his regard. If he must accept Wickham as his brother to be with her, then so be it. It would be more painful for Wickham than for him, of that he would make certain.

He rang the bell for his man, the act of which drove his thoughts to the servants' quarters, and to the unfathomable actions of his housekeeper. Mrs Reynold's betrayal was sickening. Wickham's behaviour was almost nothing in comparison, for his depravation was a well-known fact. Hers was unprecedented. Darcy, like his mother and father before him, had trusted her, implicitly, with Pemberley's intimate workings. He had never doubted her loyalty, but it was in her power to cause untold damage to the Darcy name. He shivered to think what else she had involved herself in beyond her admissions today.

Yet above and before all these concerns, there was Elizabeth. She had not left to escape his attentions. She had not sent his coat back to rid herself of any connexion to him. She had not run away from him at all. She had run *to* her youngest sister, just as she had run to her eldest, when she took ill at Netherfield. Her sublime compassion had taken her where she was needed, but *she had come to him first.* Whether for assistance or comfort or merely to say goodbye, he cared not. She had come to him, and so now he would go to her.

Vaughan entered from the dressing room. "You rang, sir?"

"I need you to pack. We are leaving for London tomorrow. Send word to Mrs Fairlight."

"Of course, sir. And so that I might know what to pack, may I ask how long you anticipate being away?"

Darcy considered for a moment. He would need to speak to Ferguson to ensure the work on the house would be in hand in his absence, though in all likelihood, his steward would be pleased he was going; Darcy knew he had been getting under the man's feet these past weeks. Then there was Wickham's chaos to set straight, and he knew not how long that might take. Then there was the simple fact that he did not wish to return to Pemberley without Elizabeth.

"As long as it takes," he replied. "Best pack well."

CHAPTER TWENTY-EIGHT

LAST GOODNIGHT

Agnes,

You know I hold you in the highest esteem, but upon my word, you can be too serious sometimes. To have forgotten the real name of a young lady you have never met scarcely warrants the ink you wasted apologising for it. I can certainly forgive you for it more easily than you seem able to. Besides, you have given me a wonderful excuse to recount the tale.

Dot is not now and never has been short for Dorothy. I confess, it amuses me to think you have gone twenty years thinking it was. I have always assumed 'Dorothy' was your own, affectionate variation of the name I use. It makes me wonder, with some trepidation, what else we have been talking about at cross purposes all these years!

My goddaughter's name is Elizabeth Genevieve Bennet. She is the granddaughter of my dear friend, Jane Bennet, née Sharpe, whom, if you recall, I met when Mr Wallis and I lived in Bishops Stortford. We were neighbours for only two years before she met and married Mr Samuel Bennet and became mistress of his home, Long-

bourn Manor, near Meryton, but we remained friends, even after Mr Wallis and I moved to Ilfracombe.

Jane was blessed with but one living child, a son, Thomas, upon whom she doted. Regrettably, she doted on him altogether too well, for he grew up apathetic and irreverent, though she was unwilling to see it for many years. Her blinkers were unceremoniously removed when he made the absurd decision to wed Miss Frances Gardiner, whom you will know better as the Termagant. Jane thought very ill of her, but she was by then a widow, and her son lord of the manor, thus she had no say in the matter. The Termagant moved in, all sense moved out, and Longbourn became, forever after, Bedlam.

Frances Bennet née Gardiner was—no doubt still is—uncommonly handsome, I shall give her that. Indeed, I must give her that, for I can give her nothing else. She is an empty-headed fop of a woman who has not, as a good mother ought to do, flattered, cajoled, or in any way encouraged her husband into providing for her children. Instead, she has left him to his indolence, and he has left her to her silly schemes, and between them they have achieved nothing greater than the woeful neglect of their children, their home, and their fortune.

Thomas Bennet named his first child Jane, after his mother. She is every bit as handsome as his wife, but that, thank the Lord, is where the similarity ends. Alas, my dear friend died weeks before her second grandchild, Elizabeth, was born. In honour of his recently deceased mother, Thomas asked me, her closest friend, to be Elizabeth's godmother. Mr Wallis and I travelled to Longbourn for the Christening—you might recall that visit, for I know I wrote several pages bemoaning the experience. From Jane's descriptions over the years, I expected the new Mrs Bennet to be awful, and she was—eye-wateringly so—but she had played her trump card. She had reproduced her husband's late mother almost identically in her second child.

I know it is why Thomas has always preferred Dot to his other girls. Indeed, it really ought to have been she who was named for her grandmother, for she is so like her in intelligence and vivacity. She has Jane's eyes, too, always sparkling. They were sparkling when I first saw her, wrapped up in blankets, so tiny one could almost have lost her in the creases. 'A wee dot of a thing,' I said to Mr Wallis at the time. It was he who began calling her Dot after that, and it stuck.

So, there you have it. My goddaughter's real name is Elizabeth, and let us thank heaven that I did agree to be her godmother, for I may be the only source of rational thought to which the child has had access from that day to this. Who is godparent to the other four girls I do not know, but they ought to be ashamed of themselves, for they have provided no guidance to their charges whatsoever that I can see. Lydia was most in need of direction yet was allowed the longest rope—which she is presently using to hang all her sisters out to dry. Thomas is showing all the signs of imminent apoplexy—the apothecary has put him on strict bed rest, apparently. It would not surprise me if it was his heart; it was that which took his father. My poor friend Jane must be turning in her grave to see her family in such dire straits.

I believe I shall write to Dot and invite her to visit me here for a while. There is nothing for her in Ilfracombe, but neither is there anyone who knows her predicament. She will be safe from scorn. Would that I could do as much to help her as you have done for your Mr D. I trust everything is well on that score, and he is faring better than last time you wrote.

Yours Affectionately,

E. Wallis

Mrs Reynolds had known the truth before she received Eleanor's answer. Reading it had still been devastating. It was a blow from which she did not think she would recover—not if she had all the time in the world, and certainly not in the time she had.

Admitting her mistake to the master was the most difficult, distressing thing she had ever done. His anger had been terrible to behold but not what upset her most, for at no point had she been frightened of him. It was the hurt in his expression that had chilled her to the core. The guilt of having betrayed him weighed like irons around her heart. Her failure to explain herself was equally painful, but what use were good intentions when the result was still ruination?

Mr Darcy was gone to London now. Her one consolation was knowing that he had taken command of the situation. More than anyone she knew, he possessed the wherewithal, influence, intelligence, and moreover the resolve to do what must be done—if not to salvage his hopes of happiness, then at least to assist the Bennets. That she was the cause of Dot's misery was almost as unbearable as being the cause of Mr Darcy's.

She stood for a moment and looked at the room before her: the mistress's chamber—perfectly proportioned and exquisitely decorated. The room that, against every probability but in answer to a good number of heartfelt wishes, could have been Dot's. The room that was once Lady Anne's.

It was in here that Mrs Reynolds had sat with her late mistress, making excited preparations for the birth of her ladyship's long-awaited second child. It had been at this bedside that she held vigil during Lady Anne's last hours. Her ladyship had begged her to help keep her young son and infant daughter safe and well after she was gone. Mrs Reynolds had given her word that she would do whatever was in her power to protect them. She supposed it was a good thing Lady Anne had not known, at the time, that her word was worthless. She touched the mattress with her fingertips, said a quick goodnight, and left, closing the door silently behind her.

In the hall, she paused to reminisce about opening the

servants' ball in 1791 with the late Mr Darcy. She had only recently been promoted to housekeeper from head housemaid, and it was the first time she had ever been called upon to dance with one of her employers. She remembered being thankful for her gloves, for her palms were clammy with fear, but she need not have concerned herself. He was so very genteel—and heavens, could he dance! With a sad smile, she twirled once, slowly, on the spot, recalling the dazzling light of all those candles, then walked on, the huge space falling back into darkness behind her.

She did not hesitate to slip quietly into the library. If it should fall down around her ears now, it would only hasten the inevitable and save her an arduous journey. The space was completely empty, every last book gone. All that remained were the walls—and myriad memories. How right the 'wise woman' had been who told the master that Pemberley was more than stones and mortar. With another stabbing spasm to her insides, she comprehended who that woman had probably been. She rested her hand on one of the mantelpieces and added an apology to her whispered goodnight.

Her candle danced about in protest when she passed through the service door to the cold, draughty passages of the servants' block beyond. There, she completed her usual round of checks, ending in her storeroom, where she laid out the up-to-date inventory on the desk and closed the door. The key, or perhaps her fingers, felt reluctant, but the lock eventually slid closed.

She went, last, to the estate office, where she placed her chatelaine on Mr Ferguson's desk. She was sorry for the work she would create for him, but it was better this way. She blew out her candle and left that also. Then she picked up her case and felt her way along the shadowy passageway to the tower door. It swung closed heavily behind her. She turned to lay her hand on the thick, weathered oak and whispered her final, heartfelt goodnight. Then she walked away from Pemberley forever.

CHAPTER TWENTY-NINE

OVERDUE CONFESSIONS

Darcy arrived in London on Saturday and called at the Gardiner residence the same day, only to discover that Mrs Gardiner was at home. Resolved to deal exclusively with her husband, he did not leave his name and instead returned home and composed an invitation. Mr Gardiner duly arrived, alone, at Astroite House on Sunday afternoon, and proceeded to demonstrate a far more obstinate sense of honour than Darcy had anticipated, even after having revised his opinion of the man's sense and worth. They argued back and forth on several points for far longer than either of the two objects of their discussion deserved, finally coming to an agreement that satisfied both and parting ways only twenty minutes before Bingley arrived for dinner.

Darcy began to rue inviting both men on the same day; he had miscalculated how draining so many unpleasant disclosures would prove. Even once dinner was over, and he and Bingley were sitting comfortably with full stomachs and a glass of the finest port each, he found himself reluctant to begin a second round.

It occurred to him that Mrs Reynolds must have felt similarly averse when she knocked on his door earlier that week —and he was instantly provoked into action in an attempt to banish her from his thoughts. He dismissed the servants, which put his friend on guard.

"Is something the matter, Darcy?"

He nodded, slowly. "I have a confession to make, and I do not anticipate that you will like it."

"Perhaps you had better not confess it then, for I do not like to be at variance with my friends—it gives me indigestion. And I have just eaten a vast amount of food."

"I dislike it too, very much, but it is overdue that I own this mistake, and if you are angry with me, that will be my punishment for having interfered in the first place." He paused, though he knew not what for. "I was wrong to convince you that Miss Jane Bennet was indifferent to you last autumn. I believe now that she was not."

Bingley sighed and scratched at a crumb on the table with a fingernail. "You did not convince me. I knew you were wrong."

Of all the responses Darcy had foreseen, that had not been one. "Why, then, did you not go back?"

"I cannot altogether account for it. First, Christmas was upon us, and there were balls and parties almost every night for weeks on end, and by the time all that was over, I was not entirely sure how I ought to explain my absence. Then Caroline told me about Miss Bennet's visit to London in January, and it rather made my mind up for me."

Shame burned Darcy's gullet every bit as much as disputes did Bingley's. "You know about that?"

"I do."

Blast! "Bingley, I am truly sorry I concealed it from you. I could try and justify it—say I thought I was acting in your best interests—but there is no excuse. It was wrong."

His friend grimaced ruefully. "I was sufficiently vexed at the time, I shall not deny it, but it served a purpose. It made me comprehend the magnitude of the opposition I would encounter if I married her. If *you* were opposed enough to the match to condescend to dishonesty to prevent it, I could only imagine the rest of society's view. I suppose it made me more clear-headed about your objections to her family."

"My objections to her family have been exposed as conceited twaddle now that I have met the Gardiners."

Bingley stroked his jaw pensively. "I rather went the other way on the matter after meeting them."

"You did not like them?"

"Oh, I thought they were a perfectly charming couple. I just...Well, as Caroline pointed out, they were exactly as you predicted they would be. Mr Gardiner was forever talking about his warehouses. Mrs Gardiner knew none of the women or places my sisters tried to talk to her about."

Darcy felt no little alarm at hearing Bingley speak so. "Gardiner is a fine gentleman."

"But he is *not* a gentleman, is he?" Bingley pressed.

"Neither are you, if we are to be pedantic about it, but you know what I mean."

"I do. And you know what *I* mean. You have only convinced yourself there is no impediment here because you do not wish there to be one."

Darcy caught the glint in his friend's eye and conceded with a small chuckle and a shake of his head that he had walked directly into a trap. "Perhaps."

Bingley returned to smiling amiably. "But you know people *will* object, Darcy. You warned *me* of that, and you were right."

"I know. But I no longer care."

"Not at all?"

"Not in the slightest." With a conscious smirk, Darcy added, "It was suggested to me earlier this year that I re-evaluate my priorities."

Bingley found this considerably funnier than Darcy expected him to and laughed heartily at it. "Is that why you were in such a bad mood all summer?"

Darcy did not deign to reply, but Bingley only smiled more broadly. "I take it you are going to make Miss Elizabeth an offer?"

"I am going to Hertfordshire to try to judge whether an offer would be welcomed."

"She is hardly likely to refuse you!"

Darcy took a long draught of port to drown the tide of memories that assailed him of Elizabeth doing just that, and his own string of internal curses for still not being sure of her regard. Gardiner had been infuriatingly circumspect, scarcely mentioning her name other than to say they were all sorry not to have been at liberty to explain their precipitous departure from Derbyshire. Darcy had assured him he understood and apologised for not being there to receive them when they called at Pemberley, hoping it might induce further revelations, but it had not.

In fairness, he had been equally guarded, but his situation in life had accustomed him to a level of independence and self-sufficiency that made the prospect of divulging his personal affairs to anyone abhorrent to him. Which made the next, necessary turn in the conversation all the more disagreeable.

"There has been a complication."

Bingley huffed a sardonic laugh. "Is not there always?"

"Her youngest sister has recently married."

"Miss Lydia? I did not think she was old enough to marry."

"She is fifteen, and she was entangled with someone who ought to have known better."

"Who?"

"Wickham."

Bingley started. "*Your* Wickham?"

"That is a ghastly epithet, but yes, I suppose so."

"Ah. Well, that does make things rather awkward."

"More than you know, but they will be gone farther away soon. I have that much comfort." As concisely as he could, Darcy summarised Lydia's elopement, the gaps in his own knowledge of the affair having been filled by Gardiner.

Bingley was appropriately dismayed. "What will become of them?"

"The money Mr Bennet has agreed to give them will scarcely cover Wickham's gambling. He has resigned his commission and has no other profession, since he refused to take orders or study the law when he had the chance. And you ought to know, the nature of their marriage has caused talk in Meryton. I hope my return will help assuage much of that, but there is always talk."

"This must have been beastly for Miss Bennet and her sisters."

"That has been my concern," Darcy agreed. "But I hope the actions I have taken today will alleviate some of their misery. I have bought Wickham another commission—well, I have said I shall pay for it at any rate. Gardiner has agreed to arrange the purchase, which we both agree will need to be somewhere as remote as possible. And I have given him an extra thousand pounds to settle on his niece in addition to what she will have from her mother, to make sure she is more comfortable, wherever she and her husband end up."

Bingley half frowned and half laughed. "That was a tad high-handed of you. You are not her brother yet."

"But I am, regrettably, the closest thing to Wickham's.

And besides," he added with a deep sigh, "none of it would have happened had I been *less* high-handed in the first place."

Thus, with the greatest reluctance and a queasy feeling in his gut throughout, he explained to Bingley how Lydia's fate had almost been Georgiana's, and how he had thought it beneath him to warn the world about Wickham. His friend listened with observable disquiet, unusually grave for a man whose response to most things was to find some good in them. By the time Darcy finished, he began to worry he had erred in telling him. "You will not think ill of my sister, I hope."

"What? Good grief, no! And never could I. Miss Darcy is quite the sweetest creature I know—an angel compared to *my* sisters."

"And I may count on your discretion?"

"Goes without saying. I wonder at you, though, Darcy. To think you have been carrying this, all these months, and said not a word to anybody."

"I do not find it easy, unburdening myself to people."

"Has it ever occurred to you that it might lessen your burdens if you asked for help now and again?"

"Why, have you some prodigious counsel to impart?"

Bingley grinned. "None whatsoever. I am only trying to impress upon you that you do not need to go through the world shouldering every problem on your own."

Notwithstanding that Darcy's discomfiture was increasing exponentially, he was not unmoved by the sentiment. "You are a good friend, Bingley."

Bingley had finished his drink and had nothing to occupy his hands—and his hands were never still. Darcy was accustomed to his friend's fidgeting and was diverted to see him reach for the nearest candle stick and begin rotating it between his fingers, scrunching the tablecloth into whirls as it turned.

"'Tis rotten that you have had to put up with the cur all these years—and are set to be saddled with him forever, now. Will not Miss Darcy object to having such a brother?"

Darcy reached to refill his friend's glass before the candlestick fell over and started a fire. "I asked her, of course, before setting out from Pemberley. She is not enamoured of the idea, it is true, but then neither am I. But she is of the same mind as I—we would rather have Wickham *and* Miss Elizabeth than neither."

Bingley looked almost proud, though if Darcy had done something to please him, he knew not what it was. "So," he said cheerfully, "you would like me to reopen Netherfield."

"I have not told you all this merely so that I can use your house, but so you can decide whether or not to join me."

"But of course I shall reopen the house!"

He did not add anything else, and after a short pause, Darcy pressed, "And will you come? For Miss Bennet? Or have you decided against her?"

"I still admire her, but I have used her ill, and Miss Elizabeth did not mention that she still admired me, did she?"

Darcy grimaced, chastened to have yet more admissions to make. "Not while she was in Derbyshire, no. But she did when I saw her in Kent in April."

Bingley tapped his finger against the side of his glass and frowned pensively for a few moments before nodding slowly. "Yes, very well, I shall join you, though I do not know what will come of it. And Caroline will spit when I tell her, but that will only add to the fun. It will take a few days to get the wheels in motion at Netherfield. Can you wait?"

Darcy assured him he could, though every part of him chafed at the delay. "I would ensure Gardiner has everything resolved with Wickham before I go, in any case."

"Yes, why are you dealing through Mr Gardiner? Would it not have been quicker to speak directly to Wickham?"

"I did not know where he was, but there are plenty of other reasons. I could not approach Mr Bennet, for he is unwell, apparently. Which provided a convenient excuse for not dealing with him at all. Much as I respect him as Miss Elizabeth's father, I do not judge him to be a man with whom I could so readily consult as his brother."

"You are probably correct in your estimation. He is amiable enough, but not serious."

"Indeed. He is insincere—and Wickham is mercenary. Were he to know I was the source of the money he would only argue for more. As long as he thinks it is coming from Gardiner, he will take what is offered. More importantly, I did not wish him to guess my interest in the matter until it is settled. I would not trust him not to make trouble."

"So, Mr Gardiner is allowed to take all the credit?"

Darcy smiled faintly. "That was a stumbling block over which we debated for some time. I expect he will ask Wickham to keep his identity secret from Mrs Wickham—which ought not to present a problem. Wickham would lie on the Bible if it meant someone would give him money."

"But you persuaded Gardiner to keep your part in it secret?"

"Yes, and I beg you would as well. I do not want Miss Elizabeth to find out. I should hate her to feel obliged to accept me." When Bingley looked as though he would say something teasing, Darcy said, emphatically, "I must get it right, Bingley. I cannot—" He stopped short of saying he could not live without her, for it sounded ridiculous, even if it was true. "I cannot be easy with the alternative."

Though he looked somewhat taken aback, Bingley reached over to gently clink Darcy's glass with his own. "I wish you luck. She would be fortunate to have you."

Darcy thanked him sincerely and sent up a silent prayer that Elizabeth would feel the same way.

CHAPTER THIRTY

BLISSFUL WHILE IT LASTED

Mr Bennet was at the breakfast table when Elizabeth came downstairs. It was a heartening sight, though she was unsure as to the wisdom of it. "Ought you to be up? You look very pale still."

"If I do, 'tis only because I have not seen the light of day for a week. But rest assured, I am much better."

Elizabeth sat down and poured them both a cup of tea. "Then I am pleased, but you must promise not to overexert yourself. You gave us all such a fright."

"Yes, yes, you are quite right. I must do as little as possible. And really, given how much I have achieved thus far without lifting a finger—nurturing my youngest children into the most senseless, selfish creatures ever to walk the earth, consenting to a marriage I knew nothing about, allowing my youngest daughter to disgrace herself and all her sisters, acquiring a morally corrupt libertine as a son, and managing my estate in such a way as to ensure there is not a penny spare to help Lydia put food on her table—I can see that the very best thing to do now is even less than before."

Elizabeth regarded him pityingly. He had lost weight, and possibly hair, and all the sport had gone out of his reflections, leaving only bitter sarcasm. "You were not to know—"

"You warned me though, did you not? You could not have said more plainly that Lydia's behaviour would get her into trouble. Would that I had listened."

Elizabeth felt again the regret that beset her upon first hearing of the elopement. Yes, she had warned her father, but only about Lydia's wild conduct. She had said nothing against Wickham. How she regretted that decision! Had she only told her father some part of his history with Darcy, or perhaps named Colonel Fitzwilliam as a second authority on the evils of his character, then Lydia might have been kept safely at Longbourn.

Time had tempered her regret with a little perspective, however. She was of the opinion now that, if the disaster in Brighton had been averted, Lydia would only have found another, somewhere else, before long. The only benefit to delaying the inevitable was that a different man would be Elizabeth's brother, and her hopes might not have perished along with her sister's virtue.

"None of us forced her into that carriage, Papa. Not even Wickham. The blame for that is Lydia's alone."

"Not so, though I thank you for trying to absolve me. But you said it yourself—I did not check Lydia's behaviour. I did not provide her with the information or understanding that would have prevented her from climbing into that carriage. What came next, I blame wholly on Wickham. Everything that came before, I must own to myself."

Elizabeth knew not how to respond, for she did not entirely disagree, but there was no point in worsening her father's shame by saying so. They ate their breakfasts without any more discussion until Mr Bennet asked a question that made it clear her silence was as strong an indictment as if she had simply concurred.

"Did your uncle think the same as you?"

"Pardon?"

"Come, Lizzy, I would think you a simpleton if you did not agree that I have let you and your sisters down. I would know what your uncle Gardiner had to say on the matter that he would not say to my face."

"He was only concerned with assisting in the search," she assured him. "If he was displeased with any party, he was too kind to say so. Unlike my aunt Wallis."

Her father let out a bark of laughter. "I can well imagine! And pray, what has she to say on the matter?"

"Nothing that I think you would consider useful," Elizabeth admitted.

"No, let me hear it. She no doubt thinks I ought to disown your sister, or something equally severe."

"Actually, she suggested that you disown Mama. She said you could send her to keep house for Lydia and install Jane as mistress of Longbourn."

"And what are her plans for you?"

"She wants me to go and stay with her." Her father seemed to think this a hollow threat, and Elizabeth judged it the wrong time to inform him she was seriously considering accepting the invitation. "I am sorry for Lydia," she said instead. "She has no idea how wretched her life will be."

"Your sister is so utterly devoid of rational thought that I think her quite capable of blundering through every tribulation in complete ignorance." He paused when Kitty came into the room, continuing once she had taken her seat at the table. "Wickham seems an equal stranger to common sense. With any luck they may not notice each other's deficiencies at all."

"They will notice when they cannot afford coal to burn."

"If you are talking about Lydia and Wickham, they have money enough for all the coal they need now," Kitty said.

Elizabeth exchanged a puzzled look with her father. "What do you mean?"

"Wickham has a new commission in the regulars. His cousin paid for it."

It was swiftly established that Kitty had received correspondence from Lydia that morning, which she reluctantly handed over for Elizabeth to read the pertinent parts aloud to her father.

> *A cousin of Wickham's has bought him an ensigncy. It means we must move to Newcastle, but I do not mind, for I am grown tired of London. It is full of foul-smelling smoke and half-finished buildings, and at night, people shout and fight in the streets and keep me awake. Mrs Younge has refunded our rent—most of it, anyway—so we have plenty of money to spend. We celebrated no longer being poor by drinking two bottles of fine wine. The whole business has put Wickham in a better humour than he has been in since we left Longbourn. I do not know why everyone had to be so horrid to him while we were there, it was quite unfair, but he is happier now, and he only got a bit cross that I have bought myself a new coat. I hope you are not too fed up being stuck there with nothing to do.*

Elizabeth let out an angry breath and handed the note back to Kitty. "Well, we can safely say she listened to none of our lessons about economy."

"We can also safely say that Wickham has more relations on hand to bail him out than any man as despicable as he has a right to," Mr Bennet added. "I am only vexed that I have ended up among their number."

"I never heard of his having any relations except a father

and mother, both of whom he told me had been dead many years."

"I thought you would both be happy that Lydia's prospects have improved," Kitty said in a bewildered tone.

"Oh, I am," Elizabeth replied with a resigned sigh. "But it does not solve as many problems as you might think. It does not make Lydia any more worldly-wise. It will not stop Wickham running up more debts." *It will not undo the fact that he is my brother!*

"You were right, though, Lizzy," her father said. "I have only been keeping my promise not to exert myself for five minutes, and I have already achieved another feat of brilliance. Your sister is saved from destitution. Lord knows what I might accomplish were I to do even less." With exaggeratedly slow actions and an expression of feigned trepidation, he set his knife and fork down and slowly leant back in his chair, clasping his hands across his stomach. At which point, the door was flung open, and Mrs Bennet burst into the room.

"Such news, everyone! Such news! Hill has just returned from Meryton, and you will never guess what she has heard. Netherfield is being reopened! Mr Bingley is coming back!"

Much of the glee that had been missing from Mr Bennet's countenance since Lydia's misadventure began returned in that instant. He pushed himself to his feet and regarded Elizabeth with a self-satisfied grin. "And on that note, I am off to my library, where I shall endeavour to do absolutely nothing for the rest of the day in the hopes that I might be able to remedy all our other troubles by dinner."

The Wickhams' windfall and Mr Bingley's intentions were the focus of endless speculation at Longbourn, though Elizabeth spent most of her time quietly assuring Jane. Her eldest sister was all apprehension for everybody's certain expectations of what was to come, and whilst she was exceedingly hopeful that Mr Bingley yet admired her, she dreaded so much attention from her family and friends.

An entire day and evening talking about nothing else was too much for Elizabeth, and at noon the next day, she escaped Longbourn and walked to Oakham Mount. She chose that destination deliberately, for it was a long way there and back, and she revelled in the bracing autumn breeze that harried her along the path, fussing at her bonnet and cuffs and loosening all her tightly held emotions.

She could congratulate or commiserate with Jane as the circumstance demanded; she could endure the whispers that came whenever Lydia's name was mentioned; she could tolerate her father's irreverence and her mother's ignorance. What she knew not how to contend with, was the sorrow that repeatedly crept over her, stinging her eyes with tears, and making her hands clumsy with tremors, every time she thought about the gentleman who was *not* coming back to Netherfield.

She did her best not to think about it most of the time, but when she returned home and heard Mr Bingley's voice in the parlour, she almost put her bonnet back on and returned out of doors, for she did not think she had the strength to feign composure for the length of a call. Only Jane's nervous attempts at conversation, emanating timorously from the parlour, prevented her running away.

She knew not what her countenance showed when she saw that Darcy was there, but his altered from a grave expression to one of fiercely restrained gratification in an instant. She doubted anyone else would notice, for as usual, he moved scarcely a muscle, but *she* saw it as clearly as if he had come to his feet and bellowed his relief to the room.

"There you are, Lizzy. Where have you been?" her mother enquired, though she did not wait for an answer before continuing, "Look who is come. Mr Bingley!"

Elizabeth curtseyed to that gentleman, said some words that she hoped were welcoming, and remembered to spare Jane an encouraging smile before turning back to Darcy. She could scarcely believe he had come, yet there he was, his penetrating gaze as intimate and familiar as if she had never stepped out of his sight.

"Oh yes, and Mr Darcy," Mrs Bennet added rudely, but Elizabeth had already left her behind and crossed the room.

"Mr Darcy. You are well, I hope."

"Exceedingly now. And you?"

"Yes, thank you. How is Pemberley?"

His mouth twitched with a small smile. "Still standing. Just about."

"Have they discovered what is causing the damage?"

"Subsidence has been confirmed."

"That sounds serious. Do they know what has caused it?"

He smiled again, clearly gratified by something, though it could not have been what they were discussing. "No."

"Can it be repaired?"

"Yes. In time."

"I am so pleased. I should have been terribly upset to hear otherwise." She wrinkled her nose in chagrin. "That is a foolish thing to say to you, is it not? I imagine you would have been a good deal more upset than I."

He shook his head very slightly.

"Is Miss Darcy still at Pemberley?"

He confirmed that she was.

"I trust she is well. I hope my note reached her safely." She detected a hint of something like annoyance in his expression, and though it was gone quickly, it nevertheless unnerved her. "It was such a pleasure to make her acquaintance—I was sorry it was curtailed. I hope the note gave her some assurance to that effect."

"Lizzy, what are you running on about to Mr Darcy? You have not stopped since you came in the door. Remember to whom you are talking and be quiet."

Elizabeth felt herself blush at her mother's coarseness—and blush again as she realised with deep mortification that she *had* been running on. She was so elated to see Darcy, had so much to say to him, wished so dearly to return to the easiness they seemed to have reached in Derbyshire, that she had quite forgotten her manners. Yet her mother was right—he had barely spoken, and she knew not whether that was because he rarely did, because he had not been able to, or because he did not wish to.

For the first time since setting eyes on him, it occurred to Elizabeth to question why he had come. Then, in the blink of an eye, all possible answers were rendered moot, for Mrs Bennet announced, "You have all heard, I suppose, that my youngest daughter is lately married? To Mr Wickham."

Elizabeth closed her eyes and lowered her chin as Mrs Bennet talked and *talked* about her new son. It had been blissful while it lasted, but whatever Darcy's reason for coming, it was sure to be his last visit now that he knew her connexions had sunk to a previously unthinkable low. As if to prove it, Mr Bingley interrupted her mother a few minutes later to announce their departure.

Before the gentlemen left, Mrs Bennet invited them to dine at Longbourn in a few days' time. Mr Bingley accepted, and Mrs Bennet clearly considered that he meant to engage his friend as well as himself for attendance. Elizabeth was under no such illusion, and her goodbye to Darcy was appropriately final. She was pleased for the opportunity to say that which precipitance had not allowed when she left

Derbyshire, but she found, when the time came, that her parting words did not convey even a tenth of her feelings, and that after he was gone, she was ten times more bereft than the last time they had been separated.

CHAPTER THIRTY-ONE

TWO VACANCIES TO FILL

"Bad news?"

Darcy looked up from his letter into Bingley's worried countenance. "Yes. My housekeeper has left."

"Surely not. Mrs Reynolds has been there since the house was built."

Too many urgent considerations churned in Darcy's mind for him to do more than smile vaguely in response. Who would replace her, why and where she had gone—whether he was pleased that she had. The latter subject vexed him too much to dwell upon, but the matter of what would be done at Pemberley in her absence was a serious problem. He must send instructions to Georgiana for how to arrange things in the meantime. And he would need to think of something to placate his steward, whose displeasure at the clandestine manner of Mrs Reynolds's departure veritably bristled off the page.

"I say, Darcy, can I ask you something?" Bingley said somewhat gingerly.

With an effort to conceal his impatience, Darcy set aside his letter and regarded his friend expectantly.

"What did you make of Miss Bennet yesterday? Think you she was pleased to see me?"

A flood of warmth instantly washed away all the discomfiture brought by Ferguson's news as Darcy thought back to the previous day. His disappointment to discover Elizabeth from home when he arrived at Longbourn had been sharp, but had amplified his pleasure when she did, eventually return. He could not have wished for a better response from her, either. Delight overspread her countenance the moment she espied him, and she had not stopped smiling until her mother embarrassed her into silence. Before that, she had talked as though they were long lost friends, frantic to reacquaint each other with every detail of what separation had cost them. It had answered all his questions, done away with all his recent indecision in an instant; Elizabeth welcomed his return. He had been in an ecstasy of relief and anticipation ever since.

"I am, perhaps, not the best person to advise on this matter," he said to Bingley, who had received no such open display from Miss Bennet. "It has been confirmed that she is serene by nature, so I daresay you ought not to be discouraged by her composure."

"True, and she has good reason to doubt my affections. I would not expect her to make her own feelings known before being sure of mine. But I would know whether she resents my coming."

"What did you talk about?"

He shrugged. "Not much. She asked after Caroline and Louisa. We spoke briefly about her cousins, whom she said were here last month. It was all terribly innocuous."

Darcy grimaced slightly. He loathed inane chatter of precisely that sort, but as Bingley said, Miss Bennet could not be expected to put forward much more at this stage. Elizabeth had asked *him* about Pemberley. He had loved her intensely in that moment. No one else had enquired—not Bingley, not Gardiner, not Pettigrew or Aldridge when he saw them at his club earlier in the week, yet it had been the first query past Elizabeth's lips. He dared to hope that was because she comprehended how deeply it mattered to him.

When she was at Pemberley, she had understood instinctively what the house represented, had spoken of it in terms entirely consonant with Darcy's own feelings. She had clearly not forgotten it in the weeks since she left Derbyshire. Her eagerness to know every detail of the structural findings showed her interest to be more than polite enquiry. If he was not entirely mistaken, Pemberley mattered to Elizabeth, also.

He knew, abruptly, what was to be done about his housekeeper.

"Miss Bennet has had time to accustom herself to your return now," he said to Bingley. "Perhaps she will be more at ease today."

"You think we should call again so soon?"

"I am going. I need to speak to Miss Elizabeth. But you may do as you please."

"No, no, I shall not stay here on my own while you dash off and make love to your lady. Let us saddle our horses!"

Elizabeth could not have looked more surprised to see Darcy when he entered Longbourn's parlour, for which he could not account at first. Only when Mrs Bennet began, again, to boast of Wickham's recent admission to their family, causing all her daughters to shrink in mortification, did he recall her panegyric on the same subject the previous day. Being already conversant with the entire sorry affair, Darcy had largely ignored her, but he recalled, belatedly, that Elizabeth was not aware of his intelligence. Evidently, she had believed the revelation would scare him off. He kicked himself for leaving her without reassurance and was thankful to have returned swiftly.

"Darcy and I thought a walk might be just the thing this afternoon," Bingley declared. "It is gloriously sunny and not too cold. What say you, Miss Bennet? Miss Elizabeth?"

Mrs Bennet declared it an excellent idea and attempted to cajole Miss Catherine and Miss Mary to join them, to 'keep Lizzy and Mr Darcy company,' by which she clearly meant, 'to ensure Jane and Mr Bingley are left in peace.' It did not escape Darcy's notice that, during the hubbub that followed, Miss Bennet quietly put the two younger girls off coming. He felt a pang of remorse for having once thought her spiritless, and a greater pang of exhilaration at the prospect of Elizabeth having said enough of her feelings for him that her sister would facilitate their being alone together.

They walked away from the village and through a small wood, emerging onto a picturesque stream. The scene reminded Darcy of the day they visited Dedman's Gorge, prompting him to relate Mr Gardiner's encounter with the river rat. Miss Bennet was greatly diverted, but Elizabeth only smiled, notably more subdued than she had been the preceding afternoon. Darcy begrudged that he would be obliged to begin what he came to say with a discussion about Wickham, but the more she frowned and bit her lips, the greater became the importance of putting her mind at rest. He slowed his pace until Bingley and Miss Bennet were out of sight.

"I beg you would not make yourself uneasy about your sister's marriage. I already knew about it before your mother mentioned it."

She looked at him sharply, then away again, just as quickly. "Oh. How did you find out?"

"Mrs Reynolds informed me."

"Your housekeeper? How did she know?"

"It is rather a complicated story."

"I see. You do not have to tell me."

"I do. It is why I have come."

She glanced at him again, warily. "Very well. I am listening."

"Mrs Reynolds came to me about a week ago and told me that you called at Pemberley the day you left Derbyshire."

It did not take Elizabeth long to comprehend the significance of this. She frowned indignantly. "Only a week ago?"

Darcy nodded and tried his best not to be distracted by how magnificent she looked when she was vexed.

"But you are wearing the coat you lent me. How did she account for that being returned?"

"She said a servant brought it to the house."

Elizabeth expelled an incredulous huff of air. "I stood in the pouring rain until I was soaked through, pleading to be allowed to speak to you! It was undignified and improper, and she was *scrupulous* in making me feel it. I suppose she did not tell you that she slammed the door in my face?"

Darcy clenched his teeth. He had not thought he could resent Mrs Reynolds any more. Apparently, he had been wrong. "She did not."

"I take it she did not give my note to Miss Darcy either?"

"No. She burnt it."

Elizabeth stopped walking. "*Burnt* it? Why?"

He took a deep breath; this part would be unpleasant. "For some reason I have not been able to unearth, it seems Mrs Reynolds took a dislike to you when you first came to Pemberley. She was quite alone in her opinion, and indefensibly presumptuous to have formed it, but form it she did, and she allowed it to affect her judgment." Elizabeth had coloured but said nothing, thus he continued. "Two letters to you from your family fell into her possession, and rather than pass them on, she read them. They contained news of your youngest sister's elopement."

She let out a wordless cry. "So you know it was an elopement. I have not even the consolation of pretending the marriage was respectable." She looked away into the trees, wringing her hands together. "This explains why I never received Jane's letters. I cannot believe this! 'Tis too much!"

"I beg you would believe *me* when I say that nothing in Mrs Reynolds's behaviour has ever led me to suspect her capable of such duplicity. Had I any inkling of what she was up to, I should have acted sooner. I can only apologise for the delay it has caused in my coming for you."

He could see she was too angry to take his meaning.

"But I do not understand! What has this to do with her not telling you that I called?"

"She apparently sought to protect me from a connexion with Wickham. When you came to Pemberley to say you were leaving, she took it upon herself to let you go without informing anybody, thinking it was for the best."

"Then not only did you not know why I had gone, but you thought I had left without even a word of farewell? What must you have thought of me!"

"The same as I have always thought."

She was still too angry. She had begun pacing back and forth across the path in front of him, and his implication went entirely unnoticed.

"She *said* she did not think anyone was good enough for you—that day she showed us the house! Had I known she was speaking for my benefit, I should not have thought her quite so generous! What right had she to decide who would make you happy?"

"None, which is why her opinion is of no importance, and her efforts to direct my affections have all been in vain. The only way in which her reprehensible interference has disadvantaged me is that I no longer have a housekeeper."

"You have dismissed her? I suppose that is well and good. I only wish she had not painted me as an unsuitable, inconstant, and ungrateful interloper before you had the chance!"

"I did not dismiss her. I had not decided *what* to do about her, but she has taken the matter out of my hands. I received a letter from my steward this morning, informing me that she has left Pemberley—under the cover of darkness and without notice."

Elizabeth stopped pacing at last, though she was evidently still in high emotion, and she looked stricken. "So now you must leave again. To appoint a new one."

"No. Indeed, that is what I wished to speak to you about. I rather hoped *you* might like to appoint one." He could not help but smile at her obvious bewilderment. "Elizabeth, you must know my affections and wishes are unchanged. I love you as much today as I did this summer, in the spring, last autumn. I shall continue to love you as long as I live, but I should be a good deal happier if you would agree to live *with* me. And Pemberley would be a good deal better off if you were its mistress."

She stared at him, myriad different emotions playing across her countenance, but gave him no reply.

Though it pained him to say it, he forced himself to add, "But if I have mistaken your feelings again, I shall not—"

"What? No! No, you have not—I am not—I was not sure I understood you properly. I was still reeling from what you said about your housekeeper. But—oh, why did you not tell me this before you made me so angry?"

Dear God, he loved her! Her countenance was an exquisite mix of annoyance, astonishment, and happiness that made him joyous just to look at it. "It was not my intention to make you angry," he replied, smiling more broadly now. "But to make it quite clear that it does not matter to me who your brother is, or how he came to be your brother. To explain why I did not come for you sooner. To tell you how ardently I still admire and love you."

He stepped closer and took her hand in his. "Elizabeth, please say you will marry me. I do not wish to be apart from you anymore."

She let out what seemed to be all her breath and smiled ecstatically. "Nor I you! I have missed you—so very much. I thought I would never see you again, and—" She huffed a conscious little laugh. "Yes, I will marry you. That would make me very, very happy."

It was Darcy's turn to be astonished. He had been reasonably confident that her opinion of him had improved during her stay in Derbyshire. He had also judged her to be pleased that he was come to Hertfordshire. He had not been expecting that she would confess to an attachment strong enough to have made her mourn their separation.

He could not easily have said how she came to be in his arms, except that it was where she belonged. At first, he only held her, rejoicing at having won the privilege at long last and jealously guarding her from anything that might wrest her from him once more. He told her how dearly he loved her, promised her everything it was in his power to give, and thanked her profusely for forgiving him. The expression of more passionate sentiments was a natural progression after she whispered his name and affirmed her affections aloud.

Her kiss was delicacy and passion entwined—a heady mix that caught him unawares, igniting a long-withstood ache into a conflagration of need. That he *could* kiss her, that she welcomed his affections at last, amplified his desire in a way he had not anticipated, and his caress was more ardent than it ought to have been. Yet, in her inimitable way, Elizabeth wasted no time on timidity, and only her innocence prevented the kiss from taking an even more heated turn. It was enough for Darcy; after the agonies of the past year, any touch of hers would have felt sublime. Such a display of regard as this was beyond anything for which he had dared hope.

They recollected themselves eventually and walked on, Elizabeth's hands wrapped around Darcy's arm and her head resting against his shoulder. It was an easy intimacy that felt as though it deserved more than a few minutes' earning, as though they had been affianced all their lives. He had never known happiness like it.

"Shall you like to be Pemberley's mistress?"

"I shall like it a great deal, though it may be a while before I can claim to be a proficient one. You ought to be aware, I do not know the first thing about how to choose a housekeeper."

"One thing is certain—you will struggle to find anyone worse than the previous candidate. I suggest you begin with a woman who knows what loyalty is and go from there." Darcy regretted the asperity that had crept into his tone.

"What made her tell you in the end?" Elizabeth asked. "It is hard enough to comprehend her deceit. Her admitting it is even more peculiar."

"I believe she was largely motivated by guilt. She claimed to have realised that she misunderstood your character."

"Well, that is something, I suppose."

It felt strange to Darcy, to be censuring a woman who had for so long been a figure of integrity and competence in his eyes. It accentuated his bitterness and left a sour taste in his mouth as he replied, "She was also anxious that your sister's marriage was not a happy one and realised I could only be of assistance to them if I were aware of it."

"How on earth did she know Lydia and Wickham were unhappy?"

"I presume she read it in your letters."

Elizabeth shook her head. "Lydia was not married when Jane wrote to me."

"I cannot answer for it in that case. I was about as angry as I have ever been in those few minutes listening to her confession. I am afraid I was not in a humour to concentrate on details. Perhaps she heard it from Wickham's mother."

"His *mother*? He told me she was dead!" Elizabeth gave an exasperated growl. "Are you sure you can tolerate him as a brother? I know I cannot."

"There is a particular advantage to me in the arrangement that makes it much easier to bear." He lifted her hand to his lips to place a kiss on her gloved fingers. "You are pleased, though, that the Wickhams are to move to Newcastle? You will not miss your sister?"

"I will always worry about her, but we are not close. I do not anticipate that the distance will cause either of us much distress. I certainly will not miss *him*. I feel such a fool for ever having tried to defend him to you. He was awful when he came here. So complacent and charming, and yet so obviously not in love with Lydia. I have no idea why he married her. Papa can only give him a hundred pounds a year. If it were not for his plethora of secret relations giving him money, they would still be stuck in Clerk—"

She stopped talking and looked at him. Darcy looked directly ahead and continued walking. She tugged on his arm to make him stop and look at her.

"It was you! *You* bought him the commission. Do not deny it—you just admitted that Mrs Reynolds only told you about the marriage so you could assist them."

"I shall not deny it, although strictly speaking, your uncle arranged the commission. I only provided the capital. And settled an extra thousand pounds on your sister to help make her more comfortable."

She was in his arms again in an instant—or rather, he was in hers as she flung them around his neck, almost dislodging his hat, and thanked him over and over. He wrapped his arms around her slender waist and held her tightly to him, revelling in the feel of her. She might not have thrown herself at him with quite such energy had she known how much, and for how long he had wanted her, but as long as she was content for him to hold her so close, he was content to continue.

"I was right, obviously, not to tell you before we reached an understanding," he said. "I was concerned you would feel obligated to me, but I had no idea of it producing so strong a sense of gratitude as this."

"That is because you do not know what I do." She stood back from him, and he was startled to see how affected she was. "I have said this to no one, but Wickham all but admitted to me that he was carrying on an affair with Mrs Younge. She is their landlady and nearest neighbour. Lydia was completely oblivious. It broke my heart that she was being so ill-used. Now you have sent them away from all that. I will not fool myself into believing he will not succumb again to temptation, but at least he is away from that woman."

Darcy regretted, now, not visiting Wickham himself to deliver a rebuke of a more memorable variety. He had wished—foolishly—to believe that some hidden vestige of decency had induced his erstwhile friend to marry Lydia. Would he never learn that the man was beyond redemption? "If there were anything more I could do to help your sister, I would, but—"

"There is nothing more to be done—and you have already

done more than either of them deserves. But you have given *me* great comfort, and I thank you with all my heart."

"I am gladder than ever to have assisted, then, though it did add a week to the time I took to get to you."

Elizabeth looked relieved to be restored to lighter matters and turned them back to the path with a renewal of her usual liveliness. "You were lucky it did not take you longer. I was about to run away to stay with my aunt Wallis in North Devon. Mrs Reynolds has been of some use after all in confessing to you when she did."

"I would have found you, wherever you had gone. And Mrs Reynolds will have none of the credit for my present happiness. I could not have stayed away from you much longer, but I was waiting for you to return home. I was told, when I called at the Plough and Horseshoe, that you had gone north. I assumed you had gone on with your holiday. I have been waiting—wretchedly, I might add—until I thought you might reasonably have returned to Longbourn."

"We had, originally, planned to go to Chesterfield when we left Lambton. They must have thought that was where we were going. We did not advertise what we were actually hastening towards, for obvious reasons. I hope it will be a comfort for you to know that we had discarded that plan some days before we received the news about Lydia. About the time that my aunt thought I might be forming an attachment to you and would prefer to stay in Lambton, in fact."

"That is both comforting and maddening. It would have saved me considerable distress had I known you felt that way."

She gave him an intoxicating look of impish contrition. "I did *try* to let you know. I could not put anything in a letter, but I did send you a message with your coat."

"Yes, but as I said, Mrs Reynolds burnt it."

"No, not the note. It might be—" She pointed to his coat pocket and asked, "May I?"

Darcy nodded and to his surprise, amusement, and rapidly increasing pleasure, she slid her hand into his pocket —in search of what, he dared not permit himself to suppose.

With a triumphant cry, she retracted her hand and waved a ribbon in the air between them. "I pushed it too far into the stitching. I am not surprised you did not notice it."

"What is it?"

"The ribbon I used at the picnic for the game of Lead Balloon. Do you not remember it?"

Darcy shook his head, nonplussed. "I was not looking at your *ribbon* that day."

"Oh." She wrinkled her nose and chuckled wryly. "So, my attempt to let you know that I admired you was a miserable failure?"

"I will admit—and only because I am now secure in your affections—had I found that, I would absolutely *not* have equated it with a declaration of your regard. I would have just thought you left your ribbon in my pocket."

Elizabeth's slight chuckle turned into full blown and hearty laughter. "How wonderfully like you that is, dearest Fitzwilliam!"

If a heart swelling with happiness was something that could truly happen, Darcy thought his might burst to see her so joyful, so beautiful, so enticingly, miraculously his. He could not kiss her again, for he had spotted Bingley and Miss Bennet coming back along the path towards them, but it was enough simply to know that she would be his wife, and that he would be endearingly hers for as long as he had on earth.

CHAPTER THIRTY-TWO

GLAD TIDINGS

Dearest Aunt Wallis,

I can scarcely believe I am writing this, but I have pinched myself until I am black and blue, and I have not woken up yet, so it must be true. I am engaged! You will think, when I tell you to whom, that I have lost my mind, but you will have to trust that I know what I am about. Remember that, as my godmother, you are obliged to nurture my happiness, and since he has made me the happiest creature alive, it behoves you to try to love him as much as you possibly can.

His real name will mean nothing to you, for you have never known it, so I shall begin by telling you that I am soon to be Mrs Starch. Yes, he is the same Starch who refused to dance with me when we were first introduced, the same Starch who persuaded Jane's Wet Lettuce to leave, and the same Starch who proposed to me so abominably earlier this year. But these recollections have now been mentioned for the very last time and are to be entirely forgot. Henceforth, you are to know him as Mr Fitzwilliam Darcy (and Wet Lettuce as Mr Charles Bingley). I shall attempt an explanation and hope that I am as convincing in my praise of him as I was in my censure.

For reasons that are no longer of any significance, my aunt and uncle Gardiner and I did not go to the Lakes this summer. We travelled only as far as Derbyshire. We may blame disappointment for my not writing to you with news of the change at the time, and I have not told you since because Lydia's misadventure overtook everything. But here it is. We travelled to Lambton, in Derbyshire, which I later found out was little more than five miles from Mr Darcy's estate, Pemberley.

(I believe I told you that he owned an estate, but I admit, I may have stinted on the details of its size and eminence. I ought to tell you, then, that it is one of the largest and oldest estates in the north of England. When I complained that Charlotte had defended his pride, this was what she meant. It suited me to omit the fact that he is one of the most illustrious men in the country. I preferred you to hate him.)

My aunt Gardiner wished to visit Pemberley. I was considerably less keen, as you might imagine, and was in agonies until we learnt from a maid that the family was not at home. Well, Aunt, we went, the maid was proved wrong, and some of the most mortifying moments of my life ensued. By the end of it, however, Mr Darcy and I were reacquainted—and by the end of another week, we were a good way to coming to an understanding. Be not disappointed by this apparently rapid resolution—I have lived up to Lydia's precedent to some degree and found a goodly number of opponents to my chosen suitor. Miss Bingley, Lydia, Peacock, Mr Darcy's housekeeper, even the rock upon which his house is built all threw obstacles in our path, but we have, at last, prevailed!

You will want me to account for how my feelings have undergone such a material change, I suppose. I never told you the contents of the letter Mr Darcy gave me in Kent, and I shall not now, for it was written in the strictest confidence, but you are aware, I know, that it had already worked to soften my opinion of him. I was further astonished in Derbyshire by the alteration in his character. The conceited gentleman who ignored me in Netherfield's library had been replaced with the gentlest, most generous man I have ever met. I anticipate that you will warn me it is but a temporary change, but I do not believe that is so. He has altered in the way he behaves towards me, that is certain, but I think only because he has learnt to comprehend me better—and if that alone is not a reason to love him then I do not know what is—but I do not consider that he is altered in essentials. Rather, I have come to better comprehend him.

The stateliness that I once derided as aloofness is better described as a deliberate self-containment that allows proper consideration and good sense to reign over imprudence. The pride I disdained so violently does not arise from a desire to be revered, but rather a sincere regard for everything and everyone connected to his family and estate. I could go on—I could tell you of all the care he took to demonstrate that he did not resent the past, and all the ways he tried to show he still loved me, after so many months and such a hurtful rejection—but suffice to say that I was as wrong as it is possible for one person to be about another. I needed only to see him properly; after that, I would have struggled not to love him.

If you are still not convinced, then perhaps knowing that he has bought Peacock a new commission and settled an extra thousand pounds on Lydia to help mitigate the very worst of their marital woes will improve your opinion of him. This he conspired to do with my uncle Gardiner in secret, lest I mistake his intentions and be made uneasy. Only once we were engaged did he admit his involvement. Now tell me you do not think him the very best of men.

My father has given us his consent. You will not be surprised to discover that he made the process as tiresome as possible for his own amusement. Several untimely recollections of my past sentiments and an unhelpful insinuation as to Mr Darcy's amiability seemed to gratify him almost as much as the knowledge that my future felicity was secured, but at least he saved his sport for me and did not trouble Mr Darcy with it. My mother was far more restrained if you can believe it. She was too shocked to say anything to me when I first told her, and she is too much in awe of her new son to speak to him. I live in constant dread of the shock wearing off and her finding her voice again.

Jane is delighted for me, but I perceive a growing melancholy in her. Mr Bingley has been all but forgotten by everyone else, but she still admires him, and my engagement has rather emphasised his more dilatory approach. I have tried to assure her it is only that Mr Darcy and I benefited from our time together in Derbyshire, but in truth, I cannot fathom Mr Bingley's purpose in coming to Longbourn so often if it is not to advance his cause. I hope he makes his mind up soon. Until he does, I am attempting to contain my joy, for it would be cruel to boast of it when Jane's is undecided. But since my joy is likely visible from the moon, it is difficult to conceal, and I hope you will not mind that I have boasted of it so shamelessly in this letter.

It goes without saying that I cannot accept your invitation to visit. I hope, however, that you and Mr Wallis will come to visit us at Pemberley as soon as it can be arranged—though not before you have decided that you approve of Mr Darcy. I cannot permit you to make him suffer any more than I have already.

On the subject of Pemberley, I have need of your counsel. Mr Darcy finds himself in want of a new housekeeper and wishes for me, as the new mistress, to appoint one. I know not where to begin! My grandmother appointed Mrs Hill before my father was married; thus, my mother has no advice on the subject—perhaps a blessing in disguise. I asked Hill directly; she said I should choose someone with good eyes and a strong back, but where I ought to find such a redoubtable specimen, she did not venture to say. I have written to both my aunt Gardiner and Charlotte for their suggestions, and now I beg the same of you. Any information you can provide, from what sort of woman I ought to employ to where I ought to find her would be most gratefully received. My dearest wishes to you and Mr Wallis.

Yours, in the most sublime contentment of spirits,

Dot

CHAPTER THIRTY-THREE

BRAVE FACES

Elizabeth turned at the sound of hooves and experienced a flutter of excitement to see Darcy approaching along the lane. She could not quite get used to the feeling, but at the same time rather hoped she never would, for it would be a sad day that she was not gladdened by the sight of her husband. It made her happier still to see her own pleasure mirrored in his countenance as he dismounted and walked his horse towards her.

"I was on my way to Longbourn to see you."

"Then this is an even more fortunate meeting. I should have been sorry to miss you."

"I would have waited for you."

He was looking at her in a way that made her acutely aware of his closeness and their seclusion. They had seen each other every day since he proposed, but never alone. There had been no opportunity, therefore, to repeat the wonderful intimacy they had enjoyed last Saturday, though that had not prevented Elizabeth reflecting on it, and not less than incessantly. Ending up in his arms had felt more than natural; it had felt necessary. She abruptly found herself wishing, somewhat wildly, that he would kiss her again.

He did not disappoint her. His attentions were less urgent than on Saturday, when he had kissed her with all the passion of a man who had been too long without hope. This caress was so tender as to be reverential, and yet somehow more rousing for it. She felt quite literally giddy from the sensations raging through her and the reckless pace at which her heart was beating. She kept her eyes closed for a moment or two afterwards, but when she did open them, Darcy was staring at her exactly as he had used to in the early days of their acquaintance. She smiled brightly to comprehend at last what had occupied his thoughts in those moments.

"I have missed you," he said, his voice gruff.

"You saw me last night."

He nodded and offered her his arm. With his horse walking obediently on his other side, they set out together for Longbourn.

"Have you been anywhere interesting?" he enquired.

"Not particularly. I accompanied Kitty to Lucas Lodge to see Maria Lucas. And before that, we were in Meryton, where I posted a letter to my aunt Wallis. I have told her our news."

"Is this the same aunt you said would not approve of me?"

Elizabeth winced contritely. "It is, but you must not blame her. I promise, she will love you almost as dearly as I do once she reads the four sides I have written in your praise."

"Do not distress yourself. If it pleases you that she should like me, then I shall make every effort to be agreeable to her, but otherwise, I care for no one's opinion but yours."

As though offended that his opinion should not be held

in equal esteem, Darcy's horse abruptly ceased walking and shook its head restlessly. It was a huge beast and looked liable to rear out of control at any moment, yet Darcy seemed wholly unperturbed and only clicked his tongue and urged it to walk on. Elizabeth let go of her held breath and did the same.

"Are you frightened of horses?" he asked her. "I can ride on and come back for you on foot if you would prefer."

"No—he is just a particularly large horse."

"I suppose he is, but I should look ridiculous riding a pony."

She laughed at the unexpectedness of Darcy's joke as much as the idea of his long legs trailing on the ground behind his mount. "I have a talent of making myself look ridiculous on most horses. It is why I prefer to walk. Jane is the natural horsewoman in the family."

"Is that why she chose to ride to Netherfield the day she fell ill?"

"That was my mother's idea. She knew Mr Bingley was dining with the officers and thought the rain would force Jane to stay at Netherfield until he returned so he could send her home in his carriage. She did not intend for her to get caught in the storm, and she only did it because she knew Jane was forming an attachment to Mr Bingley and had found so few opportunities of seeing him. It was well-intentioned, but poor Jane was mortified. I am almost afraid to ask what you must all have thought of us."

"It was a fairly transparent ruse, but I came to appreciate it more the longer you were there."

"I thought you despised me."

"I was trying exceedingly hard not to fall in love with you —and failing. It was prodigiously distracting. It is little wonder I was such poor company."

"Poor, beleaguered man."

He smiled and gently squeezed her hand with his arm.

"Can I ask, did Mr Bingley enjoy Jane's society as well as you enjoyed mine?"

"He saw less of her than I saw of you, but he was certainly concerned for her well-being—and pleased when she was recovered enough to come downstairs."

"Does he like spending time with her now, do you think?"

"So I understand," he replied cautiously, and Elizabeth did not miss his wary glance.

"Then why—" She stopped herself and tried to frame a less impetuous question. "Forgive me if this is an imposition, but as you yourself are aware, my sister has been ill-used in all of this. Pray tell me—if you can—is Mr Bingley seriously pursuing her? Because if he is not, it would be better that he ceased calling."

"I am uncomfortable speaking for him, but I do know that he is unsure of your sister's regard. She is not giving him much encouragement."

"He is giving her none."

"He is not unaware of how your sister has been hurt. It is only an abundance of respect that induces him to be so cautious. He is here, though, and came without any guarantee of being welcome. You gave him no hint of what your sister's feelings were when we were in Derbyshire."

Elizabeth grimaced in acknowledgement of that. "I dared not, after seeing him with all your friends. He was…more at ease than I have seen him before. I feared he might be attached to someone else. Miss Templeton, perhaps."

"Miss Templeton is engaged to Pettigrew."

"Really? I did not know that."

"That is, they were not engaged at Pemberley, but it did happen not long afterwards. What made you think Bingley had intentions towards her?"

"Well, to be frank, he was more of a flirt than Lydia."

Darcy smirked at that. "He has an exuberant, happy manner, but he is entirely honourable. If it helps, I will vouch for his good conduct."

"It would help *more* if you could let him know that Jane is pleased—very pleased—that he is come back."

He began to shake his head. "I have had my fill of interference, from both sides of the coin—" He stopped speaking and gave a resigned chuckle when Elizabeth fixed him with the same pleading expression she used on her sisters whenever she wished to borrow one of their prized possessions. "Very well," he said in a low voice and with a small but exceedingly affecting smile. "I shall talk to him. For you."

They arrived at Longbourn, and Elizabeth waited while Darcy tethered his horse himself, for the groom was nowhere to be found. When he emerged from the stables, he was grown altogether more serious. "Elizabeth, before we go in…"

Her stomach contracted. "What is it?"

"I had some letters of my own today. From my sister, her companion, my steward, my butler—all saying the same thing. Things are not going well at Pemberley. I am needed at home."

Elizabeth felt more than a little foolish that this news should give her such distress. She did not doubt Darcy's affections in any way. Nor did she expect that his return to Pemberley would prevent, or even significantly delay their marriage. Nevertheless, it was only with a determined effort that she was able to conceal the full extent of her dismay. She forced herself to smile sympathetically. "I understand. When must you leave?"

"As soon as I can—but I shall return as soon as possible. And then we shall make all the arrangements for the wedding, so this does not happen again."

"I should like that. Is there anything I can help with? Oh, pray, forget I asked that—stupid question. If it requires you to be there, *I* shall hardly be able to solve it from here."

He took both her hands in his and shook his head. "It was not a stupid question, and I appreciate you asking, but I cannot explain what problem Ferguson is having with the architect because I can make neither head nor tail of his attempts to explain it. With regards to the household, the head housemaid has been standing in for Mrs Reynolds, but she is, in the words of my esteemed butler, less than useless. Ferguson's wife has been attempting to assist her, but it sounds as though the two have had some manner of dispute. More than one of our regular suppliers has not been paid. And my sister lacks the confidence required to impose her will on any of them."

"Oh, Fitzwilliam, you must not wait for me to appoint a new housekeeper. I beg you would choose someone while you are at Pemberley. It makes no sense to let everything fall apart simply so that I might have the prestige of choosing her when I arrive."

"It makes complete sense," he said with some sharpness. "I will not be duped again by someone unworthy of the post. I would give you all the time you need to select somebody you trust to do her duty to Pemberley. Besides, Ferguson has already applied to the registry for applicants, and will forward the best for you to peruse."

His allusion to Mrs Reynolds was unmistakable, and for the second time, Elizabeth noticed the strain in his voice when he spoke about her. It reminded her of his claim to being 'the angriest he had ever been' when Mrs Reynolds confessed her betrayal to him. She began to suspect that he had been more hurt than angry, but she kept the thought to herself. She kept to herself, also, that she did not know to what 'registry' Mr Ferguson had applied, thinking it best to seek that information elsewhere.

"If that is your wish, then of course that is what we shall do," she assured him. "In the meantime, I assume you have a housekeeper at your London house. Might she be able to help?"

"Mrs Fairlight? Ferguson has already asked if she would be interested in the post. She said not. She has family in London."

"Why not ask her if she would be willing to step in temporarily, until we find a permanent replacement?"

He brightened a little and acknowledged it was worth a try. "You see?" he said, pulling her with him towards the house. "You are a natural."

Mrs Bennet was more vocal in her lamentations over Darcy's precipitate departure than Elizabeth had been, but Darcy bore it with commendable patience, remaining at Longbourn for cup after cup of tea. Elizabeth herself continued to be sensible about his departure, determined to show no hint of irrationality, though she would have drunk tea until she dissolved if it meant he could stay longer.

"I shall be wretched until you return," she whispered to him when it eventually came time for him to leave.

To her surprise, he broke into a broad smile. "I thought I was alone in my misery."

"You are never going to be alone in your misery again. Although I shall endeavour to make sure we share more happy times than sad ones."

That banished his smile and replaced it with the same look as that with which he had greeted her in the lane, earlier. She grinned at him and dared to kiss his cheek as she whispered that she loved him in his ear.

"You are resolved to make it as difficult as possible for me to leave, I see?"

"Only easier to return."

He kissed her hand, mounted his horse, and was gone in a trice, and Elizabeth did not mind his haste one bit, for she, too, felt that if he had not gone then, she might not have been able to let him go at all.

CHAPTER THIRTY-FOUR

A DISGRACEFUL ALLIANCE

One of Darcy's horses threw a shoe as the carriage rolled out of Netherfield's drive the next morning. Bingley offered the use of one of his bays, but none were well-matched with the other three, and Darcy could hardly empty his friend's entire stable. Much to the surprise of his coachman and manservant—both of whom were more used to his intolerance for any delay to well-laid plans—Darcy quite happily instructed them to send for the farrier and set out himself for Longbourn.

He had thought his mind would be less consumed, his spirits less agitated once he secured Elizabeth's hand. How wrong he had been! With all the shackles of awkwardness disposed of, they talked with an ease, an intimacy, that Darcy had never known with another person. It made him want to tell her everything about himself, ask her everything about herself, and discuss and debate everything in between.

Elizabeth was by turns sportive, compassionate, insightful, and challenging. Rarely was he not either diverted or intrigued by something she had said or the way she had said it, and he would swear to having laughed more this past week than in the whole of the past year. She had fairly ruined him for anyone else's company, but as if longing for her society were not distracting enough, he longed for a good deal more besides. She grew more beautiful to him by the day. She wore her happiness like jewels; her eyes sparkled with it and her countenance glowed. The pleasure of kissing her was beyond anything he had anticipated but had only inflamed his desire, occupying more of his thoughts than he would ever admit.

With his head so full of her, the prospect of leaving to attend to the mountain of problems that awaited him at home was less than appealing. He had dreamt up all manner of schemes that might enable Elizabeth to come to Pemberley with him, but there was nothing for it; he must go, and she must stay. Nevertheless, the opportunity for one last visit was an unexpected boon of which he had no objection to taking advantage.

His complacency vanished entirely upon arriving at Longbourn, for there, at the front of the house, was parked a chaise and four. The horses were post, but the equipage and the livery of the servant milling about next to it were unmistakably Lady Catherine's. Anger instantly drew every sinew in his body taut. His aunt had evidently learnt about his engagement. She would not bestir herself to travel so far, or condescend to call on such a family, for anything less important to her. Just as there was no possibility that she had come with any purpose other than to wield all her considerable consequence in opposition to it.

"Mr Darcy!" Mrs Bennet exclaimed when he was shown into the parlour. "We thought you were gone to Derbyshire today." Only she and Kitty were present, which made Darcy even more uneasy.

"There was a delay. Pray, am I right in thinking my aunt is here?"

"Yes! And how honoured we are that she is come! I am sure her ladyship will be pleased not to have missed you after all. She and Lizzy are walking in the garden."

Darcy excused himself and stalked from the house at a pace, his displeasure increasing with every step. Lady Catherine must have known she would have no influence on him, but it was unconscionable that she had come instead to hound Elizabeth.

He heard their voices as he neared the copse to which Mrs Bennet had directed him. His aunt's tone was angry, snarling almost. Elizabeth was discernibly vexed, also, but her accent was more collected. It did not surprise Darcy in the least, for her disposition was such that she was not easily intimidated, but he nevertheless respected her for it prodigiously.

Lady Catherine's words were the first to become clearly audible, and not just because he was so close; she had raised her voice. "Let me be rightly understood. This match, to which you have the presumption to aspire, can never take place. No, never. Mr Darcy is engaged to my daughter. Now what have you to say?"

"That is untrue, madam, and you demean yourself by peddling the lie," he said as he arrived in the clearing.

Both women turned to him in surprise. Elizabeth looked profoundly relieved. Lady Catherine looked shocked, but she immediately affected an air of satisfaction.

"Darcy!"

He ignored her greeting. "I am in no way bound to Anne, by either inclination or honour. If she is under the impression that I mean to marry her then it is a misapprehension entirely of your own making. Now pray tell me under what pretext you think it is acceptable that you should be here, excoriating my future wife in her own home?"

His aunt gaped at him with an expression of horror. "Future wife? You mean to say that you *are* engaged to her?"

He refused to dignify her contempt with an answer and simply glared at her with disgust.

She tottered towards him, one hand outstretched as though to touch his face like some doting nursemaid. "Darcy, I do not know what has happened, whether you are ill, or have been tricked, but you do not need to do this. Come with me, and we shall find a way to—"

Darcy stepped around her and walked to stand next to Elizabeth. "What has *happened* is that I have been fortunate enough to win the affections of the finest woman of my acquaintance, and she has done me the honour of agreeing to marry me. There has been no trickery. I am not unwell. But I am *inexpressibly* tired of other people thinking they are entitled to determine whom I may and may not marry."

Lady Catherine drew herself up tall and sneered. "The finest woman of your acquaintance? Look around you. This is the sphere in which Miss Bennet grew up—this muddy little scratch of ground her father calls his. She is of no importance in the world, Darcy. Of inferior birth and wholly unallied to our family. And who is her mother? Who are her uncles and aunts? You cannot be ignorant of their condition."

"It is not Miss Bennet's aunt who is presently standing in that mud, shouting insults like a common street hawker. Are you lost to every feeling of propriety and delicacy, madam?"

"Have you forgotten what you owe to yourself and to all your family?" Lady Catherine retorted. "You cannot possibly expect me to believe that you would allow the upstart pretensions of a young woman without family, connexions, or fortune to prevent you from doing your duty to us all."

"Your nephew has devoted his entire life to Pemberley,"

Elizabeth said angrily. "And you would struggle to find a man more concerned for the well-being of his friends and family. Of all the things you would accuse him, let it not be a dereliction of duty."

Darcy glanced at her, powerful feelings of gratitude and affection momentarily distracting from the effrontery of his aunt's attack. Oh, to be on the receiving end of Elizabeth's fierce loyalty at last!

"You are determined to ruin him in the opinion of all his friends and make him the contempt of the world?" Lady Catherine demanded, turning her ire on Elizabeth. "You will be censured, slighted, and despised by everyone connected with him."

Darcy clenched his teeth, appalled by his aunt's insolence—shame deepened by the knowledge that, though she spoke with a malice he had never felt, her objections differed very little from those he had voiced the first time he proposed to Elizabeth.

"On the contrary," Elizabeth responded. "I have met a number of Mr Darcy's friends, and I am delighted to report that they had far too much sense to join your scorn."

"They cannot know of your youngest sister's infamous elopement, then!" her ladyship replied viciously. "Is such a girl to be my nephew's sister? Is the son of his late father's steward to be his brother? Are the shades of Pemberley to be thus polluted?"

[redacted] take your conceit!" Darcy shouted. "The way things are going, Pemberley's woods will be the only thing left standing to *cast* any shade. You will not prevent me from marrying the one woman I trust to remain loyal to me whether I can put a roof over her head or not."

He felt Elizabeth touch his arm and knew not whether she meant to placate him or embolden him, but he was too incensed to let it impede his tirade. "How dare you come here, attempting to interfere in my business, to frustrate my plans, to *break my engagement*! You have overreached, Lady Catherine, and it will not be forgot. I suggest you return to your carriage."

Doubt at last flickered over his aunt's countenance. She reddened darkly and heaved a few heavy breaths. Then she abruptly turned again to Elizabeth. "Your alliance will be a disgrace. Your name will never be mentioned by any of us." With a vitriolic sneer, she turned and walked away.

Darcy watched her go until she had exited the copse then exhaled forcefully. "Elizabeth, please accept my apologies, that was inexcusable. I had no idea she was coming."

"No, of course not. I never thought you did." Her voice was distant, and she seemed stunned.

Darcy knew not what else to say. Lady Catherine had insulted Elizabeth in every possible method, but he could not tell from her expression what she thought of it. He hoped to God she was not forming a resolution to break with him.

"Well!" she declared abruptly. "I feel better about my aunt Wallis disliking you now." Then she laughed—only a soft, slightly bemused laugh, but still a pure, unaffected sound that released the iron band of dread around Darcy's chest.

With a vast sigh of relief, he pulled her into a fierce embrace. "My God, you have no idea how much I love you." She returned his embrace equally tightly but said nothing more.

He leant back slightly so he could see her face. "You are very quiet."

"I am a bit taken aback, I do not mind admitting, but you need not concern yourself. It will pass."

It was not a convincing answer and made Darcy want to get on his knees and beg her not to change her mind.

"What are you doing here, anyway?" she asked softly. "I thought you meant to leave this morning."

"One of my horses needed to be reshod, and I could not resist seeing you again while it was done." He checked his watch and cursed silently at the time. "I must go soon, though. We shall be lucky to make it as far as Baldock before dark as it is."

She nodded. "Yes, of course."

Blast it, she was so subdued! "I do not want to leave you now. Not like this, not after—"

"It is well, Fitzwilliam, I promise."

Darcy had no choice but to take Elizabeth at her word, for he really did have to go. He sent his compliments to her family rather than be held up by going indoors and returned to Netherfield in a far darker humour than that in which he had left. Would that Elizabeth's tender farewell the previous day could have been the memory he carried with him all the way to Derbyshire, rather than her brave face as she pretended his aunt's vicious attack had not deeply mortified her. Damn his aunt! Damn her and every other woman he had thought loyal to him but who was intent on sabotaging his happiness.

"Damn them *both* to hell and back."

CHAPTER THIRTY-FIVE

A MORE URGENT AFFECTION

It was strange, to go from the heights of ecstasy—with clandestine, passionate embraces, long walks, intimate discussions, and a stream of congratulatory dinners and visits—to an existence that was all but indistinguishable from her life a year ago, before Mr Bingley let Netherfield Park. Elizabeth's days were her own again; she came and went as she pleased, largely unnoticed by the rest of her family. One morning earlier in the week, Elizabeth had awoken with tears on her cheeks, having dreamt that the past year had itself been nothing but a dream. When Darcy's first letter arrived, its pages filled with expressions of his esteem, she crumpled it, quite by accident, by clutching it to her breast in happiness.

The letter was not all tenderness and sentiment, however, and the news it contained far from all good. It was with a heavy heart that Elizabeth read of the many problems Darcy had discovered upon his return—though she was gratified that he took the trouble to explain them in such detail. It proved his good opinion of her understanding, and his understanding of her growing affection for Pemberley.

The issue with the building, it seemed, was the worrying discovery of what might be sinkholes somewhere much deeper beneath the foundations. The rubble being used to underpin the wall had itself become unstable, and consequently, further excavations had been instructed. Recalling the look on his face when he told her about the first few cracks, she hardly dared imagine what he must be feeling to see such damage wrought to his home.

He was less explicit about the issues arising in the servants' ranks, which Elizabeth suspected was due to it involving some of the younger housemaids and being therefore a uniquely feminine problem. Neither the butler nor the steward had been able to resolve it either, presumably for the same reason, and Elizabeth shared Darcy's relief that Mrs Fairlight would be at Pemberley in a fortnight to assist.

She would not like what she found when she arrived if things were half as bad as Darcy described in his letter.

Bills have gone unpaid, wage books have not been balanced, and some stores are running low. I can live with my fires not being set properly, my bed not being made, and my clothes being held hostage in the laundry. What I cannot abide is watching Pemberley's reputation being squandered because Mrs Reynolds had not the decency to work her notice.

The housekeeper's departure had seriously distressed his sister, also, it seemed.

Who can blame Georgiana for being hurt and confused that a previously loyal servant, whom she has known all her life, should have left without any farewell, and whilst she was present in the house?

Elizabeth wondered whether Darcy was aware that almost half of his letter was taken up with grievances against Mrs Reynolds. His anger was evident not only in what he wrote but in the deep gouges his pen had scratched in the paper beneath each word. It was obvious to her, if not to him, that he was deeply wounded by her desertion. It surprised her, even with her new knowledge of him, that he should be thus affected by the actions of a servant. She strongly suspected it would surprise him more, thus she stored the information away and hoped it would never need to be re-examined.

"Did you hear what I said, Lizzy?"

Elizabeth looked up from the path and grimaced apologetically at Kitty. "Sorry, I was miles away."

"I said Lydia has asked me to write to her again. But I only wrote last week when you got engaged, and I do not have anything new to tell her. I think she is bored."

"Things will improve for her when she makes some new friends."

"*You* have had a lot of letters lately."

"Yes, everybody has been very generous with their congratulations. Although, most of the letters were in reply to those I sent out, asking for advice about housekeepers."

"Did you get any?"

"I did, and more than I was expecting, for none of the people I asked have one of their own. Charlotte could tell me only that the housekeeper at Rosings Park is one-and-thirty, and that is apparently young for the position—but I was pleased for the information, for if the Dread Lady Catherine approves of a younger housekeeper, who am I to argue?"

Kitty agreed, wide-eyed, having been fully apprised of and horrified by Elizabeth's exchange with her ladyship.

"Aunt Gardiner explained about servant registries, where people looking for work can apparently list their credentials for employers to view. But then my aunt Wallis warned me in her letter not to use a registry."

"What does Mrs Wallis know about housekeepers? She cannot have one. 'Tis only her and Mr Wallis in the house."

"True, but she has servants. And according to her, nobody who needs to advertise themselves at a registry is good enough for Pemberley." Affecting a silly imitation of her godmother's voice, she added, "Only recommendation will do, apparently."

Kitty screwed up her face in doubt. "I know she likes to know things, Lizzy, and I grant you, she may have hired a servant or two in her four hundred years, or however long she has been alive. But she cannot possibly claim to know anything about Mr Darcy's estate."

"I did not think so either, until she reminded me that she grew up in Castleton, which is near enough to Pemberley for her to have heard something of its size and reputation."

"That hardly makes her an expert."

"She did not claim to be an expert. She only advised me that such an establishment must have a queue of women wanting the position of housekeeper, and that I ought to take no one who had not worked at a senior level in a house of a similar size before. She listed seven other large country houses in the area that might have maids interested in advancing their positions—three of which I am to ignore any application from, for risk of giving offence to the mistress of a house of greater consequence than Pemberley." With a grin, she added, "Servants from the other four are apparently mine to poach."

"Are you supposed to just knock on the door and ask the lady of the house to hand them over?"

"I do not know," Elizabeth replied, laughing. "She seemed to think *they* would apply to *me*, but I shall not know whether that is true until I am there." Elizabeth was rather hoping

Mrs Fairlight would recommend someone and that would be the problem solved.

Kitty regarded her with a mixture of fear and pity. "I am glad it is you doing this, and not me. It sounds altogether too exhausting."

Elizabeth did not bother to tell her that this constituted less than half of Mrs Wallis's advice. There was also a warning against taking recommendations from either the butler, the steward, or her future husband, for 'it could not be sensible to allow a man to choose who ought to do a woman's work'. A list of essential skills had been provided, from numeracy, jam making, and distilling, to appearance, judiciousness, and discretion. She had even given guidance on what could be considered an acceptable range for a housekeeper's salary. Had Elizabeth been the sort of person who succumbed to spells of self-doubt, she might have wished Mrs Wallis had not written such a daunting list of considerations. As it was, she was exceedingly thankful for it.

"My aunt has been of infinite use. All I need her to do now is agree to like my husband as well as she seems to like my house."

"Aunt Philips is a much easier godmother to me than your Mrs Wallis is to you. The only advice she tries to give me is about the length of my sleeves. And *she* approves of Mr Darcy very much."

"Does she?" Elizabeth said brightly.

"Why yes! She and I agree that he is much handsomer than Mr Bingley, although much scarier, too."

"You think Mr Darcy is scary?"

"Well, you know—he is so tall, and stern, and he does not say very much. 'Tis unnerving."

Elizabeth smirked. 'Unnerving' was not the word she would use to describe Darcy's formidable presence, though it often left her breathless for other reasons. "You could learn from his example, Kitty. If you talked a little less, people might pay more attention when you did speak, then they might decide that you had something interesting to say."

Kitty scoffed at the notion and then, with a surprisingly knowing look, which emphasised her likeness to Jane, asked, "Do you love him?"

"Yes, I do. Very much."

"And it does not worry you that his aunt is so horrible?"

"It does not give me one moment's concern. Besides, it was rather wonderful to hear him defend me in the way he did."

"Aye, from what you told us, it sounded awfully romantic. Has he kissed you yet?"

Her sister obviously expected that this would shock her, and it did, thoroughly, but only because she was wholly unprepared for it to make her cry.

Kitty was all confusion. "La! Lizzy, I was only teasing!"

"I know, ignore me, I am being silly." She pressed the heel of her palm to her eyes to soak up her tears with her gloves. "I just miss him."

"Thank goodness! I thought I had said something wrong. It is very unlike you to cry."

Elizabeth shrugged. "I miss him a great deal."

After a slight pause, Kitty said, "I hope I love whomever I marry as much as you love Mr Darcy."

"Oh, so do I, Kitty. I wish it for all my sisters."

Though her wish was too late to help Lydia, it seemed to work wonders for Jane, for when they arrived home, it was to the news that Mr Bingley had proposed. Celebrations flowed warmly and sincerely between the sisters. It was wonderful to see Jane at peace at last. The little frown that had marred her handsome features of late was gone, her countenance returned to its natural serenity now that all her doubt was banished. Mr Bingley, too, was the picture of contentment.

He beamed at Elizabeth when she took his hands and wished him all the joy in the world.

"I am sure to have it now, for not only shall I be blessed with the loveliest wife, but the best brother and sister, too." He leant towards her slightly and said under his breath, "You and Darcy have been invaluable in your services to my happiness. I thank you for your words of encouragement and beg you would pass on my gratitude when you next write to him."

Elizabeth assured him she would, and though she spent the rest of the day agreeing with her mother and sisters' praise of all Bingley's finest qualities, her private thoughts were dedicated entirely to Darcy. That he had kept his word about speaking to Bingley when he had so much else on his mind showed a generosity of spirit that suffused her with pride and made her feel his absence ever more keenly.

Bingley's sisters arrived in Hertfordshire less than forty-eight hours later. Jane thought it a fine compliment that her future relations should come so soon to express their joy. Elizabeth was not fooled into thinking they had come for any other purpose than to judge whether they could yet persuade their brother to change his mind. It rendered her barely civil when they called at Longbourn.

"I hear congratulations are in order for you as well, Miss Eliza," Miss Bingley said. "How amazed we all were to hear of your engagement, after you left Derbyshire without even a farewell."

"Thank you."

"But now it is Mr Darcy's turn to abandon you. How sad that he had to leave you so soon after you came to an understanding."

Elizabeth gave no reply at all this time, but Miss Bingley would not be put off.

"Be assured, I know him to be honourable. Let me advise you, therefore, that you must not let it upset you that some people will question his commitment."

"Very well, I shall not."

Miss Bingley pursed her lips. "Although, nobody could blame you for being unsure of his regard. I should be most put out if my betrothed prioritised a house over me."

How glad Elizabeth was that Miss Bingley had never succeeded in inveigling herself into Darcy's affections, then! It would have been tragic indeed had he ended up with a wife who understood so little what Pemberley meant to him. *She* understood, and Darcy's letter proved that he knew it. It made her value more his insistence on her choosing the new housekeeper, for she supposed it was his way of asking her to share Pemberley's custodianship. Comprehending that only made her wish to be there more, instead of here at Longbourn, listening to Miss Bingley's snide remarks and Mrs Bennet and Mrs Hurst's debate on wedding dates.

"It cannot be before Michaelmas," Mrs Hurst said in a vexed tone.

"Why not?" replied Mrs Bennet indignantly.

"Because that is next week!"

"Well? They can marry by licence."

"I do not think there is any harm in waiting for the banns to be read," said Miss Bingley. "There is no particular rush in this case, is there?"

Bingley took up Jane's hand, smiling at her warmly. "I am not going anywhere, and I have nowhere I should rather be."

"October then," Mrs Bennet said impatiently.

"It cannot be October," Mrs Hurst replied. "Mr Hurst and I will be in Northampton for most of next month."

"Oh, well, November is a nice month for a wedding," Mrs Bennet persisted. "Not too cold, not too close to Christmas."

"Close to Christmas would be ever so romantic," Kitty opined. "Especially if it snowed."

Elizabeth could not fathom the serenity with which Jane was watching everybody talk her wedding into next year. She leant to whisper to her quietly. "You ought to say something if you wish to be married before you are old and grey."

"I have no objection to fitting in with everyone else's plans, Lizzy. There is no rush."

Elizabeth straightened once more in her seat. No rush? What were they waiting for? Did they hope to stumble across a more passionate attachment while they ambled their way towards the altar? This gentle, unhurried affection bore no resemblance whatever to the ardent feelings that raged like a permanent storm in her heart. Whether born of their particularly arduous passage to understanding or an extraordinary, natural affinity, her feelings for Darcy were more profoundly urgent than any sentiment she had experienced before, or any she could perceive in those around her. She needed him —just as he needed her at Pemberley with him.

She excused herself, claiming a headache, and set herself up in private with a pen and ink. Without thinking too much about what she would write, she addressed it to Darcy and then allowed her feelings for him, already overflowing, to spill onto the page. First, an admission of her struggle to be reasonable when he said he must go home—that she had not wished to add a teary-eyed lady to his troubles, but that she had been one sob away from begging him not to go. Next, a confession to not being troubled in the least by his aunt's absurd visit, only by the difficulty of pretending for the second time that her heart was not breaking to say goodbye. Then, that she could not think why she had ever let him leave without her. That she wished he would come back for her, take her home with him to Pemberley, put an end to both their suffering, and make her his wife. She dared not read it back to herself, lest that stole the courage required to send it. She sealed it and begged her father to send it express, having entirely run out of patience for anything slower.

CHAPTER THIRTY-SIX

CERTAIN FELICITY

Darcy waited at the window in Netherfield's saloon, too focused to concentrate on any of the chatter behind him. Bingley made a remark about his poor company, but he only smiled vaguely. Miss Bingley said something teasing, and he ignored it entirely, for a carriage had pulled through the gates, and he was already halfway out of the door.

He met Elizabeth's eye through the carriage window and could barely constrain the exultation that threatened to spread itself stupidly all over his face. With impatience he hoped did not show, he handed Jane down and offered his congratulations on her engagement. Then he took Elizabeth's hand and without a word, but with a look that he trusted she understood perfectly, pulled her away from the house, towards the formal gardens.

He took her as far out of view as his endurance allowed, which was probably not as far as propriety would have preferred, then tugged her hand to bring them face to face. He almost crowed at the eagerness with which she welcomed him. Need drove him forward, walking her backwards several steps before her ardour caught up, and she pressed herself with equal force against him. Her passion was exhilarating, her soft warmth beneath his hands, intoxicating. This was his life now—this woman, this passion, this unfettered joy! This was why he had raced back at her beck and call, for what man would not gladly submit to this ecstasy?

"You did not mind that I wrote, then?" she whispered.

"It was the finest letter any man, past or present, has ever received. I have been out of my senses since I read it." He kissed her again, briefly, but with considerably less reserve, to demonstrate it. "Are you sure you are ready to leave Longbourn, though? I would not like you to regret the haste."

"More than ready."

He inhaled deeply, relieved to hear her confirm that which doubt had whispered might be but the impetuous outpourings of frustration. "That is fortunate, for I brought some things with me that would have been entirely wasted had you changed your mind."

"What things?"

"Come. I shall show you."

Elizabeth's delight upon finding Georgiana and Fitzwilliam in the saloon was gratifying indeed. Darcy did not expect that she would comprehend the significance of Linseagh's coming too, but he was grateful for both his cousins'—and, by extension, Lord and Lady Matlock's—choosing to stand by him in the face of Lady Catherine's opposition. Darcy introduced them and stepped back slightly to allow them to become acquainted.

"Nice of you to join us," said Bingley wryly, appearing at Darcy's side.

"We had something to settle in private before we spoke to anybody else," he replied quietly.

"And pray, what was so important it could not wait?"

"What else?" Fitzwilliam interposed, sidling up to join them. "That thing pressing a hole in his pocket, of course."

Bingley made a choking sound. Darcy levelled a baleful glare at his cousin, but Fitzwilliam only grinned devilishly and tapped Darcy's jacket, causing the folded paper in his inside breast pocket to rustle.

"You might as well tell him, Darcy. He must be wondering why you have dragged us all here with you."

"I am, rather," Bingley agreed. "Not that you are not all most welcome."

Darcy did not have time to prevent Fitzwilliam from blurting, "We have come for the wedding."

The rest of the room quieted, all eyes turned on them in surprise—except Elizabeth's, which shone with happiness.

"The wedding?" Bingley replied, his smile become somewhat fixed. "How long are you planning to stay?"

"I do not know. What say you, Darcy—a day or two?"

"A *day* or two? What—"

"Keep up, Bingley! That is what's in his pocket. A marriage licence."

Darcy moved closer to Elizabeth and said quietly, "That is the other thing I brought with me."

"You are going to marry by licence?" Bingley asked. He looked unduly perturbed. "When?"

"Hopefully, within the week."

"Upon my word, that *is* soon. Jane and I had a November wedding in mind."

Darcy knew not why this should be relevant. He understood better when Elizabeth addressed her sister, who looked even more disturbed than Bingley.

"You will not mind too much, will you, Jane? It would have been wonderful to stand up together, but Darcy is needed at Pemberley. He cannot keep travelling between here and there to see me. It makes much more sense for me to be there with him. We shall come back for your wedding."

"Of course," Jane replied with no conviction at all, and frowning at her sister in a manner that suggested she had more than a few qualms.

"It was very good of you to come all this way for the sake of just a few days, Miss Darcy," Miss Bingley said.

"I would not have missed my brother's wedding for the world." There was a hint of rebuke in Georgiana's answer that banished the sneer from Miss Bingley's face, for which Darcy silently congratulated her.

His sister's delight when he told her of his engagement had been deeply touching. She had perceived his recent sadness, it seemed, and was overjoyed to see him happy at last—and with Elizabeth in particular, who was apparently, 'by far and away the nicest of all the ladies she had thought might one day be her sister.' He had not asked who else she had considered to be a contender, but if Miss Bingley was one, she need not have been worried.

"Besides," Fitzwilliam said, "it will not be a few days for us, will it, Georgiana? Darcy and Miss Elizabeth might be scooting back up to Pemberley, but we three are off to London for a spell. Thought we might take in a few plays, perhaps enjoy a few exhibitions. Whatever takes our fancy while the happy couple enjoy some well-deserved time alone."

Elizabeth squeezed Darcy's arm. "That is excessively kind of everyone," she whispered when he bent closer, "but your sister should not have to leave her home on my account."

"It is only for a week or so."

"Even so, it is not necessary."

"Yes, it is. Unless you wish to share the journey home with her."

He was diverted to see the blush that danced briefly

across her cheeks once she took his meaning, and not a little encouraged when she made no further argument and walked, with a coy smile, to speak to Georgiana.

Miss Bingley stepped immediately into her place. "Charles tells me Mrs Reynolds has left your employment, Mr Darcy. I hope it had nothing to do with her dislike of Miss Eliza."

Darcy fixed her with an incredulous glare. "Excuse me?"

"Caroline, desist at once!" Bingley hissed.

"No, I insist. What is your meaning, madam?" Darcy made no effort to constrain his displeasure, and Miss Bingley floundered in the face of it.

"Only that my maid mentioned Miss Eliza seemed to be in disfavour with your housekeeper while we were there last month. But I…I know nothing more than that. Forgive me, I ought not to have mentioned it."

"No," he said darkly, and turned his back on her. He could hear Bingley admonishing her in hushed tones behind him, but he found he was less angry with Miss Bingley than he was with Mrs Reynolds. That the woman had plotted against him was bad enough. That she had spoken openly against Elizabeth amongst the other servants, exposing her to God knew what rancour and dissent in her new home, was entirely another. Not that it would be tolerated. He would sooner dismiss the entire household and start from scratch before he subjected Elizabeth to any unpleasantness of that sort.

"Is something the matter?" Linseagh enquired quietly.

"I have just been reminded of what awaits me at Pemberley."

His cousin cast a quick, quizzical look in Elizabeth's direction. "I must say, I think what awaits you at Pemberley now is a darned sight pleasanter than that scowl implies."

Fitzwilliam grinned. "Careful, Brother. He will have you out on the lawn at sunrise if you say much more."

Their teasing ran long, but since it mostly consisted of praise for Elizabeth, Darcy gave no complaint and instead allowed it to rally him back into good humour.

A delightful hour was passed before Elizabeth and her sister were required to return home. Darcy rode alongside their carriage to Longbourn, where he and Elizabeth petitioned Mr Bennet together. Notwithstanding that they had his permission to wed, prudence demanded that, after Lydia's misadventure, he be allowed to sanction the licence. It was more a courtesy than a true entreaty, but it would place a necessary distinction between Darcy's conduct and Wickham's.

Mr Bennet turned out not to be the problem; it was his wife who threw up all manner of obstacles to their plan. Elizabeth privately expressed her vexation at it until it became clear her mother's resistance was born more of affection than obstinacy, how far away she would be at Pemberley becoming an oft-repeated lament. When there were no objections left, Mrs Bennet appealed to Darcy directly to take care of 'her sweetest Lizzy'. He gave his word. It was the easiest promise he had ever made.

The only other objection came, surprisingly, from Bingley.

"Are you quite certain Lizzy is happy with all this haste, Darcy?" he asked after dinner the next day. The ladies had withdrawn, but not before Miss Bingley and Mrs Hurst had bored the whole table with talk of the many obligations and invitations they felt must be honoured before their brother could even contemplate saying his vows.

"Are *you* sure Miss Bennet is happy with all this delay?" Fitzwilliam replied. "Anyone would think your sisters are attempting to defer your nuptials for so long you forget you said you would marry her in the first place."

"Oh, they probably are," Bingley replied. "They are never content with whatever makes me happy. But a November wedding suits Jane and me well. So I must ask you again, Darcy, are you sure Lizzy is not feeling rushed? Apparently, you are not even granting her the comfort of your house in town on your wedding night."

"That would rather defeat the object of marrying in haste so that we might return to Pemberley."

"I suppose, but would one night make that much difference?"

"My London housekeeper is presently en route to Pemberley. We deemed it more sensible not to open the house again." He sipped his drink and tried not to be provoked by his friend's prying. "Are there any other of my plans for which you would like me to account?"

Bingley winced contritely. "Her sister is concerned that she has agreed to all this only to please you."

Darcy could not help but smile. "You may tell Jane not to concern herself. Marrying quickly was Elizabeth's idea."

After a brief pause of obvious surprise, Bingley chuckled lightly. "In that case, I propose a toast to your certain felicity, my friend."

Darcy accepted the toast, as he accepted a swathe of others over the next few days, both before and on the day of his wedding, though he was not truly interested in anyone's approbation by then. He wanted only to take Elizabeth home, and even the blessedly short time he had to wait to do it was too long for his liking.

It was on a crisp, sunny morning in early October that Darcy and Elizabeth drove away from Meryton as husband and wife.

For a good while after the carriage passed out of view of their friends and family, Darcy simply held Elizabeth. She had removed her bonnet and nestled against him beneath the travel blanket without a word. He marvelled at the way she had fitted herself against him, her form sinuously aligned with his and not a stitch of daylight between them. She had hooked her foot over his shin to hold herself in situ. It was artlessly done, and effective, but achingly arousing. Her hair smelled of perfumed soap, and he treasured this new freedom to cleave her to him for long enough to heed it. He savoured the easy familiarity that existed between them—a stark and exquisite contrast to the awkwardness that had marred so much of their acquaintance. He pressed a kiss to the top of her head and said a silent prayer of thanks.

She took a deep breath and let it out slowly.

"You are not too sad to be leaving, I hope," he said softly.

"I am not sad at all. I shall miss Jane dearly, but I am so happy, it will be an age before I notice."

"I cannot tell you how well I like to hear you say you are happy."

"Are you?"

"Happy does not do justice to what I feel. I thought this day would never come."

"As did I—it seemed to take forever."

"And yet Bingley asked me whether you felt rushed into marrying."

"Jane asked me the same."

Elizabeth was toying with the buttons on his waistcoat. Innocently, he knew. Still.

"She does not know that you wrote to me?"

She glanced up at him, revealing a heightened colour to her countenance. "No."

"Or that you were impatient for me to make you my wife?"

She neither answered nor looked up this time. Her hand had stilled and now rested, flat, on his stomach.

He slid his hand over hers, caressing her wrist with his thumb. "There are more ways to interpret what you wrote than just an exchange of vows."

She moved slightly—a shrug, or a nod, or some other vague acknowledgement that was not a denial, and which made Darcy altogether too hot for the blanket.

"Did you mean…*that*?"

"I do not know," she said in a hushed voice that was barely audible over the thundering of the carriage's wheels. "I did not *not* mean it. I do want to be with you at Pemberley. But I suppose I…"

"Yes?"

"Well, I…I want to be with *you*."

He exhaled heavily, and brought his hand to cradle her face, tilting it until she was looking at him. "God, not as much as I want to be with you."

Her eyes flashed, and she cocked her head by the smallest degree as though bestowing a challenge, and that was Darcy's undoing. Thereafter, the inside of his carriage became the stage for the fiery, transcendent prelude to the denouement that followed that night, and the next, so that by the time they reached Pemberley, Elizabeth was his wife in every conceivable way.

CHAPTER THIRTY-SEVEN

BELOVED IMPERFECTION

'Mrs Darcy' had an elegant ring to it that Elizabeth liked very well, and she would be forever proud to be known as the wife of such an honourable and generous man. Nevertheless, she was not sure she would ever grow accustomed to the effect her new name seemed to have on other people. No one had ever flushed in fright, bobbed absurdly deep obeisance, or scrambled to do her bidding at the mention of Elizabeth *Bennet*. She could not think how to prevent it, for all attempts to dismiss such behaviour as unnecessary had drawn only further grovelling apology from those doing it.

She wondered how the servants at Pemberley would treat her. Not a thing would get done if everyone was resolved to start bowing and scraping each time she walked into a room. She was somewhat worried that Darcy expected them to do just that, but she was hopeful it was a whim that would pass once he was assured of her contentment. After all, it was for him, not the servants, to treat her like a princess—a job which, to her vast pleasure, he was performing commendably.

The past few days had been wholly unlike anything Elizabeth had anticipated. Pleasures she had never known existed, intimacies she could never have supposed, human frailties for which she had been wholly unprepared, had all been discovered with the loving guidance of a man who treated her as though she were the most precious gift he had ever been given. She ended the journey to Pemberley more in love with Darcy than she had understood was possible.

Occasionally, she forgot. Every so often, in the midst of buttering a muffin, or lacing a boot, or looking at a clock, a recollection would pop into her head of this or that nuptial revelation, and she would grow hot and lose her train of thought. More often than not, Darcy would guess what had crossed her mind and worsen her plight by smiling at her in that particular way he had that seemed to melt every bone in her body. It was outrageously unfair. As the carriage neared Pemberley, she began to imagine herself catching his eye halfway through her introduction to the servants and being reduced to a blushing, mumbling bottlehead. That idea was promptly usurped by the even sillier notion that none of the servants would notice anyway, for they would all be too occupied with preposterously exaggerated genuflections to look at her.

"What amuses you?" Darcy enquired.

"I was just imagining all the ways in which my reception could go awry."

It was the wrong thing to say; his countenance clouded. "Any servant who does not treat you with the respect you deserve will be dismissed. You have my word—you will not have to tolerate insolence of any sort."

"That was not my meaning. I was thinking of all the ways I might embarrass *myself*."

"I do not employ servants so they may judge my behaviour, or that of my wife."

Elizabeth did not press the point, for he was evidently determined to misunderstand. She comprehended why: Mrs Reynolds's disloyalty had left an ever-lengthening shadow. She asked him, instead, to remind her of everyone's names and was relieved to see the storm clear from his eyes somewhat as he obliged her.

They arrived late in the afternoon, and Elizabeth was touched that despite the gathering gloom, several servants had congregated at the front of the house to greet them. They looked respectable and orderly, precisely as she recalled. Matthis, the butler, introduced the first and second footmen, both of whom Elizabeth recognised, three housemaids, whom she did not, and explained that the other servants would be presented at whatever time was convenient to her.

"Where is Mrs Fairlight?" Darcy enquired.

Matthis cleared his throat in a disgruntled manner. "Unwell, sir. She arrived yesterday with a fever and...other disagreeable symptoms. I have ordered her to remain abed until she is recovered, for I would not have contagion running rampant throughout the house."

Darcy gave no response but to scowl.

"Please tell her I hope she feels well soon," Elizabeth said. "It cannot be pleasant to be ill in unfamiliar surroundings."

Matthis thanked her, informed them that dinner would be in an hour, and dispatched the footmen to begin unloading the trunks. Darcy led Elizabeth inside. He was still scowling.

"I hope you are not planning to dismiss Mrs Fairlight for not clambering out of her sickbed to welcome me."

Darcy looked at her sharply but relaxed upon meeting her gaze. He was, she was pleased to observe, learning admirably quickly to be laughed at.

"I should have preferred that she was not indisposed, but not as much as she, I am sure. Should you like to rest before dinner?"

"Unless you would prefer to rest, I should like to see some more of the house while there is still a bit of daylight left."

Darcy agreed readily and directed her to a room beyond the stair hall, which he informed her was known as the Derwent room. "A few of the portraits from the gallery are being stored in here while the underpinning is done. I can show you my mother and fa—" He stopped speaking when the action of opening the door caused something beyond it to bang, scrape, and then smash loudly. He muttered something that sounded divertingly ill-tempered and used his shoulder to force the door more widely open. "What in blazes?"

Elizabeth followed him into what little space there was left in the room. She could not see the perimeter, but it was clearly a large space, and it was full to bursting with stack upon stack of crates. One had been toppled off its pile and was wedged, upside down, between two other stacks, its contents—what looked to have been a vase and a large quantity of books—emptied onto the floor.

Darcy closed his eyes briefly, then stepped back to the open door and called loudly for somebody to attend them. Behind him, Elizabeth quietly bent to rescue those books that had fallen with their pages open, stacking them carefully on the floor, then picked up the pieces of broken vase.

"This room was not being used for storage when I left less than a fortnight ago. Pray explain why it is now full of the contents of my library," Darcy said severely.

Elizabeth stood up; the footman James had arrived.

"Mice got to the crates where they were before, sir. Mr Ferguson wanted them put somewhere secure until alternative storage could be arranged. We had to use the Chesterfield and Hadrian rooms, too."

"*Both?*" He sighed. "So be it. Where are the portraits that were in here?"

"Still here, sir. At the far end of the room."

Elizabeth stepped forward and handed the footman her collection of broken porcelain. "Would you see whether this can be rescued?"

He took it with a rather bemused expression and darted away. Darcy began to apologise, but Elizabeth dismissed it with a wave of her hand and edged along the nearest wall in the direction James had pointed. "This is why we are here. We knew everything was going wrong. If it were not, we would still be in Meryton, suffering the most drawn-out courtship in history with Jane and Bingley. I should much rather be here, clambering over boxes to meet your mother, than at Longbourn, listening to mine eulogise about which warehouses are best for wedding clothes. Oh! I have found your father!"

She could not see Darcy anymore, and therefore could not tell what caused the delay before he replied, but when he did, all trace of vexation was gone from his voice, and that made her smile.

"How do you know it is my father?"

"Because if it were not for the wig, I would have thought it was you."

"Elizabeth, he was forty-two when that was painted. I am not yet thirty."

"That is something for me to look forward to, then."

After another pause, Darcy said, "If you are quite finished, I would show you our rooms now."

Something in his voice made Elizabeth's stomach flutter. She sidled back out from behind the crates towards the door. As she passed in front of Darcy, he rested his hand on her back to guide her towards the stairs. She wondered whether he knew what effect the slightest touch of his hand had upon her. Then she wondered what the touch of hers did to him. Then she became aware that she had, once again, succumbed to indelicate reveries and forced herself to stop thinking about either of their hands and pay attention to the house.

She had not been to the upper floors since Mrs Reynolds showed her around, and she could recall almost nothing of what she had seen that day. There were too many pictures, ornaments, and chandeliers to take in at once, but the overall impression was of elegance and taste, and she felt again the sense of Pemberley being a comfortable home, despite its grandeur.

Her room, when Darcy showed her into it, was somewhat less cosy—the fire was not lit, and there was a distinct chill in the air. She said nothing of it, but she could tell Darcy was displeased. He rang the bell and stood in brooding silence while she explored the space. Eventually, his summons was answered by one of the maids who had been outside before.

"Hannah, why has Mrs Darcy's fire not been lit?"

"Begging your pardon, Mr Darcy, none of the bedroom fires have been lit. We've run out of coal."

Elizabeth bit the insides of her cheeks to prevent herself from laughing, Hannah's expression of terror and Darcy's palpable disbelief persuading her this was not the time.

"*Run out of coal?*" Darcy repeated incredulously.

"Yes, sir."

"Do you comprehend the absurdity of that statement? This is a coal-producing estate. You must be mistaken."

"I wish I was, sir. But it were Mrs Reynolds who used to arrange for the coal to be brought in when it were running low, and no one who's been taking it from the stores thought to tell anyone else when it got low, 'cos they all assumed it'd just turn up like it usually does. Only then it din't, and this morning, there were none left. We've had to take all the coal from the bedrooms to heat the dining and drawing rooms, for we thought you'd rather be warm while you was eating."

"Matthis said nothing of this to me just now."

"I don't know as Mr Matthis knows, sir. I've sent word to Mr Gabion, and he's coming first thing wi' more. I'm sorry, sir. Truly."

"If Matthis does not know, then I can only assume it is because *he* still has coal in his grate."

Hannah reddened and looked at the floor. "I don't know, sir. I din't think to look for any in there. We're not allowed in the men's rooms."

"So, you took it from your new mistress's room instead?"

"A-and yours, sir. I would've brought up some logs, but they won't burn proper in a coal grate."

"I am aware of that," Darcy snapped. "Find some coal from somewhere and light this fire this instant."

Hannah hastened away to see to it. Elizabeth waited only for the door to click closed behind her before she let out the laughter she had been holding in throughout the interview.

"How is this remotely amusing?" Darcy exclaimed.

"Because having enough coal to heat her cottage is what I lectured Lydia about before she left Longbourn. And now we do not have any in the whole of this enormous house."

"That makes it less amusing, not more."

"Poor Hannah, she did what she thought was best. And I own, I should rather a cold bed than a cold dinner." She looped her arm around Darcy's and placed a hand on his chest. "I promise to keep you warm."

He raised an eyebrow but had not the time to act upon whatever thought had occurred to him before two other maids burst in carrying one of Elizabeth's trunks between them. They dropped it in fright when they espied their master and mistress embracing in front of them. Preempting Darcy's certain anger, Elizabeth asked him to leave her to change. She enlisted the maids' help in refreshing herself after her travels and readying for dinner, satisfying herself in the process that, friendly though they were, neither they nor Hannah were contenders for the role of housekeeper.

Dinner might as well have been cold for all that she enjoyed it, but she was resolved to reveal no hint of her dissatisfaction to Darcy. The food aside, she relished sharing a meal with him at his table. He fitted into his surroundings as well as he did his clothes, as though Pemberley had been tailored to suit him. They conversed unceasingly, laughed often, and several times startled the servants with the liveliness of their discussion. It was all going swimmingly, in fact, until Darcy had an unfortunate recollection.

"You do not like ragout," he said, looking up from her still half-full plate. "I recall you talking to Hurst about it at Netherfield."

Elizabeth gave him a crooked smile and shook her head. "But it does not matter. It is perfectly wholesome. I shall not go hungry."

"It does matter. This is your first meal here as mistress, and I did not even think to notify Chef of your preferences. I shall have him send something different up."

"You will do no such thing!" Turning to the servants, Elizabeth said, "And you will not repeat a word of this to Monsieur Dubois if you have any compassion. Indeed, I beg you would give him my regards and tell him I enjoyed the meal very well. I will not offend the poor man on my first day here."

Matthis assured her of their secrecy. "There is a blancmange for dessert, Mrs Darcy. Would that be to your taste?"

Her heart sank. She cast a rather desperate glance at Darcy, who took her meaning directly. "Pray tell Chef neither of us are overly hungry this evening and to save dessert for another day."

"Very good, sir. Should you like some coffee in the drawing room?"

Elizabeth agreed that she would and stood to go through together with Darcy, wishing the evening had not soured so quickly. "I assure you I am not particular—I will eat most things. It is just rotten luck that those are two of my least favourite dishes. I hope I have not offended you."

"Not at all. *I* am sorry that it was not a more enjoyable meal."

"It was enjoyable! Just not the food part."

He smiled vaguely but did not seem much cheered.

"I *have* offended you."

"Are we to argue on our first evening at home, Mrs Darcy?"

"No. Not if you admit what is upsetting you."

Darcy tucked a curl behind her ear and stroked her cheek. "I have waited a long time to bring you to Pemberley as my wife. Yet the servants are indisposed, half the house is packed into crates, the other half is freezing cold, and you have eaten three slices of potato and a carrot for your dinner. Not even you can convince me this is a perfect beginning."

"You are forgetting all my previous visits, which, if you include being framed as an interloper by your guests, reprimanded by your butler, and shut out in the rain by your housekeeper, serve as an invaluable contrast." She reached for his hands, entwining her fingers with his. "Whereas this time, I am here with you. You have made me your wife, and I have never felt as though I belonged anywhere as much as I do here. In my humble opinion, that makes it perfect."

Elizabeth wished she had known sooner in their acquaintance that when Darcy stared at her as piercingly as he was at present, it was a good thing. It would have saved a significant number of misunderstandings and afforded her a great deal more pleasure.

"Have I mentioned how dearly I love you?" he asked.

"Not for at least an hour. You are slipping."

They forewent the coffee in favour of giving Darcy the opportunity to catch up with his endearments and Elizabeth the chance to prove that she could, indeed, keep Darcy more than adequately warm.

CHAPTER THIRTY-EIGHT

AN UNEXPECTED ALLY

Darcy glanced at Elizabeth, hunched pitiably at his side. "You look frozen."

She regarded him sheepishly. "I did not realise how much colder it would be with the wind blowing in our faces."

He did not point out that he had warned her, though he did not attempt to hide his smirk. "Should you like to turn back?"

"Is there any point? We must be at least halfway by now. It would surely be as quick to keep going."

"The park is ten miles around. We have gone about two and a half."

She grimaced. "Maybe, then. Would you be terribly cross?"

Darcy tugged gently on the reins, for this was a better place to turn the curricle than any other for the next mile. As to being angry with his wife—the very notion was ridiculous. It seemed as though everything that could go awry at Pemberley was doing so, and were it not for her, he was sure he would presently be in the bleakest of spirits, but despondency was impossible in Elizabeth's company. It mattered not what calamity beset them, she never failed to find some way of solving, or evading, or laughing at it. She was simply not formed for ill humour.

It was at her insistence that they had ventured out to drive around the park this morning. He did not doubt that she wished to see it, but neither did he doubt she would have preferred a warm, sunny day for the excursion to this blustery autumn morning. She had done it, he knew, to get him away from the house, where it had been discovered that the mouse that prompted the Derwent room to be repurposed as a warehouse had come *with* the crates and subsequently chewed a hole in the portrait of his great grandmother, and the task of unpacking every crate to check for more mice was under way. Elizabeth had been entirely right: a blast of fresh air and the pleasure of her radiant, windswept complexion had done wonders for his equanimity.

Once the horses had walked the curricle a full one-hundred-and-eighty degrees, he pulled them to a halt. Holding the reins in one hand, he slid his other around the back of Elizabeth's neck to cradle her head and kissed her soundly. "There is nothing you could do or say that would make me cross with you."

It was true, although a few minutes after they set off again, he regretted arming her with the information.

"I have had a letter from my aunt Wallis," she said in altogether too airy a tone. "She made a suggestion, which I dismissed as silly at first, but after a bit more thought, I have begun to see its merit. She thinks I ought to seek a rapprochement with Lady Catherine."

"No." He was not joking, though he supposed it was a

good thing that Elizabeth was diverted rather than offended by his brevity.

"I have not told you why yet," she objected, laughing.

"It does not matter why. Her behaviour to both of us has been unpardonable."

"I shall not argue that she has been difficult, but—"

"*Difficult?*"

She grinned. "It is a word with a broad gamut of meaning —but that is not the point. My aunt thinks that Lady Catherine would be the ideal person to help me find a replacement for Mrs Reynolds."

Darcy clenched his teeth and said nothing. A discussion of *both* of the most objectionable women of his acquaintance would rapidly leach his enjoyment of the outing.

"And I need to find someone soon," Elizabeth pressed. "For Mrs Fairlight is not happy."

"Why not?"

"I do not believe the work suits her. Pemberley is a much larger house than she is used to, and I get the impression the extra responsibility does not sit well with her. And she is worried about her relations in London. Unless we wish to find ourselves short of two housekeepers, we shall have to make haste and find a replacement."

"I have every faith you will find one."

"The trouble is, Mrs Reynolds is proving to be exceptionally hard to replace. The more I discover about her work here, the more insufficient all the other applicants seem."

Darcy concentrated on driving, staring hard at the ground ahead.

"When I spoke to her in Hertfordshire, Mrs Annesley told me that your sister's contributions to the running of the house have been minimal until very recently."

"She is only sixteen."

"Of course. I do not mean it as a slight. But I understand, too—from Mrs Fairlight, and Mrs Ferguson, and generally everybody I speak to—that Georgiana, and you, and your father before you, have all benefited from having somebody to perform those tasks that would ordinarily have fallen to the mistress of the house. What I am trying to say is, that, since your mother's death, Mrs Reynolds has fairly run the household by herself."

"Perhaps, but Pemberley *has* a mistress now, therefore the need for another 'Mrs Reynolds' has been eliminated. You may find someone with different talents."

"I appreciate your faith in me more than you can possibly know, but I have not been the mistress of *any* house before, let alone one this size. It will take time for me to learn all that I need to know, and I need a competent woman to manage it with me." After a brief pause, which Darcy could not deny worked to good effect, she added, "I think my aunt Wallis has a good point. Lady Catherine seems an obvious person to ask for help. Unless Lady Matlock could be of assistance?"

"Dear Lord, no! Lady Matlock is a kind woman, but she is not somebody to whom I would direct anyone for counsel. I would not speak ill of her but...you will see what I mean." They were travelling to Lord and Lady Matlock's home the following week to introduce Elizabeth and collect Georgiana, whom his cousins planned to return there after their sojourn in London. He had no idea what to expect from the visit, but he doubted Branxcombe Court could be any less enjoyable than Pemberley at present.

"I presume she has a housekeeper, though," Elizabeth said. "She must have found her from somewhere."

Darcy sighed with chagrin and admitted, "I believe Lady Catherine chose for her."

It was Elizabeth's turn to say 'I told you so' with only a smirk.

"That does not mean I am in any way reconciled to the abuse she directed at you," he insisted.

"I would not expect you to be. But, unless you are explicitly forbidding it, I should like to write to her."

Darcy almost wished he could be cross, but it was impossible when Elizabeth was so clearly right. "Very well. Only do not hold your breath. I doubt she will condescend to help us."

Elizabeth broke into a smile. "Nonsense. Lady Catherine loves to be of use. And I fully anticipate that she will take advantage of the opportunity to call attention to all my deficiencies, by which method I shall be able to return the favour. Everybody will be happy, except maybe you, but I can make up for that by other means."

She kissed him on the cheek and changed the subject, and Darcy supposed that if he must be so thoroughly worked on, it might as well be by a woman who made him nigh on giddy with happiness.

They arrived home to find they had received an invitation to dine with Connelly and his cousin that Thursday. It pleased Darcy that Elizabeth not only recalled them but was also clearly delighted by the invitation.

"Miss Reid and I got on famously at your picnic," she said as they walked towards the saloon. "I did think at the time that she would make a delightful neighbour, but I scarcely dared hope it would ever come true."

"I spent the whole of that day wondering how I would ever convince you to come and live here. Had I known Miss Reid was the key, I should have introduced you both a lot sooner."

The way she gently bumped into him to dismiss his nonsense whilst letting him know she enjoyed it with an indulgent smile was enchanting.

"It is fortunate they have not dropped the acquaintance

altogether," he added. "I have been ignoring their invitations to dine at Delamont since you left in the summer. I could not face going without you."

Elizabeth opened her mouth to reply but sucked in her breath and stepped backwards instead when a mouse scurried across her foot. She did not scream, as her uncle had at the river rat, though she did yelp in surprise when one of the hall boys dashed after it, obliging her to jump from his path to avoid being hit by the broom he was wielding with intent. Then, of course, she dissolved into peals of laughter.

"For crying out loud, look where you are going!" Darcy shouted after him. "Elizabeth, I am sorry."

"You really must cease apologising. I am used to chaos. Longbourn is always like this. Aunt Wallis calls it Bedlam."

"Your aunt Wallis seems an eminently sensible woman."

"She has decided you are the best man in the world, so she must be."

"What has brought on that change of heart?"

"Probably my endless letters telling her so. And now I have another letter to write, to *your* aunt, if you will excuse me."

She began to walk away, and Darcy came to a decision. "Elizabeth. Let me know when you have finished. I shall send a letter with yours."

It took him a moment to recognise the emotion that suffused her countenance, softening her eyes and bringing her lips together in a tender, contented smile. When he comprehended that it was pride, it pleased him so well that he did not even cavil when there came a panicked shrieking and a loud crash from beyond the nearest door.

CHAPTER THIRTY-NINE

INFLUENCE & AUTHORITY

Lady Catherine's need to prove herself an authority on all matters did, in the end, outweigh her disdain for her new niece. In little more than a week, Mrs Lovell, formerly of Chisholm Park in Buxton, was installed as housekeeper at Pemberley. Chisholm Park was one of the houses from which Mrs Wallis had warned Elizabeth to disregard applications. Yet, it was also the place where Jennifer Lovell had been employed for three unhappy years, wasting what appeared from her testimony to be a wealth of potential.

Lady Catherine had proved invaluable in securing her services. Elizabeth knew not what Darcy's aunt had written in her letter, but on receipt of it, the mistress of Chisholm Park had sent Mrs Lovell to Pemberley with expressions of delight that her protégé had gone forth into the world to better it. It was yet to be confirmed whether this intervention from her ladyship signalled a thawing of her resentment—no direct communication had been received from Rosings Park

—but to Elizabeth's mind, it could only be a good sign that her plea for assistance had not been entirely ignored.

Mrs Lovell was in her mid-forties and a delightful mix of youthful energy and seasoned competence. Rather than command that people do her bidding, she steamed through the house with great enthusiasm, acting as though everybody already was, and with a few exceptions, all the servants fell into line in her wake. Most of the maids appeared to be relieved by the return of some direction to their work. Some were less content.

The previous head housemaid, Hannah, had done her best to manage things over the last few weeks, with extremely limited success. The mishap with the coal had been the final straw before she left to find easier work. Martha had been promoted to head housemaid. Edna remained the stillroom maid—something by which she apparently felt vastly aggrieved.

"She thinks she was better suited to head housemaid," Mrs Lovell reported. "More than once, she has remarked about knowing better than Martha the way Mrs Reynolds used to do things. I hope she will settle down with time, but I wanted to make you aware, so it does not come as a surprise should a problem occur."

"Thank you, and please continue to keep me informed. Is this matter with the house books one of the things troubling her?"

The management of the household accounts was the reason Elizabeth had met with Mrs Lovell this morning. Darcy had warned her before she arrived at Pemberley that they were in disarray. He blamed this solely on Mrs Reynolds's precipitous departure, but after some meticulous investigation, Mrs Lovell had determined that her predecessor left matters in a far better state than was first thought.

It seemed Mrs Reynolds had, in fact, annotated the house books in minute detail before she went, giving clear indications of what was owed, and by whom. The true problem, in Mrs Lovell's opinion, was that Mrs Reynolds's system of payment was one that had been a quarter of a century in the making. She had different agreements with almost every supplier, some recorded as being paid upon delivery, others as infrequently as once a year. In her absence, the other servants had been obliged to guess what arrangements were in place to ensure the smooth running of the household did not falter. The consequence was endless confusion, with some bills and labourers not being paid at all, several being paid twice, and the cash in the house safe being over one hundred pounds short.

"And your preferred solution is to pay everything and everyone quarterly?"

"Yes, ma'am. It will make it much easier to oversee. And keeping in mind what you have said about finding economies to offset the cost of the building work, I know I can find savings if I can only get a better understanding of what money is going where."

"That is well, but some of these immediate payments will have been made this quickly because the recipients could not afford to wait. Will you draw up a list of everyone who has received prompt disbursement and continue to pay them in the same manner until you can confirm from your own observations that it is not necessary?"

The housekeeper agreed, and thus they continued, Elizabeth making all manner of suggestions, from how to mollify those suppliers most affected by the mismanaged payments, to the best method of assuaging the pride of Pemberley's senior male servants, who had been put out by the alteration to the status quo.

"I suggest you ask Matthis, Ferguson, and Chef to name their most trusted suppliers. Tell them you will see what you can do to make special arrangements with those people. I see no reason why everybody else should not be paid according to your new method."

"Thank you, Mrs Darcy, I shall do as you say—and happily, for if I may say so without sounding impertinent, this is wise counsel indeed."

Elizabeth agreed; it all sounded exceedingly wise. Regrettably, not a word of it was her wisdom to claim. Every suggestion that passed her lips had come from her aunt Wallis. Having found herself writing almost daily to one or other of her friends or relations with reports of her latest travails, it was Elizabeth's godmother whose replies had consistently proved the most insightful, every letter bringing shrewd suggestions of what she might try, always couched in affectionate assurances of her ability to implement them.

She was not inclined to admit any of this to Mrs Lovell, perfectly content to let the woman continue under the impression that she had been employed by the most intelligent twenty-year-old in the country until such time as Mrs Wallis ran out of advice, and the mistress of Pemberley was exposed as a fraud.

"I had better return to the main house. Mr Darcy will be wondering what has become of me."

Mrs Lovell held the door open for her. "Might I ask how you are finding Miss Garrett?"

"I like her very well. Thank you for recommending her," Elizabeth replied, leading them along the passageway. "My hair certainly approves. I am lucky I have any left after having it yanked about by Sarah these past weeks. I hope she is happier than Edna to be returned to her usual duties. A lady's maid is not her calling, poor girl—" She stopped talking and let out a little grunt when she rounded the corner and collided with an immovable object that turned out to be her husband.

"My apologies," Darcy said, looking quite alarmed until she assured him that she was unhurt, whereupon his expression changed from concerned to distinctly irritated. "I had not realised you were in this part of the house. What brings you here this time?"

"I needed to speak to Mrs Lovell."

"Again?"

"Yes." Elizabeth might have been vexed by Darcy's surliness had not she then noticed the architect and steward behind him, both looking equally grim-faced; she decided he had enough on his mind to justify a little ill humour. "On business less irksome than yours, I imagine." She stepped out of his way and with a serious nod, he went on.

"I apologise if I have yet to make a good impression on Mr Darcy," Mrs Lovell said quietly.

"He is only concerned about the house. We are both excessively pleased to have you at Pemberley." Elizabeth hoped it sounded more convincing to Mrs Lovell than it did to her own ears. In truth, she suspected Darcy was unimpressed with the new housekeeper. Unlike Mrs Lovell, however, she did not think it had the slightest thing to do with the woman herself, but rather the woman she was not. Whomever Mrs Reynolds's successor had been was doomed to be tarred with her traitorous brush, making it impossible for Darcy to approve of her—or, it would seem, any time his wife spent with her.

Elizabeth smiled as she passed through the service door into the main house. Perhaps Darcy had been right to be wary of dissent amongst the servants, but she had not anticipated that it would come from one who was no longer even in his employment. She was sorely tempted to haul Lady Anne's portrait from beneath the pile of crates in the Derwent room and hang it somewhere prominent in the hope that her ladyship would exert some of her former authority over the ever-pervading ghost of Mrs Reynolds.

CHAPTER FORTY

THE SOUND OF SILENCE

The journey to Branxcombe Court took three hours, and Darcy relished every second of it. With the building work behind them, his relations not yet upon them, and Elizabeth in his arms, it was like a small holiday in itself.

He could not entirely banish his woes from his mind. According to Jacobs's latest reckoning, the fault in the ground did, indeed, extend beyond the east wing. If one extrapolated its trajectory, it would pass beneath the morning room, saloon, and music room in the central section of the house, and the kitchen and stillroom in the west wing, putting them in equal danger. It was a dismal prospect that had instilled in him a persistent sense of dread. Their inspection of the servants' quarters had, thankfully, revealed nothing alarming, which was just as well, for if Darcy was forced to close off any more rooms, then he, Elizabeth, and all the servants would be living together in the dining-parlour by Christmas.

"What is the matter?" Elizabeth asked softly.

"What is always the matter? But let us not speak of that now. I would give you a few days' respite from thinking about buildings."

She nestled more snugly against him, and he noticed she did not attempt to deny the respite was necessary.

"Would that I could have taken you abroad on a honeymoon. Or at least to the Lakes. I was cripplingly jealous when you mentioned in Kent that you were going there with your aunt and uncle."

"And I thought you were quiet because you disapproved."

"I did. I disapproved of anyone who was not me, taking you anywhere."

Elizabeth was silent for a moment or two before abruptly rearranging herself with some impressively economical manoeuvres until she was sitting in his lap. Then she slid her arms around his neck, told him she treasured the way he loved her, and kissed him—with thrilling vigour. It was some time before Darcy recalled how near they were to Branxcombe and reluctantly disentangled himself, but it was not before he had made it abundantly clear that he was equally enamoured of the manner in which Elizabeth loved him.

"I shall take you to the Lakes one day."

"I should like to see them."

"And I should like the exceptionally long carriage ride to get there." He enjoyed the look that earnt him. It was only as he helped her down from the carriage in front of his uncle's house that he comprehended the complete respite Elizabeth had given *him* from all his worries, and he knew instantly it had been entirely deliberate. He whispered his thanks in her ear and cherished the knowing smile it induced.

The introduction to Lord and Lady Matlock went well enough. His uncle was his usual contemplative self, and Darcy quietly assured Elizabeth not to be offended if he seemed aloof. This amused her for some reason, though she did not elaborate as to why. Lady Matlock's diffidence made her equally quiet. Linseagh had not come at all, having been detained in London, but Fitzwilliam and Georgiana welcomed Elizabeth with unaffected delight, more than making up for any perceived reticence from other quarters.

"You are happy, then," Fitzwilliam said to him in a private moment that afternoon.

Darcy smiled slightly and nodded, but a glance at his beaming cousin cracked his usual reserve, and he could not hold back the bubble of joy that escaped him as a burst of laughter. "I am!"

"'Tis a fine thing to see. I confess there have been times this last year when I have been worried for you."

"Not as worried as I."

"And Elizabeth? Is she settling in at Pemberley?"

Darcy winced. "She is doing everything that could be asked of her and more, but Pemberley is in such blasted disarray. She says she is not troubled by it, but she cannot be content."

"She does not seem particularly *dis*contented."

"Because we are here, away from it all. It just feels so one-sided. I have gained all the pleasure and she has made all the sacrifice."

"That is not quite true. You sacrificed a large fortune to marry her."

"So I told myself once upon a time, but there was no guarantee I would have found a woman of good fortune who would have me."

"I shall have to respectfully disagree with you on that point."

"You cannot deny it would be even less likely now, for who would volunteer their inheritance that I might literally pour it into the ground to keep Pemberley standing? To think —I almost did not marry Elizabeth because my condition in life was superior to hers. Now she is living on a building site." He shook his head in disgust. "Master of one of the finest houses in the county, and all I have to offer is rooms full of boxes and an abyss in lieu of a garden."

"This might be a legitimate concern had you married almost any other woman of your acquaintance, but you and I both know, Elizabeth did not marry you for your house."

"I know. But I dislike that I cannot give her the things a wife of mine ought to have—parties, dinners, balls. A single day that is not interrupted by some new disaster."

Fitzwilliam chuckled and slapped him soundly on the shoulder. "I am sure you will have the chance soon enough. In the meantime, take it from a man who has known plenty of miserable women—your wife is the very opposite of downcast. I shall not insult you by asking how you put such a magnificent smile on her face, but whatever it was, I daresay if you keep doing it, all will be perfectly well."

Darcy had time to do no more than glare at this indelicacy before his cousin continued, "Speaking of the pleasures of marriage, Georgiana received a fair amount of interest while we were in town."

"From whom?"

"Mostly just pups, gazing longingly across the theatre, but there were some more notable names sniffing around. Londonderry, Prinsep, the youngest Duncan-Bryre. She did not seem to notice, but I thought I should mention it, for it will not be long before we must begin to consider an alliance. And after last summer, it may be prudent not to wait too long."

Darcy stared grimly at the carpet. Fitzwilliam and he shared the guardianship of Georgiana, but as her brother, the onus of ensuring her well-being weighed particularly heavily upon him.

"Yes, I share your enthusiasm for the matter," Fitzwilliam

went on. "Would you like to know what conclusion I have come to?"

"Go on."

"It is that this gives us both even more reason to rejoice in your connubial bliss, for surely Elizabeth will manage this business better than you or I could ever hope to."

Darcy brightened instantly. "That is a heartening thought. Just when I thought she could not bring me any more joy."

"I am beginning to see your point, though. It does seem an exceedingly one-sided arrangement, this marriage of yours."

The latter part of this exchange, which Darcy relayed to Elizabeth later that night as they sat together before the fire in their bedchamber, diverted her no end.

"This is rich! You despised my mother for her hopes of Jane marrying Bingley. Now you would have me do the same for Georgiana."

"I take it all back. Pray do not abandon me to the task. You have seen the extent of my romantic abilities. Do not condemn my sister to the same fate."

"That would be cruel indeed!" She nudged him affectionately, in her sweet way, and he tried to pull her closer but could scarcely get his arm around her.

"Why are you wrapped in so many blankets?" He tried to peel one back, but she fought him, laughing.

"Because I am cold—get off!"

He gave up and settled for letting her rest her head on his shoulder. He kissed her crown and asked, "What did you make of my aunt and uncle?"

"I see what you meant about Lady Matlock. She is very kind, but a little like a rabbit caught in lantern light. I was worried I would frighten her if I spoke above a whisper."

"As long as she *was* kind."

"She was certainly not *un*kind. I am not sure either of

them knows quite what to do with me. It is as though they want to approve but think they will be in trouble if they do." Elizabeth yawned deeply as she added, "Perhaps with Lady Catherine."

"Enough talk," Darcy said. He scooped Elizabeth up, blankets and all, and carried her to the bed. "You are going to sleep, Mrs Darcy."

Elizabeth made no objection, except when he unrolled her from the blankets, but she was easily placated when he wrapped her in his arms instead. He watched her for a long while after she fell asleep, feeling every bit of the happiness his cousin had observed in him, and praying that Elizabeth's would last beyond their return to Pemberley.

After breakfast the following day, he and Elizabeth walked with Fitzwilliam and Georgiana into Matlock Bath. On their return, Darcy left Elizabeth to enjoy a peaceful afternoon in the saloon with his aunt and sister while he spoke to his uncle. It was a conversation he was obliged to grit his teeth throughout, for Lord Matlock wished to advise him about matters at Pemberley. It was not that he did not appreciate his uncle's concern, but such counsel as 'do not trust architects, they are all imbeciles,' and 'do not be tempted to sell Pemberley at a reduced price,' were unhelpful, to say the least.

Dinner was a more enjoyable affair. Darcy was seated next to his aunt, an arrangement they always favoured, for both were content with the other's silence. He was surprised, therefore, when she leant to speak to him quietly.

"We are delighted for you, Darcy. It is about time you had some good fortune. Your marriage will surprise people, of course, and some will be immoveable in their contempt, but society in general is not as shallow as Lady Catherine believes. Nobody cares anymore that Mrs Prestbury was an actress before she married, do they? You never hear of anybody slighting Lady Aubrey, despite her uncle owning a string of abattoirs. It is the shock of the thing that will cause a stir. Once that dies down, and the world sees what a treasure you have in Elizabeth, it will all be forgot."

"You think Elizabeth is a treasure?" It filled Darcy with pride to hear her say it, though it seemed a hasty turnabout from the uncertainty Elizabeth claimed to have perceived in her the previous day.

"She is a charming creature. Quite lively, I will not deny, but that is a good thing in this modern world. We all need shaking up a bit, I think."

"Thank you. I welcome your support, though I confess, I am curious what Elizabeth has said to you that has made your mind up so decidedly."

"It is not what she has said to *me*, dear boy. It is the change she has wrought in *you*. Your uncle and I could never disapprove of anyone who made you this happy."

Perhaps understanding that he knew not how to respond, Lady Matlock chose that moment to indicate to Georgiana and Elizabeth that they ought to withdraw.

"Nay, I say we do not separate this evening," Fitzwilliam objected.

"You can say what you like, boy, I want my port," Lord Matlock replied stoutly.

"Bring it with you. My cousins are all off home tomorrow. Let us enjoy the evening together."

Lord Matlock grumbled a bit more but levered himself to his feet with his cane and limped out of the room, shaking his head as he went.

"Come, Mother," Fitzwilliam said, taking Lady Matlock's

arm. "Do not look so concerned. Father will survive the indignity."

Lady Matlock continued to fret but submitted to being led into the drawing room while she did so. The others followed behind.

"I cannot remember the last time I had such a pleasant day," Georgiana said to Darcy.

"How is that for gratitude?" Fitzwilliam said over his shoulder. "That is the last time I take you to London!"

"He is teasing," Darcy said quickly, knowing she would baulk otherwise. "It has been a most agreeable day. I suggest you make the most of it. Things are not quite so peaceful at Pemberley."

"Is it truly that bad?"

"Unfortunately, yes."

"But Lizzy has found a new housekeeper. She must be helping to settle the household, at least."

Darcy considered how to phrase his response.

"What is that face for?" Fitzwilliam enquired, dropping onto the sofa.

"He does not approve of my choice of housekeeper," Elizabeth answered, lowering herself more demurely to sit next to him.

"That is not true," Darcy objected. "But you do seem to spend an inordinate amount of time with her."

"She has only just begun."

"My mother never needed to spend as much time with Mrs Reynolds."

Fitzwilliam snorted. "How old were you when Mrs Reynolds began working at Pemberley—three? Four? What can you truly recall from that long ago beyond how your nursemaid conducted herself?"

"I was seven when she was made housekeeper. I recall plenty."

"Your mother might not have spent much time with Mrs Reynolds, but you certainly did."

Darcy looked at his uncle in surprise. Lord Matlock had not seemed to be paying attention to the conversation, occupied as he was with the footman pouring him a glass of port. The footman departed, and his lordship met Darcy's eye. "You were forever pestering her. For food, mostly, since you were too terrified of the cook to ask for it yourself."

"Lady Anne's cook *was* terrifying," Fitzwilliam said, feigning a shiver. "I do remember though, Darcy, you could always persuade Mrs Reynolds to give us biscuits."

"It was not biscuits that had you in the servants' quarters all the time," Lady Matlock interposed. "It was the kitten you rescued from the stables, which your mother forbade you from having in the house. Mrs Reynolds let you keep it in her sitting room until it recovered."

"Upon my word, I had forgotten all about Dung!" Fitzwilliam exclaimed.

"Dung?" Elizabeth said, laughing.

"Darcy called it that because it is what everybody thought it was—a little brown thing lying in the straw. It was only when it started mewling that anyone noticed it."

Darcy realised he was grinning. Then a more recent memory assailed him: the same woman who had let him look after a kitten in her sitting room when he was nine, scheming, twenty years later, to separate him forever from Elizabeth. It was a betrayal that was in no way compatible with happy reminiscences, and he wished everyone would stop talking about her. He turned to Georgiana and asked her if she would play for them. She did, as did Elizabeth and Lady Matlock, more than successfully salvaging his contentment.

It was raining heavily by the time they retired. While Elizabeth clambered into bed, stubbornly refusing to relinquish the blanket in which she had once again wrapped herself, he walked to the window. "Shall I open it so we can listen to the rain?"

"Do not dare! It is cold enough in here already."

He shrugged and removed his banyan. "It is not that cold."

"Well, I am!"

"I cannot stoke the fire much more without risking burning the house down." An alarming thought occurred to him as he climbed into bed, and he leant over Elizabeth, trying to make out her complexion in the gloom. "You are not ill, are you?"

"No, I am not ill. Your uncle's house is just freezing. What a relief we are going home tomorrow!"

That caught him by surprise. "Even with the state Pemberley is in? With all that noise?"

"I have quite missed the sound of people shovelling rubble. It is so quiet here. Your aunt and uncle have been exceptionally welcoming, but Branxcombe is...pardon me if I sound ungrateful, but it is a little staid. I have had a lovely time, but I miss Pemberley dreadfully."

"I was worried you had decided you hated it."

"How could anyone hate Pemberley?"

"At present? I could think of a few who might. It is not the house it once was."

"Fitzwilliam, I do not love it because it is a fine house. I love it because it is inviting, and comfortable—and *warm.* I love it because of what it means to you, and what you have made of it. I love it because it is yours."

Darcy ought to be used to the strength of his feelings for Elizabeth by now, but there were occasions when the power of his sentiments still took him by surprise. It was a moment before he was able to respond, and even then, he managed to say only, "Ours."

She understood. No more words were said, but they neither of them left the other in any doubt of their affection.

The journey home, which Darcy had worried would be fraught with the disinclination to return to chaos, was instead a happy blur of anticipation. Elizabeth and Georgiana chatted merrily about all they had done these past few weeks, and all that they planned to do together now they were reunited. Darcy listened contentedly and even dozed for a short while.

They might all have felt a greater measure of trepidation had they known what they were travelling towards. Matthis opened the door to them, and with a look that robbed Darcy of all his good cheer.

"What is it?"

"Lady Catherine is here, sir. She is waiting for you in the saloon."

CHAPTER FORTY-ONE

UNWELCOME HOUSEGUESTS

Elizabeth was sorely tempted to laugh but thought better of it. Darcy looked about as amused as a man just arrived at the gallows. This served her right for complaining that Branxcombe Court had been too quiet!

"Georgiana, perhaps you ought to let your brother and me deal with this. Why do not you run upstairs and change?"

Georgiana required no convincing and all but ran across the hall.

Darcy waited only until she reached the stairs before he began to rage. "Of all the insolent, presumptuous—Who in their right minds turns up uninvited to the house of a newly married couple in the midst of a major building restoration without sending word?"

"Lady Catherine did not invent the notion of unwelcome houseguests. She may claim the honour of being our first, but I doubt she will be our last. You may rest assured that the only reason my father has not yet shown his face is because he knows your library is packed away into crates."

Darcy was unmoved. "I shall tell her to leave."

"Let us at least find out why she has come. She did help me secure Mrs Lovell after all. She may be more tractable than she was in Hertfordshire."

She *did* laugh at the look Darcy gave her in response to that. He really was proficient at exuding disdain. "Come. We shall get nowhere standing about trying to guess at her purpose. Let us ask her why she is here."

Lady Catherine did not mince her words. "To judge for myself exactly how terrible a mistake my nephew has made."

"Might I suggest that you would have more time to make your assessment if you did not immediately provoke him into evicting you from the house?" Elizabeth replied with cool composure.

"You have lost none of your impertinence I see!"

"*Your ladyship* would speak of impertinence?" Darcy replied incredulously.

Elizabeth placed a hand on his arm and tried to disarm him with a look, but she could see straight away it had not worked. He continued to seethe as she spoke. "Lady Catherine, you have travelled a long way. Can I offer you some refreshments?"

Her ladyship reluctantly conceded that she would accept some tea, adding unhelpfully, "Since your servants did not see fit to offer me any such courtesy while I waited for you."

Elizabeth rang the bell then turned to Lady Catherine. "We are in a period of upheaval. I know your ladyship is sensible enough to comprehend that there may be the odd interruption to the smooth running of things."

"That is a sanguine evaluation of the situation, Mrs Darcy. 'Upheaval' implies a temporary inconvenience, not one that lasts until death do you part."

Darcy's countenance had darkened alarmingly. "You know

perfectly well Elizabeth was referring to the problems with the house."

"Do I?" his aunt retorted. "It seems to me that your wife has more foresight than you, Darcy. She is at least aware of the turmoil surrounding her. You seem blind to every dire consequence of this scandalous alliance."

"I am painfully aware of the turmoil surrounding us. I do not need it pointed out to me."

Elizabeth listened to them rail at each other, her mind racing to think of a way to prevent an all-out war, when the door opened, and James poked his head into the room. She hastened to him and whispered, urgently, "Please have some tea sent up. Ask Mrs Lovell to come too. But first, find Mr Ferguson, and tell him to invent an emergency. I do not care what it is, but it must require Mr Darcy's immediate presence. Do you understand?"

He nodded and hastened away.

"And what do you propose by coming here?" Darcy was saying when she turned back to the room. "Do you think you can somehow undo my marriage?"

"Would that were possible! Alas, I cannot work miracles."

"I see. I must conclude, then, that your design is to burn every bridge that exists between us to ensure we need never speak again?"

"It would be better if we could all remain reasonable," Elizabeth tried, to no avail. She only drew Lady Catherine's ire back upon herself.

"Oh, but I *was* reasonable while I accounted to my friend the Marchioness of Shrewsbury, why my nephew had overlooked my daughter in favour of a penniless nobody from Hertfordshire. I was the *epitome* of reason when Lady Alcroft uninvited me from her soiree."

"Lady Shrewsbury, who slighted Anne at court?" Darcy replied angrily. "Lady Alcroft whose husband could not trouble himself to attend Sir Lewis's funeral? These are not your friends, madam. Are you truly more concerned with appeasing them than looking to my happiness?"

James cleared his throat from the doorway. "Pardon the intrusion, Mr Darcy. Mr Ferguson has requested that you join him at the dig site."

"Tell him I shall come presently," Darcy snapped.

James glanced fretfully at Elizabeth.

"Did he say it was urgent?" she asked him. James nodded feverishly, making her feel bad for having embroiled him in the first place. To her husband, she said, "I think you ought to go. I can manage things here."

Darcy did not move immediately, but at length he muttered what Elizabeth did not doubt was an imprecation and took a step towards his aunt. "Do not allow it to slip your mind in my absence that Elizabeth is the mistress of this house. If I hear that you have caused her more insult, I will personally see you turned out." Then he left, and it felt for a moment as though he had taken all the air from the room with him.

Lady Catherine recovered first. "A few weeks of marriage to you and he has become a savage! Never have I heard such language from him."

"I think it fair to say that he was equally dismayed by your behaviour. It was hardly civil." Mindful of her aunt Wallis's recent advice to make an ally of her ladyship if she could, Elizabeth forced herself to adopt a more collected tone. "I can see his anger has surprised you. Perhaps you thought he would tolerate your unashamed invective against his wife, and indeed, he might have done had he married a woman for whom he felt nothing. But you must know that is not the case."

"I cannot deny that he is completely under your spell. Do

you care what injury you have done to my relationship with him?"

That Lady Catherine thought anybody other than herself was responsible for the schism with her nephew only demonstrated the magnitude of the conceit Elizabeth was battling. Nevertheless, she persevered.

"Please, let us sit." When they were both seated—something that took longer than it needed to thanks to her ladyship's stubbornness—she continued. "It goes without saying that Darcy holds you in extremely high regard. If he did not, we would not be having this discussion. He would have dropped the acquaintance after what transpired at Longbourn."

"Do not remind me! His behaviour towards me that day was unpardonable!"

"And what was yours to him? You came, hoping to persuade me—or scold me, or scare me—into forsaking him. I wished at the time that he had not discovered you there, for it hurt him deeply to know that was your object. Yet even then, I doubt he would have spoken so intemperately if your attempt to separate us had been the first. But Mrs Reynolds had already tried—and almost succeeded. Coming so soon after her betrayal, yours was all the more painful."

"Are you comparing me to a housekeeper in my nephew's affections?"

"No, not at all." Elizabeth sincerely doubted that Lady Catherine would ever have allowed Darcy to keep an injured kitten in her sitting room. "But the fact remains that both of you have peopled his life since he was a child. He trusted you both, and you both schemed to destroy his happiness. He is not made of stone, madam. You cannot use him ill and expect that it will not distress him."

"You have a nerve, preaching to me about using people ill. You who stole my daughter's husband."

The chances of preserving Lady Catherine as even a passing acquaintance, let alone an ally, felt to be vanishing into the farthest distance. Elizabeth took a deep breath. "There is no point revisiting that matter. Your ladyship wished that your nephew would marry your daughter, but he chose otherwise. It is done. Darcy and I are married. Therefore, let us be frank. There is nothing to be achieved by your coming here other than to decide whether or not you will condone his choice. That is the only power you have remaining. And if your decision is to cut ties with him, then you *will* be no better in his estimation than the housekeeper who also abandoned him, and it will be for no reason but to satisfy your own pride."

"It will be because *you* made it impossible for me to do otherwise!"

"We must both hope, then, that your observations do not bring you to any such conclusion."

Elizabeth breathed a sigh of relief when the door opened, and Mrs Lovell arrived. Matthis entered behind her with a tray of refreshments, which he laid out on the table and, at Elizabeth's signal, departed.

"You wished to see me, Mrs Darcy?" Mrs Lovell said, glancing anxiously at Lady Catherine.

"I did." Elizabeth deliberately began preparing the tea to avoid having to meet her ladyship's eye as she spoke. "Lady Catherine, might I introduce you to Mrs Lovell, whom you recently helped bring to work for us from Chisholm Park."

She was obliged to look up eventually, for no answer was forthcoming. Her ladyship was glaring at her sullenly, her expression a poor imitation of Darcy's far more skilful contempt, and Elizabeth was in no way intimidated. "Since you have expressed such a keen interest in observing the running of the house, I thought perhaps you might like to stay while I conduct my business with her?" It was a risk, but

Elizabeth calculated that, if Lady Catherine were determined to find a reason to despise her, it would be better to get it done and send her on her way than have her loitering about the house making Darcy miserable while she made up her mind.

Her ladyship grudgingly conceded, and even seemed to approve of Mrs Lovell at first, for the housekeeper gave a good account of herself. Elizabeth did not take this as any sort of victory, for it was unlikely anyone would object to the servant they themselves had contrived to install. She was more hopeful of success when Mrs Lovell was able to give favourable answers to her initial enquiries. Yes, the distribution of Pemberley's latest charitable donations had been made and gratefully received. Yes, the other senior servants had accepted the proposed alteration to the household expenses. After that, her luck ran out.

"Tell me, Mrs Lovell," Lady Catherine said. "What was it that caused the furore I overheard in the orangery when I arrived earlier? Something to do with flowers, I understand."

Mrs Lovell glanced uneasily at Elizabeth.

"Do not look to your mistress for assistance. It was she who invited me to join this meeting. Answer my question."

Elizabeth indicated with a nod that Mrs Lovell should do as her ladyship asked, though she was unreasonably gratified when the housekeeper addressed the explanation to her instead of Lady Catherine.

"Martha instructed one of the younger maids to gather some fresh flowers to be arranged in preparation for your return, Mrs Darcy. The instructions were not clear enough, I fear, for Sarah apparently cut the flowers herself rather than ask one of the gardeners to do it. Mr Howes was unhappy that some of his plants had been damaged."

"Oh dear, that is unfortunate," Elizabeth replied. "I assume you have dealt with the matter?"

"I have, ma'am. It will not happen again."

Lady Catherine made a little noise in her throat that might have been a laugh or a bark of triumph. "Are there any other problems brewing amongst your ranks, Mrs Lovell?"

"No, ma'am."

Elizabeth thought it pitiable that her ladyship should look so disappointed to hear it. She poured a solitary cup of tea, not caring that it was likely not steeped properly, pushed it across the table towards Lady Catherine, and stood up.

"The work on the east wing is regrettably disruptive. I shall have a room made up for you as far from the noise as possible."

"I can tolerate noise perfectly well. You will not scare me away by that method."

"I did not think for a moment that I would. But there is no profit in allowing you to be deprived of sleep, for it would only put you in a worse humour than you already are. Pray remain here and enjoy your tea while the room is readied. Mrs Lovell, the Mahogany Bedroom, I think." With a gesture for the housekeeper to follow, Elizabeth left the saloon and her husband's vexatious aunt behind.

Outside the room, she stopped walking and turned to face Mrs Lovell. "I apologise. That was…unpleasant. Now tell me, was Mr Howes *very* cross?"

"Livid, I am afraid."

"Oh Lord. I shall ask Mr Darcy to speak to him."

"There is something else," Mrs Lovell said. "It seems William told Edna that you did not enjoy dinner on your first night here, and Edna has been taunting Chef with the information."

"Has she now? She is sailing perilously close to the wind, is she not? Thank you for telling me. Pray tell Monsieur Dubois to pay her no mind."

"You must not concern yourself on that score, Mrs Darcy.

I am fast learning that Chef is an inveterate gossip. Edna's petty tittle-tattle will not trouble him."

"It ought not to be troubling Mrs Darcy, either."

Both women jumped at the sound of Darcy's voice—unexpectedly close and unusually cold. Elizabeth turned to greet him but faltered when she saw his expression, unsure what was wrong. It soon became clear.

"This incessant pestering of my wife must stop, Mrs Lovell," he said icily. "You are paid to manage this household. If you are determined to run to Mrs Darcy for assistance every time you encounter a difficulty, I see no reason for us to employ you at all. My wife has had an exceedingly trying day. Pray leave her alone and get on with the work you are being paid to do."

Elizabeth was so stunned by this outburst that the housekeeper retreated before she had the opportunity to defend her. Her shock ignited into burning hot anger when Darcy began to apologise for *Mrs Lovell's* behaviour.

"Elizabeth, I am sorry you had to deal with that as well as—"

"Upon my life!" she interrupted. She was attempting to keep her voice at a level that Lady Catherine would not hear, but her pique was such that it made her sound as though she was growling. "Mrs Lovell was only here at my request! She has just saved me the brunt of your aunt's derision. And I *asked* her to keep me informed of Edna's conduct! If you have just cost us the best thing that has happened to Pemberley since we got married, you may find the replacement yourself. I am done with the whole business!" She strode away at a pace.

"Where are you going?"

Darcy sounded utterly bemused and a little panicked, and Elizabeth almost stopped to reassure him, but the danger of encountering Lady Catherine again if she lingered too long decided her against it.

"For a walk!" she answered without stopping. And since nobody had given her the time to so much as change out of her travelling clothes since she arrived home, it was the easiest thing for her to march directly out of the front door and away into the park.

CHAPTER FORTY-TWO

THE PRAISE OF AN INTELLIGENT SERVANT

Darcy knew not which way Elizabeth had gone and therefore wasted half an hour searching in vain on the wooded north slope. He eventually spotted her from the top of the rise, walking back towards the house along the riverbank, and set off to intercept her at the bridge.

He was not concerned that there was any insurmountable disharmony between them, but he was dismayed to have vexed her. His intention had been to lessen the demands on her time, not create yet more difficulties for her to overcome. Either way, he was relieved that, when she saw him approaching, she did not strike off angrily in another direction.

"Will you allow your fool husband to walk with you?" he asked when he reached her.

She shook her head at him fondly. "You are not a fool. I know you were thinking of me. I ought not to have stormed off, but I needed some air."

"I am a fool if I have made matters worse for you." He reached to toy with the curls at her temple. "I would give you the world, but all I seem able to do is make more problems for you." When she looked as though she would argue, Darcy pulled her into his embrace and kissed her as he had wished to kiss her when he met her at this same spot in the summer —penitently, with all the tenderness of a man begging for forgiveness, and all the warmth of a man violently in love. "Am I pardoned?"

"A girl could pardon an awful lot for a kiss like that." She wrapped her hands around his arm, setting them in the direction of the house. "I do wish you were less determined to dislike Mrs Lovell. She truly is an asset. Even your aunt approves, though she will never admit it."

"How was my aunt?"

He knew it was unfair. He could see Elizabeth had hoped for more, but it would only distress her if he voiced his true opinion—that everything had run smoothly before, and if only everything could be managed properly again, she would not be required to superintend the havoc, and he would be able to rest easy, knowing she had the life she deserved. Would that Mrs Lovell could be half as efficient at the business that Mrs Reynolds had made look elementary.

With a slight sigh, Elizabeth submitted to the change of subject. "She was her usual delightful self. That said, she can surely only be here to reconcile with you. If she truly despised us, she would not have taken the trouble of coming so far. I think she only wishes to punish us for not doing as we were told."

"Her presence here is ample punishment."

"It will not be for long. She says she will not be frightened off by the noise, but she may not be so complacent after a few days of it."

They emerged onto the lawn. From this angle, the shoring that leant at five-and-forty degrees to the end of the east wing was silhouetted against the low sun and made the house looked like a giant, ungainly grasshopper. Following his gaze, Elizabeth asked how things were progressing with the works.

"The new foundations seem to be holding at last. Which makes it all the more difficult to explain why the original crack is getting larger."

"It *was* an emergency then?" Elizabeth asked, all alarm.

"Not as such—it has not happened suddenly. But it has widened by four sixteenths of an inch since it was last measured, when the underpinning ought to have ceased all movement." Her distress made him regret telling her. "Ferguson has it well in hand."

"I am sure he has. I am sorry—of all our silly little tribulations, Pemberley is the only one that truly matters." In a lighter voice, she added, "But for heaven's sake, do not tell your aunt. She would be seriously displeased to know she was not our utmost priority."

Lady Catherine certainly tried to be their chief agitator, finding endless things about which to be displeased. By noon on Saturday, she had twice insisted on being moved to a different bedroom, demanded food that was out of season at both dinners, accused Pemberley's servants of bullying her lady's maid, offended the stonemason, and picked a fight with Matthis. When her derogatory comments about Georgiana's pianoforte practice made his sister cry, the last of Darcy's forbearance evaporated. He ordered Georgiana and the footman out of the music room and rounded on his aunt.

"Since you have been dissatisfied with every aspect of your stay, I trust you will have no objection to my insistence that you leave."

"Indeed, I do object! I have no wish to go."

"What possible reason can you have to stay? You have demonstrated a total want of regard for every person in this house and have done nothing but cast malicious aspersions and make petty complaints since you arrived. And to what end? You cannot change anything. Has it all been done in some perverse attempt to vindicate your unfounded objections to my choice of wife?"

His aunt stiffened and her voice grew colder. "If you must know, I came with the hope of being proved wrong. It is a source of deep regret for me that the opposite has occurred. I am profoundly sorry for you, Nephew. Mrs Darcy is every bit the disaster I feared she would be."

Darcy would have railed had not his fury been subsumed by incredulity. "Madam, what fictitious world have you been inhabiting these past two days that you have not seen what I can see? Elizabeth is the one thing holding this disaster together at the seams."

"Never mind what I can *see*. What I *know* is that there would *be* no disaster if she were not your wife."

"You blame her, do you, for Pemberley sinking into the ground?"

"Of course not. But the rest of it, the mismanagement of the servants, the disarray within the house, your discomposure, can all be laid squarely at her door. She was not born to this sphere and has no idea what she is doing."

"It is not for Elizabeth to corral the servants. That duty ought to be the housekeeper's, but Mrs Lovell, whom you so kindly foisted upon us, seems unable to fasten her own shoes without asking for help."

"In blaming Mrs Lovell, you might as well blame your wife, for it was she who chose her! I did not review the woman's application or interview her. It was not I who decided she possessed the qualities Pemberley required of her. You let your young, inexperienced wife do that. If she has chosen unwisely, then you must see it is only further proof of her ineptitude, not Mrs Lovell's!" She stopped and frowned at him before continuing more composedly. "I am sorry if you are distressed, but it is about time you heard these hard truths."

Darcy felt unpleasantly ill at ease. His aunt was right. Not about most of the drivel she was spouting, but on one, salient point. In disapproving of the housekeeper, he was, essentially, distrusting his wife's judgment. It pained him to think that Elizabeth might have perceived his misgivings as having anything to do with her.

He tried but could not, in that moment, recall the basis on which his objections to Mrs Lovell were formed, and that pointed to a lapse of reason that he found abhorrent. He had used to pride himself on never allowing his feelings to influence his decisions, but he had fallen foul of that moral before, when he separated Bingley from Jane. The prospect that he had done so a second time, and yet again to Elizabeth's detriment, was disagreeable, to say the least.

"Do you think Anne would have had the strength of character to endure all this—to help *me* endure it as Elizabeth is doing?" he demanded. In a more agitated tone, he added, "Do you think I do not need help? That I could wake up every day and face this alone? Never mind that Elizabeth is holding Pemberley together—for God's sake, she is holding *me* together. If you cannot be civil to her, you must leave. I need her. I do not need you."

He walked with purpose towards the servants' quarters, through a house of closed-off rooms stacked high with mouse-chewed heirlooms and priceless artifacts shoved into cupboards.

The doors to all those rooms, however, were all neatly closed. In truth, nothing could be seen of the disarray. Everything that was not packed away was pristine—dusted and polished to perfection. The fires in all the principal rooms were lit. The windows all shone in the late afternoon sun, with not a streak to be seen on any of them. Even the sound of workmen was absent from this part of the house. Odd, that he had not noticed order restoring itself.

It was a very different picture on the other side of the service door. Raised voices reached his ears immediately and grew louder as he made his way farther along the passage. There was some manner of disturbance occurring in the servants' hall, it seemed; he kept to the shadows of the doorway to observe it. Mrs Lovell was standing with Matthis at her side and a gaggle of wide-eyed maids and hall boys surrounding her. A housemaid whose name Darcy did not know stood red-faced and defiant on the other side of the table.

"This in't fair! Why are you accusing me not her?" she demanded, pointing at another maid.

"Because Martha does not fly into a rage every time I mention the account books," Mrs Lovell answered calmly.

"Neither do I!"

"That is precisely what you do, Edna. You have frustrated my attempts to unravel the housekeeping payments at every turn."

"Prove it!"

"I have. I have interviewed everybody involved, and my findings are that on three separate occasions, between the day that Mrs Reynolds left and the day that I arrived, you were given money and charged with the task of settling outstanding bills. Mrs Fairlight, Mr Matthis, and Hannah all recorded that they gave you cash from the safe." She pointed to an open book on the table. "You recorded that you paid those bills. It was also recorded that Mr Ferguson gave you money to purchase supplies for the stillroom. None of the suppliers you claim to have paid had received a penny when

I spoke to them. And these supplies are not in the stillroom."

"I've used them, an't I!"

"You could not have, because according to the shop keepers, you never bought them. And according to your own brother, you gave the money to him. On his own testimony, and that of his friends, he has received more money from you than you could save in a year. You stole it, did you not?"

Darcy was furious, though as much with himself as the maid. A thief in the house was something about which he would never object to being kept informed, yet he had berated Mrs Lovell for bringing the girl to Elizabeth's attention. Would that he had taken half as much trouble as she had to ensure his charges were founded!

"You had an excellent position here," the housekeeper continued in an unshakeable voice. "There are girls who would give their eye teeth to work at Pemberley, but rather than be thankful, you have chosen to steal, and at a time when savings are already having to be made to pay for the work on the house."

Edna screwed up her face in disdain. "They wouldn't need to save money if the master han't married a commoner, would they?"

A gasp ran around the hall that drowned the furious breath Darcy sucked in through his nose. Only his wish to see what the housekeeper would do prevented him from revealing himself, though his entire frame thrummed with the tension of remaining still.

Mrs Lovell closed the account book. "And that, Edna, has sealed your fate. Mrs Darcy asked me not to dismiss you until I had definitive proof of your crime. She hoped, at the very least, to be able to send you on your way with a good character. You will leave now with nothing. And to ensure it really is nothing, you will sit here while I have your room searched."

"You can't do that!" After a panicked glance around the room, Edna skirted around the table, but Matthis flicked a hand at one of the hall boys, who stepped into her path. Edna swung her foot at his shin and darted for the door. Darcy stepped out of the shadows. One of the boys swore and somebody dropped something that clanged loudly on the flagstones. Edna almost ran headlong into him, but she came up short, the words 'get out of my way' frozen on her lips when she looked up and saw who was blocking her escape. She backed away until she was pressed against the table. Darcy continued to glower at her until she scrambled into a chair, where she sat, shaking her head as though she might yet persuade him of her innocence.

He transferred his gaze to the housekeeper. "Do not let me interrupt, Mrs Lovell. You appear to have the matter in hand. Come and see me in the Argyll room when you are done." With a last, dark glare at Edna, he left, walking quickly lest the temptation to drag the insolent wretch all the way to the magistrate's door by her ear grew too strong to resist. He halted mid-stride when he espied his manservant in the boot room and, on a whim, stepped inside and closed the door.

"Tell me, Vaughan, how is Mrs Lovell settling in?"

Vaughan put down the shoe he was polishing. "Finding her feet, sir. She is certainly very competent, but she ought to be, coming from Chisholm Park."

"Is she well regarded?"

"In general, yes. It has taken some of the servants time to accustom themselves to a housekeeper who answers to the mistress of the house before the master. Mrs Reynolds was very much your creature, sir. Mrs Lovell is very much Mrs Darcy's."

"That is natural, given that Mrs Darcy was not here when Mrs Reynolds was in post."

Vaughan inclined his head and resumed his polishing in a way that gave Darcy the distinct impression he had missed the point. It irritated him and with a grudging mumble of thanks, he left to await Mrs Lovell in the Argyll room.

"I am sorry you had to witness that, Mr Darcy," she said when she eventually joined him there.

"Was anything found in her room?"

"Yes, sir. Ten guineas, a dozen beeswax candles, a large pouch of tea leaves, and some fine soap bars that were recorded as gifts given to Mrs Reynolds. She evidently took advantage of the period when there was no one in charge to make some money on the side."

"What have you done with her?"

"One of the grooms is escorting her off the estate. If it pleases you, Mr Darcy, I thought it better not to send for the magistrate. If Edna were to be prosecuted, it would likely be reported in the papers, and I cannot see that such attention would help repair our reputation with suppliers, as Mrs Darcy has asked me to try and do."

"A sensible decision, Mrs Lovell, thank you." He took a deep breath. "I must apologise for the incident on Thursday. Mrs Darcy has explained the situation to me. I ought not to have questioned your competence. I hope I did not make you feel as though your position at Pemberley was in question."

She observably struggled to decide upon her answer, settling at length for, "I am glad to hear you confirm it is not, sir."

He had, then. That was regrettable. "I would not have you concern yourself a moment longer. You have more than proved your loyalty to this house today."

"I am honoured you should think so. I have grown excessively fond of working here in a very short time. Mrs Darcy is an exceedingly kind and judicious mistress. I have learnt much from her already. Would that all mistresses could understand their houses so well."

Darcy had no wish to deny Elizabeth her due, but this was nevertheless surprising praise, given that her tenure at Pemberley barely exceeded Mrs Lovell's.

He thanked and dismissed her, frowning at the closed door after she was gone. It was preposterous that he should be in any way affected by his housekeeper's opinion of his wife. Yet, he could not deny that he liked Mrs Lovell better for hearing her speak so well of Elizabeth. And that only made him angrier with Mrs Reynolds for never recognising her worth.

CHAPTER FORTY-THREE

A PERVERSE TWIST OF FATE

Elizabeth paid a call on her aunt's friends in Lambton on Saturday. Having seen neither Mrs Whitaker nor Miss Tanner since she and the Gardiners left Derbyshire in the summer, she was pleased to be able to pass on her aunt's apologies for their abrupt departure. The call afforded a blissful hiatus from Lady Catherine's incessant cavilling, though when she arrived back at Pemberley, Elizabeth felt rather bad for having abandoned Darcy to it, for it seemed that matters had come to a head in her absence. Her maid, Garrett, filled her in on most of it, and the rest, she determined to learn from her husband. She found him in the Stag Parlour, reading a book, which he set aside the instant he saw her in favour of pulling her down next to him for a kiss.

"That was a very enthusiastic welcome home."

"I am excessively pleased you are back."

"Yes, I heard that you have had a rather unpleasant time of it."

At her behest, Darcy related the morning's goings-on,

ending with an enquiry as to why she had not informed him about the business with Edna.

"I did not know she was a thief, only that she was a malcontent."

"Then you ought to have told me *that*. You need not shield me from these matters. When I asked you to choose the new housekeeper, it was so you would feel that the household was your domain, not because I expected you to take on everything, straight away."

"'Tis not as onerous as you seem to think. It has taken some time to get to know everyone's faces and understand how things work, but Mrs Lovell is very much running the show."

"Mrs Lovell was all praise of your judiciousness and understanding. She insists that she has learnt a good deal from you already."

Elizabeth bit her lip guiltily. "I ought to make a confession, but you are sworn to secrecy, do you understand? All these wonderful suggestions that Mrs Lovell thinks are mine have in fact come from my aunt Wallis."

"Your godmother?"

She nodded. "She even chose Mrs Lovell from the applications I sent her. I hate to break it to you, but Lady Catherine is right. I really do not know what I am doing."

Darcy reached for her hand. "You are not giving yourself enough credit. Mrs Lovell, Matthis, Ferguson—they all approve of you." He kissed her fingers. "Even Vaughan approves, and his good opinion is scarcely ever bestowed."

"Now I need only to convince Lady Catherine."

"No, you do not," he replied, stiffening. "I was about to say that *I* approve of you, and that is all that matters. Anyone who disagrees—my aunt, Mrs Reynolds, the lot of them can take their disapproval to the [redacted]."

Elizabeth was taken aback by the incongruous mention of

Mrs Reynolds. Her name was spat out so reflexively, it seemed as though Darcy was not aware he had said it. His enduring bitterness ought not to have been a surprise. He had admitted early in their acquaintance that he found it hard to forgive other people's offences against him—but she knew he had meant people who were important to him. Though, she supposed Mrs Reynolds had been the nearest thing to a matriarch at Pemberley since Lady Anne died, and there was no doubt that Darcy must have felt the warmth of her devotion.

The thought made her heart heavy for him, for it confirmed something she had long suspected: his anger towards Mrs Reynolds was born of more than displeasure at a servant's misconduct; it was born of real hurt. Elizabeth had assumed Darcy disliked Mrs Lovell because he had decided all housekeepers were untrustworthy, but it occurred to her now that there was a simpler explanation. He *missed* Mrs Reynolds but was too angry—and undoubtedly too proud—to admit it.

She cupped his face. "I wish I could cheer you up."

"You do. Constantly."

"Mrs Whitaker mentioned that the Lambton assembly is next week. I think we should go." She dissolved into laughter to see Darcy's expression. "I would not be so cruel! But I might insist that you let me invite Mr Connelly and Miss Reid to dinner, to liven us up a bit."

"You can invite Napoleon to dinner if you like. Anything but an assembly, I beg you."

They parted ways thereafter, Darcy to speak to his steward and Elizabeth to see whether Georgiana was recovered from her earlier upset. She was halfway up the stairs when Mrs Lovell called her name from below. She waited for her to catch up, then continued with her to the landing.

"I was planning to come and see you in a short while, Mrs Lovell. I understand you have had a rather trying day."

The housekeeper waved away her concern. "It is all resolved, Mrs Darcy. I shall happily answer any questions you have, but that is not what I came to speak to you about." She held out several bundles of letters, each tied with string. "I was unpacking some more of my belongings this morning, and I found these at the back of one of the cabinets in my room. I presume they belonged to Mrs Reynolds. I was not sure what you would like me to do with them."

Elizabeth took them and was about to jest that perhaps she would save them for the next time they ran out of coal when she was arrested by the familiarity of the handwriting on the uppermost letter. Frowning, she slid it out of the binding to look at it more closely—and inhaled sharply when the post mark confirmed the identity of the sender.

"Is anything the matter, ma'am?" the housekeeper asked, all concern.

"Um, no. No, I…thank you for these." She walked away, her heart pounding and her mind racing. Georgiana would have to wait, for these letters could not. Not when, by the looks of it, every single one had been sent to Mrs Reynolds from her own aunt Wallis. She hastened to her room and tore open the first one. Ten minutes later, she was cross-legged on the floor, sheafs of opened letters spread all around her as she attempted to fathom what on earth she had uncovered.

The two women were clearly the best of friends; the earliest letter Elizabeth had found thus far was dated 1776 and was full of Mrs Wallis's descriptions of her new home in North Devon. Many of the letters meant nothing to her, full of references to people she did not know and incidents that were unrelated to her, all written in her aunt Wallis's distinctive style, with daft names for everything and sarcasm largely obscuring the gist of the message. But in a letter dated 1799 the line, 'Dot has recovered!' caught her eye, and her heart sank. That was the year she contracted whooping cough, and what were the chances that her aunt knew two Dots, both of whom were ill in the same year?

Having seen her name once, she saw it everywhere. In another letter, dated 1801, Mrs Wallis had written about Elizabeth's first visit to Ilfracombe with her father and Jane. In 1807, she had filled two pages with her raptures at having spent a week in Bath with Mr Wallis and 'dear Dot'. A quick perusal of a dozen more letters revealed multiple mentions of the events of Elizabeth's formative years. Her whole life was here, in snippet form, for Mrs Reynolds to play voyeur to!

The prospect that her aunt Wallis, one of the most beloved people in her life, should have been privy to that woman's scheming was inexpressibly painful. She was tempted to burn the lot in anger, but unwillingness to believe it of her aunt compelled her to read on in search of some other explanation.

There were many reports of happy events. Births were mentioned frequently, from Georgiana's—

How Pemberley must be rejoicing at this happy news!

To Lydia's—

The Termagant has birthed a fifth girl. She is officially useless.

Childhood antics seemed a favourite topic, and a few of the allusions to Darcy's misadventures made Elizabeth laugh aloud despite her distress. She knew not which of the women had coined his nickname but given that she herself had heard Mrs Reynolds describe him as a good-natured boy, she suspected 'The Cherub' had been the housekeeper's epithet.

It did not take long to work out that 'The Wastrel' must be George Wickham.

Some of the letters contained more distressing news. In one, her aunt sent her condolences for the death of Lady Anne, expressing her pride that Mrs Reynolds had shown such compassion to her 'friend and mistress' in nursing her steadfastly through her final hours. Did Darcy know Mrs Reynolds had done that? In another, Mrs Wallis had written of her own grief at the death of 'her dear friend Jane', whom Elizabeth comprehended with a start was probably her grandmother. Another—a distressingly candid communication—contained advice on how Mrs Reynolds might assist Lady Anne through her repeated miscarriages, based on Mrs Wallis's own numerous experiences.

Tears stung Elizabeth's eyes when she read the letter that her aunt had evidently written in response to the news that Darcy's father had died. It was full of pity and sadness and spoke volumes as to the sorrow enshrouding Pemberley at the time. She noticed, also, that Mrs Wallis did not refer to Darcy with his childhood nickname in any letter dated after that day.

An hour was not enough to read a fraction of the correspondence Mrs Lovell had found, and when her clock chimed four, Elizabeth was no closer to understanding how her godmother and Darcy's housekeeper had come to know each other, nor what part each had played in separating them in the summer. She sifted about in the sea of open pages for more unread letters and uncovered a whole cache, still bound with string, behind the leg of the chaise. These were dated more recently, and as she read them, a far more detailed picture began to paint itself.

August 1811, You always said that Mrs Younge was a canny one, and you were right! It is probably best not to know the details of what transpired in Ramsgate if it has given Mr Darcy such pain, but you were right to dismiss the fools who were whispering about it. Your master would thank you if he knew.

October 1811, A stupid man, whom Dot has very aptly named Starch, refused to dance with her and said she was not handsome enough to tempt him—can you credit it!

December 1811, Dog Collar has proposed to Dot (she refused him), Wet Lettuce has run away, never to return, and Peacock has turned his attentions to an heiress. Pray send your Mr Darcy quickly, Agnes, and save Dot from all these insincere Lotharios!

April 1812, Starch has proposed to Dot! It is preposterous enough that he should think himself worthy of her, but he added insult to injury by doing it in the most contemptible, hurtful manner imaginable!

May 1812, I am sorry to hear Mr Darcy's spirits are so low. I agree with Mrs Fairlight; he is probably lonely. I know you think no one is good enough for him except my Dot, but really, you must not judge all other young ladies by her standard, it is most unfair. She is a rare creature.

August 1812, Clarabelle sounds utterly delightful. What a charming mix of guile and impudence for a young lady to possess! Her connexion to George Wickham is something of which to be wary, to be sure. I hope, for all your sakes, you see no more of her.

"Am I Clarabelle?" Elizabeth cried indignantly.

August 1812, Dot, my precious, undeserving goddaughter, has been dealt the most unjust and injurious of blows. Her youngest sister has eloped!

"*This* is how she found out about Lydia and Wickham!"

August 1812, Dot is not now and never has been short for Dorothy. My goddaughter's name is Elizabeth.

"She did not know it was me!" Elizabeth scrabbled to her feet, relieved beyond measure to discover that her aunt Wallis had not been party to Mrs Reynolds's interference. It was still unclear what had induced the housekeeper's intervention, though from the fragments she had read, it seemed as though her main objection was that she—or rather Clarabelle—had not been enough like Dot.

Elizabeth let out a small, slightly hysterical laugh. "She disliked me because I was not as wonderful as myself!"

Little wonder that Elizabeth had not appeared to her best advantage when she first arrived at Pemberley, tongue-tied with dread at the possibility of encountering Darcy and thereafter mortified to have obtruded into his life again uninvited. But of far more significance was that Mrs Reynolds *had* approved of Dot—the version of her that Mrs Wallis had portrayed in her letters; the version that was far closer to her true self; the version with whom Darcy had fallen in love.

She had to tell him! If he knew Mrs Reynolds would have heartily approved of their marriage, it might ease the hurt of her betrayal. It might not, of course, for he would first have to admit to *being* hurt, but that was a bridge Elizabeth could cross at a later date. At the very least it must lessen the sting, to see written in these letters such immutable proof of the devotion with which Mrs Reynolds served him up until that point.

The clock struck the half hour, and Elizabeth noticed how gloomy the room and sky outside had become. She hastily gathered up all the letters and threw them in a drawer, snatched a shawl from the back of a chair, then walked briskly to the front of the house.

"James, is Mr Darcy still outside with Mr Ferguson?"

The footman confirmed that he was, and she dashed through the door, along the path and around the corner to where the east wing jutted out from the back of the house. She smiled to herself as she thought of how, in one of the letters, her aunt Wallis had referred to Pemberley as Mrs Reynolds's pride and joy. How it would surely please Darcy to know she had thought so well of it!

She took a wide berth around the trench and the scaffolding and wove her way between the many piles of earth and rubble. The workmen were packing up for the day, more of them milling about on the lawn than were still working on the footings. A few of them doffed their caps, and she smiled and wished them good afternoon, but she was in too much of a hurry to stop and speak to them.

She did not spot Darcy until she was almost at the back of the house. He was standing at the foot of the north slope with several other men, all of them looking back at the north elevation. Her heart leapt at the sight of him, not least because she was anxious to tell him what she had discovered, but also because, even at this distance and in the waning light, he cut an exceedingly fine figure—taller, more stately, more masterful than any of the people to whom he was speaking. She allowed herself a small smile of complacency and quickened her steps, eager to reach him.

She jumped and almost stumbled when someone bellowed something at her from close by. She turned to see who. Several men, all of them shouting, came scrambling with unnerving urgency out of the trench beneath the scaffolding. At the very instant that she comprehended they were screaming "Run!" there came a noise unlike anything she had ever heard, and to her horror, the entire east wing abruptly shrank away from the sky in a flood of tumbling, crashing, cascading stone. Scaffolding pinged away from the walls like snapping twigs; the ground shook; and a roiling bank of dust and rubble bubbled up from the ground to engulf her, the sky, and everything in between. It filled her eyes and ears and lungs with grit and turned the whole world black.

CHAPTER FORTY-FOUR

THE MASTER OF PEMBERLEY

The last thing Darcy saw as Pemberley fell was Elizabeth, being swallowed by the rubble. Abject terror gripped his heart in an iron fist, preventing him from breathing. He knew not for how long, but when he next tried to inhale, nothing came into his lungs but debris. He hacked and spat the dust from this mouth and called her name until he was hoarse.

The collapse had ceased—over in the blink of an eye—but the patter of falling scree was an unambiguous signal of the persisting danger. Darcy cared nothing for it. He ran towards the sound, towards the ruins, towards the last place he had seen Elizabeth. Other noises began to fill the air; coughing, shouting, swearing, but they seemed far away, as though he were in a waking dream, aware of things but not present enough to affect them.

"Fitzwilliam!"

He whirled around, his heart exploding back to life with painful force to see Elizabeth stumbling through the haze towards him. "Thank God! I thought—" He took her by the shoulders, in need of the contact but scared to embrace her lest she was injured. "Are you hurt?"

She tried to speak, coughed, and shook her head. After a deep breath, she found her voice, unsteady though it was. "What should we do?"

"You must go inside. Have Mrs Lovell fetch you some wine and send for the physician to attend you." Before she could object, he added, "Pray, give me the comfort of knowing you are safe. You were almost—" He could not say it. "You are caked in dust."

"As are you. And you *are* injured." She lifted her hand to touch his forehead, which hurt in a way he was not anticipating, then showed him her bloodied fingers. Someone let out a pained cry nearby. Elizabeth held his gaze. "*Our* house, remember? Tell me what to do."

She looked shaken, filthy—and utterly determined. Darcy had never loved her more.

"Very well. Summon the physician—for the men if not you."

She gave a quick nod and left to see it done.

Darcy turned to the wreckage of his house and began shouting for people to identify themselves. Men all started calling their names, some adding that they were injured, one yelling in a strained voice that he was trapped. Darcy set off in his direction but stopped when Howes appeared at his side with more bad news.

"Mr Ferguson is badly hurt, sir. Hit by the same bit of scaffold as flew at you and me by the look of it."

"Show me." Howes was also bleeding, Darcy noticed. They had none of them escaped unscathed.

The steward was in the same spot upon which they had been standing when the collapse occurred, only now supine on the ground, dazed and groaning. Darcy crouched next to him. "Ferguson, can you hear me?"

Evidently, he could not. Darcy removed his jacket and laid it over him, then stood up. "We must get him inside. Do you know if Mr Jacobs is well?" He had been standing with them.

"I shall live," answered he, limping up to join them through the gloaming. "But *they* might not if you do not stop them."

Darcy looked to where the architect was pointing. With twilight leaching the colour and clarity out of everything, all he could make out was the roiling shadow of men at work at the base of the collapsed wall, toiling to free their fellow ground worker. Underscoring the seriousness of Jacob's warning, a torrent of loose stones abruptly cascaded down over the rubble, sending the men scattering across the lawn.

"Get away!" Darcy yelled. "We will get him out, but do not get yourselves crushed trying!"

"It is not only the danger from above, sir," Jacobs said. "It is whatever is beneath it that brought it all down. There is no way of knowing what ground is safe."

"Then we must find out, for we cannot leave him there! Is he the only one? Hell's teeth, we need some light!"

"It is coming," Howes said, nodding over Darcy's shoulder to the house.

Darcy turned to see a wall of bobbing lanterns approaching. One came directly towards him, revealing Matthis's steely face.

"Where would you like these, sir?"

Behind the butler and the line of lantern-wielding footmen, Darcy saw a host of maids hurrying across the lawn bearing armfuls of blankets and what looked like casks of beer. Elizabeth peeled away from the troops she had evidently rallied and came to stand at his side. An image of her pink gown disappearing beneath an avalanche of falling stone flashed before his eyes and hollowed out his stomach biliously. He stepped closer so their arms were pressed together, touching her the only thing he could think of that would drive away the horrible feeling. They exchanged a fleeting look, a tiny, conspiratorial nod, and then they were both swept forward again in a relentless churn of frantic activity.

Darcy tasked the butler with illuminating the mountain of toppled stonework. Howes was charged with accounting for every man's whereabouts. James was sent to fetch a pallet to convey Ferguson inside. Jacobs and the stone mason were despatched to see whether anything could be discerned about the integrity of the remaining structure. Maids dispersed across the lawn, distributing drinks and blankets to those in need and shepherding the walking wounded into the house. Elizabeth must have given that instruction. Darcy lost track after a while of which of them had given what commands. He lost track of Elizabeth more times than he liked, too, each time, the same, empty feeling welling in the pit of his stomach.

He found her when he went to oversee the footmen lifting Ferguson onto the pallet. She was kneeling next to the steward, gently encouraging him to drink from the cup she held to his lips. She stepped away to allow the footmen to reach him.

Darcy touched her arm. "Are you bearing up?"

"I am if you are."

That was all they had time for before Howes appeared with his report.

"Six hurt, one trapped, two unaccounted for, sir."

"Then danger or no danger, we must get them out. Where is Jacobs?"

The four footmen hefted the pallet bearing the steward off the ground and set off for the house, Elizabeth in tow, but she paused as she passed Darcy and laid a hand on his arm.

"I shall not ask that you do not help them, but I beg you would take care. Every care. Please."

He saw it again; the cloud of debris engulfing her with sickening speed. He gave her his word and strode away in search of Jacobs in the hope that he might outrun the memory.

The architect was clambering over what was left of the east wing, assessing what still stood as best he could by lantern light, what had been exposed beneath, and what was safe to move. At length, an approach of minimal risk was agreed upon and the task of shifting rubble began, but with every new cascade of scree prompting a swell of panic among the men, it was a fraught undertaking. Darcy had no idea how long it took to free the man whose foot was trapped. It seemed too long. He had stopped yelling in pain and gone quiet by the time they pulled him out, which boded abominably ill for the two men buried further underneath the ruins.

Darcy followed the men who bore him inside to see that he was properly attended, but as he neared the house, a figure came darting towards him out of the darkness, distinguishable only by her wailing. He swore under his breath and was schooling himself to be as gentle as possible when someone else dashed from the house and intercepted them. *Elizabeth!* Of all the ways she had assisted him that day, Darcy thought he might be most grateful for this intervention. Mrs Ferguson, heavy with child and distraught with worry for her husband, was not something he relished dealing with. After a quick, reassuring smile at him, Elizabeth put her arm around the steward's wife and led her inside, murmuring soft words of comfort. Darcy inhaled deeply in a vain attempt to dispel the unrelenting but nameless feeling gnawing at his guts and followed.

Inside was not much less chaotic than out. Household

servants and labourers had taken over the saloon. Maids were attending to cuts and bruises; Mrs Lovell was pouring hot drinks that Mrs Annesley was distributing; Georgiana was washing the grit from a young lad's eyes. It did not escape Darcy's notice that someone had covered all the furniture with sheets, and the fleeting thought that Mrs Reynolds would have approved made him smile in spite of everything.

His smile vanished when he saw Lady Catherine, standing at the edge of the room with a shawl pulled tightly about her shoulders, watching the fray with an inscrutable expression. When her gaze met his, her countenance shifted, and he thought he saw pity in her eyes. It was not a sentiment for which he had any use at the present moment, and he turned hastily away.

"Is everything well?" he asked his sister.

"Yes—oh! You are cut!"

"It is just a scratch. Is the physician here yet?"

"Yes, he is with Mr Ferguson. And the apothecary has come up from Lambton. He went to attend to the man who was just carried in."

"I told them to put him in one of the visiting footmen's rooms for now," said Elizabeth, appearing at Darcy's side. "Here, drink this." She handed him a cup of beer.

He immediately drained it. "Thank you. I had not realised how thirsty I was."

"Or cold, I should wager. Put this on before you freeze." She held out his green coat, which she must have had Vaughan bring down from his dressing room.

Darcy did as she bade him, though it was not the coat that produced the powerful feeling of warmth in his breast, but her beloved compassion. That warmth was instantly usurped by the same lurching feeling that had plagued him all night, and since he could not seize her to him to eradicate it, as he wished to, his only other recourse was to keep running away. "I must return to the search. Two men are still unaccounted for."

Another hour passed before anyone remarked on the futility of the exercise. Even if they were fortunate enough not to have already suffocated, the sheer amount of rubble was more than this many men could shift in a fortnight, and as the night wore on, more and more mutterings to that effect reached Darcy's ears. With a mounting sense of repugnance, he comprehended that the instruction to cease the search could only come from him.

"They will not stop until I tell them to," he confided to Elizabeth on one of her many forays out of doors to help distribute refreshments.

"Then pray tell them. They are exhausted. *You* are exhausted."

"And condemn two men to death? I cannot do it."

She squeezed his hand. "Yes, you can, because you must."

He closed his eyes for a second, taking strength from the feel of her grip and bracing himself for the grim task, when a shout went up from the other side of the toppled wall. Darcy heard Elizabeth suck in her breath, and he held his with her while they waited to hear what had been found. It was not a body. It was not a person at all.

"There is a bloody great hole down here!" someone shouted.

"We know that you clodpole! Where do you think the rest of the library disappeared to? Up the [redacted] arse?" shouted Howes.

Elizabeth tried unsuccessfully to stifle a laugh and hastily marshalled the girls back indoors.

"No, sir," the man called back. "I don't mean downwards. I mean alongways. Looks like a tunnel."

"How far underground is it?" came another voice—Jacobs's.

"Hard to tell in the dark."

In short order, a lantern had been lowered into the newly exposed cavity, and the architect had peered down after it.

"It is impossible to say with any certainty until I can look in the daylight," he reported to Darcy. "But from what I can see, it bears a very striking resemblance to a drift mine."

"That is not possible," Darcy replied flatly. None of his forebears were fool enough to dig a mine under their own house.

Jacobs shrugged. "As I say, sir, I shall have to investigate more in the daylight. But it would explain an awful lot."

It explained nothing to Darcy. He felt as though he were back in the dream state of earlier, where nothing made sense, and he had no power over any of it. So preoccupied was he with attempting to recall whether his father had ever mentioned mines on this part of the estate that it was a moment before the rising tide of shouts around him broke into his consciousness.

"Is it true?" Howes bellowed furiously from nearby.

Following his gaze, Darcy saw someone jogging towards them from the house. The shape materialised into Matthis.

"They have been found, sir!" he puffed as he arrived in front of Darcy. "According to his wife, Mr Ferguson has complained about these two lads before, for being work-shy. We sent a few footmen to look for them in case they were never here. And it turns out they were not. One was in his bed, the other was in the alehouse."

A chorus of extremely vulgar oaths passed around the men, along with the clatter of two dozen tools being thrown down. Darcy did not object in the slightest. He would have shared their outrage had not he felt a bone-deep relief that he would not be required to give the command to cease searching for them.

The men quieted themselves when Elizabeth and her

trusty legion of maids returned, this time with steaming hot toddies for everyone. As Darcy watched her move among the men, handing them drinks and thanking them all with her indefatigable vivacity, the strange feeling he thought had finally gone returned with a vengeance. It did not help that the ruin of the east wing loomed over her in the darkness like some monstrous beast with a mouthful of broken teeth —a hellish memorandum of what almost was. It disposed him to keep his departing speech brief, though he doubted any of the men would object, given the hour. He expressed his and Elizabeth's sincere gratitude, commended their endeavours, and sent them home with very little ceremony.

He returned inside to discover that the saloon had been returned to perfect order. As he perched on one of the sofas, holding the plate of food Matthis had given him, he fancied he could be forgiven for thinking he had dreamt the whole disaster. If his wife were not moving about the room covered from head to foot in mud and dust, he would almost have believed it. He set the plate aside, his appetite long fled.

"I have had a room made up for you, Mr Jacobs," Elizabeth said. "Matthis will show you."

Jacobs thanked her and, also declining any supper, excused himself directly to bed, leaving the family alone. The room was so silent, Darcy's ears began to ring, but then Georgiana said, quietly, "I never thought it would actually fall down."

"None of us did," Elizabeth replied.

"How sudden it was in the end! Was there any warning?"

Another flash of pink, vanishing in a sea of dust, filled Darcy's vision. "Yes, there was a twenty-foot crack in the wall, Georgiana, but I think I can be forgiven for assuming the several tonnes of shoring would hold it up."

"Of course! I only meant, was there any warning today, before it fell. A noise or a—"

"No, there was no warning!" Darcy rubbed a hand over his face in frustration, regretting his incivility. He had not meant to shout, but he wished Georgiana would cease forcing his mind back to that damned moment!

"Your brother is very tired," Elizabeth said. "Perhaps it would be best if we all went to bed now."

"A very sensible suggestion, Mrs Darcy. I shall go up as well."

Darcy had not even noticed his aunt was still there. She inclined her head solemnly and left without another word. Georgiana hastened after her.

Elizabeth came to stand in front of Darcy and held out her hand for him to take. "Come. Vaughan and Garrett will never get to bed if we do not go up soon."

Upon arriving, alone, in his bedroom, the surreal quality settled even more oppressively over Darcy's world. He tried not to picture it again, but when Elizabeth walked through the door, he could do nothing to ward off either the memory of crashing stone or the appalling feeling that accompanied it. He did not think he made any sound, but he must have done something, for Elizabeth cried his name and dashed across the room to him.

"For heaven's sake, sit down!"

He let her push him into a chair. He heard her ask Vaughan to leave them, and the door close behind his man. He watched her kneel on the floor in front of him and listened as she told him how profoundly sorry she was for him. She began saying things about Pemberley, and legacies, and rebuilding, and—

"I know all of that, Elizabeth. That is not—" He was obliged to stop speaking because he was either going to be sick or start crying. He shook his head to clear it, but he could not bring his breathing under better regulation and was all but panting as he forced himself to say what had been haunting him all evening. "I thought you were underneath it. I thought I had lost you."

There was so much pity in the way she said his name it made him squeeze his eyes shut against it.

She picked up his hands and brought them to her own face. "I am perfectly safe. See?"

When he could not answer, she grew more insistent, smoothing his hair and stroking his face as she repeated her assurances. He did not stop her because he had never needed reassuring of anything more than this, but her words were not enough. With something inside him howling for her, he kissed her—harder than he meant to, but not as hard as he wanted to. He made himself stop.

"'Tis well, my love," she said softly. "I am flesh and blood, not stone. I'll not crumble. I promise."

Darcy might have wept in earnest, then, except he wanted her too badly. He put his hand at the back of her head and pulled her back into the kiss. She met him with urgency that matched his own, her hands on his chest, then around his shoulders, then in his hair. When he kissed her neck, she tasted of rubble, and though it wrenched his gut to be reminded of why he felt this way, it only inflamed his need for her. Nothing but being as close to her as it was possible to be would suffice now. With an arm cradling her shoulders, he slid forward off the chair and lowered her onto the hearth rug.

He still felt as though he were in a dream—an intense, unsettling, impassioned one. He had never been as in love, never been as terrified, never been as aroused, never *felt* as much in his life. Elizabeth welcomed him to her, let him love her with unfettered emotion, whispered to him again and again that she was safe, she was well, she was his, until words failed her, too. Firelight caught her rapture in glorious relief, and in that moment, still in her pink dress, still covered in the dust of his ruined house, Darcy's beloved wife banished his fear completely.

"I shall never be able to put into words what you mean to me, Elizabeth," he told her quietly. "I would not have survived today without you. I have never known anybody with your courage or strength."

He was not expecting a response and was taken aback when she took his face in her hands and lifted his head until he was looking down at her.

"I was *terrified* today, Fitzwilliam! I was terrified when the wall fell, I was terrified that people were hurt and missing, and I knew not what to do or how to help. Do you know how *I* survived? I had you! We *all* had you. Every servant, every labourer, every man and woman in this house was looking to you, taking your lead, following your instructions. And you let none of us down." She let out a small huff of the tenderest laughter and shook her head. "Never known anybody with my courage and strength? You foolish man. Try looking in a mirror."

He settled for carrying her to his bed and looking at *her* while he loved her again—less urgently but no less ardently, until her fears were banished as incontrovertibly as his own had been.

CHAPTER FORTY-FIVE

THE MISTRESS OF NOTHING BUT RUBBLE

"I have already looked in that pile," Elizabeth said. She lifted the stack of papers off the desk and replaced it with a different one. "Try these."

Colonel Fitzwilliam duly began rifling through his new commission. "What exactly are we looking for, again?"

"I do not know," Darcy replied, closing the folder on the desk before him with a contemptuous flick. "Every record of Pemberley's mines, past and present, is accounted for, and I have never set eyes on any document relating to works this close to the house. Ferguson swears blind that neither has he, and the plans show nothing. But I must look. I cannot sit idly and do nothing."

"And if we cannot find anything?"

"Then the next task will be to unpack every crate from the library and look there."

Elizabeth repressed a sigh. It was a hopeless task. They had already searched every drawer, cupboard, and shelf in the estate office that Ferguson had suggested from his sickbed—and every one that he had not—to no avail. They had turned their attention this morning to the Argyll room, where the contents of Darcy's study, formerly in the east wing, were being stored. After this, it would indeed be the library contents, followed by Darcy's attorney's office in Derby. All because Mr Jacobs was immovable in his conviction that there was a mine under the house, and Darcy would not rest until he had found something to discredit the theory.

The architect was due at any moment with a report, having spent the morning inspecting the site with Darcy's own Principal Colliery Viewer, Mr Regis. If anybody could identify a drift mine, it would be the man responsible for superintending all the others on the estate, and Elizabeth had no doubt the imminent meeting was the chief source of Darcy's present agitation. The anguish in his voice saddened her deeply, yet she could think of no other way to support him but to help look for that which she was entirely unconvinced existed.

The colonel heaved a great sigh and dropped into a chair. "Had I known, when you sent for me, that you wanted me to do your filing, I might have stayed at Branxcombe." He pulled out a hip flask, took a swig and offered it to Darcy, who refused. The colonel waggled it at him again, attempting to persuade him, but desisted when someone knocked on the door. At Darcy's instruction, Mr Jacobs entered, followed by Mr Regis.

"Well? What is the verdict?" Darcy enquired.

Mr Regis cleared his throat. "I am inclined to agree with Mr Jacobs, sir. Looks like a drift mine."

"How is it possible that nobody knew about it?" Fitzwilliam asked incredulously.

"How is it possible that the vast trench you dug in my lawn did not expose it?" Darcy demanded of the architect.

"Our excavations were not deep enough, Mr Darcy. We dug well below the level of the foundations but stopped when we hit solid limestone. Even when we thought there might be sinkholes, we did not suspect so large a cavity, and we could not have investigated deeper without the use of explosives, which would have done untold damage to the house."

Mr Regis took up the explanation, pointing at the colonel. "And, in answer to that gentleman's enquiry, Mr Darcy, it is very easy to see why nobody knew about it. It is old. Much older than the house. Could even be Roman."

"Roman?"

"Aye, for it has all the hallmarks of the lead mine over at Lower Kympton. 'Tis certainly not modern at any rate—far too irregular, and though it is hard to be sure without climbing all the way down, there look to be scorch marks, which would indicate the use of fire-setting for ore extraction."

Darcy rubbed his face with both hands and came back up shaking his head. "Where is the entrance to it?"

"Could have been buried more than a thousand years ago. Or if the mine between this point and the entrance has collapsed, could look like nothing more than just another cave by now."

"But this bit has remained intact until now," Elizabeth said, frowning. "If it is that ancient, and Pemberley has stood on it for over a century without issue, why has it collapsed now?"

"I believe," said Mr Jacobs, "it has to do with the blocked culvert that was discovered on the north slope in the summer. Rainwater *will* erode limestone given enough time, but even so, I thought it could not have so great an effect on solid bedrock. But I did not know there was a pre-existing void there. It must have eroded the roof of the mine until the weight of the east wing eventually became too great."

"Can it be backfilled?"

"Any cavity can be filled, given enough materials, money, and time, Mr Darcy. The question is, how far under the house does the mine extend, and how much of it has been compromised by erosion? If the answer to either of those questions is unfavourable, then the cost may prove prohibitive. Grandchester Abbey down in Somerset had a similar problem—not with a mine, but subsidence, nevertheless. Lord Inbrooke ended up pulling the whole house down and rebuilding on another part of the estate."

The look on Darcy's face made Elizabeth heartsick. Colonel Fitzwilliam did not look much better as he watched Darcy, his eyebrows drawn together in a deep frown and pity twisting his mouth askew.

"What do you suggest?" Darcy asked in a strained voice.

"Investigate what is down there. It is all we can do."

"Is the house safe to live in?"

Mr Jacobs's shrug gave Elizabeth no comfort. "There are no visible cracks on any other part of the building as there were on the east wing. It warrants careful monitoring, but there is no sign of an imminent problem."

"I understand you are returning to Sheffield this afternoon, Mr Jacobs. May I presume I can retain your services for the foreseeable future, though?" Darcy asked the architect, who agreed that he could. "In that case, I thank you both. That will be all for today."

The two men departed, and a pall fell over the room. Colonel Fitzwilliam offered Darcy his flask again, and this time, he took it. "That was not the news you were hoping for, Darcy, I know."

"It may not be as terrible as they made it sound," Elizabeth tried. "Remember, Pemberley is far more than just a house."

"Mayhap, but it is nothing without *any* house," Darcy replied bitterly.

"Do not jump the gun, old boy," his cousin interceded. "There is a decent chunk still standing, and your man Jacobs has declared it safe to inhabit."

"I suppose we shall have to find somewhere more permanent to store everything now. At least then we can get back to living properly in the house that remains. For as long as it does remain."

Elizabeth wished there were something she could say to alleviate Darcy's obvious distress, but she would not insult him with more platitudes. The want of sanguinity sat ill with her; she was used to being able to laugh herself out of despondency, but laughing oneself, one's husband, and one's entire household out of a literal hole in the ground was quite another.

"I must call on Ferguson," Darcy said, coming to his feet. "I promised I would tell him what Jacobs discovered."

Elizabeth offered to join him, to see how Mrs Ferguson was faring, but they had not made it to the hall before Matthis intercepted them with a letter, just arrived for her. She took it eagerly, a rush of anticipation quite outstripping her reason for a moment.

"Would you mind if I did not come after all?" she asked Darcy before even looking at it properly. He readily agreed and went on his way, leaving her to read her letter in peace and quiet.

She regretted her decision intensely upon inspecting it more closely. She had hoped it might be from her aunt Wallis or Jane. To the former, she had sent an express, begging for an explanation of her connexion to Mrs Reynolds. Of the latter, she had begged for words of solace, for despite Darcy's insistence that she was the panacea to all his woes, Elizabeth had never felt so helpless in all her days.

Alas, the distinctively careless hand marked it very clearly as having been sent by Lydia. She did not need to open it to know what it said, for it was the third such plea she had received; but open it she did. When she passed the saloon door and heard someone call her name, she could not decide which was worse—continuing to read Mr and Mrs Wickham's appeal for money or stopping to hear whatever it was Lady Catherine wished to say.

Ultimately, it was the modesty of her ladyship's request that induced Elizabeth to slip her letter into her pocket and agree to spare a moment of her time. Apart from coming downstairs to greet the colonel when he arrived the day before, Darcy's aunt had kept herself to herself since the wall collapsed, even eating all her meals in her room. It had been useful, for there had been much else to occupy their time, but Elizabeth felt a little guilty now for having ignored her so thoroughly.

"I shall not prevaricate," her ladyship began. "I wish to apologise. As you know, I came here to see how you were conducting yourself as mistress. You will also know that nothing escapes my notice, and that I have therefore observed all the ways in which you have erred in your duties, not to mention your failure to court the esteem of any of the ladies of eminent neighbouring families. Until two days ago, the best I could have said of you was that you displayed a willingness, perhaps even a capacity to improve."

Elizabeth said nothing. She had already admitted to Darcy that she was relying on other people's wisdom to pass herself off as competent. That somebody as determined to find fault as Lady Catherine had also noticed was no great surprise.

"But that was before this tragedy occurred," her ladyship continued. "Darcy asked me, two days ago, whether I thought Anne would have had the strength to support him in the way you have. It offended me, of course, but I must answer now that no, I do not believe she would. My daughter has a delicate temperament. She would have struggled with such adversity as you faced two nights ago. For so young a woman, you betrayed a remarkable presence of mind and a pleasing degree of good sense."

Elizabeth had not gathered her wits enough to reply before Lady Catherine continued. "Events of such significance as this often induce periods of reflection. I have spent the last day asking myself what my sister would have made of the situation. She was a fine lady, and excessively proud of her children and her position as mistress of this house. She was also fair, and I find that I have not been.

"You have made some mistakes, yes, but you will learn from them. I see now what my nephew has been attempting to tell me—that you have other talents which far surpass those I came here to judge. Courage, compassion, and intelligence. The respect of your household. Most importantly, you have demonstrated in the most incontestable way that you will always put my nephew's interests first. My sister would have said that these are the things that truly matter."

Of all the praise Lady Catherine could have given, this was the least expected and most valuable, and Elizabeth found herself feeling unexpectedly tearful—and that diverted her no end. She had been so dearly hoping for the comfort of a letter from Jane, and it seemed she would have to make do with the dubious consolation of Lady Catherine de Bourgh's approbation. It made her cry and laugh at the same time.

"Forgive me." She swiped away a tear and sniffed. "I am not generally given to sentimentality. Only it is all rather daunting."

Lady Catherine replied with surprising gentleness. "It is, but I shall not abandon you or Darcy to it. None of us will. My nephew is by no means friendless. And neither are you, Mrs Darcy."

On reflection, Elizabeth decided that reading Lydia's

letter had definitely been worth postponing. "Thank you. Will you tell him that?"

"Tell me what?"

Elizabeth turned around at Darcy's voice, and regretted not wiping her tears before she did, for when he saw them, his countenance darkened alarmingly.

"What is happening here?" he demanded of her ladyship.

"You aunt has been very kind," Elizabeth said hastily.

"I was apologising to your wife, Darcy, and now I apologise to you. I judged you both unfairly—and incorrectly. Your mother and father would have been exceedingly proud of the way you have responded to this disaster. I am exceedingly proud of you. I would have you know that you may rely on all your family to help restore Pemberley to what it was."

Darcy's transition from furious to dumbfounded was so abrupt and so complete, it made Elizabeth laugh again. Lady Catherine was less forbearing this time and gave her a withering glare as she informed them that she would make arrangements to leave that week, then left the room.

Darcy sat, somewhat dazedly, next to Elizabeth. "What prompted that?"

"She said she had been thinking about what your mother would have made of it all."

Darcy smiled a small, far-away smile that disappeared with his next question. "Why were you crying?"

"It has been a week of surprises. I think it must have been one too many."

He laughed lightly, and it was on the tip of Elizabeth's tongue to tell him about Mrs Reynolds and her aunt Wallis, but he forestalled her.

"Who was your letter from?"

"Oh! It…it does not matter."

"It clearly does."

Elizabeth sighed heavily. "Very well. It was from Lydia,

asking for money—but you are to ignore it, as I mean to do. I would not have troubled you with it at all if you had not asked."

"Good Lord, the Wickhams are the least of my concerns. How much do they want?"

"You are not giving them a penny!"

"How much?"

"Thirty pounds," she admitted reluctantly.

"Just send it. Thirty pounds is nothing to what I must spend now."

Elizabeth reached for his hand. "Can you afford the work?"

He shrugged despondently. "I ought to be able to raise the capital to rebuild the east wing, for I was halfway there already with the underpinning. But I do not see how I could afford to rebuild the entire house. And it would take a decade." He sat forward abruptly and pulled her hand into his lap. "Do you know, I do not wish to even think about it. To blazes with it—should you like to go dancing, Mrs Darcy?"

"Pardon?"

"I am of a mind to take you to the Lambton Assembly. It is tonight, is it not?"

"Are you serious? The master of Pemberley at a public assembly?"

"I might be the master of nothing but rubble soon. I should like to dance with the mistress of Pemberley while Pemberley is still standing."

Elizabeth wanted desperately to repeat her assurances that Pemberley would endure, but the more she said it, the less Darcy seemed to be convinced. Besides, she would not like him to change his mind. "In that case, I should be delighted to accept your invitation, Mr Darcy. Though I hope it does not mean that you would no longer dance with me if I were the *mistress* of nothing but rubble."

He smirked devilishly. "Fortunately for you, I have discovered that you taste sublime covered in rubble. I should do more than dance with you."

CHAPTER FORTY-SIX

HEART-WARMING DEDICATION

It was not an exaggeration to say that the people of Lambton were astonished to see their party enter the assembly rooms. Darcy was recognised instantly, and Georgiana and Fitzwilliam not long after, but it soon became clear that Elizabeth was the true object of interest. Every woman seemed desperate to glimpse the new mistress of Pemberley—and every man desperate to dance with her. On a promise to exert himself, Darcy consented to be introduced to everyone who asked for the privilege, danced with two of Mrs Gardiner's friends, and spoke to the master of ceremonies for a full ten minutes.

He enjoyed the rest of his evening better, not least the final set with Elizabeth. She danced in the same way she played the pianoforte—the same way, indeed, that she did most things—with such captivating élan that any imperfections only served to render the whole more pleasing. She teased him as they danced, her eyes alight with mirth, her countenance radiant with exercise, and he was so utterly bewitched that he quite forgot his troubles.

"I congratulate you, Darcy," said his cousin afterwards. "No other woman of our acquaintance would have looked that dazzlingly happy to have been mistress of Pemberley for less than two months before half of the house collapsed, the other half was condemned, and she was taken for a spin at a *public assembly* in consolation."

Somebody behind them gasped at the mention of the collapse, which served only to exacerbate Darcy's consternation. "Thank you, Fitzwilliam. I am obliged to you. I was in danger of forgetting that my house is in ruins."

He knew his cousin had meant only to compliment Elizabeth, but he did not need reminding of how wonderful his wife was; he was well aware of that already. What he needed was to forget about the threat of demolition to his ancestral home. To go but one hour without the remembrance of his father's austere instruction—repeated almost daily while he was alive—never to allow Pemberley to fall into debt or decay. For, now, one had happened and the other was inevitable, and he was sick to his core with guilt and grief.

It did not help that in the course of the evening, he had met more and more people who relied on Pemberley, either completely or in large part, for their livelihoods. He watched them all dancing merrily and was hard pressed not to dwell on how they would pay for a subscription to the next season's assemblies, or indeed anything else, if their chief source of income was extinguished overnight.

Elizabeth and Georgiana's exuberant and profuse thanks on the way home went a long way to restoring his good humour. It was impossible not to be buoyed by such cheerfulness, nor the gratification of finally giving Elizabeth something about which to smile. Nevertheless, when morning came, he found he did not wish to face the day. Given a choice between remaining where he was, with Elizabeth in his arms, and getting up to spend another day in painful deliberation about the future of Pemberley, he was unsurprisingly reluctant to push back the covers.

When Vaughan sidled discreetly up to the side of his bed and quietly informed him that his presence was required at the east wing, Darcy groaned and told him to go away. The last thing he wanted was to look upon the wreckage—even more devastating in daylight than it had seemed when it happened. His despair upon first viewing it, the morning after the collapse, was something he would never forget. Shattered glazing, still caught in its twisted lead beading, had hung limply from shattered mullions. Irreplaceable marble fireplaces had lain in pieces amid the rubble, and the remains of the roof had been left swinging precariously over the whole of it like the skin of a congealed custard, dripping from the lip of a jug. If he was never required to set eyes on it again, he would be happy.

"I beg your pardon," Vaughan persisted, "but I think you ought to see this."

Elizabeth, hiding under the covers at Darcy's side, mumbled that perhaps he ought to go.

Vaughan cleared his throat. "If I may, sir, I believe Mrs Darcy might also wish to see."

With a vast sigh, Darcy conceded; he and Elizabeth dressed as quickly as they could. They said nothing to each other as they walked through the house, and he did not doubt that, like him, she was rather too jaded by recent events to be provoked to any great anxiety by the prospect of another problem. Her only concession before they passed through the door to outside was to cast him a small, tender smile of encouragement.

Darcy could not immediately comprehend what he was looking at as they approached the site, but the heaving mass before them was slowly revealed to be a line of people.

Indeed, more than one line of *dozens* of people. The closer he got, the more faces he recognised. Almost every one of his tenants was here, even old Mr Mason, who had been caught poaching in the summer. Sheldon, with all the gamekeepers; Howes, with his gardeners; and Regis, with a handful of his pitmen. All three of the rectors whose preferments were in Pemberley's gift. Both teachers and a group of children from the Shepsbrook schoolhouse. The innkeeper of the Plough and Horseshoe. Many others Darcy could not name or did not know.

Every single one of them was moving bits of rubble, varying in size from pebbles in the hands of children, to great slabs carried between strong men, away from the site of the collapse to neat piles, or barrows and carts, under the careful direction of a still-bandaged Ferguson.

Fitzwilliam turned as Darcy and Elizabeth approached, an expression of deep appreciation on his countenance. "This is quite something, is it not?"

Darcy was moved beyond words. There was a moment when he might have summoned something vaguely articulate to say, but then Vaughan walked past him and joined the line of workers, and he was silenced completely.

Elizabeth's voice, when she spoke, was soft with wonder. "Now do you believe me when I say that Pemberley is more than stones and mortar? We shall find a way. We cannot fail with so many people willing us to succeed."

Though he could not conceive of how they might achieve it, for the first time, Darcy felt a glimmer of hope that she might be right. He nodded and let out a breath that it felt as though he had been holding for a very, very long time.

"I am feeling moved to shift a rock or two myself," Fitzwilliam announced and, without waiting for a reply, set off towards the workers, removing his coat as he went.

"You had better join him," Elizabeth said, still sounding greatly affected. "I shall see whether Chef can rustle up enough refreshments for them all."

After the upheaval of the last few days, Darcy did not much feel like exerting himself, but in the end, he was required to do nothing more than talk to people. It was not the sort of conversation he despised—the sort that passed around dinner tables and ballrooms and obliged a person to appear interested in the concerns of strangers. On the contrary, every person to whom he spoke had a memory of Pemberley to share with him, and that was a topic on which he could happily converse indefinitely.

After Elizabeth's show of sentiment for the turn-out, it struck Darcy as odd that she did not come back to join him in talking to everyone when the maids brought out the refreshments. When she still had not appeared over half an hour later, he thanked the volunteers sincerely for their hard work and dedication to Pemberley and went in search of her.

"An express arrived about an hour ago, sir," Matthis informed him. "I understand Mrs Darcy went into the park to read it in private."

"An express? Do you know where from?"

"I do not, sir, but Mrs Darcy seemed rather agitated by the receipt of it."

Darcy clenched his teeth. Could they go no more than an hour without more bad news? He thanked Matthis and asked him to direct Elizabeth to the saloon when she returned, then went there to await her. "And send some coffee."

Elizabeth arrived before the coffee did, and she was, as Matthis had warned, all agitation. He went to her directly. "Is everything well? Matthis said you received an express."

"Nothing is *wrong*. But there is something I need to tell you about. Can we sit down?"

No sooner had they done so than Elizabeth was back on her feet, pacing nervously before him. Matthis appeared with the coffee, and Darcy waited impatiently for him to serve it and go away again before reaching for Elizabeth's hand and pulling her down next to him. "Just tell me."

She took a deep breath and nodded. "Do you remember, just before the wall collapsed, I was running to see you?"

"I am not ever likely to forget it."

"I had just made a discovery. That is, Mrs Lovell had. She found a stash of old letters in her room that belonged to Mrs Reynolds. I almost threw them away until I realised they had all been written by my aunt Wallis."

"They knew each other?"

"They have known each other since they were children, apparently. I was concerned at first that it meant my aunt was party to Mrs Reynolds's attempts to separate us, but she was not, because she did not know—well, neither of them knew—that *we* were who they were writing to each other about. It sounds ridiculous, but they did not know that we were us."

"Ridiculous is one word for it."

"It is almost impossible to explain, but that is hardly the point anymore. What matters is what else I have found out. After everything that happened with the house, I decided against telling you until I had written to my aunt for an explanation. Well, she has written back, and...Mrs Reynolds is with *her*."

Darcy could quite happily have gone the rest of his life never knowing the whereabouts of his perfidious erstwhile housekeeper and was entirely unsure how Elizabeth expected him to respond. Mrs Reynolds being with her godmother meant only one thing to him: that his opinion of Mrs Wallis was in need of review.

He was, perhaps, silent too long; Elizabeth observably reined in her enthusiasm. "I know you are angry with her, but you may not be after I have explained it all."

"She no longer works here. That is all there is to it."

"That is not quite all. You see, it seems it was Mrs Reynolds who arranged for Lydia and Wickham to marry."

"What?"

"Apparently, she took steps to ensure they wed on the assumption that if Wickham was my brother, you would never marry me, and that would keep you safe."

Darcy stared at her incredulously, at a loss to understand why she was so much better pleased by the revelation than he. "Pardon me if I am missing something," he said stiffly, "but this is not news likely to make me *less* angry with the woman."

She winced. "I am not presenting it well. The material point is that she did it for *you*. And to do it, she went to a lot of trouble and spent every farthing of her life savings. And now she has nothing left on which to live."

"Then she ought not to have done it!"

"But cannot you see that she did it because she cared so deeply for you?"

Darcy rubbed both hands over his face. Why Elizabeth was attempting to defend the actions of a deceitful, and more to the point *departed* servant, he could not fathom. "Mrs Reynolds perfectly demonstrated the care she felt for this house, this family—and me—when she left."

"My aunt says she only left because when she realised her mistake, she was too ashamed to stay. She was devastated to have injured you when she only meant to protect you."

"It was never her place to protect me. She was my housekeeper, not my mother!"

"No, she was not your mother, but she was devoted to

you. If you would read the letters I found, you would see that."

"I will not condescend to reading someone else's correspondence merely that I might forgive a servant their misdemeanour. Have you any letters belonging to the larcenist we dismissed last week that I might read and absolve her of all guilt, too?"

Elizabeth's countenance lost its cajoling aspect and took on a more reproving turn. "Edna was a petty thief who worked at Pemberley for less than eighteen months. Mrs Reynolds was a devoted housekeeper, who served this house and this family faithfully for quarter of a century before making one mistake, for which she has been trying to atone ever since."

"In what possible way can she claim to have been trying to atone?"

"That is what I am trying to explain. She is with my aunt Wallis, who has been the source of every piece of invaluable counsel I have received since you proposed to me. It has all been Mrs Reynolds! Every decision, every suggestion, the rapprochement with Lady Catherine, even Mrs Lovell's appointment, it has *all* been her. I could never have made such a strong beginning as mistress without so much help. I am indebted to her, but I do not think for a moment she did it for me. It has all been done out of affection for you."

"Then she has betrayed a degree of presumption equal to her perfidy."

"It would be more accurate to say she has betrayed a degree of dedication that is heart-warming. She could have chosen to have nothing more to do with Pemberley. Instead, she has helped write several letters a week with advice on how to run it."

Elizabeth began fighting with the folds of her gown in search of something. "My aunt writes that she wept when they received my letter with news of the collapse. She has sent a whole list of places you might look for information about the estate that might help." She pulled a letter from her pocket and flicked hurriedly through its pages. "Yes, here. Two specific crates from the library, an old picture on the wall in Mrs Wickham's cottage, and some documents in your mother's writing desk in the Chesterfield room."

She looked up. "Do you see? She is still trying to help you."

Darcy wished profoundly that Elizabeth would desist, but he would not be uncivil—not on account of Mrs Reynolds. He had nothing kind to say, however, so he said nothing at all. That turned out to be a mistake, for Elizabeth seemed to take it as a softening of his resentment. She lowered the letter to her lap and adopted a gentler tone.

"And do not you think, that if Wickham's mother should be allowed to live in comfort at the expense of the estate, then Mrs Reynolds might, also?"

"What are you suggesting?" he demanded, disgusted.

"That we invite her home."

"Absolutely not!"

"Why not?"

He was positively itching with discomfort, his collar too tight and his face burning. "Elizabeth, I beg you would let this matter drop."

"But you would not have her be destitute, would you? She spent her entire fortune, if it could be called that, attempting to keep you safe. I cannot believe you would more willingly give money to the Wickhams than to the woman who has served you faithfully your whole life."

"I do not have time for this—I have a house to rebuild. Send her the blasted money if it pleases you, but pray do not mention her name to me again!"

He left, barging directly past his aunt, who was hovering

about outside the door, without stopping to speak to her. Throwing his coat at James as he exited the house, and rolling his sleeves up as he walked, Darcy went to join the line of volunteers, of the opinion that he would be far more agreeably engaged hefting about the ruins of his house after all.

CHAPTER FORTY-SEVEN

A LITTLE PERSPECTIVE

Elizabeth watched with dismay as Darcy stormed out of the room. Her heart sank further still when Lady Catherine sauntered ominously into it and settled herself with exaggerated state in a chair.

"That was quite a display. Had you envisaged that my nephew would be overcome with sentiment for a former housekeeper who used him infamously and then abandoned her post?"

"I merely thought it might please him to discover that her actions were not as disloyal as we believed," Elizabeth replied tightly.

Lady Catherine shook her head, her lips pursed. "Mrs Reynolds was a servant. Your concern for her is absurd. This is not the way to put my nephew's interests first—this is the way to inconvenience and embarrass him."

"That is your ladyship's opinion. It is *my* opinion that this will give him comfort. I know he was distressed by what appeared to be Mrs Reynolds's treachery."

"Insolence in one's inferiors is always distressing. It

should not be mistaken for apprehension about her future living arrangements. She is nothing to him. I may have praised your compassion, but you must be careful not to confuse liberality with radicalism."

Elizabeth gave an incredulous laugh. "I am not trying to incite a revolution, madam. Only to recognise a very real attachment between two thinking, feeling people."

"That is precisely the sort of connexion that the mistress of a great house is expected to discourage! Pray cease embroiling my nephew in matters so far beneath him and concentrate your efforts on properly supporting him."

Elizabeth ought to have known better than to engage Lady Catherine on the subject. Her pique was up, however, and she was not ready to recede fully. "I shall. And since you promised your nephew that you would do the same, I hope I may prevail upon you to help. I mean to locate the documents Mrs Reynolds has mentioned, and since one of the places that she suggested I look is Lady Anne's writing desk, it makes sense that your ladyship should accompany me. You will comprehend better than anyone what your sister has written, and which parts of it pertain to the estate."

She had not truly expected the application to succeed, thus she was not a little surprised to find herself in the Chesterfield room a short while later with Lady Catherine, rifling through the forgotten paperwork of Darcy's late mother. They were not at it for long before both agreed there was nothing of use to be found. Neither was there anything helpful in the two crates Elizabeth asked James to bring up from the Derwent room that Mrs Reynolds had identified.

"Your *Mrs Reynolds* has not been as useful as you pleaded after all," her ladyship said with a note of triumph. "The presumption of thinking she knows this house better than Darcy!"

"She was only trying to help."

"I cannot understand why you are so intent on defending her when you are fully aware of how abominably she used Darcy."

Elizabeth gripped the top edge of the crate, her forbearance worn paper-thin. "Pray, were her attempts to 'save Pemberley's shades from my pollution' any less abominable than your ladyship's? If Darcy and I can forgive you, why should not we forgive her?"

Lady Catherine puffed up with affront. "Because I am Darcy's aunt, and she is a housekeeper. And you, Mrs Darcy, are at serious risk of destroying the accord we have reached with this preposterous fascination."

"I am not 'fascinated' with Mrs Reynolds, but I am vastly grateful to her. Other than my husband, nobody has done so much to help me make a success of becoming mistress of this house. And my gratitude does not stop there. Whatever your ladyship may think of my youngest sister, and whatever I may think of her husband, their marriage was arranged for the best. Mrs Reynolds saved my sister from ruin at the hands of a man who was brought up on *this* estate by *this* family. Had not she acted as she did, I and all my sisters would have shared in Lydia's disgrace. I do not know how I am expected to turn a blind eye to such a reprieve.

"And it bears mentioning that, unlike *others*, who attempted to interfere in Darcy's business in a way that would ensure he never discovered it, Mrs Reynolds told him what she had done. Even though it meant leaving the only home she had known for most of her adult life. It is the reason that Darcy and I were reunited, and there are no words strong enough to convey my gratitude for that."

Lady Catherine's lips were thinned almost to extinction with displeasure. "For somebody who professes to like advice so well, it is a wonder that you will not take this from me. You must preserve the distinction of rank to have a hope of success. I urge you to keep some perspective. Mrs Reynolds was a *servant*."

"Yes! The servant who nursed your ladyship's dying sister on her deathbed!"

Elizabeth instantly regretted her outburst when it drained the colour from Lady Catherine's countenance. With a sigh, she dragged the chair from the writing desk and sat in front of her. "Her correspondence with my aunt shows that Mrs Reynolds cared for Lady Anne through all her miscarriages, through her daughter's birth, and through her final days. And afterwards, it seems that she wrapped this whole house in cotton wool, doing everything she could from afar to look after Darcy, his father, his sister—and now me."

"And Pemberley, too, it would seem."

They both started at the interruption. Elizabeth knew not how long Darcy and his cousin had been stood in the doorway, or how much they had overheard, but she was vastly relieved to see that he no longer seemed angry. On the contrary, he looked happier than he had in some time.

"What is your meaning?" his aunt enquired, reverting to cold austerity.

Darcy came farther into the room, followed by Colonel Fitzwilliam, who began lifting the crates off the table.

"I sent someone to fetch the drawing from Mrs Wickham's cottage." The table cleared, Darcy unrolled a sheet of paper onto it, pinning it open with books and pointing at what he had unveiled. "This used to hang on the wall in my father's study. I remember it being there, though I never looked at it closely, and I certainly never noticed it was gone."

"What is it?" Lady Catherine asked impatiently.

"One of the original design proposals for Pemberley, dated 1660—five years before this house was built, and drawn by a different architect. It shows a house in the same spot, but with only two wings. And this—" he moved his finger, "—shows the mine."

"We were not sure at first," the colonel said. "It could easily be mistaken for a feature of the landscape if one did not know what was underground, but Darcy's steward agrees that it aligns with what we know is there."

"So, they knew about it?" Elizabeth asked. "Why, then, did they build over it?"

Darcy shrugged—an uncharacteristically carefree gesture that matched his buoyant mood. "This architect may have resigned before telling anyone what the lines represented. Or been dismissed. Or died. Or been kidnapped."

"Or your ancestor ran roughshod over his advice not to build there. It is scarcely unheard of for a Darcy to like to have his own way," the colonel interjected, grinning almost as widely as his cousin. Their joint ebullience was extraordinary—and infectious. Elizabeth found herself smiling with them.

"Or they gambled that the rock was sufficiently sound foundation regardless," Darcy went on. "Which technically it was, for the house stood for almost a century and a half before a blocked culvert upped the ante."

Fitzwilliam agreed. "Particularly if they knew this was where the mine ended."

"Did they know that?" Lady Catherine enquired.

"It seems so. The *entrance* is not shown—the mine heads off the page in an easterly direction," the colonel replied, wiggling his finger over the plan in vaguely the right place.

Darcy took up the explanation, jabbing at the page triumphantly. "But this clearly shows the passage *ending* here, *before* what is the central part of the existing house."

Elizabeth looked up at him in surprise. "So, the rest of Pemberley is safe?"

He nodded and then laughed slightly, as though he could

not contain his relief. "It is the most hopeful indication to that end that we have found so far. And I am more than ready to believe it."

She gave a little cry of happiness and flung her arms around him, heedless of the apoplexy it was sure to give Lady Catherine. "I am so happy for you!"

Her ladyship made a noise of disgust, and Elizabeth laughed quietly into Darcy's shoulder before relinquishing her hold on him. He was less eager to relinquish his on her, she noticed, which pleased her very well.

"Come, madam, this news is worthy of celebration, surely?" Colonel Fitzwilliam said soothingly to his aunt.

"Perhaps, but I have been treated to a glut of Mrs Darcy's *excess of feeling* already this morning. I have no desire to witness any more." She hauled herself to her feet and turned to Darcy. "I am delighted for you, of course, but you must excuse me. My head is aching." She narrowed her eyes at Elizabeth for a moment, before adding, "I daresay you will do well enough, Mrs Darcy. Only pray do less of it near me."

It was as close to a joke as Elizabeth had ever heard the woman come, and she liked her better for it, despite how clearly it vexed her husband. The colonel rose to escort his aunt out of the room, giving Elizabeth a wink as he went. As soon as they were gone, Elizabeth returned to embracing Darcy. "This is the most wonderful news!"

She shrieked when he lifted her off her feet and spun her around. "Not quite the best news I have had all year, but as near as blazes."

"What was the best news?"

He put her down and pierced her with a look that made her breathless. "You. Not for one minute did you doubt a happy outcome, did you?"

"I do not know about that. I had faith that your family's

legacy would prevail. I was not quite so sanguine about the walls. Thank goodness for that drawing."

"What you mean to say is thank goodness for Mrs Reynolds." Darcy loosened his hold and stepped back. "I heard your defence of her."

"I know you asked me not to talk about her, but your aunt was nettling me, and I—"

"It is evident that she has given you many reasons to be thankful. And we may add my gratitude for this to your extensive list," he added, pointing at the plan on the table. "But I cannot reconcile myself to her interference. I know you think otherwise, but it *was* worse than Lady Catherine's."

"How so?"

"Because it came so much closer to working. Because she was so much more intimately involved in this house and therefore my business than my aunt has ever been."

Because you cared more about her than your aunt! Elizabeth longed to say, but knew he was not ready to hear it. "Would you like to know why she did it?"

"Not really."

Elizabeth inclined her head and set about repacking the crates from the library. She did not have to wait long before she heard Darcy exhale sharply and say, "But if you are going to punish me with your silence until I have heard it, you had better get it out of the way."

She wanted to laugh at his petulance but thought it best not to waste the opportunity. "I gather her main objection was born of an older concern—what happened at Ramsgate."

"What does she know of that?"

"No details, I understand, but what *you* do not know, and what my aunt has told me, is the lengths to which Mrs Reynolds went to extinguish the gossip it caused amongst your servants.

Or her sadness at seeing you so affected by it. Or the guilt she felt for not having reported to you her misgivings about Mrs Younge's character. It was her wish not to allow a repeat of any of that which apparently motivated her to protect you from me."

"How could she ever think you like Mrs Younge?"

"More easily than you would think when you hear the objections laid out. On my first visit to Pemberley, I committed the capital offence of appearing surprised when Mrs Reynolds spoke in your favour. It made her think I did not like you. My aunt Gardiner compounded the matter by letting slip that we were acquainted with Wickham—and because I had not told her what I learnt from you about his character, she referred to him as a friend.

"Then Miss Bingley's maid had some rather unflattering opinions to share about me when she arrived, for which I do not entirely blame either her or her mistress. My behaviour to you in Hertfordshire was always bordering on the uncivil, and I never spoke to you without rather wishing to give you pain than not. I cannot justly say that their ill opinion was unfounded. Then there was my uninvited foray into the library, which Mrs Reynolds did not know was orchestrated by Miss Bingley." Elizabeth stopped putting books away and stood up to face Darcy. "To be sure, she knew no actual good of me—only that I was trouble, and you were too smitten to see it."

"That did not give her the right to interfere."

"Is it truly any worse than your interference in Jane and Bingley's affairs?"

"Much worse. Bingley is my friend. Mrs Reynolds had no claim to such familiarity."

"It does not mean she was not motivated by affection. You would see, if you read her letters, that she was all too aware of her position. That she could not so much as hug you if you cut your knee, because she had not the right to play nursemaid, even."

He frowned and mumbled, "She did actually."

"Did what?"

"When I was a boy. She used to hug me if I hurt myself."

"There you are, then."

He stood silently for a moment or two longer then said, quietly, "Very well. I shall read the blasted letters if it will please you."

She did laugh then. "I do not want you to read them to please me. I am very grateful to Mrs Reynolds, but it was not me she doted on for four-and-twenty years."

"Why are you so determined to convince me of her esteem?"

She smiled tenderly and took his hands. "I could not prevent your house from crumbling. I know not how to organise a renovation. Apparently, I cannot even be mistress without significant assistance. But I can, and I do, understand you. I can see quite clearly that Mrs Reynolds's actions distressed you, and it pleases me that I can do something to ease your pain."

"I did not marry you because I wanted you to fix things for me, despite everything I have brought to this marriage being in need of repair."

"All *I* have brought to this marriage is my dreaded compassion. Will you not let me put it to some better use than vexing your aunt?"

He rolled his eyes but allowed her to lead him to her bedroom and station him on her chaise longue while she retrieved the correspondence from her drawer and began explaining to him her aunt Wallis's strange method of naming things. Much the same as when she first read it all, they both ended up on the floor with open letters strewn about them.

"I would never have believed Wickham would settle for so little." Darcy was leaning against the chaise, reading Mrs Wallis's most recent express. He looked up sharply and added, "No offence to your sister."

"None of us could understand why he married her, either. I am sure if his debts had not been quite so pressing, and had a mysterious benefactor not appeared just at that moment offering immediate relief, he might have waited for a more lucrative match."

"Impatience always was his greatest weakness, after greed."

"And Mrs Reynolds had apparently saved hundreds of pounds. It was a good offer. Although, it seems to have been the goldsmith's idea that some of the money was given by way of a down payment on their rent, to prevent Wickham gambling it."

"And the licence bond?"

"There cannot have been one, but they must have known my father would never contest the marriage. In truth, it was a remarkably cunning scheme."

"Yet you approve of her?"

"I could not but approve of anyone who thought so highly of you that they would make themselves destitute in your defence. But I am probably biased."

He smiled and reached for her hand, tugging her closer so he could kiss it. Unbalanced, Elizabeth squawked and fell sideways, her eyes alighting on one of her aunt's more diverting letters as she did. She held it out for him and had sat up and turned to search for another when he exclaimed, "I was 'Starch?'"

She snorted inelegantly with laughter. "'Tis better than being named for a dairy cow."

"Is it?"

"Would you hate me if I told you I came up with that name?"

He regarded her for a moment before reaching to grab her waist and slide her back towards him. "No," he said against her lips. "As long as you never stop smiling at me like that." He kissed her until she admonished him to attend to the task.

Snatching up the first letter her hand touched, Elizabeth lay back on the floor parallel to his legs and crossed her ankles on the chaise behind him. "This one says 'Agnes, you must stop feeding The Cherub biscuits or he will get fat, and there is nothing worse than a fat little lord, taking tithes from hungry villagers'. Mrs Reynolds spoiled you rotten! No wonder you disliked Mrs Lovell at first. She did not give you any biscuits."

"Mrs Wallis has a way with words," he said dryly.

Elizabeth agreed with a laugh and picked up another letter. "What is this about you not being in your own portrait?"

Darcy smirked, though he looked very much as though he was trying not to. "I hated the thought of sitting for it. The artist was a swaggering fop. I told Wickham I would settle his debts if he dressed as me and sat for it in my place. It was two weeks before anyone noticed."

"I thought disguise of every sort was your abhorrence!"

"Youth must be my defence—I was but sixteen."

"Anyway, it was not two weeks before *anyone* noticed. It says here, 'You ought to tell someone what he is up to, Agnes, for it will only make his punishment worse if it goes on too long. It does not matter how ill he likes being looked at—he had better get used to it if he is turning out as handsome as you say'."

Darcy looked vaguely disgusted, which diverted her, then interrupted her mirth by reading his own letter.

"'Dot has fallen out with the Termagant again and tried to run away to me here in Ilfracombe. Her father caught up with her in the village and took her home. She is refusing to eat in protest.'"

"Refusing to eat! I said no to one meal, then cried and cried until Jane snuck down to the kitchen to get me some bread."

"And how old were you?"

"I do not know. I think I tried to run away at least once every year from the age of about two." Darcy looked less amused by this than she was expecting. She sat up and rested her hands and chin on his bent knee. "I have stopped running now."

He did not respond except to smile her favourite, enigmatic smile, and stroke her cheek.

"Come. One more letter each, and then we must find Georgiana and give her the good news about the house. We are cruel to have made her wait this long." She picked one at random and gave it to Darcy, then crawled away, collecting the letters back into a pile as she searched for one that looked interesting. She dropped them all in fright when Darcy cried, loudly, "Collins proposed to you?"

That set her off laughing again. "He did. The day after Bingley's ball."

Darcy tossed his letter aside and lunged across the floor to kiss her possessively. She submitted to it willingly, utterly light of heart to be enjoying such an unguarded, playful half an hour with him, lounging on the floor, exchanging memories as readily as kisses. It was an intimacy she cherished profoundly. No one else ever saw him thus; this was *her* Darcy. And Elizabeth loved him completely.

"You are right of course," he said abruptly.

"About what?"

"We must ask her to come home. I am not sure why I said no."

She smiled broadly and cupped his face with both her hands. "Because you are Starchy."

He gave a wry chuckle. "I am not as good at this as you. I am still learning."

"So, you admit you do need me to fix *something*."

"I need every bit of you, all the time."

And since they had all the time in the world, they took some more of it for themselves, and made Georgiana wait a little longer to hear that her house was not going to be demolished and her former housekeeper would soon be coming home.

CHAPTER FORTY-EIGHT

THE HAND THAT FATE DEALT

At the end of November, Darcy took Elizabeth and Georgiana to Hertfordshire for Jane and Bingley's wedding. His letter to Mrs Reynolds had been sent, along with instructions to reply to London. Elizabeth had yet to see Astroite House, and with things more settled at Pemberley and the weather maintaining a mild turn, they had decided a visit was in order before they returned north.

For two days and three nights prior to the wedding, they stayed at Netherfield, and during that time, Darcy scarcely saw Elizabeth at all. She had said, after their own wedding, that she would be too happy to notice if she missed Jane. As it turned out, she had merely been too busy, but he had easily perceived, the closer they travelled to Hertfordshire, how dearly she anticipated the reunion. Upon arrival at Longbourn, she had disappeared entirely, sucked back into her old world of petticoats and gossip.

His reprieve came at night-time when Elizabeth became his, and only his, once again. On the first night, she was bubbling over with excitement and news. On the second, she was complaining of an aching head and expressing wonder that she had ever tolerated the noise of so many people talking at once. On the third, she was troublingly quiet.

Such she had been since she returned from Longbourn that afternoon, though he had given up attempting to discover what was wrong, for every enquiry resulted in an airy assurance that naught was amiss and an anxious glance at whomever else was in the room. Anticipating, therefore, that she was waiting for privacy, Darcy felt a frisson of alarm when Garrett and Vaughan both departed for the night, and instead of coming to bed, Elizabeth asked him to sit with her by the fire.

"I received a letter today," she told him gently. "From my aunt Wallis." She said no more—only handed it to him.

With no expectation of pleasure, Darcy opened it and began to read.

To my precious Dot,

I trust you are well and that you have arrived safely at Bedlam. I hope this letter reaches you there before you leave for London. It is not an easy letter to write—indeed, it breaks my heart, for I am about to betray the confidence of my oldest friend—but it must be written.

Agnes has received Mr Darcy's letter, promising to refund all her expenses for Peacock and Peabrain's wedding, and inviting her to return to Pemberley to live in a cottage on the estate. I know full well this was your idea, but I do commend him for consenting to it. I know from Agnes what mortification such a condescension will have cost him.

She has sent her reply to his London house—he will get it when you arrive there. She has refused both offers. The reason she has given is the deepest shame. That part is not a lie. I have witnessed the depths of her regret and can easily believe that she would find it inexpressibly difficult to face Mr Darcy, his sister, you, or any of the servants she left behind. I also believe, however, that her devotion to Pemberley would eventually have outweighed the ignominy of her disgrace, were it not for another impediment, which she has not mentioned in her letter.

Agnes is too unwell to make the journey to Pemberley. She does not think it is an illness from which she will recover, and I am reluctantly inclined to agree. I was shocked by many things when she arrived at my door last month, but none so much as her appearance. She has been unwell since long before you arrived at Pemberley, though she has confessed that knowing how ill she was added force to the other inducements which led her on in attempting to separate you from Mr Darcy. She wished to do all that was in her power to secure his happiness before her time ran out. You can imagine her despair when she discovered that she had done the opposite and was unlikely to see the matter rectified before she departed this world.

She kept her illness well hidden, revealing nothing of it in her letters to me nor telling anybody at Pemberley. It must have been more easily concealed at that time, but the events of the past months have hastened matters cruelly. There is no longer any mistaking that she is gravely ill. Her reasons for keeping it a secret are as irrational as they are obstinate, but I can summarise them for you: she is too ashamed to come home, and her illness is denying her both the time required to overcome her shame, and the strength to make the journey.

I know not how far Mr Darcy's condescension—or dare I say affection—will extend, nor what he can truly be expected to do to help, but I beg you would tell him. At the very least, he ought to know that his kind offer meant the world to Agnes. Not many things make her smile these days. Only your letters with news from Pemberley, and now Mr Darcy's, calling it her home. I shall do what I can for her, Dot. That I promise.

Pray wish Jane all the best for her wedding.

All my love,

E Wallis

Darcy stared at the page, unsettled by the power of its effect on him. A memory of Mrs Reynolds stumbling in the library wedged a knot of emotion in his throat that made him wish he had never consented to reading the damned stash of her letters in the first place.

"We tried," Elizabeth said quietly. "I am sorry we were too late."

He attempted to speak and was dismayed to discover he could not.

"Shall we go to bed?"

He nodded, inordinately grateful that Elizabeth did not intend to press him to say any more on the subject, for what more was there to say? She merely curled up next to him and held him tightly. He was reminded of the assurance she gave him, early in their engagement, that he would never be alone in his misery again. He had been deeply touched by the sentiment but had not truly understood the breadth of her promise, nor the gamut of adversities capable of causing him misery. This was certainly not something he ever anticipated would be one, and he thanked God, yet again, for Elizabeth's treasured compassion. He pulled her more firmly against him and waited for what felt like an eternity for sleep to come and extinguish his uncomfortable, distant sense of sorrow.

Elizabeth referenced the matter but once, indirectly, the next morning. As they readied themselves for the ceremony, she asked whether he was well, accompanying her enquiry with a significant look. He answered that he was and then silenced her with a compliment and a kiss—because she deserved both, and he had no wish to dwell on anything else.

The wedding was a more extravagant affair than his own to Elizabeth had been, no doubt a consequence of the extra time Mrs Bennet had been afforded to make it so. Darcy felt in no way deprived. He had almost fully acquainted himself with all the pleasures of marriage to his new bride in the time it took Bingley to get around to cutting into his wedding cake.

"We were dreadfully sorry to hear about Pemberley," Mrs Gardiner remarked at the wedding breakfast. "It is such a handsome house."

"Is it?" Mrs Bennet said airily. "I would not know. Not all of us have had the pleasure of an invitation."

"You must take the hint, my dear," said Mr Bennet. "As excuses go, razing half one's house to the ground to avoid a visit from one's new mother shows a resolve I can only admire."

Darcy did not contradict him. If there were any positives to be taken from the disaster, he was in no position to refuse them.

"Will you put it back exactly how it was?" Gardiner enquired.

"Nay, I say you should leave it as it is," Bingley interposed. "Caroline has always wanted me to build a house that was modelled on Pemberley. I shall save a fortune if I do it now, while half of it is missing."

"What rooms were lost?" Jane enquired of Elizabeth, who listed the library, study, gallery, bedrooms, and attic rooms.

"Oh well, at least the nursery did not fall down, for you will need that soon enough," said Mrs Bennet. "And this is a fine opportunity to decorate the rest of the house. But attend, you must never put chinoiserie in a dining room. It plays havoc with the digestion."

Darcy glanced at Elizabeth, expecting her to be diverted. Instead, he found her with heightened complexion, staring at her plate with uncommon intensity, a small frown pulling at her forehead. He thought back over all that had been said, anxious to know what had given her such pause. His heart lurched when he thought he had hit upon the answer, and the longer Elizabeth remained still, the more certain he became.

"Darcy? Are you listening?" Bingley said loudly. "What say you? Will you let Lizzy paint the dining room purple?"

"She can knock it down and build a new one if she likes. I should not object."

"He is positively blasé about knocking walls down now! You may never get an invite, Mrs Bennet, for there will be no house left at this rate."

"If the house was to be painted purple, that may not be a bad thing," Hurst opined.

At length, Elizabeth shook off her distraction and added her customary wit to her family's banter. Darcy found it harder to shake off *his* and grew impatient for the celebrations to end, yet no opportunity presented itself for private conversation with Elizabeth, either before the time came to wish the happy couple well and depart, or on the carriage ride to London with Georgiana. And the letter that awaited Darcy on his desk when they arrived at Astroite House momentarily drove all other considerations from his head. Elizabeth left him to open it in private, though it took very little time to read the short and shakily written note.

To Mr Darcy,

You do me great honour, but I cannot accept your money or your invitation to return to Pemberley. I shall not worsen my offences by attaching my disgrace to you. I am profoundly sorry for the harm my misdirected and presumptuous interference caused. No excuse I can offer compensates for the egregiousness of my actions, but I do offer you my sincerest, most heartfelt apology. If it is not too impertinent, I congratulate you on your marriage. I wish you and Mrs Darcy all the happiness in the world. Never have there been two people whom I wished so well.

With all the esteem you will permit me to send,

A. Reynolds

Darcy inhaled deeply and held his breath as the far off, unsettling feeling that had been plaguing him since the previous evening swooped closer, made itself fully felt, and resolved into something vastly more governable. After all, among the many other things a certain wise woman had once told him, was that it was always better to take charge than sit about, waiting for Fate to play its hand.

He found Elizabeth in front of the window on the upstairs landing, tracing her finger over one of the sea lilies in the stone mullion. The afternoon sun fell on her face in a way that illuminated her complexion and showed him her small, contented smile in flawless profile. She looked absolutely beautiful.

She turned to regard him when he came abreast of her. "Was my aunt Wallis correct?"

He nodded.

She lifted a hand to caress his cheek, and he regretted that pity had stolen her smile away.

"You are allowed to be sad. It is permissible to be fond of a servant, despite what your aunt says. Mrs Wallis is no real relation to me, either, yet I have benefited from her affection all my life. You might think of Mrs Reynolds in the same way. An honorary aunt."

He smiled faintly. It was a quaint notion, but his mind was on other things. "Why did your mother's mention of the nursery make you so pensive?" His heart was pounding in his chest, and if he might judge from the blush that instantly overspread her countenance, hers was doing likewise.

"I knew you had not missed that."

"Well?"

Her agitation was striking, her eyes darting all over his face and her voice breathless. "I do not know. We have barely been married two months, and so much has happened, I have not given it a second thought."

"But?"

"But, well, Mama's comment made me think what I had not stopped to think before—that, I suppose, there is one thing that has *not* happened in that time."

He gave in to the smile that was desperately pulling at his lips. "You have not bled."

She gave in to a very tentative smile of her own. "No."

"Are you, then?"

"I suppose I might be." Her smile slowly broadened into a more assured one. "I suppose I must be."

Darcy was, by now, accustomed to Elizabeth's ability to utterly fell him with sentiment. This, though, was beyond everything. *This* was the reason Pemberley would endure. He kissed her forehead reverently and then looked her in the eyes. "That will give you something to tell Mrs Wallis when you see her."

She frowned endearingly in puzzlement.

"I am taking you to Devon to see your godmother. And to bring Mrs Reynolds home myself."

She fixed him with a look he had come to cherish—one that betrayed her pride in him. Though, that was absurd, for if anyone had a right to be proud, it was him, of his magnificent wife, who had shown him in the kindest, most courageous way conceivable that every one of his early prejudices had been unfounded. The very idea that she was in any way inferior was insupportable. Elizabeth was quite simply perfect. And Darcy loved her completely.

CHAPTER FORTY-NINE

TO HAVE HIS OWN WAY

The view out to sea was Eleanor's favourite. She talked constantly of the tall ships sailing by, the changing clouds, the water that was sometimes choppy, sometimes smooth and glistening. Aloud, Mrs Reynolds agreed, for her friend had done too much for her to hear any manner of complaint, but privately, she could never perceive anything extraordinary in the monotonous, grey vista. Her eyes were no longer strong enough to see the distant specks of boats, and her heart was too fragile not to be terrified by the vastness of the disappearing horizon. She longed for Derbyshire, to be once more grounded betwixt rocks and mountains.

Yet, here she sat, as she did most mornings, at the rickety table outside Eleanor's cottage, wrapped in shawls to ward of the wind that whipped up over the cliffs as she and her friend drank chocolate and observed the view. If she did not, there was every chance she would forget what fresh air tasted like, for she never left the house otherwise. Mr Wallis had procured a bath chair for her use, but neither he nor Eleanor were strong enough to push it up and down the steep hills of the town. This was as far as she ever got.

Eleanor had gone inside to fetch some biscuits when a movement at the head of the cliff path caught Mrs Reynolds's attention. Her failing sight showed her only the silhouette of a man in a hat, but as she watched him approach, her eyes filled with disbelieving tears, for she would be blind before she failed to recognise that stately stride. She had never been given to flights of fancy, but she wondered whether she had drifted to sleep in her chair and begun to dream. Then the figure drew near enough that the shadows receded, and a little cry escaped her lips to see his dear face. Mr Darcy had come to see her!

"You know how I like to have my own way, Mrs Reynolds," he said gently but firmly. "I am afraid I must insist that you come home to Pemberley. Where you belong."

He had not lost his piercing gaze, though it no longer had the haunted quality from the summer and instead contained a warmth that gladdened her heart to see. She held out a shaking hand and the dear man took it. She smiled unsteadily. "You always were the most sweet-tempered, generous-hearted boy in the world."

Somebody else appeared at his side. Mrs Reynolds suffered a moment of apprehension when she recognised Clarabelle, but there was no hint of censure in her countenance, only a hopeful smile as she took Mrs Reynolds's other hand and asked, "Will you come?"

Eleanor had evidently returned as well, for she said from somewhere behind, "Did not I tell you, Agnes? Not a bone of resentment in her body, my Dot."

Eleanor *had* told her, repeatedly, but it had been difficult for Mrs Reynolds to imagine anyone forgiving her when she could not forgive herself. Yet, Mr Darcy evidently had. He truly was the best master that ever lived. And he had found the only woman in the world who was good enough for him, and she had forgiven her as well. Thus, although she assured Mr and Mrs Darcy that she would be honoured to accept their generous offer, and though the prospect of seeing Pemberley again before she departed this world gave her pleasure such as she had never felt before, Mrs Reynolds thought that if she had died there and then, she would have died happy.

EPILOGUE

Elizabeth stepped out of the way of a passing footman and craned her neck to locate Darcy. He saw her first, peeling away from a group of clerks to greet her. In her arms, their young son pulled his thumb out of his mouth and squealed, his hands held out in anticipation of being passed into his father's doting embrace.

Darcy obliged him, then kissed Elizabeth's cheek. "Are you feeling better?"

"Much better, thank you." Taking George's hand and waggling it gently, she added, "It ought to pass soon. I was not sick for so long with this little man."

"Do you hear that?" Darcy said to his son. "Your brother or sister is set to be a mischief-maker. You will have to be on your guard."

George smiled brightly as he did at most things Darcy said to him. Never had there lived an infant more besotted with his father, and Elizabeth did not know of any father prouder of his son than Darcy. It gladdened her heart to see it.

"It looks as though things are progressing well in here," she remarked, looking around the library with wonder. Almost two years since the east wing collapsed, the restoration was finally complete—structurally, at least; the upper floors were still hollow shells. Now, the meticulous task of unpacking the library from storage had begun. For a week, a constant stream of servants had been coming and going as crates were emptied and furniture brought back in. Gradually, the vast stone chamber was being returned to the enchanting, elegant space Elizabeth had briefly glimpsed in the moonlight what felt like a lifetime ago.

"It seems ridiculous to say that I missed these books, but seeing them returned feels like seeing an old friend come home," Darcy said. There was a wistful quality to his countenance at which Elizabeth did not wonder. The new wing was the culmination of a vast amount of work and no small quantity of tribulations, and this reinstatement of the library signified far more than merely an exercise in filling shelves; it signified the triumphant salvation of Pemberley.

"It does not seem ridiculous to me. This collection is as much your family's legacy as the house itself. I am just delighted to see it at last. When you told me, that day we stood out on the lawn, that you would show it to me in daylight as soon as the library was secure, I did not think I would have to wait quite so long as this." She placed a hand on his arm and said, earnestly, "It was worth the wait. It is magnificent."

George babbled a string of utterances that sounded awfully sincere but made no sense, his endearingly serious expression making him look even more like Darcy than usual.

"I am glad you agree," Elizabeth said to him. "This will all be yours one day, and you must take as much care of it as your papa has done."

"Starting with not allowing it to fall down," Darcy said sardonically.

George blew a raspberry.

"Quite," he added in reply.

Elizabeth laughed at them both and asked Darcy whether he had time to join her for some tea.

"Just you? Where is Georgiana?"

"Miss Reid invited her to Delamont again, though I do not doubt that her cousin will be there as well." When Darcy only nodded, she asked, "Do you approve?"

"I do. Connelly is a fine gentleman."

"And if Georgiana marries him, she will be settled less than five miles from Pemberley, which I know would make you happy."

Darcy fixed her with an indulgent smile. "It would indeed, though she may not be the only relation we are pleased to have in such close neighbourhood. Ferguson informed me this morning that Grassbury Manor, north of Kympton, is for sale. I have written to Bingley, inviting him and Jane to stay with us while they look at the place, if they choose to. But I think he will take it if he can. It is an excellent prospect."

Elizabeth could scarcely contain her excitement and kissed him on the cheek enough times between all her exclamations of happiness that George began to grow jealous of her attention. "Forgive me, precious," she cooed, taking him back into her arms. "But you will see how fine it is to have your aunt and uncle so close by." To Darcy she added, "How wonderful for the children to grow up so near each other!"

Someone knocked over a marble pedestal, and the loud bang reverberated around the chamber and made George cry.

"I had better take him back to the nursery. But thank you, dearest Fitzwilliam! You have made me so very happy with this news."

"I must have a turn at making *you* happy now and again." He kissed first the baby then Elizabeth on their crowns and promised to join her in the saloon shortly.

She left without troubling herself to contest his point, for he knew perfectly well that he gave her reason to be happy every day. "He and you both," she said to George, squeezing him to her. "And you too, soon enough," she whispered, touching the slight swell of her stomach.

She delivered George back to Nanny and returned downstairs, pausing to peek into the Stag Parlour upon hearing voices as she passed the door. Mrs Lovell was within, explaining the provenance of the hunting tapestry to two wide-eyed visitors. The housekeeper did not possess the same breadth of knowledge about Pemberley as her predecessor, but she was learning fast, and the couple seemed satisfied with her information. They certainly looked more attentive than Elizabeth herself had been the day she first came to Pemberley, when the fear of encountering Darcy had rendered her deaf to everything that was said about the house. Diverted by the memory, she backed away from the door to leave Mrs Lovell to her more appreciative audience, but she was halted in her steps by an enquiry from one of them about the miniatures that hung above the mantelpiece.

"That is the late Mr Darcy," Mrs Lovell answered. "And that one is my present master, that one is my mistress, and that one is their sister, Miss Darcy."

"And this one?" the gentleman enquired.

"That is Mrs Reynolds. She was housekeeper here before I took the position."

The couple both exclaimed at the uncommon condescension of so distinguished a family displaying a servant's picture next to their own. Elizabeth grinned; Lady Catherine was of the same mind. Darcy's aunt had never reconciled herself to Mrs Reynolds coming back to Pemberley, and that she was still held in such high esteem, even now, was a source of enduring displeasure for her ladyship.

"Mrs Reynolds had a special connexion to the family," Mrs Lovell explained. "She served them for quarter of a century, and Mr and Mrs Darcy were both excessively fond of her. It was a sad day indeed when she died."

A wave of sadness washed over Elizabeth. Despite Darcy's best efforts to find a physician who could help her, Mrs Reynolds's disease had been too advanced, and she succumbed less than a year after they brought her home. All that had been in their power was to make her final months as comfortable and agreeable as possible. The former had become increasingly difficult towards the end, but Elizabeth was confident they had achieved the latter—in large part because George had been born in time for Mrs Reynolds to meet him. She would remember for all her days the pride with which Darcy introduced them. Though no substitute for Lady Anne, when Mrs Reynolds spoke, with authority, of the affection her former mistress had felt for her son and would unquestionably have felt for her grandson, it had moved both Elizabeth and Darcy exceedingly.

The gentleman peered more closely at the miniatures. "Some servants work their whole lives for the same family and are not so well regarded. Mr and Mrs Darcy must be excellent employers."

Mrs Lovell nodded seriously. "They are the best master and mistress that ever lived, and not one of their tenants or servants will tell you otherwise."

Feeling awkward to be eavesdropping on such talk, Elizabeth hastened away, but with a blossoming sense of the deepest contentment. Mrs Reynolds had once said the same to her of Darcy, marking the hour, the spot, and the words that set her off towards falling in love with him in the first place. Little had Elizabeth known with what intimacy she would come to understand the truth of the commendation. Even less had she imagined that she would ever share in it. Yet Pemberley was her world now, and she had come to love it almost as dearly as she loved Darcy. It was pleasing to know Mrs Lovell perceived her devotion.

She smiled to herself. Mrs Reynolds had also said, long before she ever actually met her, that nobody was better suited to be mistress of Pemberley than Dot. She had been right about that, too.

ACKNOWLEDGMENTS

I spent a disproportionate amount of time in 1812 instead of 2022 whilst writing this book, so I must thank my wonderful family and friends for not giving up on me or forgetting what I looked like while I was missing in action. Special thanks to my mum who, as always, has suffered every high and low of this process with me, cheering me on when I was flagging, and making sure to slap me down when I got too cocky. To my dad, whose vast knowledge of the building industry has been invaluable in making sure *Unfounded* had its footings in reality and thus did not disappear down its own hidden crevasse of implausibility. To Amy D'Orazio for her unstinting and invaluable advice on writing, publishing, and generally surviving life as an author, as well as her enviable skill at wielding her editing axe with precision and sensitivity. To Kristi Rawley, for her patience, her grammatical prowess, and for loving this version of Darcy as much as I do.

Last but by no means least, I thank Jane Austen: for her razor wit, stunning turns of phrase, and captivating characters; for the honour of incorporating some of her inimitable writing into this alternative journey for Darcy and Elizabeth; and for inspiring me to write.

ABOUT THE AUTHOR

Jessie Lewis enjoys words far too much for her own good and was forced to take up writing them down in order to save her family and friends from having to listen to her saying so many of them. She dabbled in poetry during her teenage years, though it was her studies in Literature and Philosophy at university that firmly established her admiration for the potency of the English language. She has always been particularly in awe of Jane Austen's literary cunning and has delighted in exploring Austen's regency world in her own historical fiction writing. It is of no relevance whatsoever to her ability to string words together coherently that she lives in Hertfordshire with two tame cats, two feral children and a pet husband. She is also quite tall, in case you were wondering.

Check out her musings on the absurdities of language and life on her blog, **LifeinWords.blog**.

facebook.com/JessieLewisAuthor

bookbub.com/authors/jessie-lewis

amazon.com/Jessie-Lewis/e/B075S864GF

ALSO BY JESSIE LEWIS

A Match Made at Matlock (*with Jan Ashton, Amy D'Orazio, and Julie Cooper*)

Epiphany

Fallen

Mistaken

Speechless

Multi-Author Anthologies

Rational Creatures: Stirrings of Feminism in the Hearts of Jane Austen's Fine Ladies

Made in the USA
Monee, IL
22 March 2023

30303042R00236